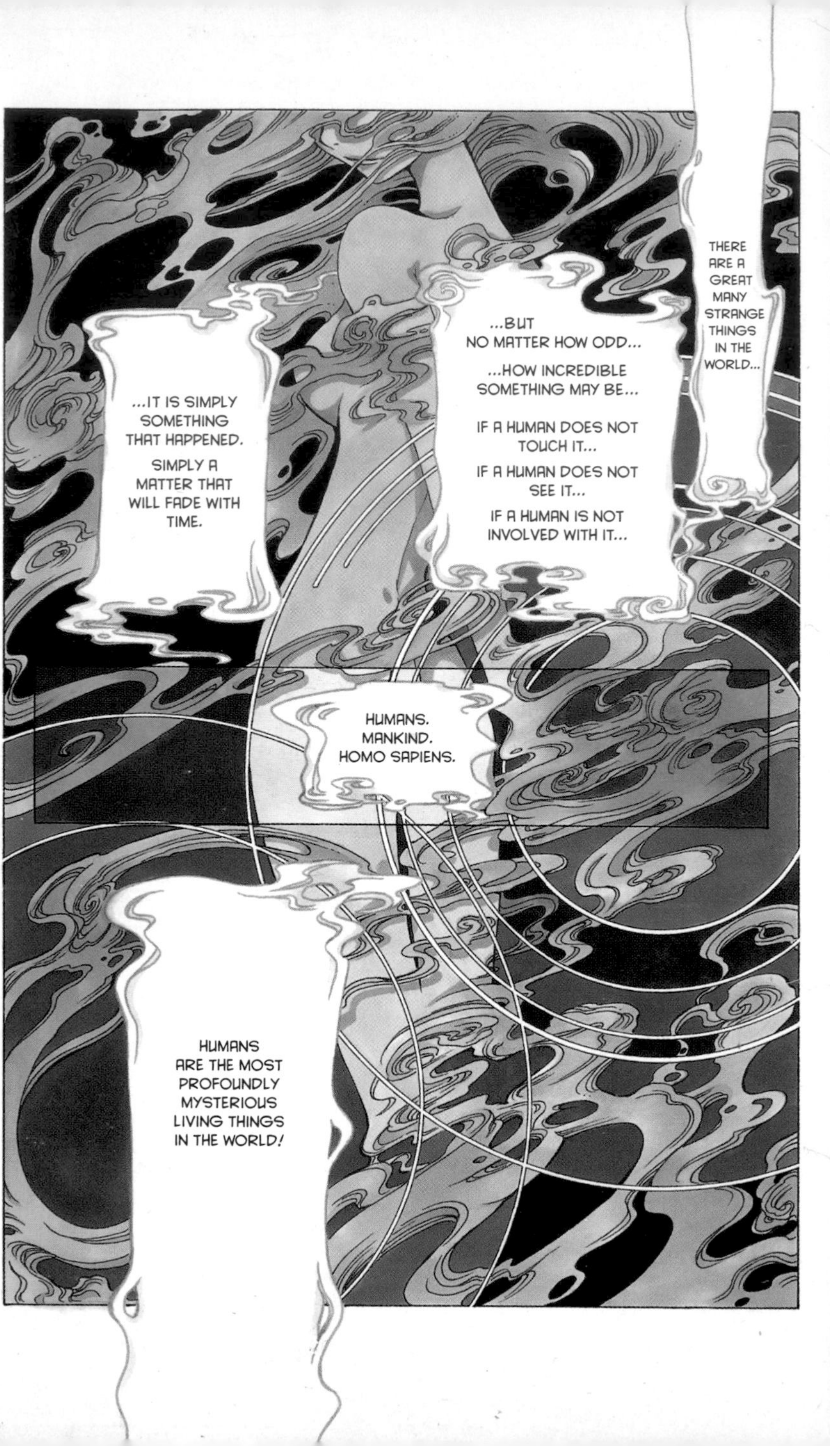
THERE ARE A GREAT MANY STRANGE THINGS IN THE WORLD...
...BUT NO MATTER HOW ODD... ...HOW INCREDIBLE SOMETHING MAY BE... IF A HUMAN DOES NOT TOUCH IT... IF A HUMAN DOES NOT SEE IT... IF A HUMAN IS NOT INVOLVED WITH IT...
...IT IS SIMPLY SOMETHING THAT HAPPENED. SIMPLY A MATTER THAT WILL FADE WITH TIME.
HUMANS. MANKIND. HOMO SAPIENS.
HUMANS ARE THE MOST PROFOUNDLY MYSTERIOUS LIVING THINGS IN THE WORLD!

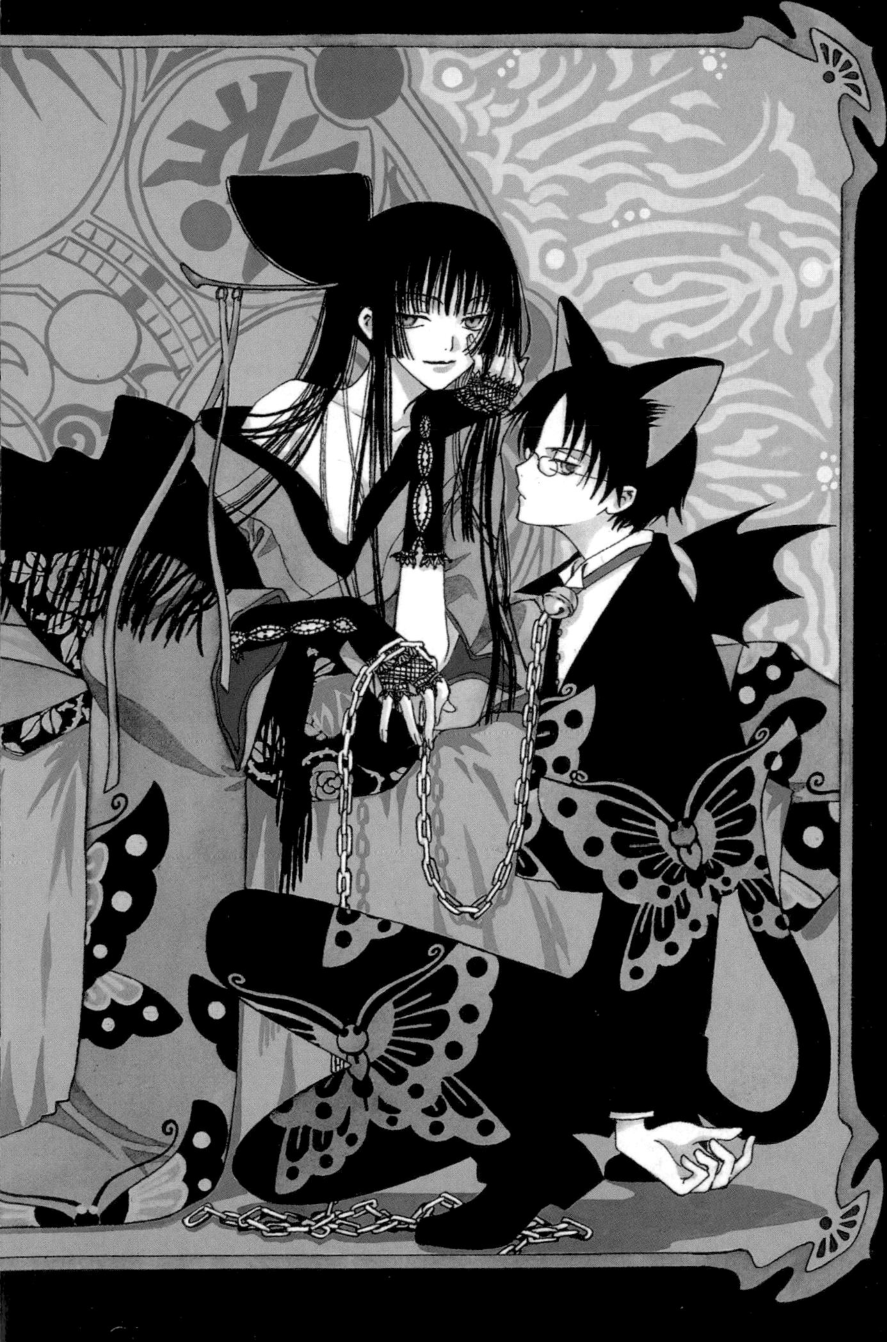

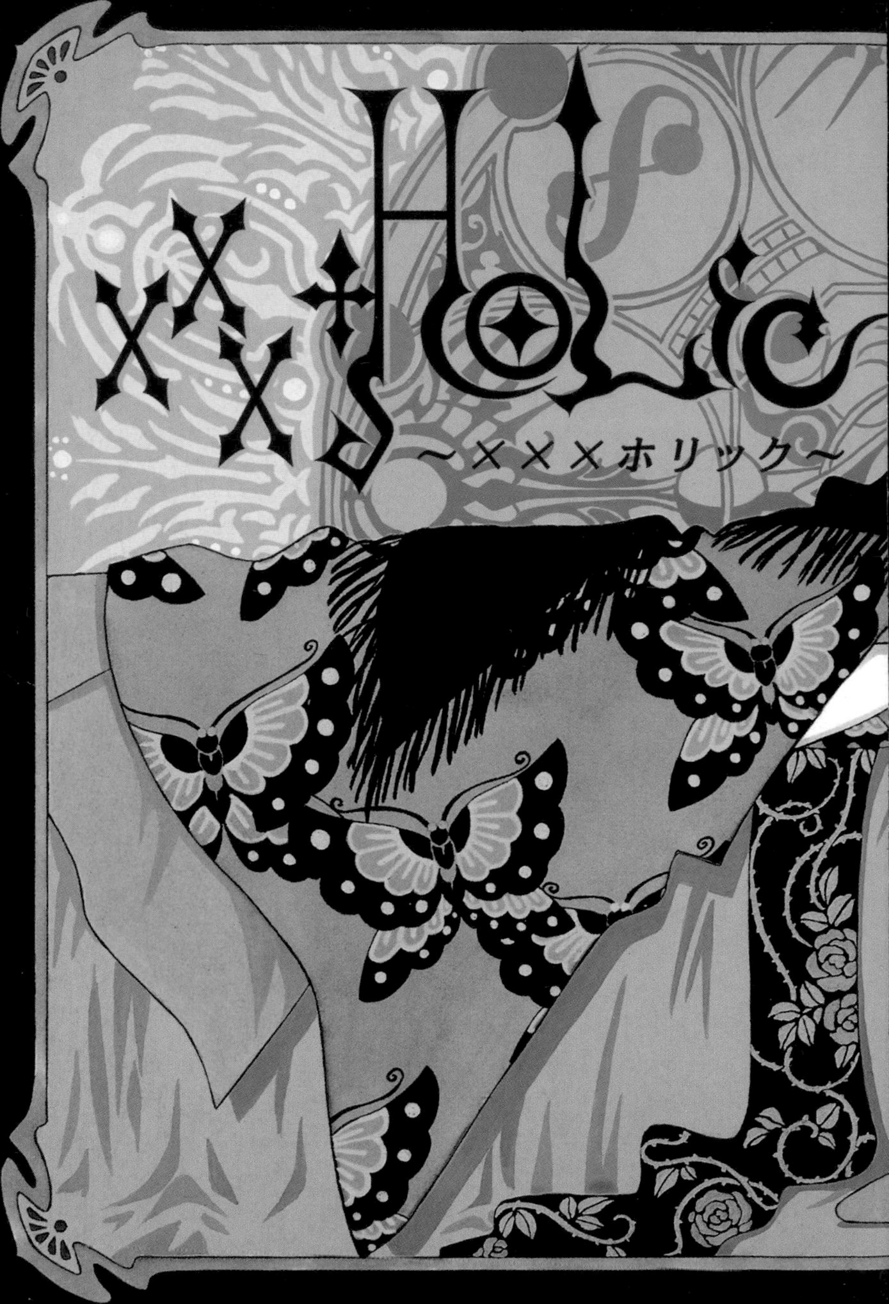
xxxHOLiC
～×××ホリック～

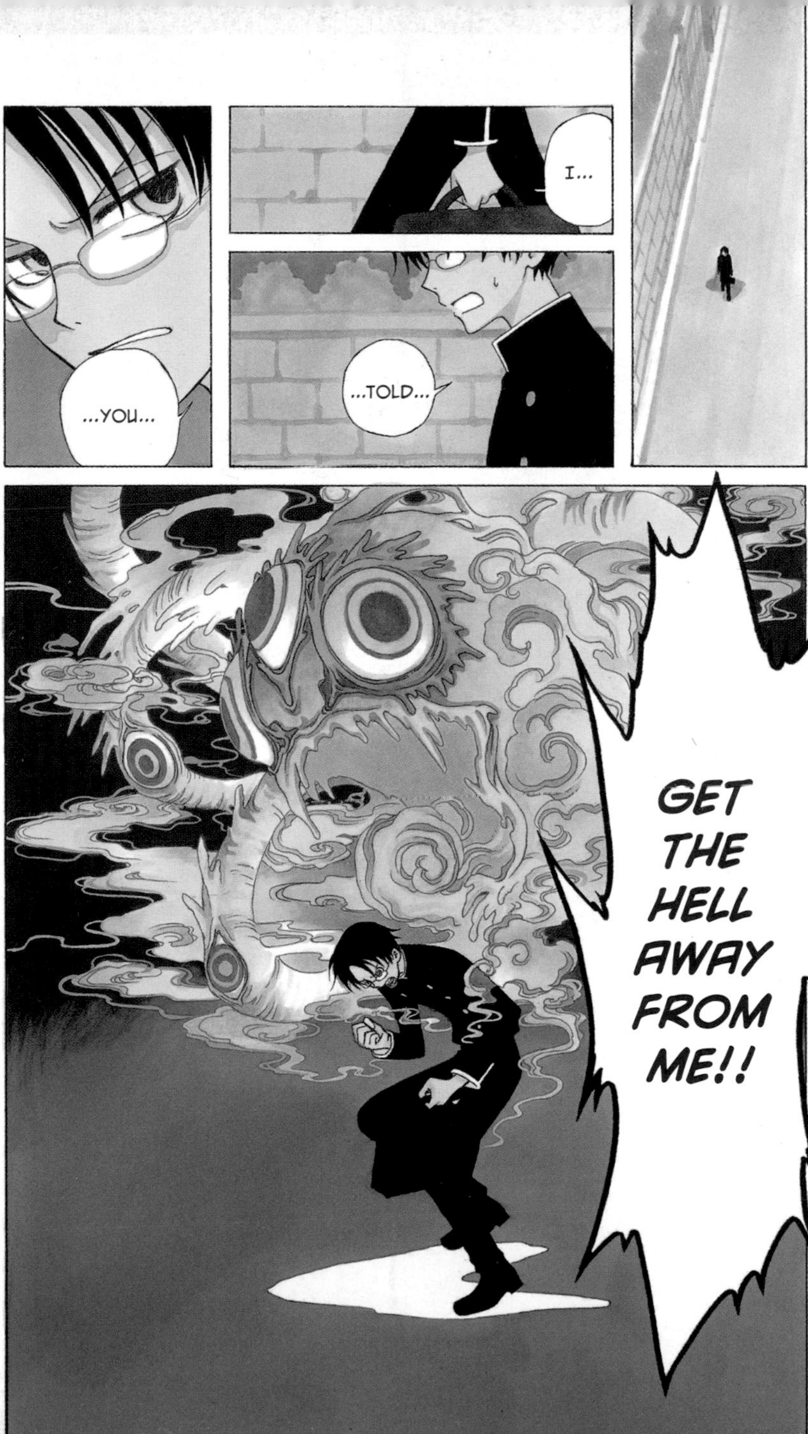
I...
...TOLD...
...YOU...
GET THE HELL AWAY FROM ME!!

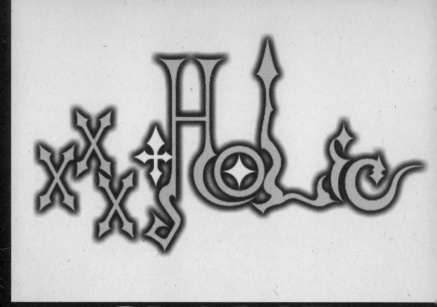

CLAMP

TRANSLATED AND ADAPTED BY
Anthony Gerard

LETTERED BY
Dana Hayward

BALLANTINE BOOKS • NEW YORK

xxxHOLiC Volume 1 crosses over with *Tsubasa* Volume 1. Although it isn't necessary to read *Tsubasa* to understand the events in *xxxHOLiC*, you'll get to see the same events from different perspectives if you read both!

A Del Rey® Book
Published by The Random House Publishing Group
Copyright © 2004 CLAMP. All rights reserved.
First published in Japan in 2003 by Kodansha Ltd., Tokyo
This publication — rights arranged through Kodansha Ltd.

All rights reserved under International and Pan-American Copyright
Convention. Published in the United States by The Random House
Publishing Group, a division of Random House, Inc., New York, and
simultaneously in Canada by Random House of Canada Limited, Toronto.

Del Rey is a registered trademark and the Del Rey colophon is a
trademark of Random House, Inc.

www.delreymanga.com

Library of Congress Control Number is available upon request
from the publisher.

ISBN 0-345-47058-3

Translator and Adaptor—Anthony Gerard
Lettering—Dana Hayward
Cover Design—David Stevenson

Manufactured in the United States of America

First Edition: May 2004

1 2 3 4 5 6 7 8 9 10

Contents

Honorifics

Throughout the Del Rey Manga books, you will find Japanese honorifics left intact in the translations. For those not familiar with how the Japanese use honorifics, and more important, how they differ from American honorifics, we present this brief overview.

Politeness has always been a critical facet of Japanese culture. Ever since the feudal era, when Japan was a highly stratified society, use of honorifics—which can be defined as polite speech that indicates relationship or status—has played an essential role in the Japanese language. When addressing someone in Japanese, an honorific usually takes the form of a suffix attached to one's name (example: "Asuna-san"), or as a title at the end of one's name or in place of the name itself (example: "Negi-sensei," or simply "Sensei!").

Honorifics can be expressions of respect or endearment. In the context of manga and anime, honorifics give insight into the nature of the relationship between characters. Many translations into English leave out these important honorifics, and therefore distort the "feel" of the original Japanese. Because Japanese honorifics contain nuances that English honorifics lack, it is our policy at Del Rey not to translate them. Here, instead, is a guide to some of the honorifics you may encounter in Del Rey Manga.

-san: This is the most common honorific, and is equivalent to Mr., Miss, Ms., Mrs., etc. It is the all-purpose honorific and can be used in any situation where politeness is required.

-sama: This is one level higher than "-san." It is used to confer great respect.

-dono: This comes from the word "tono," which means "lord." It is even a higher level than "-sama," and confers utmost respect.

-kun: This suffix is used at the end of boys' names to express familiarity or endearment. It is also sometimes used by men among friends, or when addressing someone younger or of a lower station.

-chan: This is used to express endearment, mostly toward girls. It is also used for little boys, pets, and even among lovers. It gives a sense of childish cuteness.

Sempai: This title suggests that the addressee is one's "senior" in a group or organization. It is most often used in a school setting, where underclassmen refer to their upperclassmen as "sempai." It can also be used in the workplace, such as when a newer employee addresses an employee who has seniority in the company.

Kohai: This is the opposite of "-sempai," and is used toward underclassmen in school or newcomers in the workplace. It connotes that the addressee is of lower station.

Sensei: Literally meaning "one who has come before," this title is used for teachers, doctors, or masters of any profession or art.

[blank]: Usually forgotten in these lists, but perhaps the most significant difference between Japanese and English. The lack of honorific means that the speaker has permission to address the person in a very intimate way. Usually, only family, spouses, or very close friends have this kind of permission. Known as *yobisute*, it can be gratifying when someone who has earned the intimacy starts to call one by one's name without an honorific. But when that intimacy hasn't been earned, it can also be very insulting.

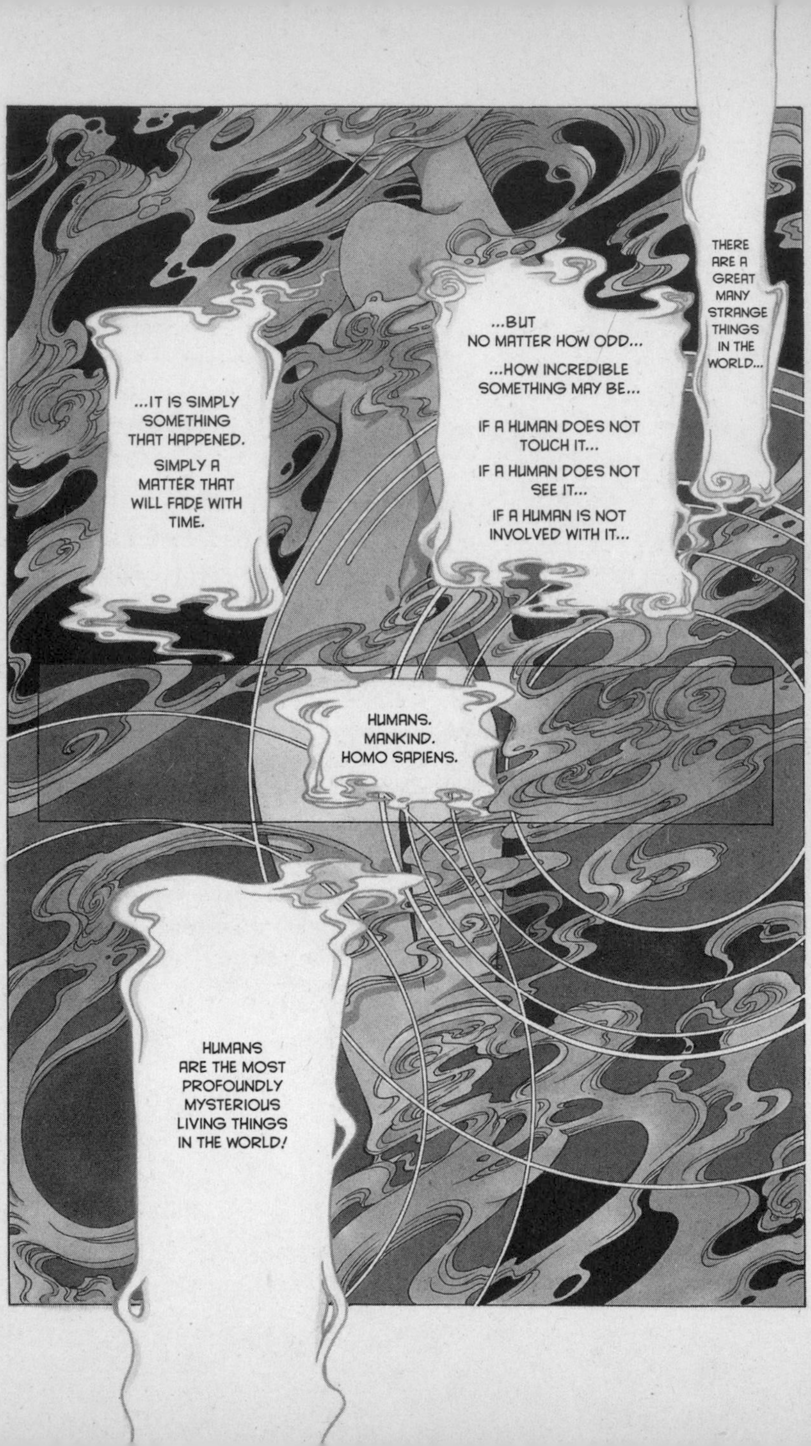
THERE ARE A GREAT MANY STRANGE THINGS IN THE WORLD...
...BUT NO MATTER HOW ODD...
...HOW INCREDIBLE SOMETHING MAY BE...
IF A HUMAN DOES NOT TOUCH IT...
IF A HUMAN DOES NOT SEE IT...
IF A HUMAN IS NOT INVOLVED WITH IT...
...IT IS SIMPLY SOMETHING THAT HAPPENED.
SIMPLY A MATTER THAT WILL FADE WITH TIME.
HUMANS. MANKIND. HOMO SAPIENS.
HUMANS ARE THE MOST PROFOUNDLY MYSTERIOUS LIVING THINGS IN THE WORLD!

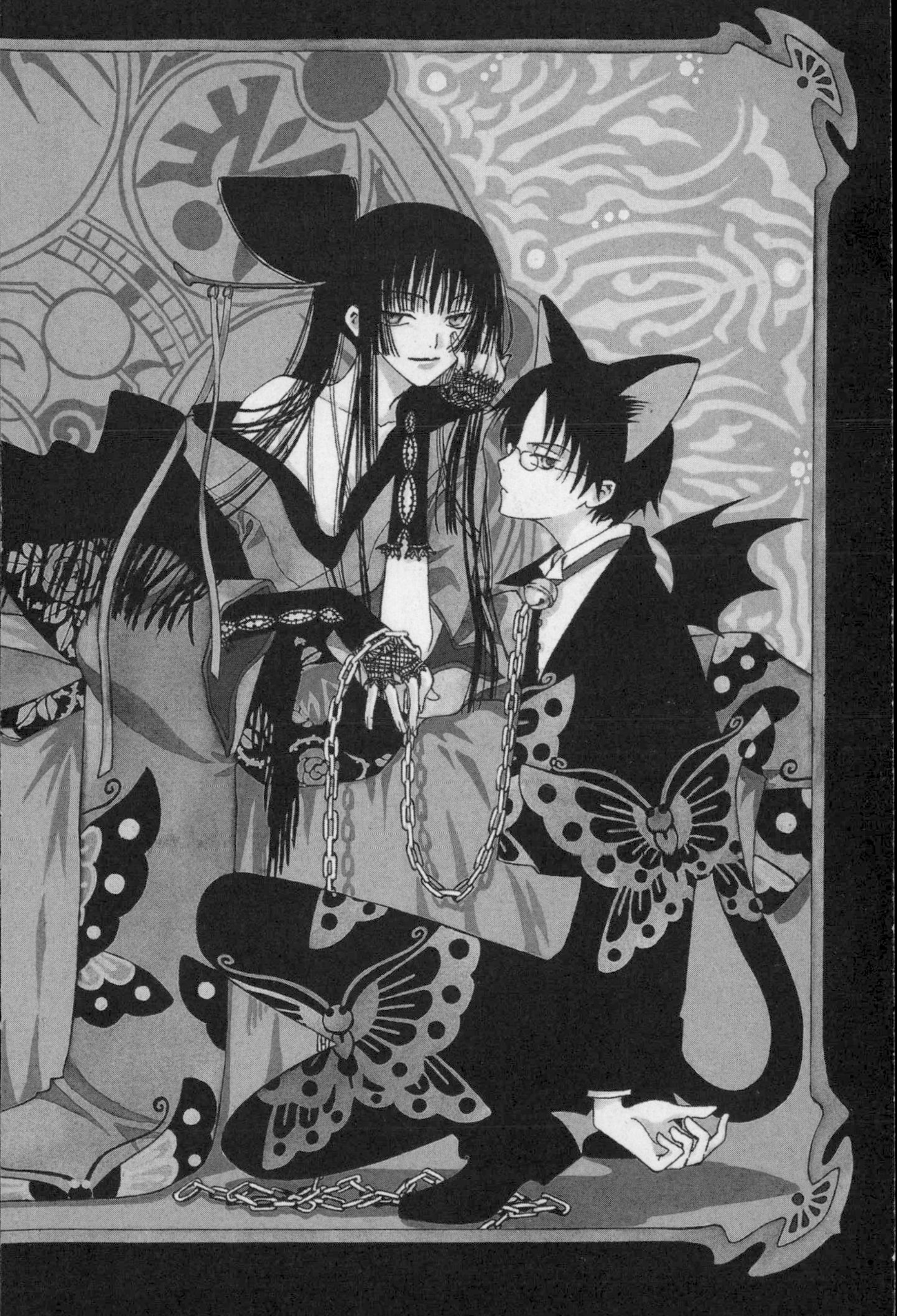

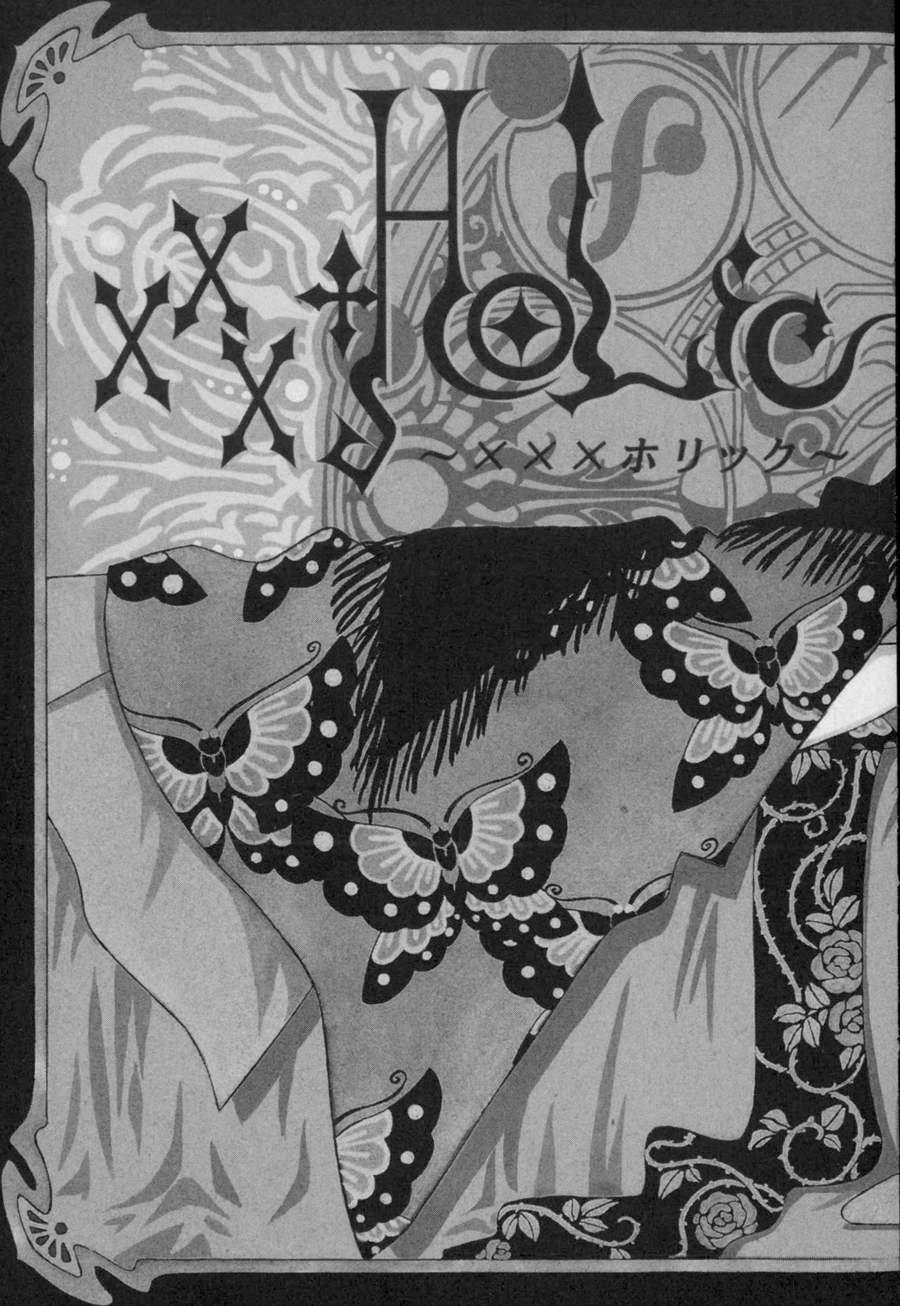
xxxHOLiC
～×××ホリック～

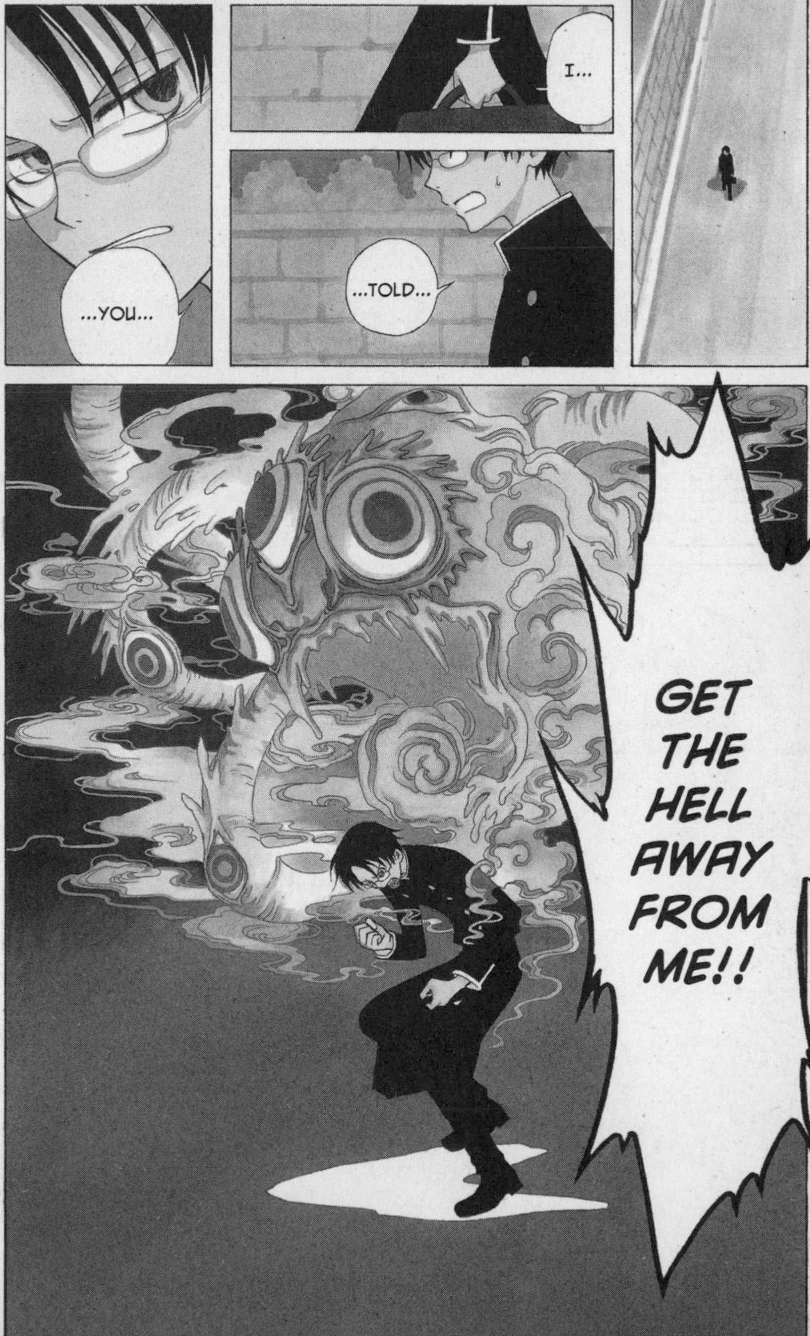
I...
...TOLD...
...YOU...
GET THE HELL AWAY FROM ME!!

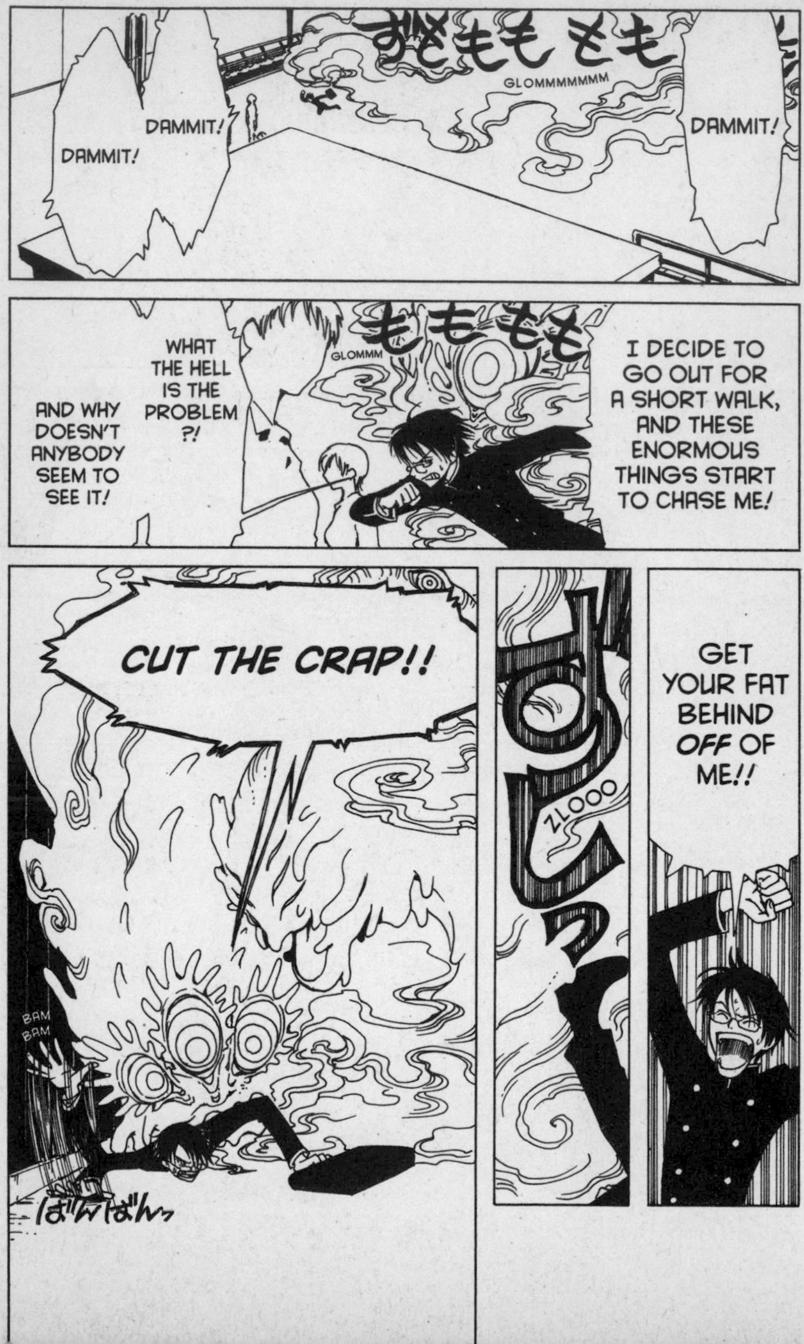
GLOMMMMMMM
DAMMIT!
DAMMIT!
DAMMIT!
I DECIDE TO GO OUT FOR A SHORT WALK, AND THESE ENORMOUS THINGS START TO CHASE ME!
もももも
GLOMMM
WHAT THE HELL IS THE PROBLEM?!
AND WHY DOESN'T ANYBODY SEEM TO SEE IT!
GET YOUR FAT BEHIND OFF OF ME!!
ZLOOO
CUT THE CRAP!!
BAM BAM
ばんばんっ

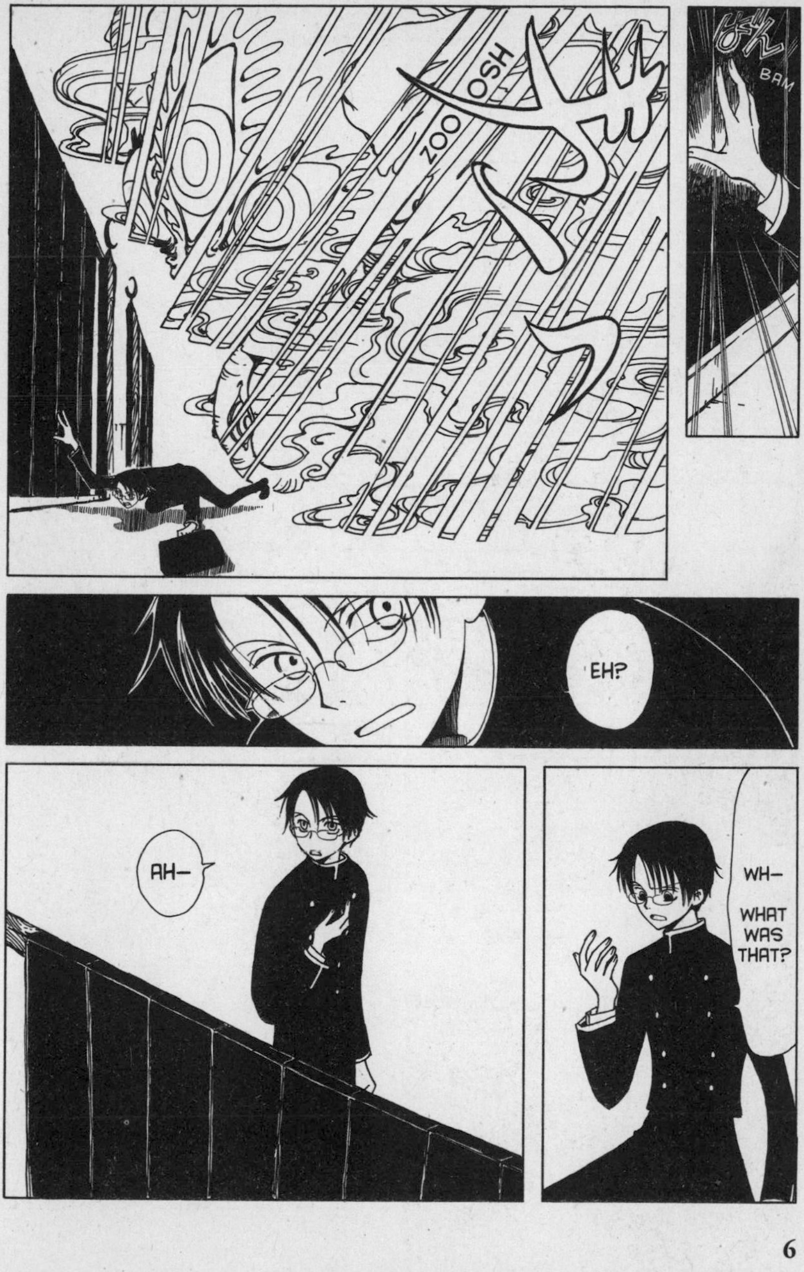
ばん
BAM
ZOOOSH
EH?
WH—
WHAT WAS THAT?
AH—

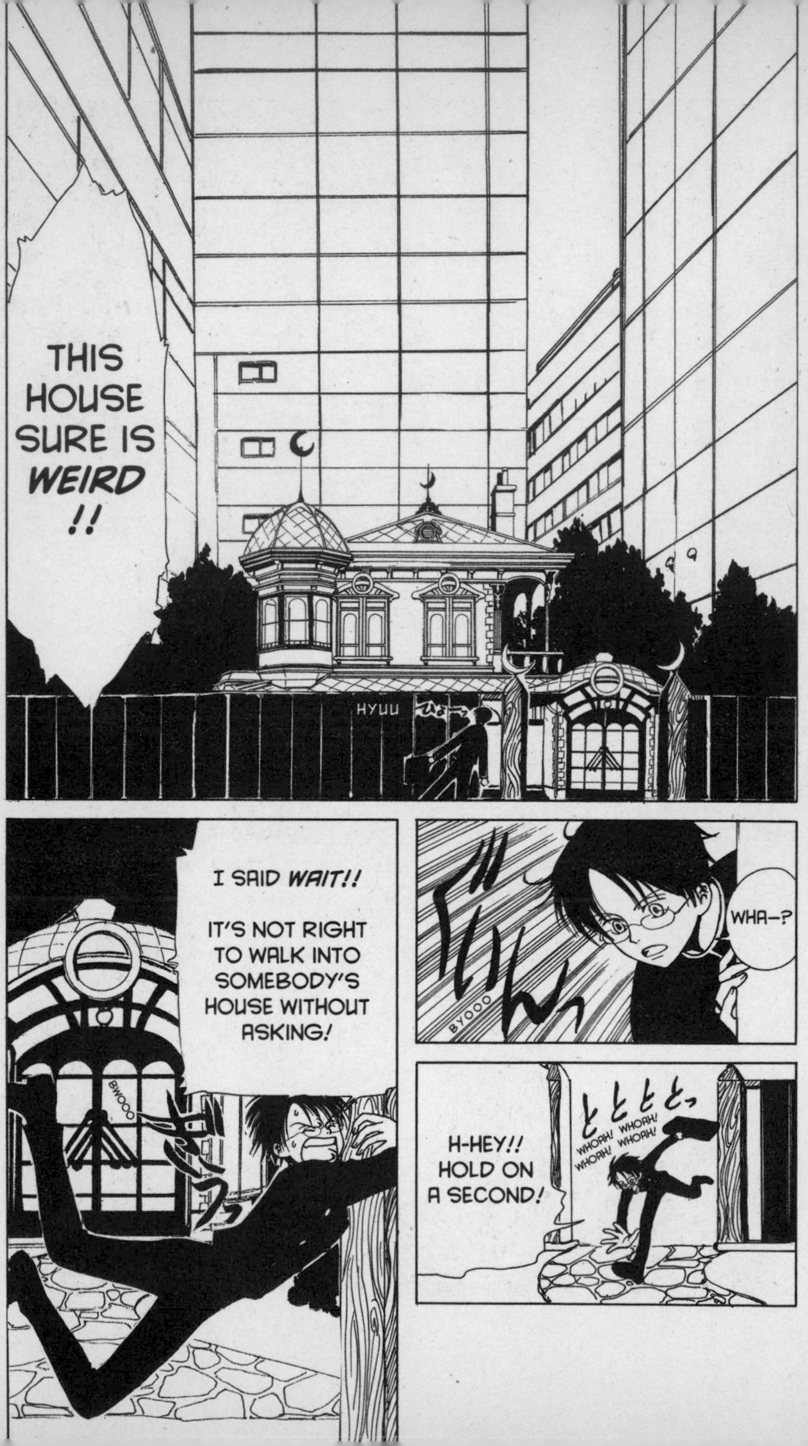
THIS HOUSE SURE IS WEIRD!!
HYUU
WHA-?
BYOOO
H-HEY!! HOLD ON A SECOND!
とととっ
WHOAH! WHOAH! WHOAH! WHOAH!
I SAID WAIT!!
IT'S NOT RIGHT TO WALK INTO SOMEBODY'S HOUSE WITHOUT ASKING!
BYOOO

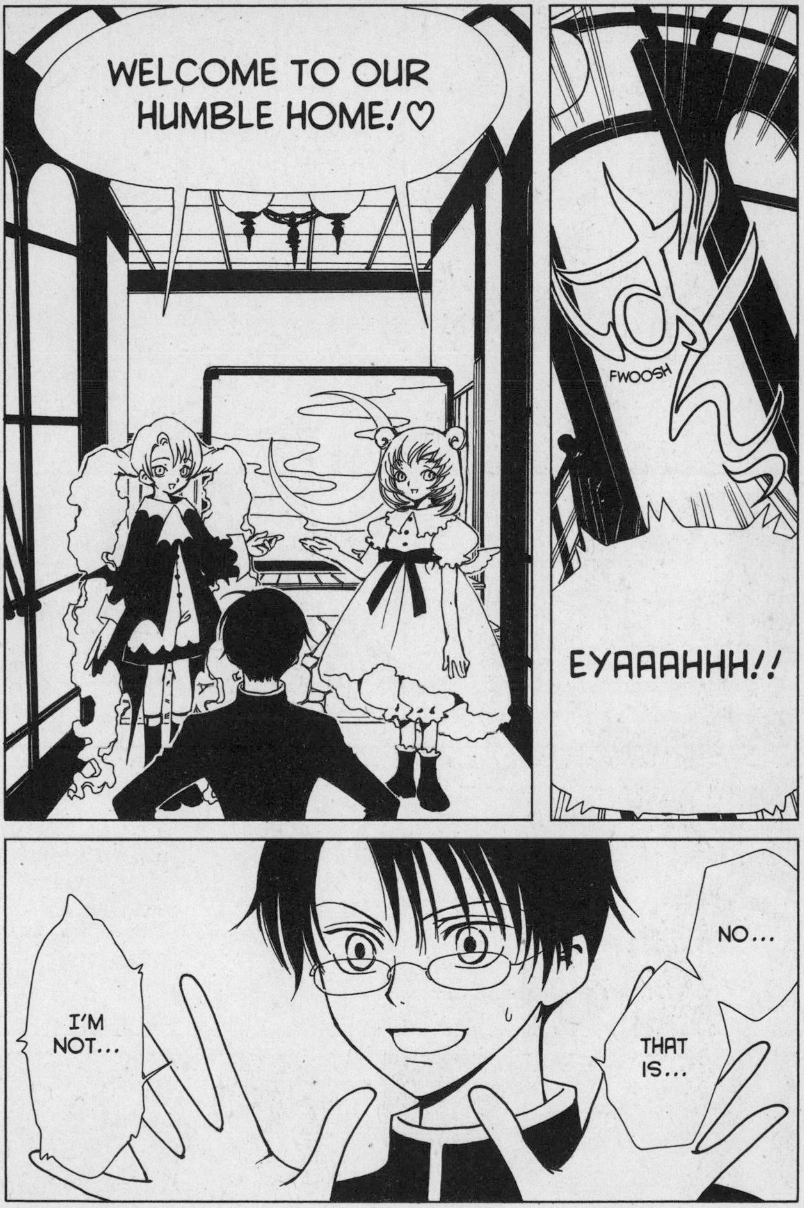
FWOOSH
EYAAAHHH!!
WELCOME TO OUR HUMBLE HOME! ♡
NO...
THAT IS...
I'M NOT...

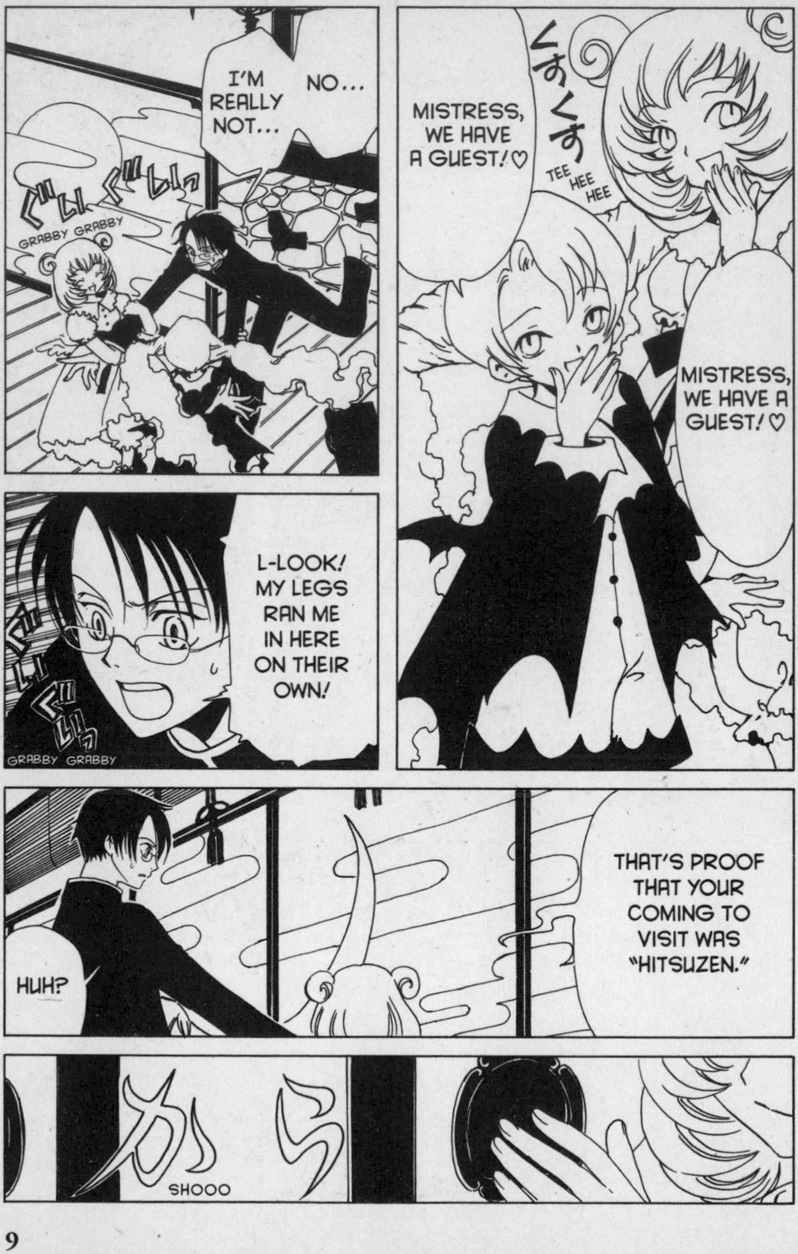

くすくす
TEE HEE HEE
MISTRESS, WE HAVE A GUEST! ♡
MISTRESS, WE HAVE A GUEST! ♡
NO...
I'M REALLY NOT...
ぐいぐいっ
GRABBY GRABBY
L-LOOK! MY LEGS RAN ME IN HERE ON THEIR OWN!
GRABBY GRABBY
THAT'S PROOF THAT YOUR COMING TO VISIT WAS "HITSUZEN."
HUH?
から
SHOOO

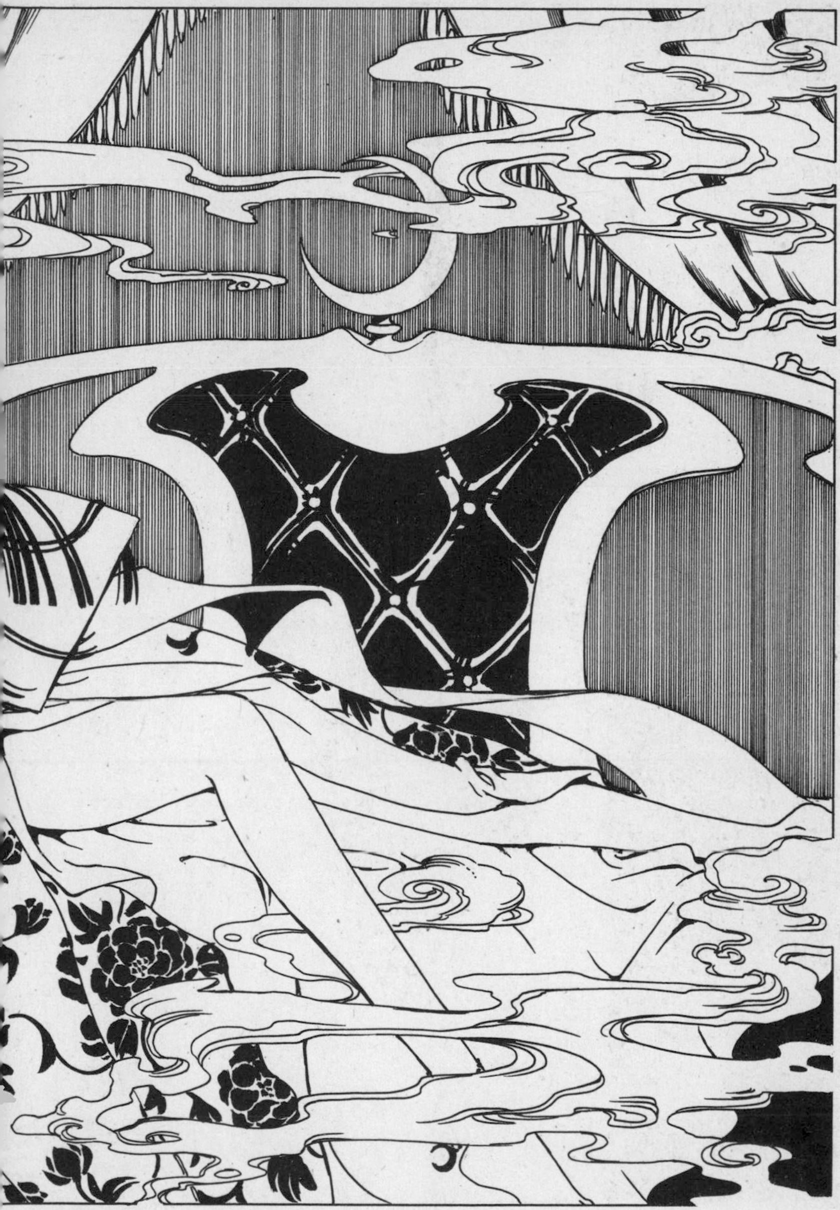

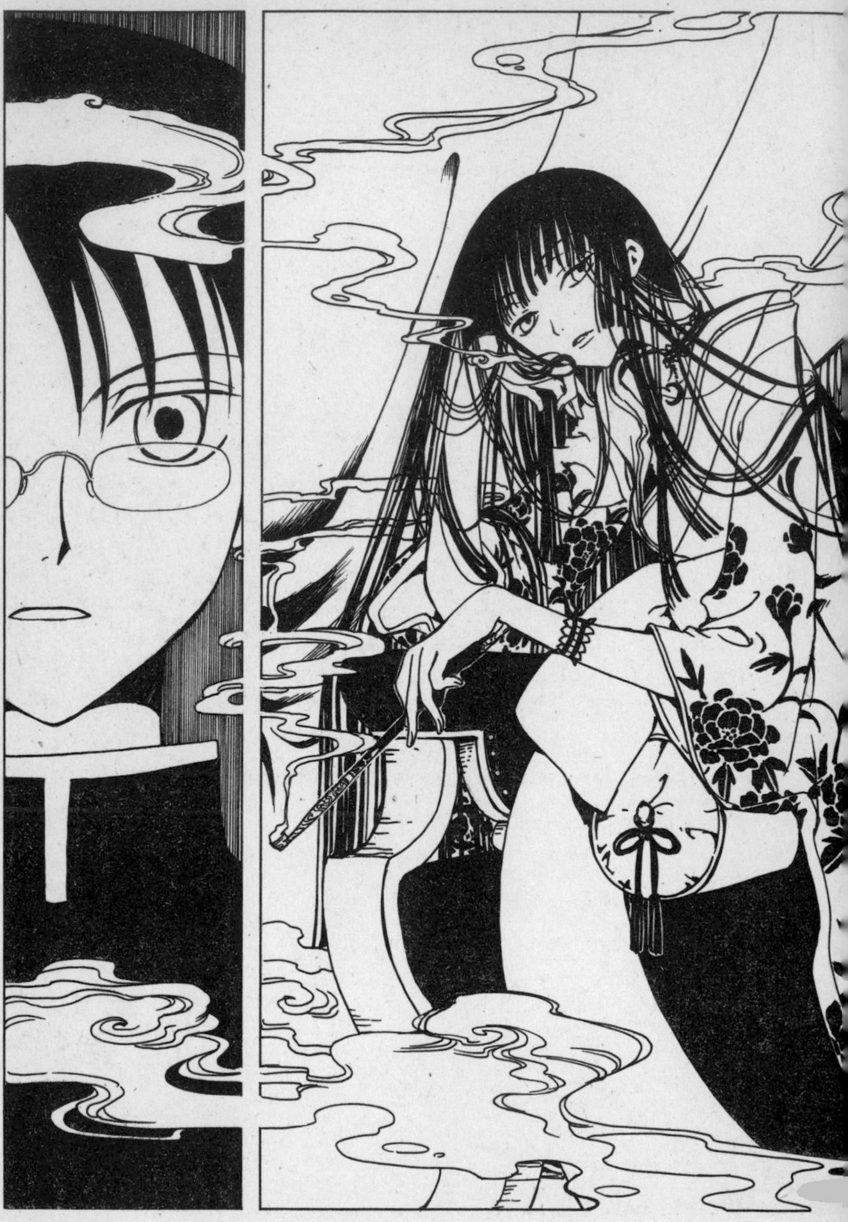

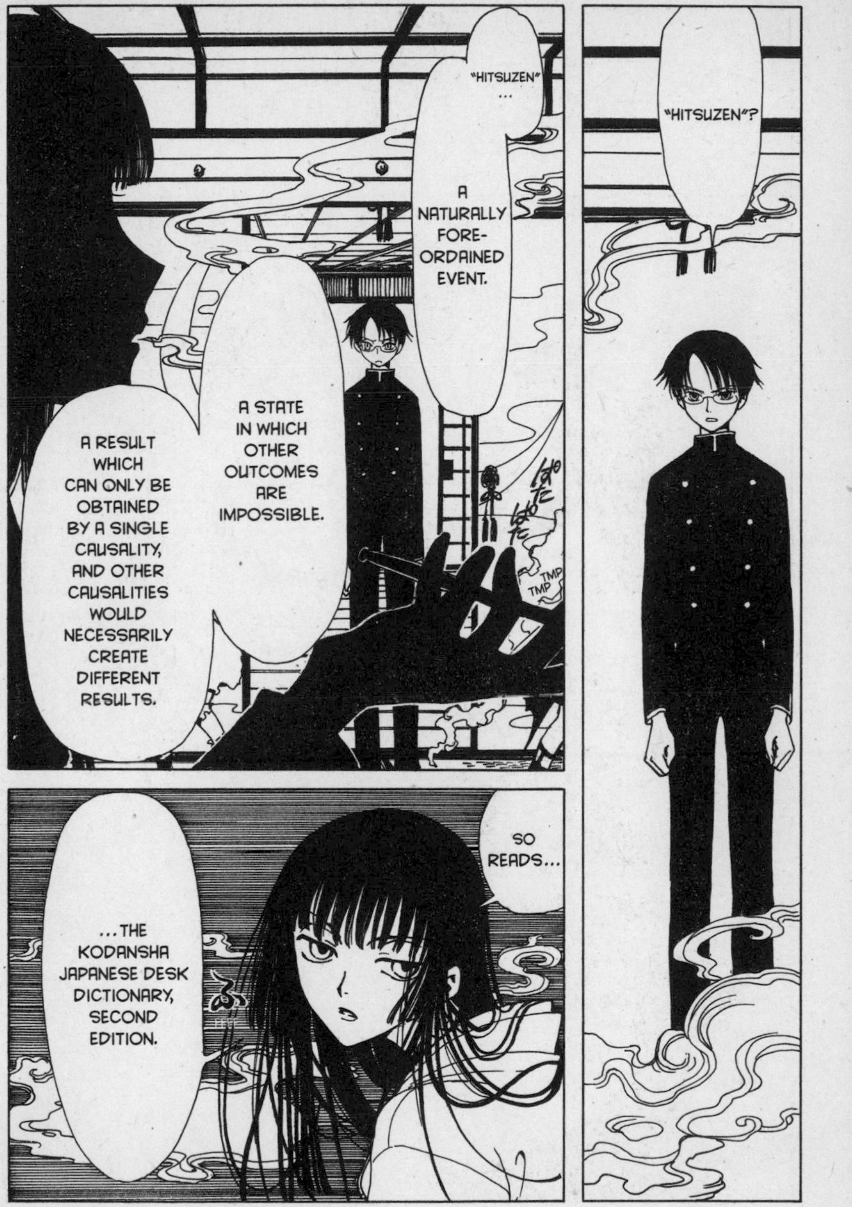
"HITSUZEN"?
"HITSUZEN" ... A NATURALLY FORE-ORDAINED EVENT.
A STATE IN WHICH OTHER OUTCOMES ARE IMPOSSIBLE.
A RESULT WHICH CAN ONLY BE OBTAINED BY A SINGLE CAUSALITY, AND OTHER CAUSALITIES WOULD NECESSARILY CREATE DIFFERENT RESULTS.
TMP TMP
SO READS...
...THE KODANSHA JAPANESE DESK DICTIONARY, SECOND EDITION.

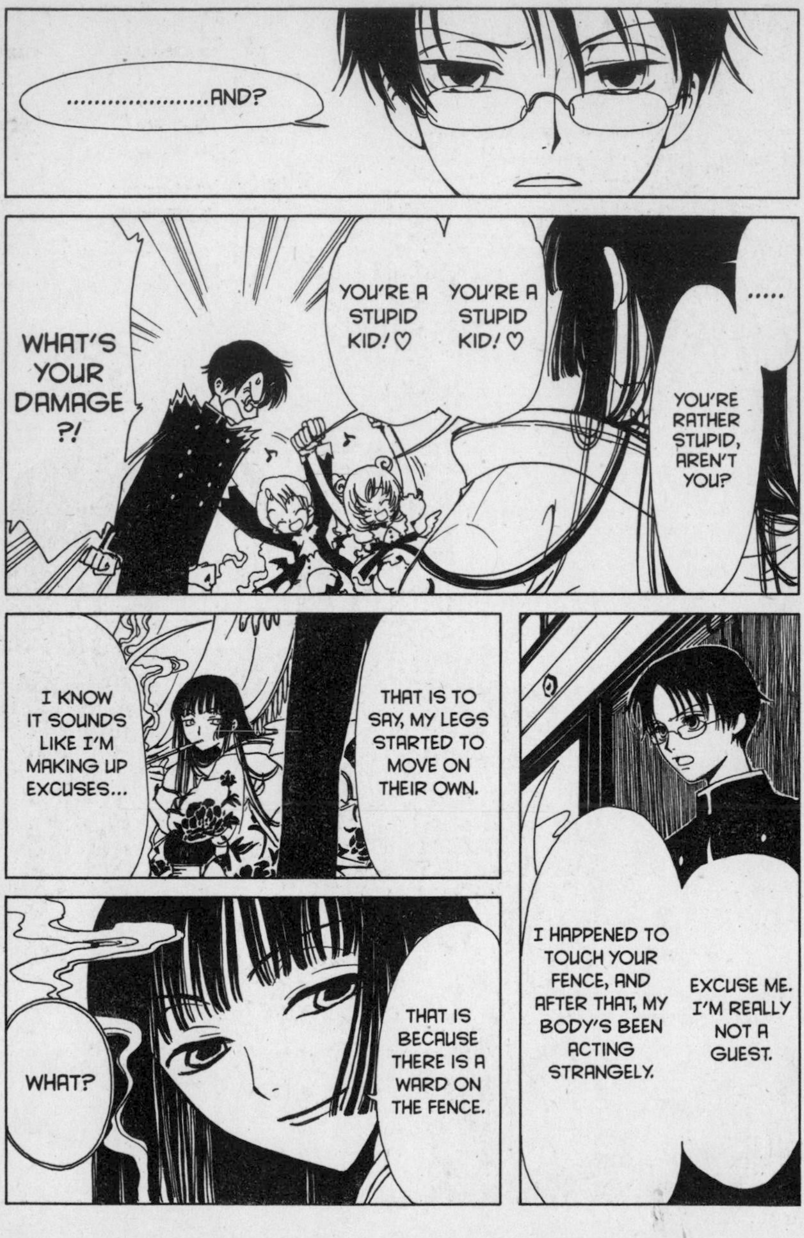

....................AND?
.....
YOU'RE RATHER STUPID, AREN'T YOU?
YOU'RE A STUPID KID! ♡
YOU'RE A STUPID KID! ♡
WHAT'S YOUR DAMAGE ?!
EXCUSE ME. I'M REALLY NOT A GUEST.
I HAPPENED TO TOUCH YOUR FENCE, AND AFTER THAT, MY BODY'S BEEN ACTING STRANGELY.
THAT IS TO SAY, MY LEGS STARTED TO MOVE ON THEIR OWN.
I KNOW IT SOUNDS LIKE I'M MAKING UP EXCUSES...
THAT IS BECAUSE THERE IS A WARD ON THE FENCE.
WHAT?

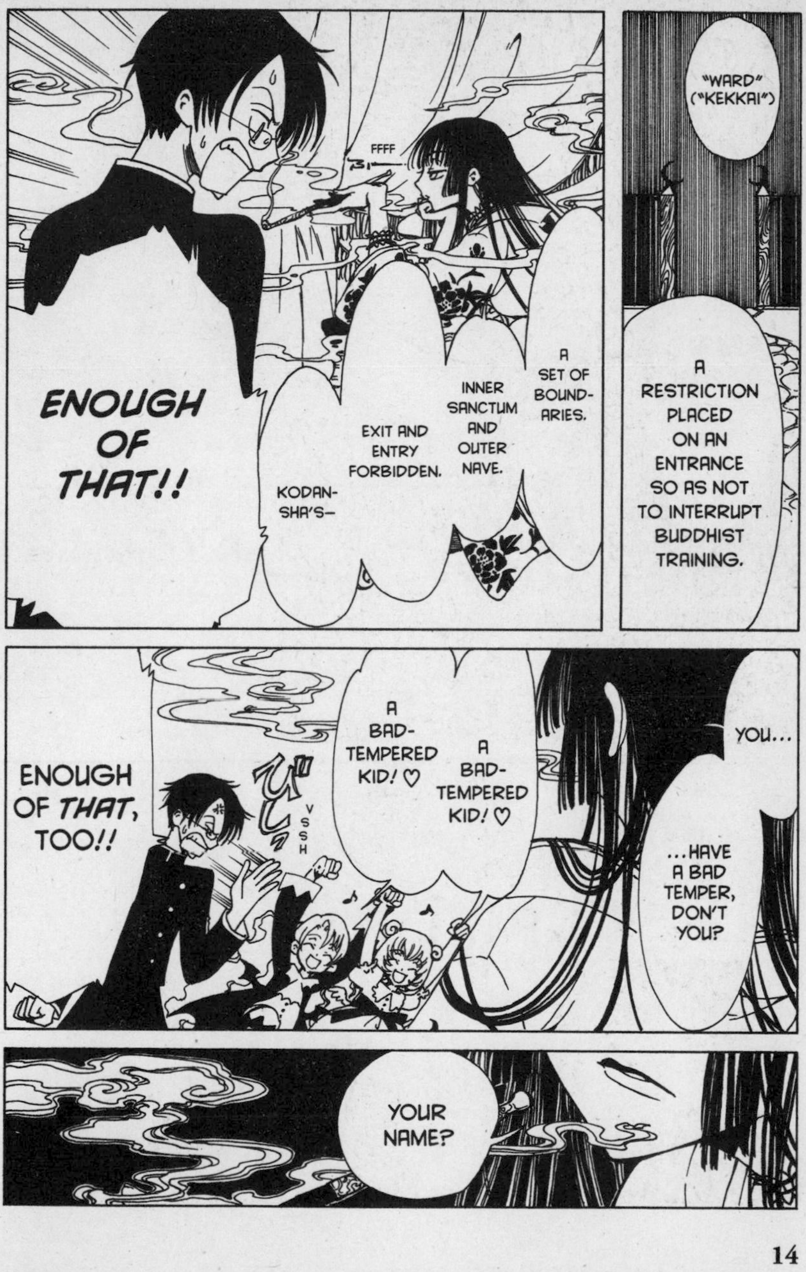
"WARD" ("KEKKAI")
A RESTRICTION PLACED ON AN ENTRANCE SO AS NOT TO INTERRUPT BUDDHIST TRAINING.
FFFF
A SET OF BOUND-ARIES.
INNER SANCTUM AND OUTER NAVE.
EXIT AND ENTRY FORBIDDEN.
KODAN-SHA'S—
ENOUGH OF THAT!!
YOU...
...HAVE A BAD TEMPER, DON'T YOU?
A BAD-TEMPERED KID! ♡
A BAD-TEMPERED KID! ♡
VSSH
ENOUGH OF THAT, TOO!!
YOUR NAME?

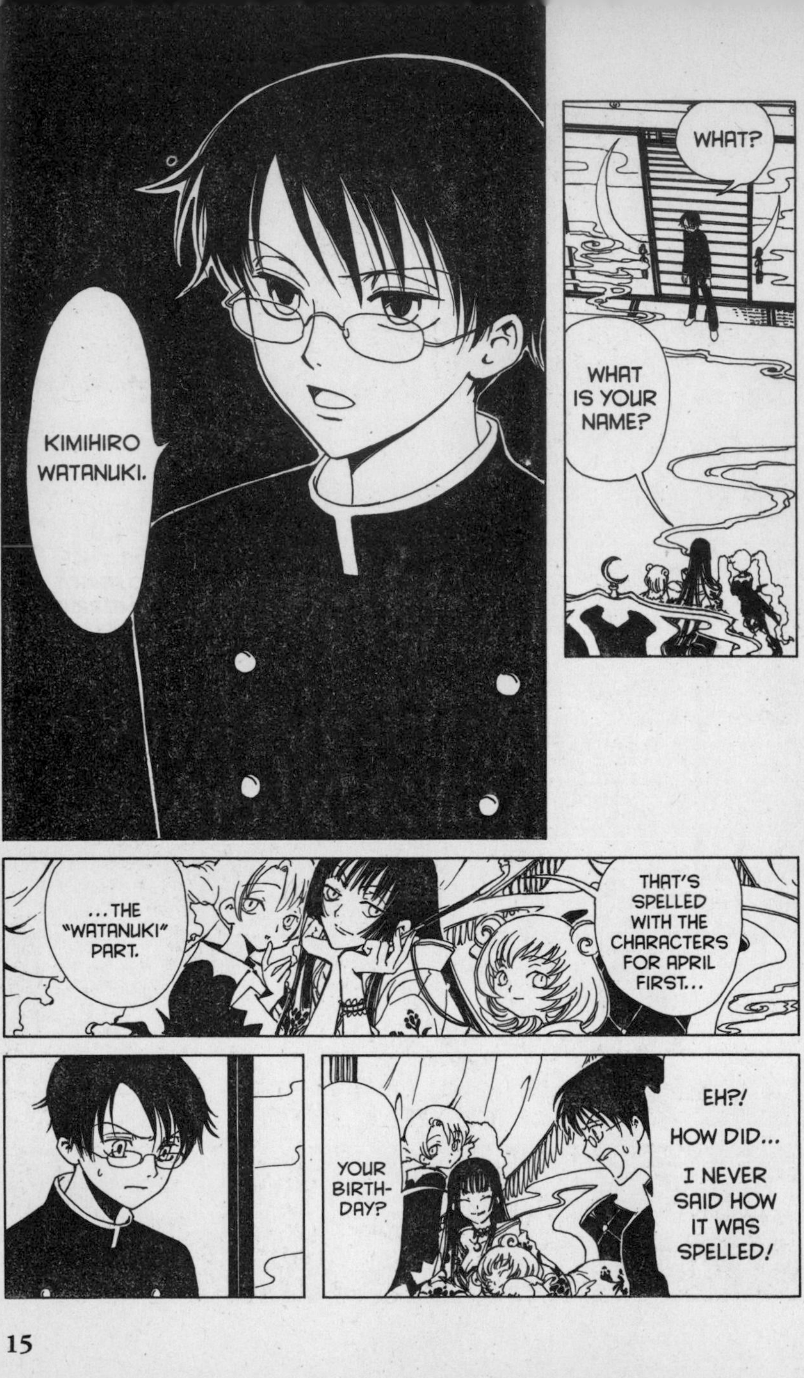
WHAT?
WHAT IS YOUR NAME?
KIMIHIRO WATANUKI.
THAT'S SPELLED WITH THE CHARACTERS FOR APRIL FIRST...
...THE "WATANUKI" PART.
EH?!
HOW DID...
I NEVER SAID HOW IT WAS SPELLED!
YOUR BIRTH-DAY?

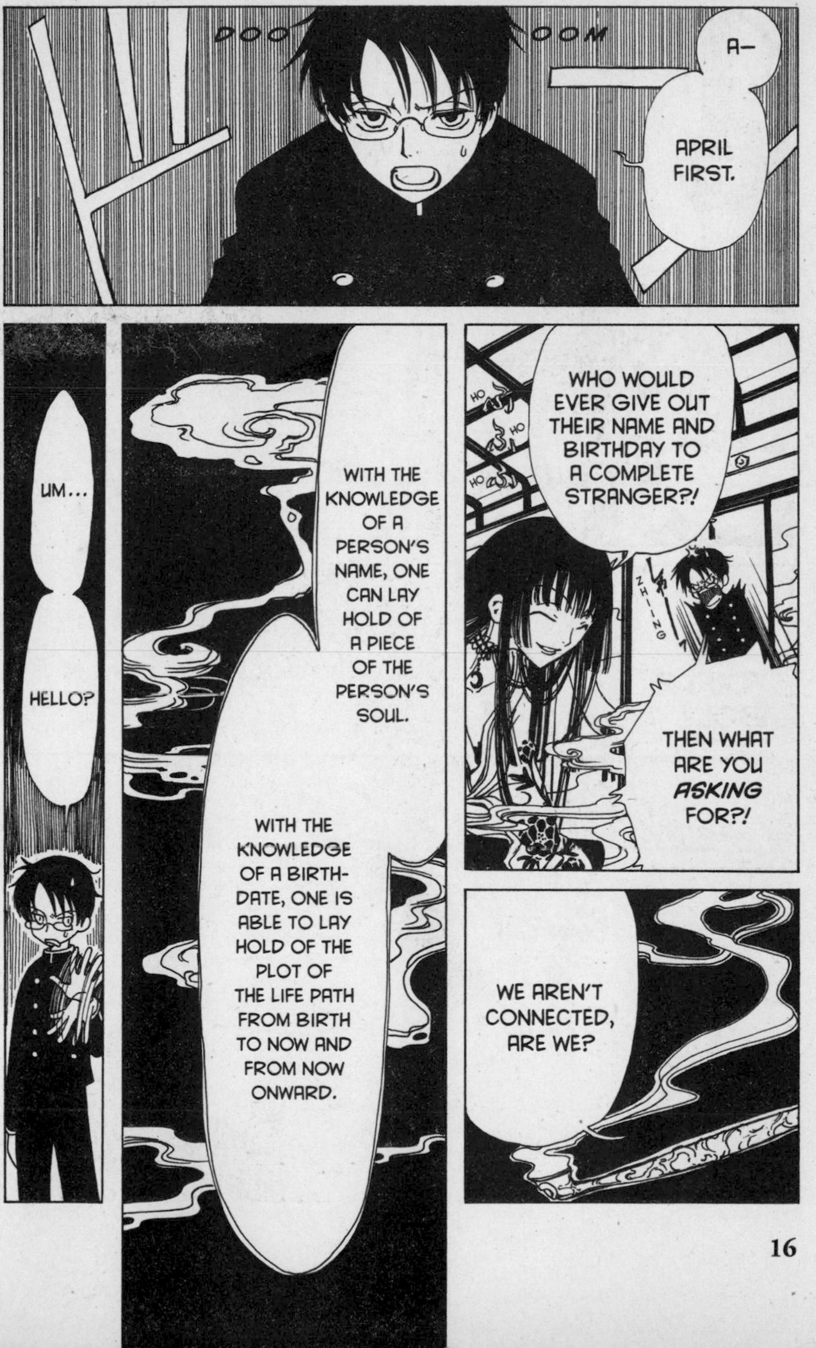
DOO OOM
A—
APRIL FIRST.
HO HO HO
WHO WOULD EVER GIVE OUT THEIR NAME AND BIRTHDAY TO A COMPLETE STRANGER?!
ZHIING
THEN WHAT ARE YOU *ASKING* FOR?!
WE AREN'T CONNECTED, ARE WE?
WITH THE KNOWLEDGE OF A PERSON'S NAME, ONE CAN LAY HOLD OF A PIECE OF THE PERSON'S SOUL.
WITH THE KNOWLEDGE OF A BIRTH-DATE, ONE IS ABLE TO LAY HOLD OF THE PLOT OF THE LIFE PATH FROM BIRTH TO NOW AND FROM NOW ONWARD.
UM...
HELLO?

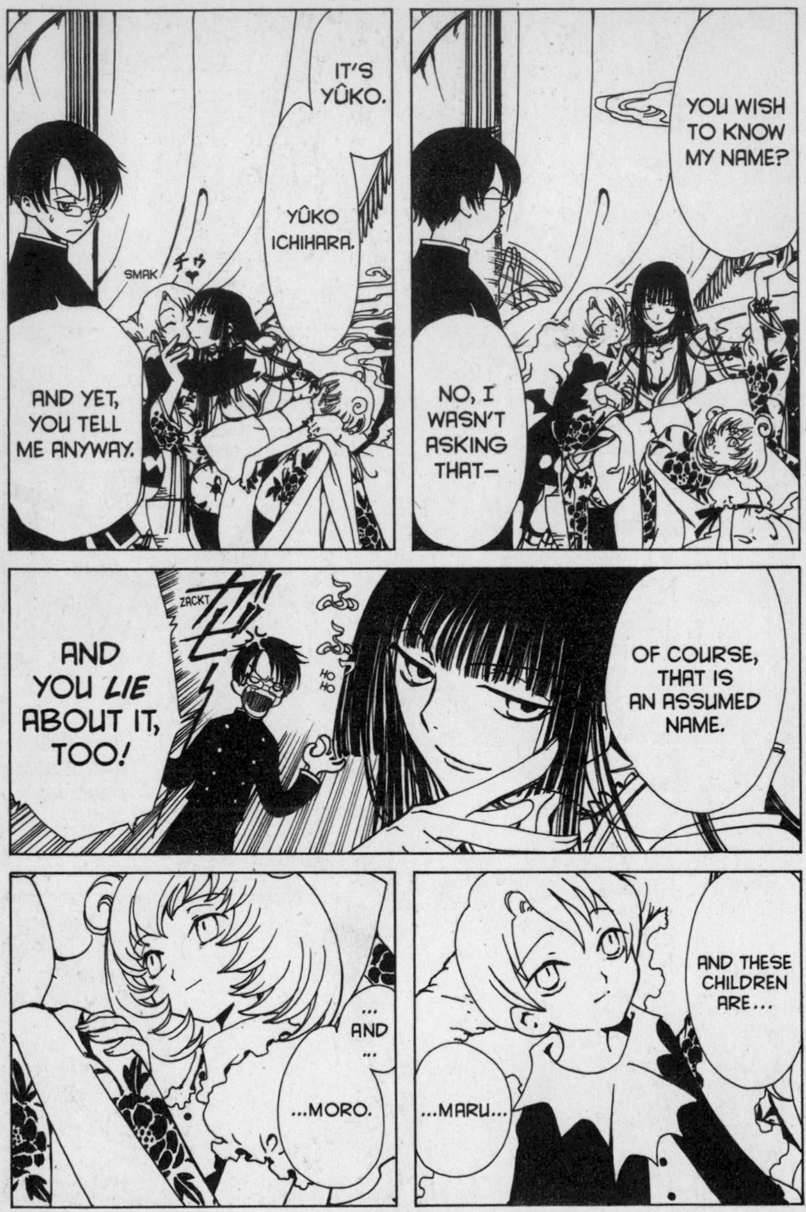
YOU WISH TO KNOW MY NAME?
NO, I WASN'T ASKING THAT—
IT'S YÛKO.
YÛKO ICHIHARA.
SMAK
AND YET, YOU TELL ME ANYWAY.
OF COURSE, THAT IS AN ASSUMED NAME.
HO HO
ZACKT
AND YOU LIE ABOUT IT, TOO!
AND THESE CHILDREN ARE...
...MARU...
... AND ...
...MORO.

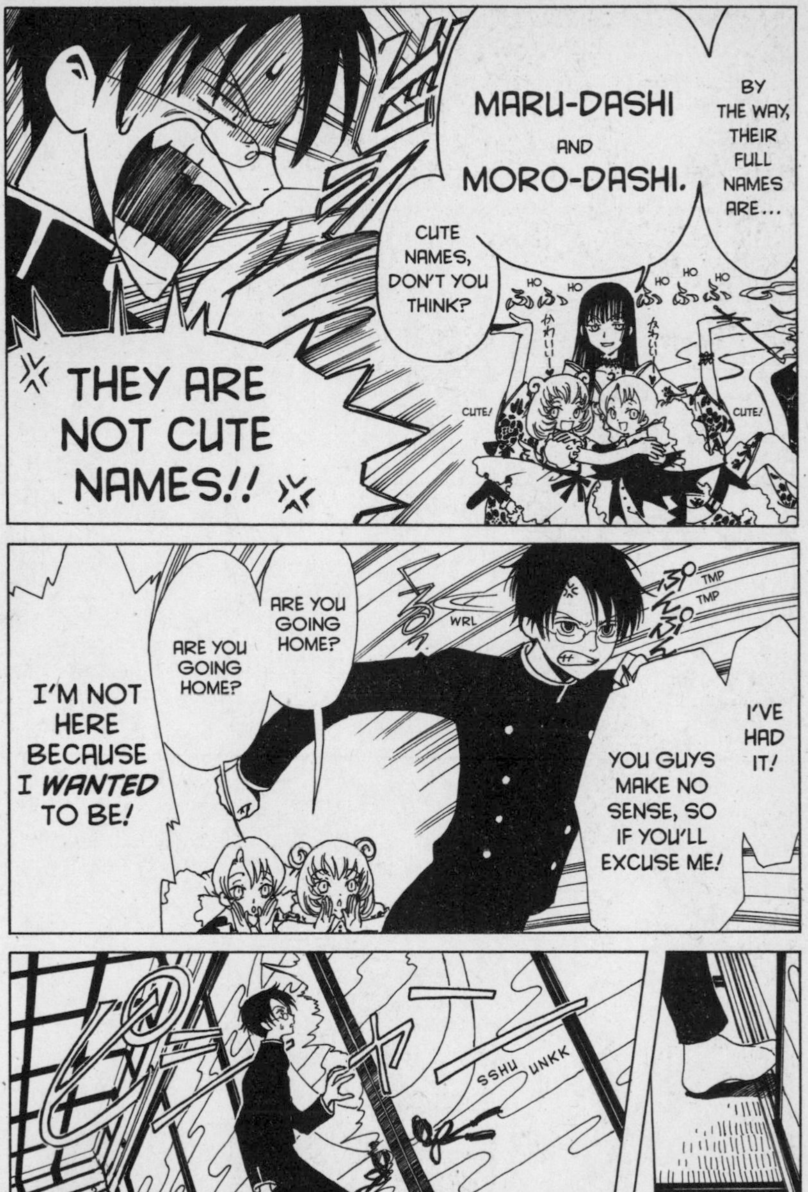

BY THE WAY, THEIR FULL NAMES ARE...
MARU-DASHI AND MORO-DASHI.
HO HO HO
CUTE NAMES, DON'T YOU THINK?
HO HO
CUTE!
CUTE!
THEY ARE NOT CUTE NAMES!!
I'VE HAD IT!
TMP TMP
YOU GUYS MAKE NO SENSE, SO IF YOU'LL EXCUSE ME!
WRL
ARE YOU GOING HOME?
ARE YOU GOING HOME?
I'M NOT HERE BECAUSE I *WANTED* TO BE!
SSHU UNKK

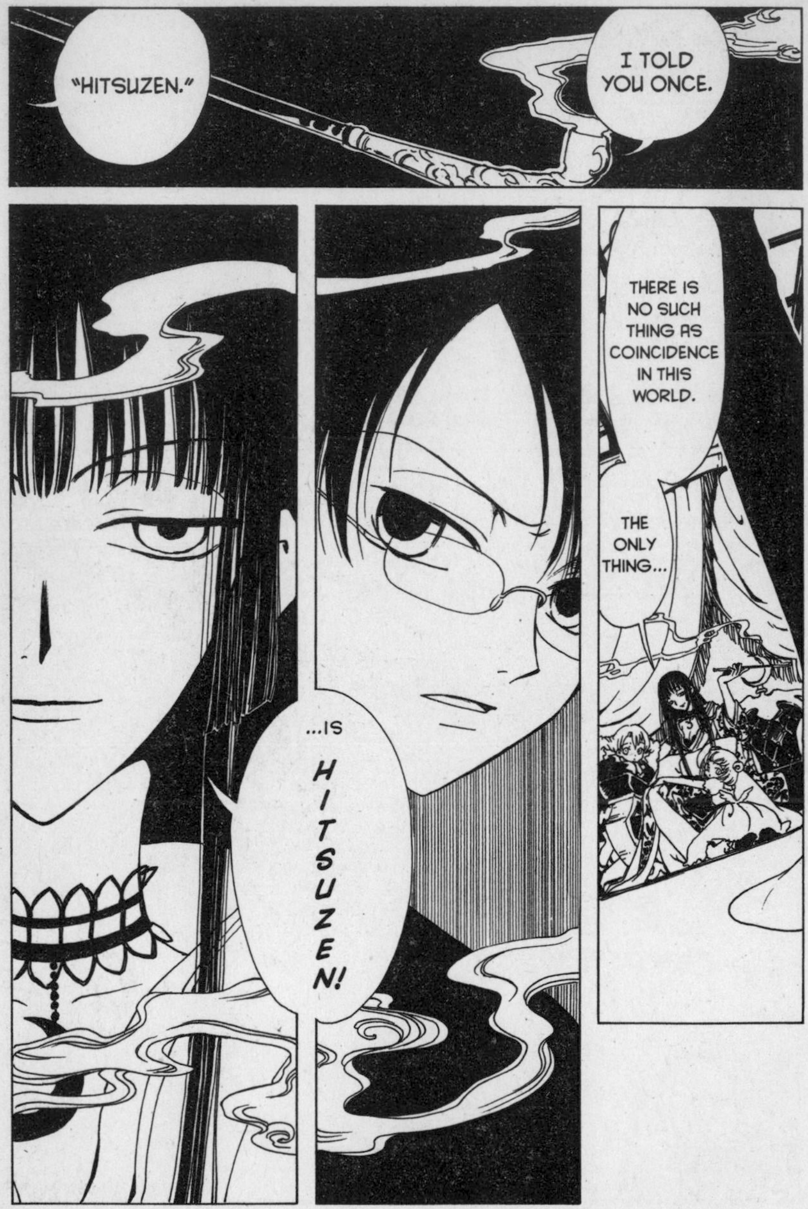
I TOLD YOU ONCE.
"HITSUZEN."
THERE IS NO SUCH THING AS COINCIDENCE IN THIS WORLD.
THE ONLY THING...
...IS HITSUZEN!

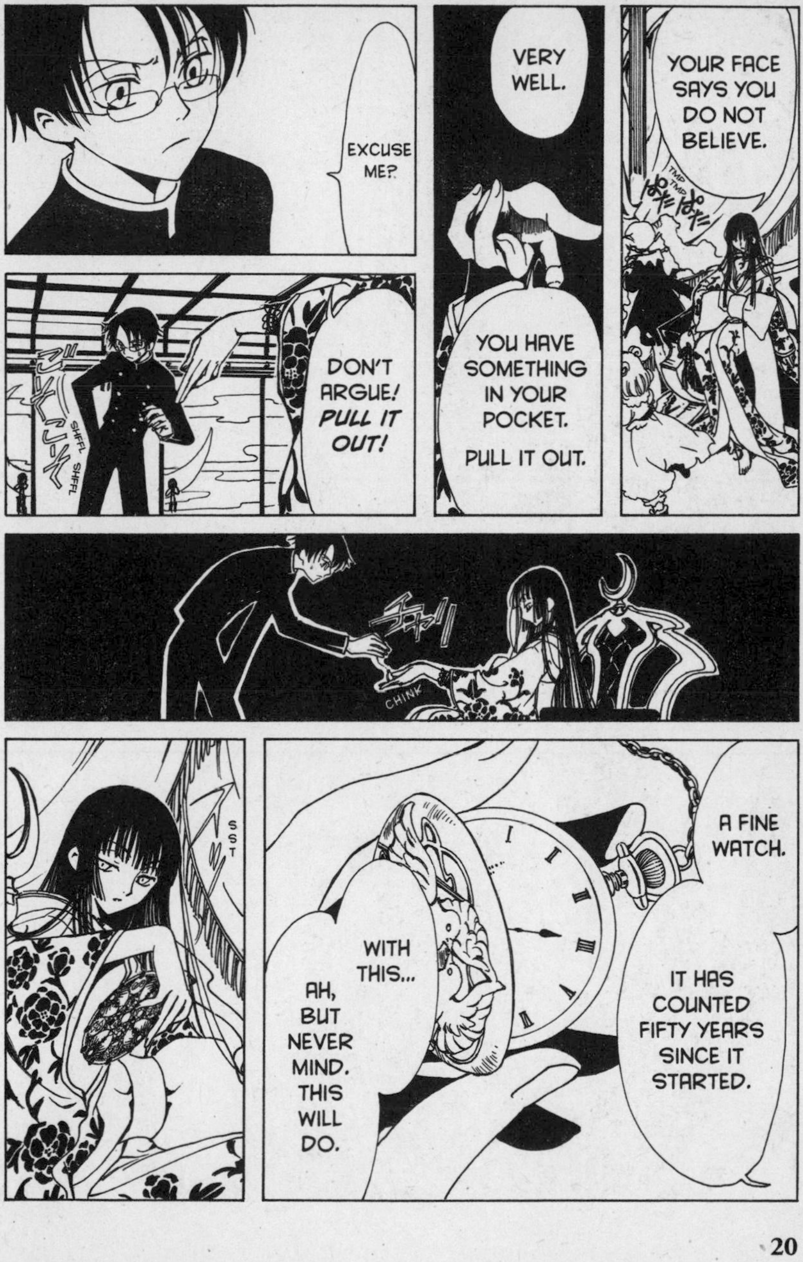
YOUR FACE SAYS YOU DO NOT BELIEVE.
TMP TMP
VERY WELL.
YOU HAVE SOMETHING IN YOUR POCKET.
PULL IT OUT.
EXCUSE ME?
DON'T ARGUE! *PULL IT OUT!*
SHFFL SHFFL
CHINK
A FINE WATCH.
IT HAS COUNTED FIFTY YEARS SINCE IT STARTED.
WITH THIS...
AH, BUT NEVER MIND. THIS WILL DO.
SST

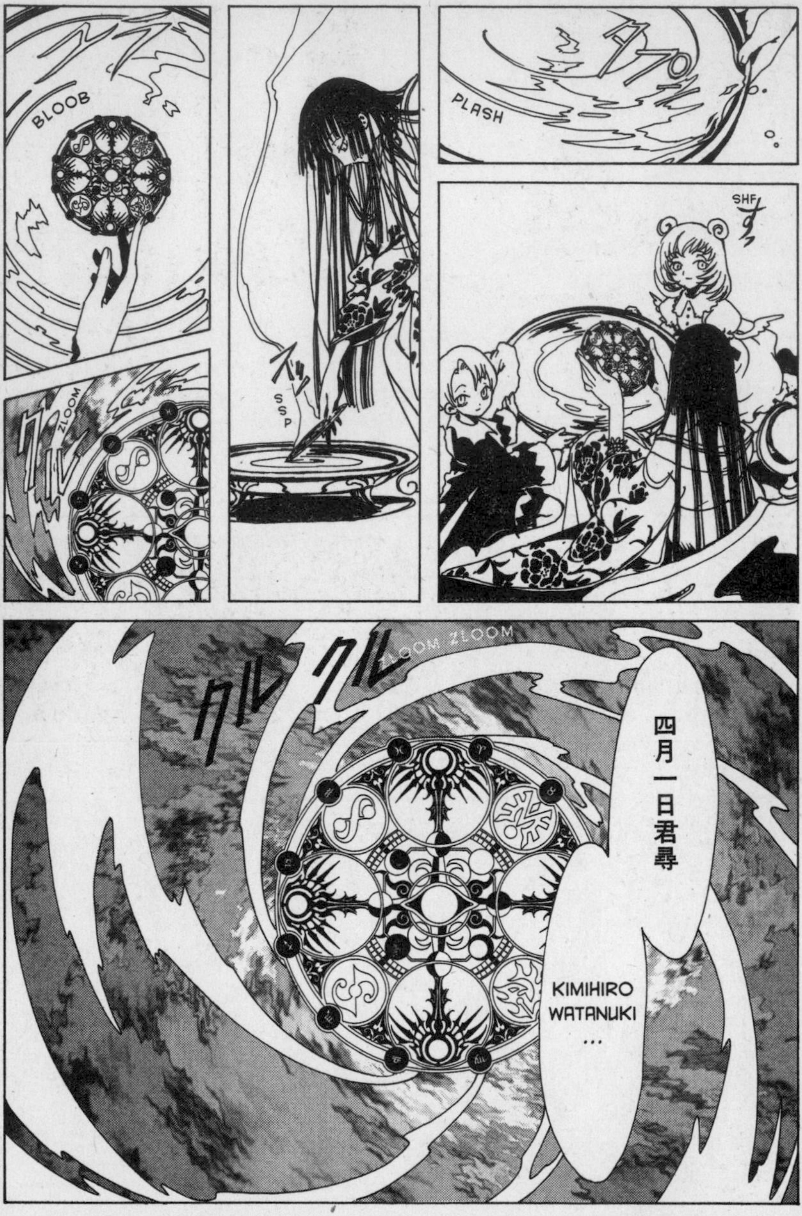
PLASH
SHF
SSP
BLOOB
ZLOOM
ZLOOM ZLOOM
四月一日君尋
KIMIHIRO WATANUKI
...

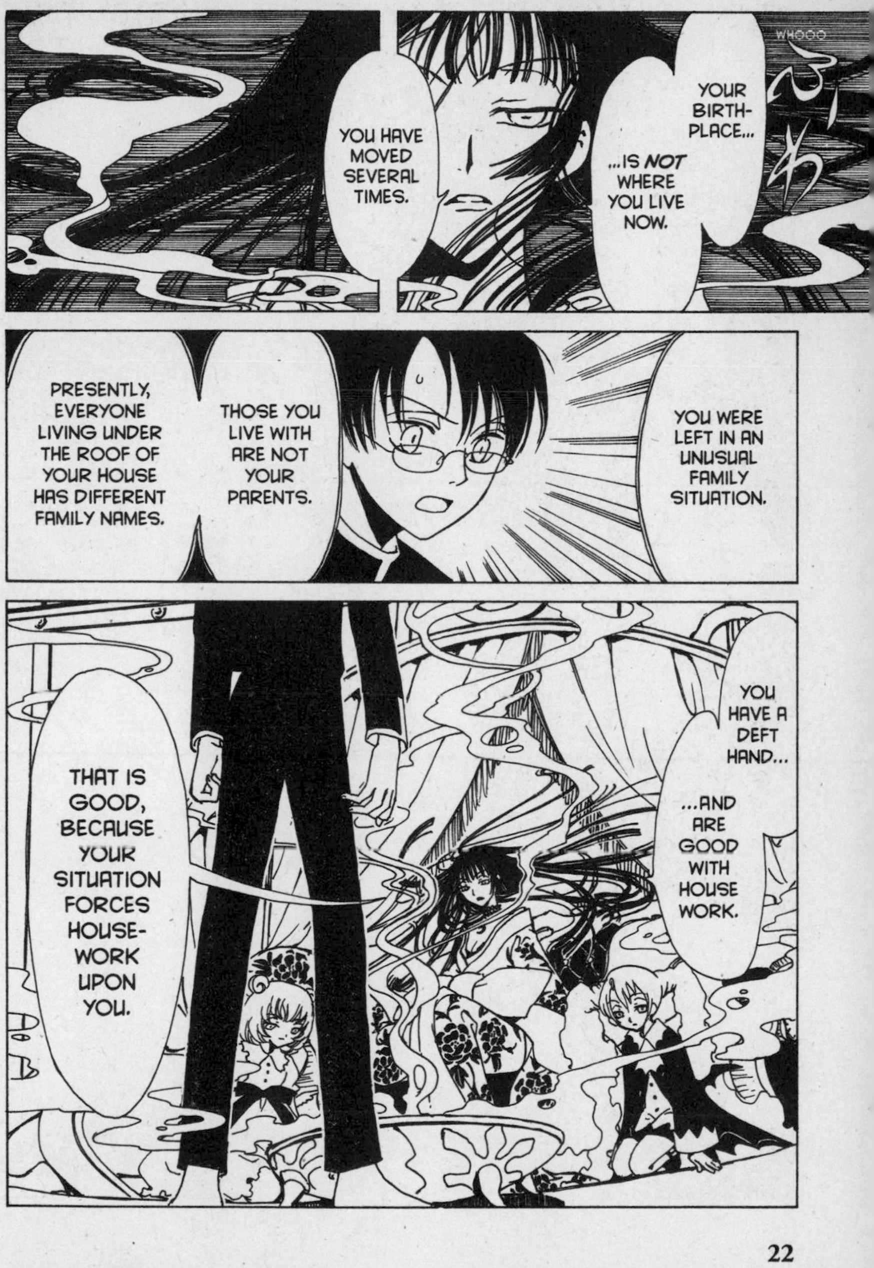

WHOOO
YOUR BIRTH-PLACE...
...IS *NOT* WHERE YOU LIVE NOW.
YOU HAVE MOVED SEVERAL TIMES.
YOU WERE LEFT IN AN UNUSUAL FAMILY SITUATION.
THOSE YOU LIVE WITH ARE NOT YOUR PARENTS.
PRESENTLY, EVERYONE LIVING UNDER THE ROOF OF YOUR HOUSE HAS DIFFERENT FAMILY NAMES.
YOU HAVE A DEFT HAND...
...AND ARE GOOD WITH HOUSE WORK.
THAT IS GOOD, BECAUSE YOUR SITUATION FORCES HOUSE-WORK UPON YOU.

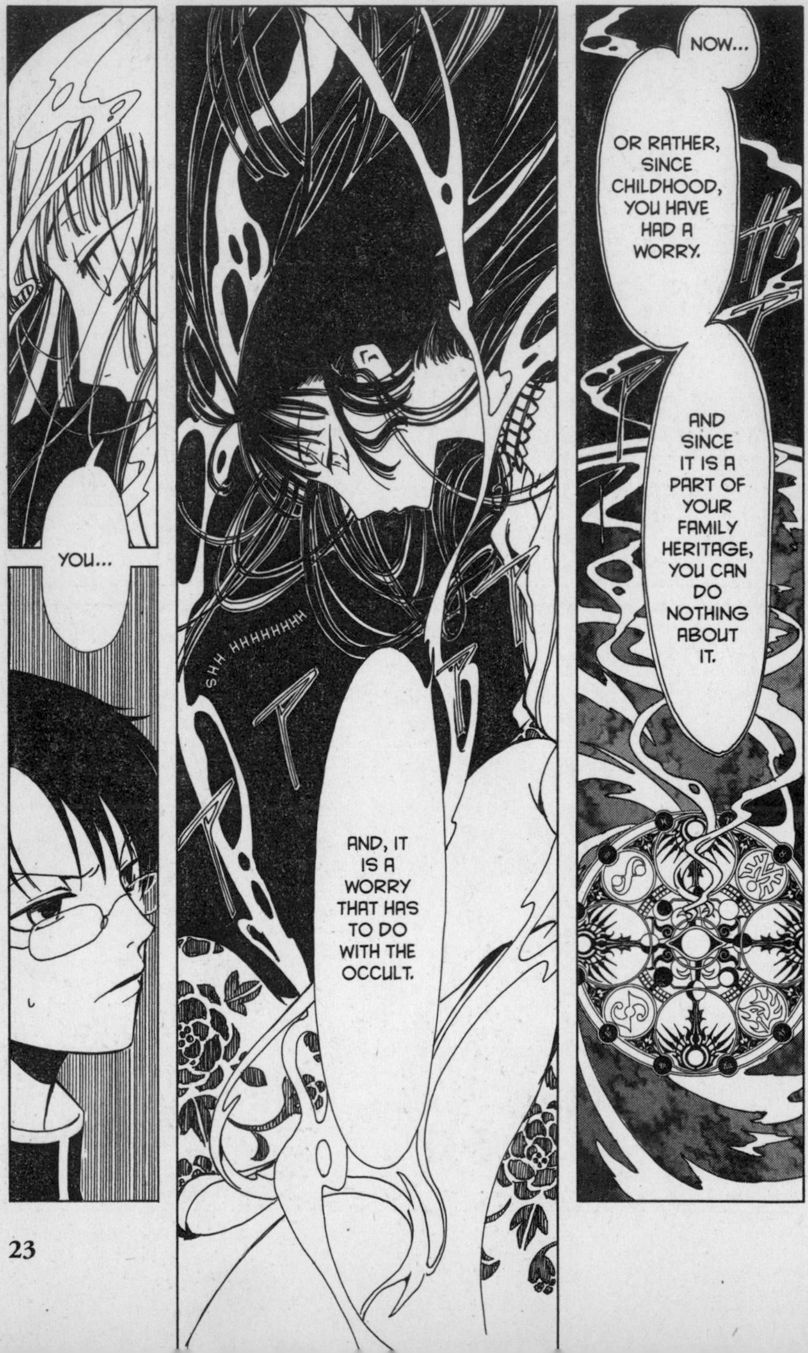
NOW...
OR RATHER, SINCE CHILDHOOD, YOU HAVE HAD A WORRY.
AND SINCE IT IS A PART OF YOUR FAMILY HERITAGE, YOU CAN DO NOTHING ABOUT IT.
SHH HHHHHHHH
AND, IT IS A WORRY THAT HAS TO DO WITH THE OCCULT.
YOU...

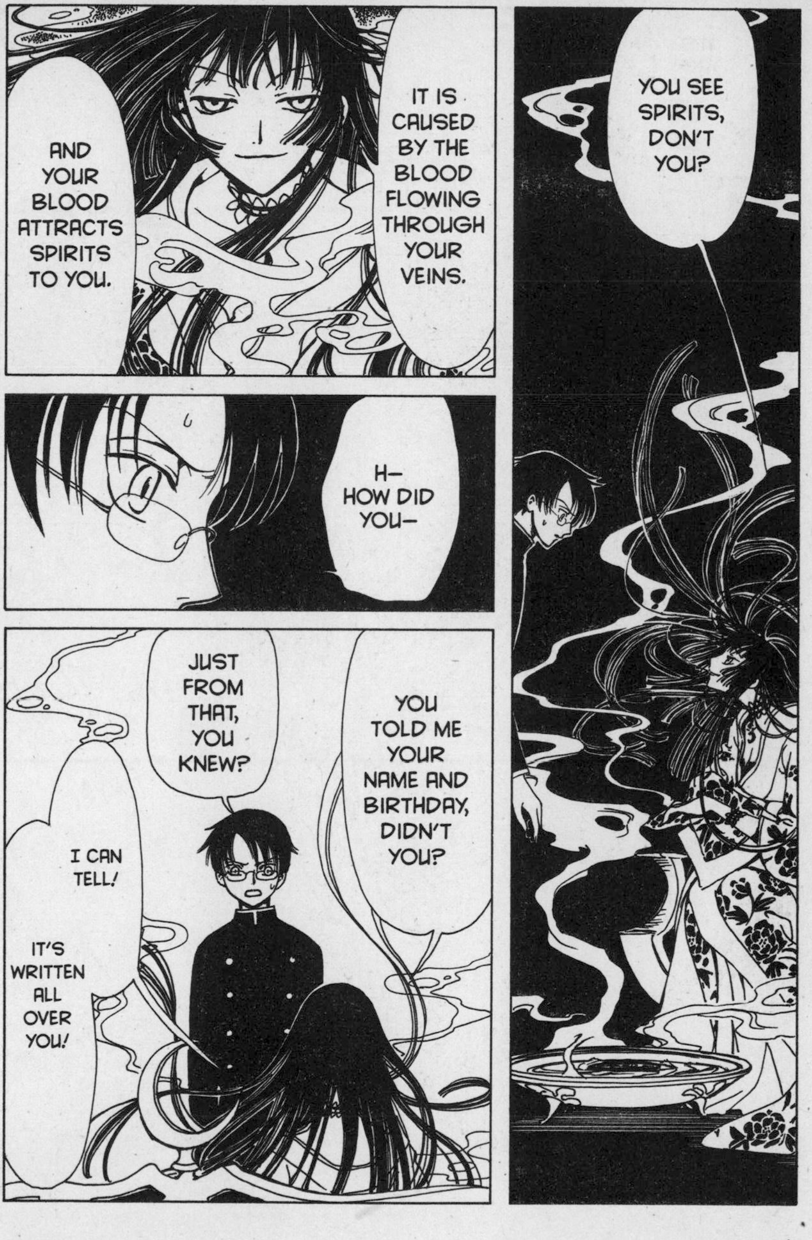
YOU SEE SPIRITS, DON'T YOU?
IT IS CAUSED BY THE BLOOD FLOWING THROUGH YOUR VEINS.
AND YOUR BLOOD ATTRACTS SPIRITS TO YOU.
H— HOW DID YOU—
YOU TOLD ME YOUR NAME AND BIRTHDAY, DIDN'T YOU?
JUST FROM THAT, YOU KNEW?
I CAN TELL!
IT'S WRITTEN ALL OVER YOU!

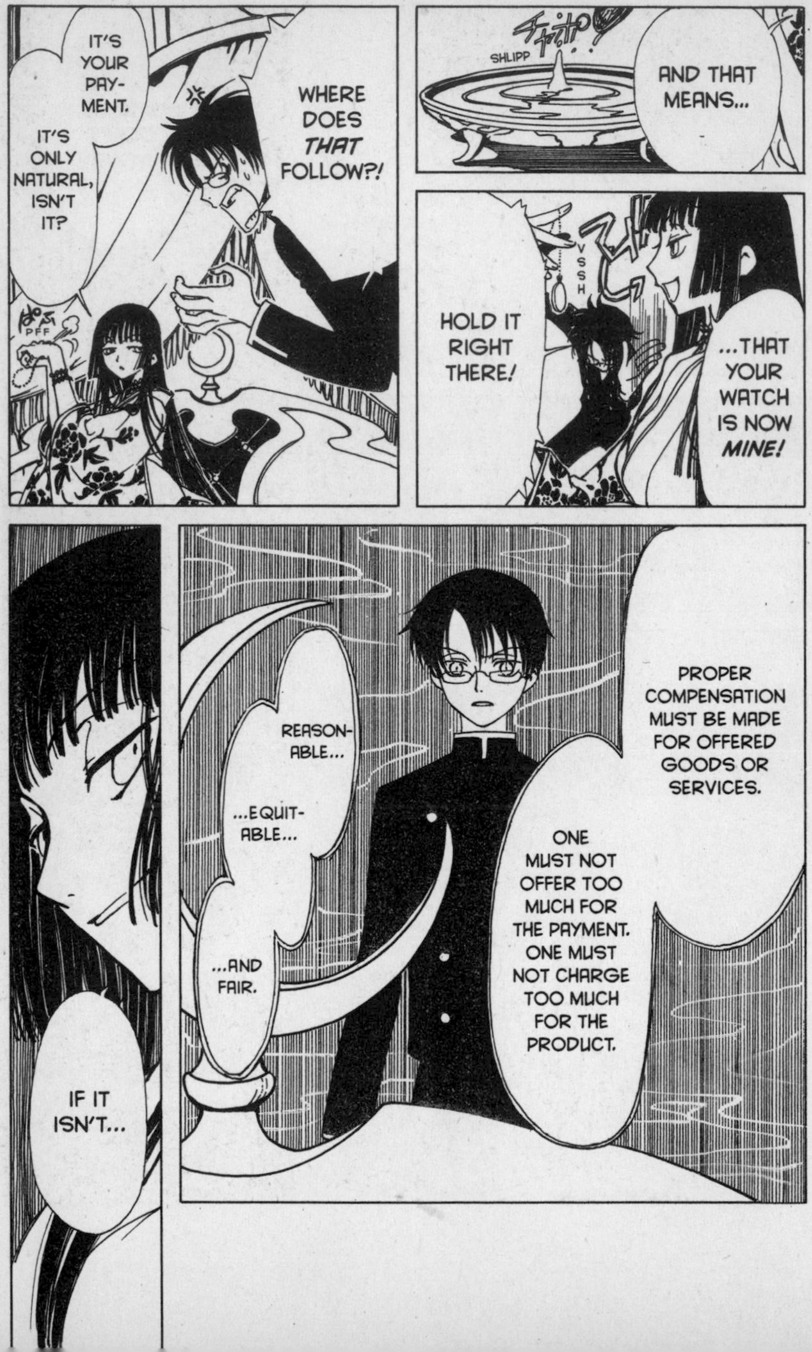
SHLIPP
AND THAT MEANS...
VSSH
...THAT YOUR WATCH IS NOW *MINE!*
HOLD IT RIGHT THERE!
IT'S YOUR PAY-MENT.
IT'S ONLY NATURAL, ISN'T IT?
WHERE DOES *THAT* FOLLOW?!
PFF
PROPER COMPENSATION MUST BE MADE FOR OFFERED GOODS OR SERVICES.
ONE MUST NOT OFFER TOO MUCH FOR THE PAYMENT. ONE MUST NOT CHARGE TOO MUCH FOR THE PRODUCT.
REASON-ABLE...
...EQUIT-ABLE...
...AND FAIR.
IF IT ISN'T...

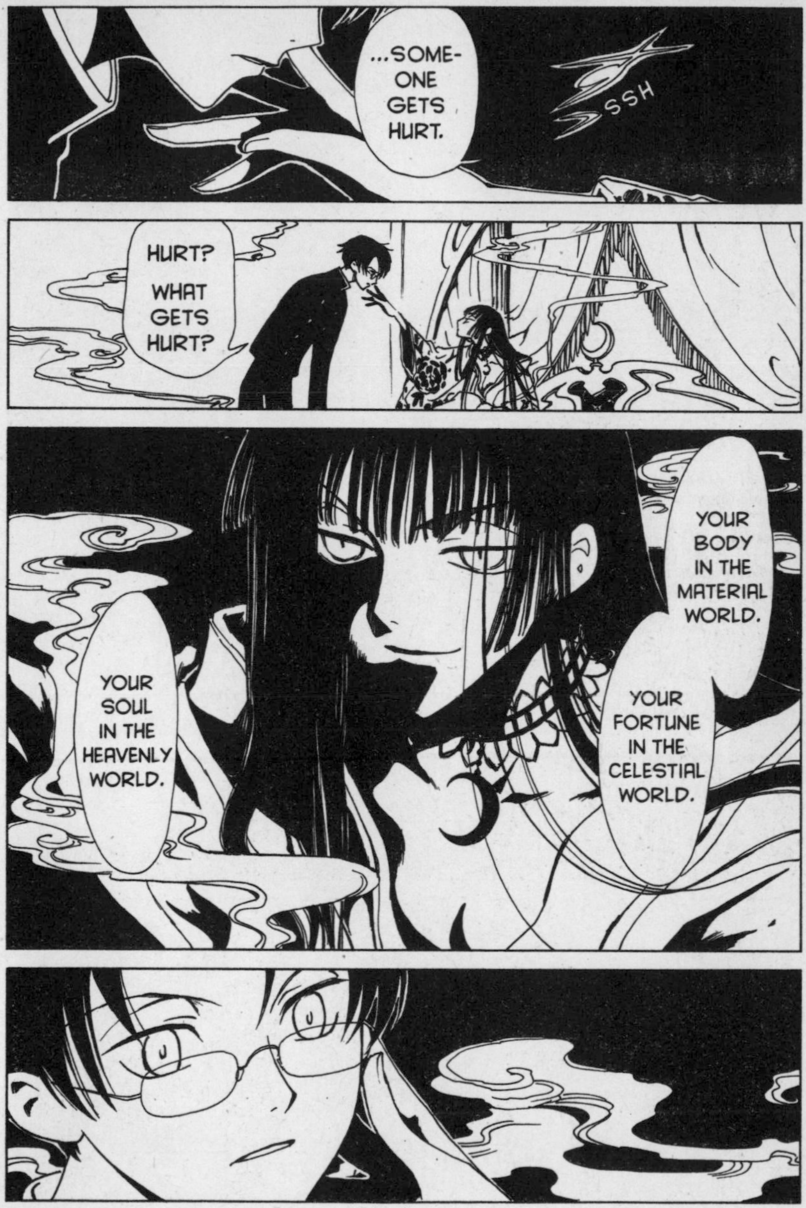
...SOME-ONE GETS HURT.
SSH
HURT? WHAT GETS HURT?
YOUR BODY IN THE MATERIAL WORLD.
YOUR FORTUNE IN THE CELESTIAL WORLD.
YOUR SOUL IN THE HEAVENLY WORLD.

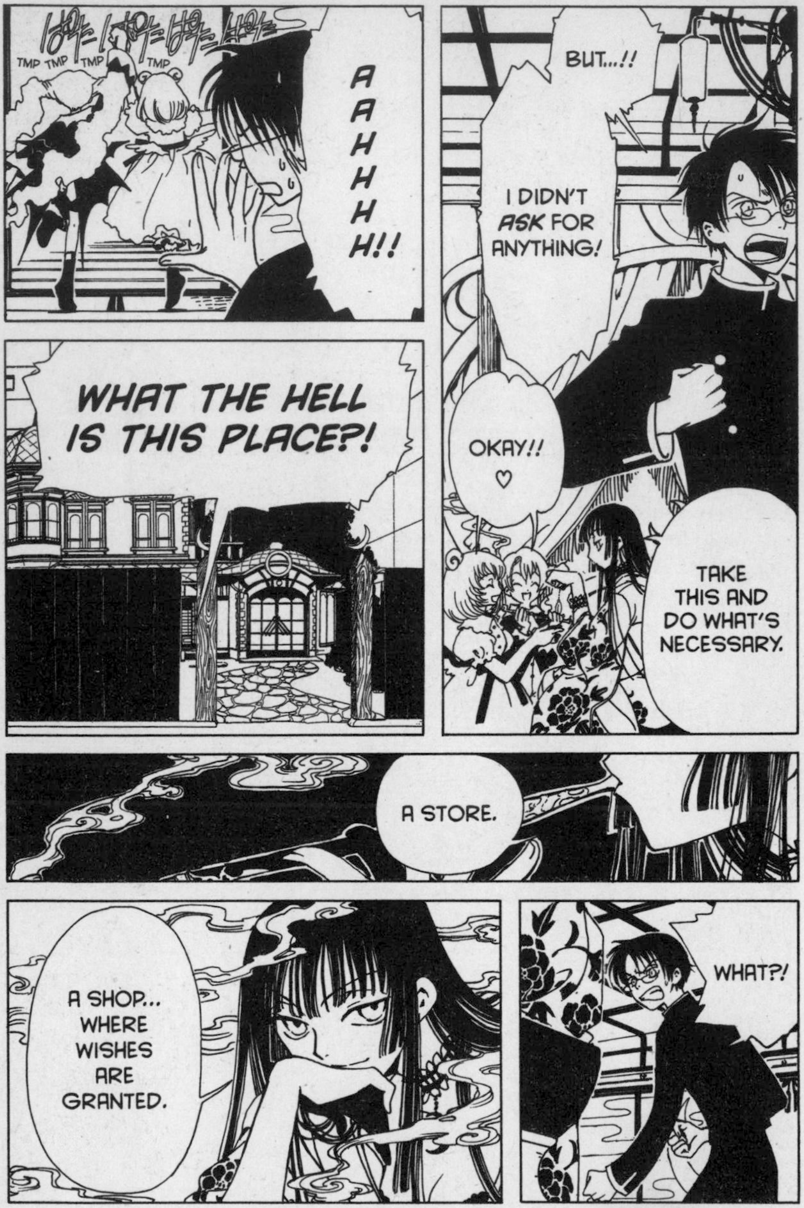
BUT...!!
I DIDN'T *ASK* FOR ANYTHING!
TAKE THIS AND DO WHAT'S NECESSARY.
OKAY!! ♡
TMP TMP TMP TMP
AAHHHHH!!
WHAT THE HELL IS THIS PLACE?!
A STORE.
WHAT?!
A SHOP... WHERE WISHES ARE GRANTED.

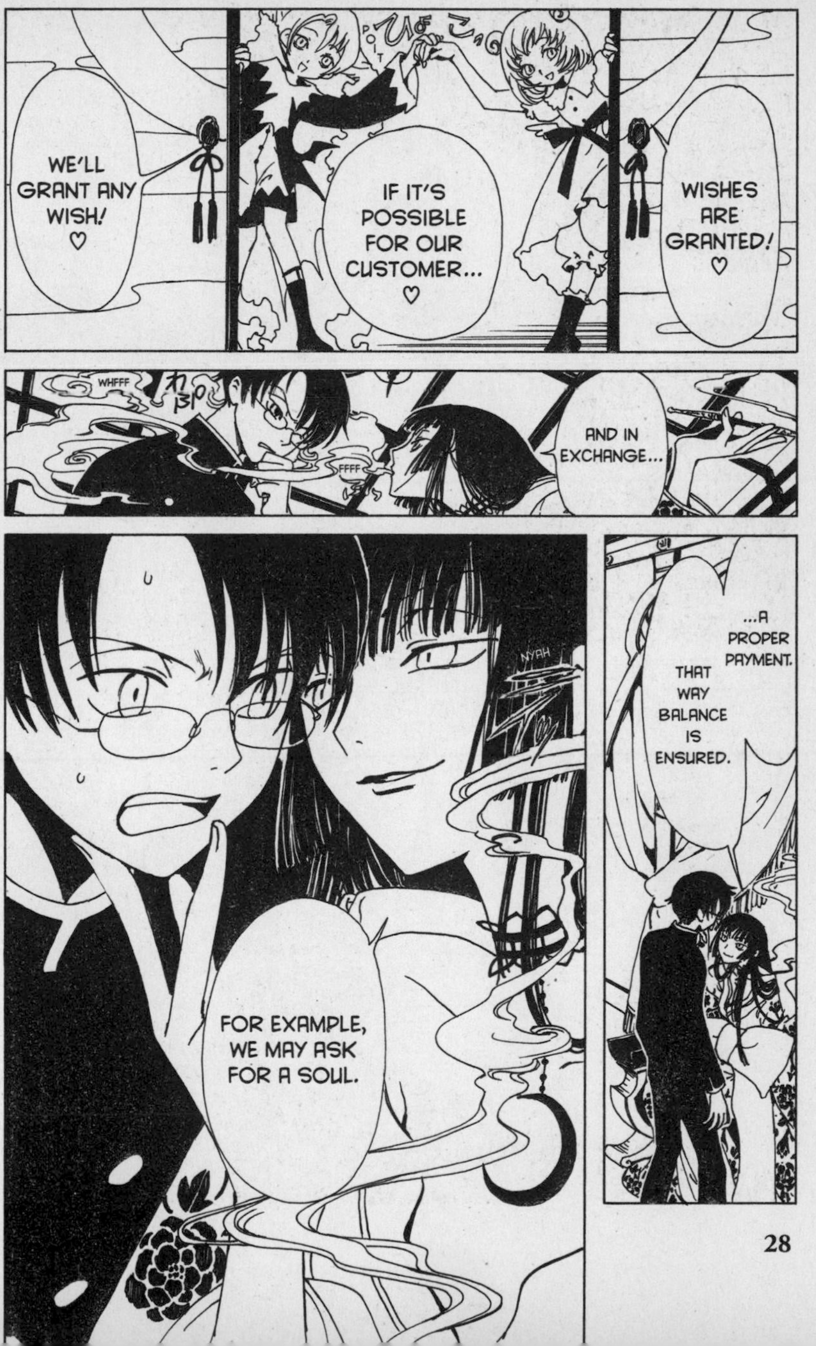
POIT
WISHES ARE GRANTED! ♡
IF IT'S POSSIBLE FOR OUR CUSTOMER... ♡
WE'LL GRANT ANY WISH! ♡
AND IN EXCHANGE...
WHFFF
FFFF
...A PROPER PAYMENT.
THAT WAY BALANCE IS ENSURED.
NYAH
FOR EXAMPLE, WE MAY ASK FOR A SOUL.

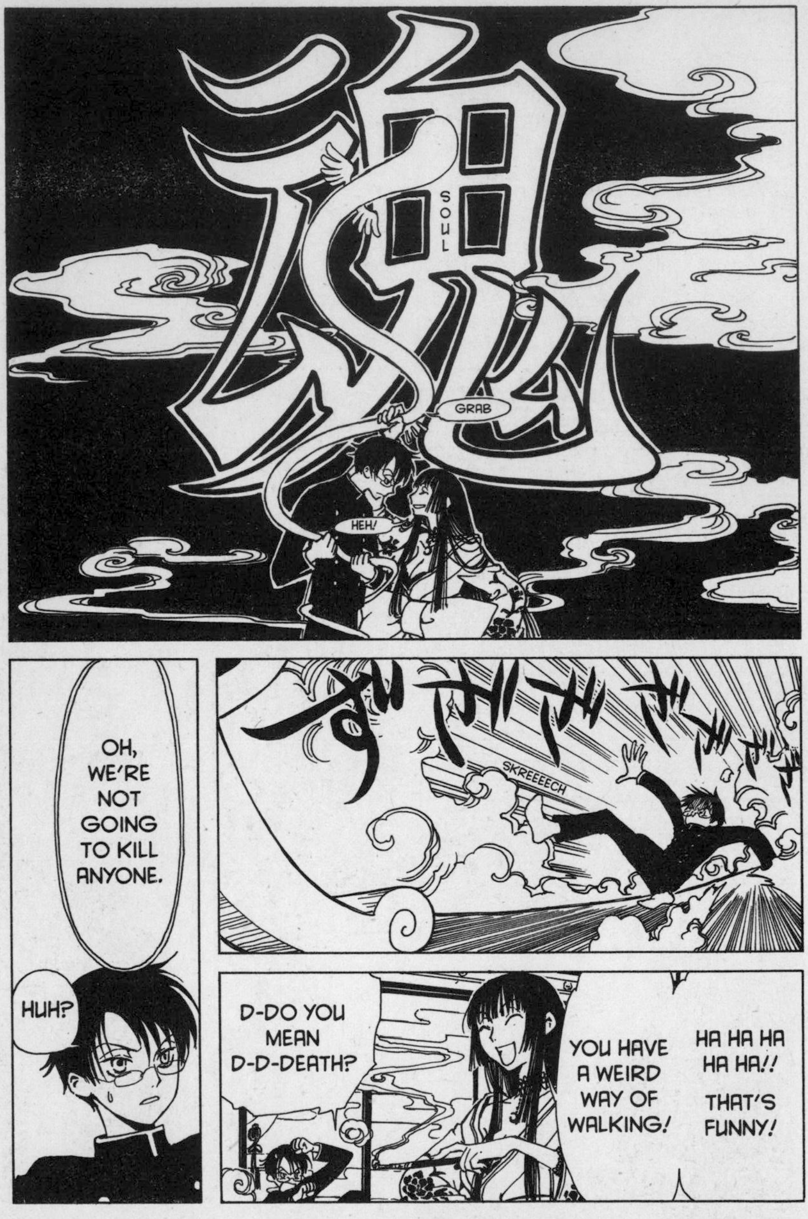
SOUL
GRAB
HEH!
SKREEEECH
HA HA HA HA HA!!
THAT'S FUNNY!
YOU HAVE A WEIRD WAY OF WALKING!
D-DO YOU MEAN D-D-DEATH?
OH, WE'RE NOT GOING TO KILL ANYONE.
HUH?

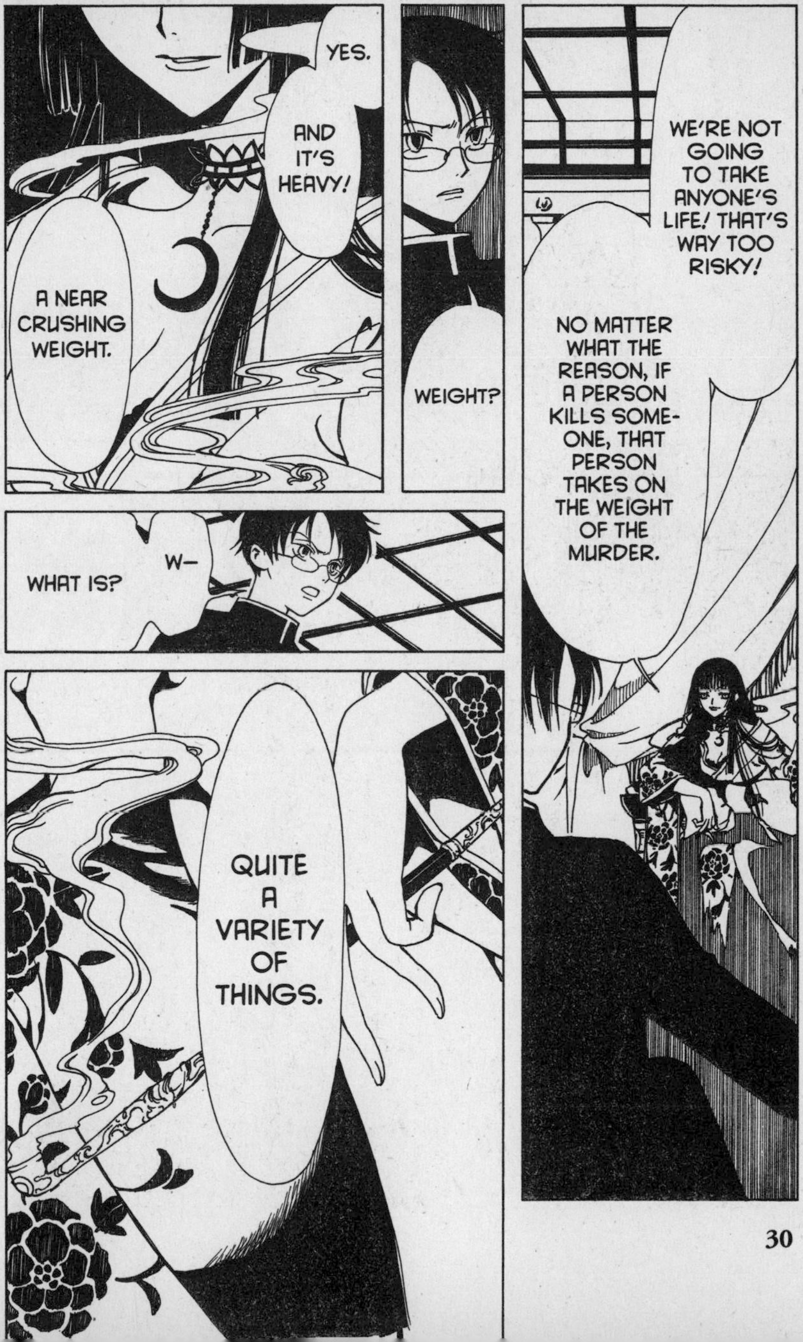
WE'RE NOT GOING TO TAKE ANYONE'S LIFE! THAT'S WAY TOO RISKY!
NO MATTER WHAT THE REASON, IF A PERSON KILLS SOME-ONE, THAT PERSON TAKES ON THE WEIGHT OF THE MURDER.
WEIGHT?
YES.
AND IT'S HEAVY!
A NEAR CRUSHING WEIGHT.
W-
WHAT IS?
QUITE A VARIETY OF THINGS.

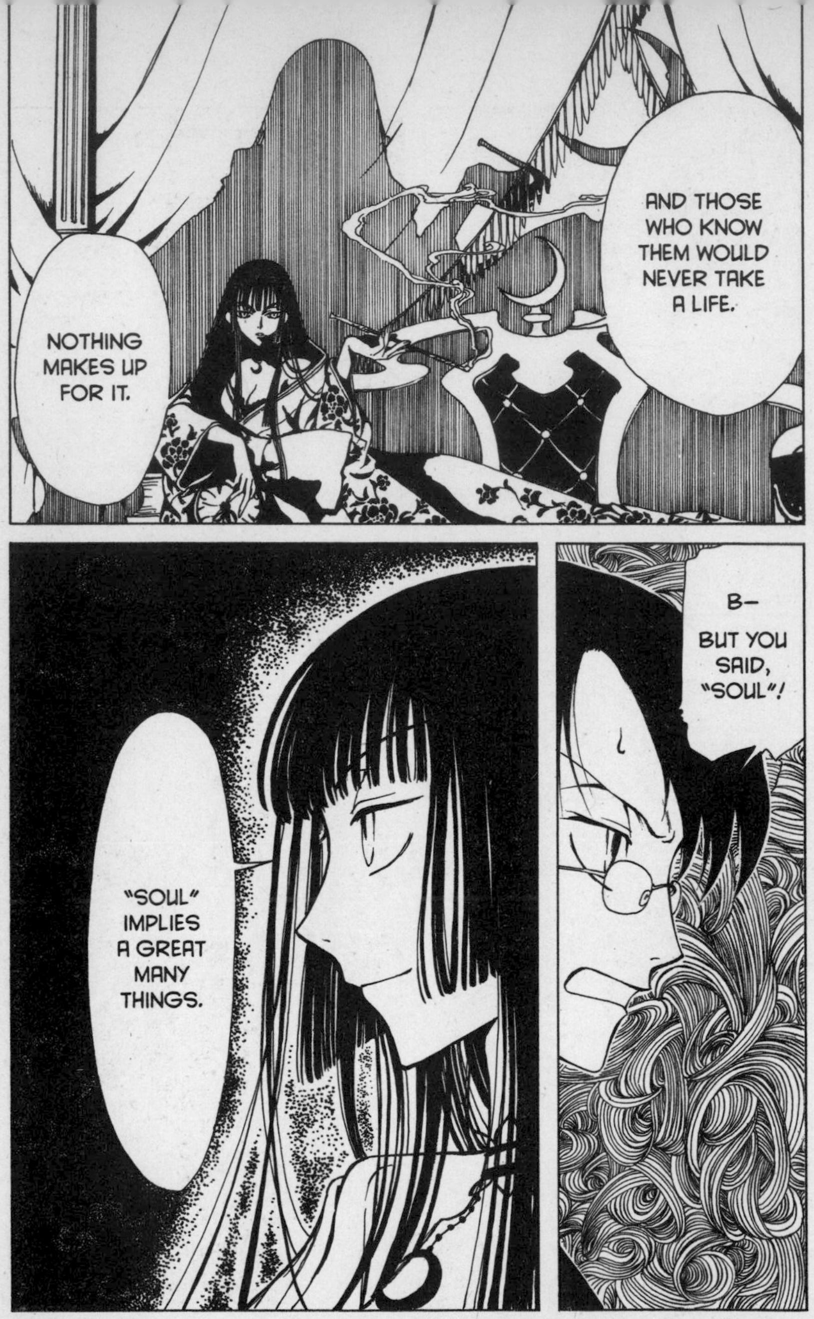
AND THOSE WHO KNOW THEM WOULD NEVER TAKE A LIFE.
NOTHING MAKES UP FOR IT.
B—
BUT YOU SAID, "SOUL"!
"SOUL" IMPLIES A GREAT MANY THINGS.

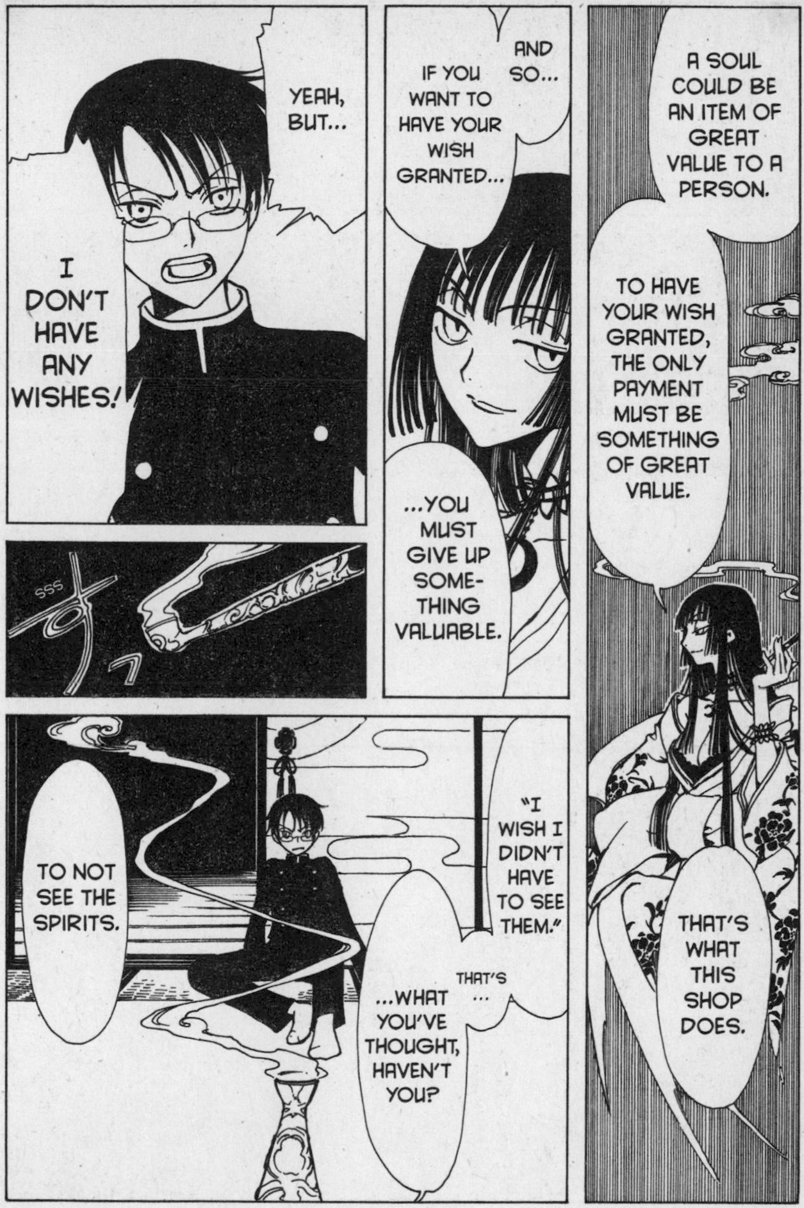
A SOUL COULD BE AN ITEM OF GREAT VALUE TO A PERSON.
TO HAVE YOUR WISH GRANTED, THE ONLY PAYMENT MUST BE SOMETHING OF GREAT VALUE.
THAT'S WHAT THIS SHOP DOES.
AND SO...
IF YOU WANT TO HAVE YOUR WISH GRANTED...
...YOU MUST GIVE UP SOME-THING VALUABLE.
YEAH, BUT...
I DON'T HAVE ANY WISHES!
SSS
"I WISH I DIDN'T HAVE TO SEE THEM."
THAT'S ...
...WHAT YOU'VE THOUGHT, HAVEN'T YOU?
TO NOT SEE THE SPIRITS.

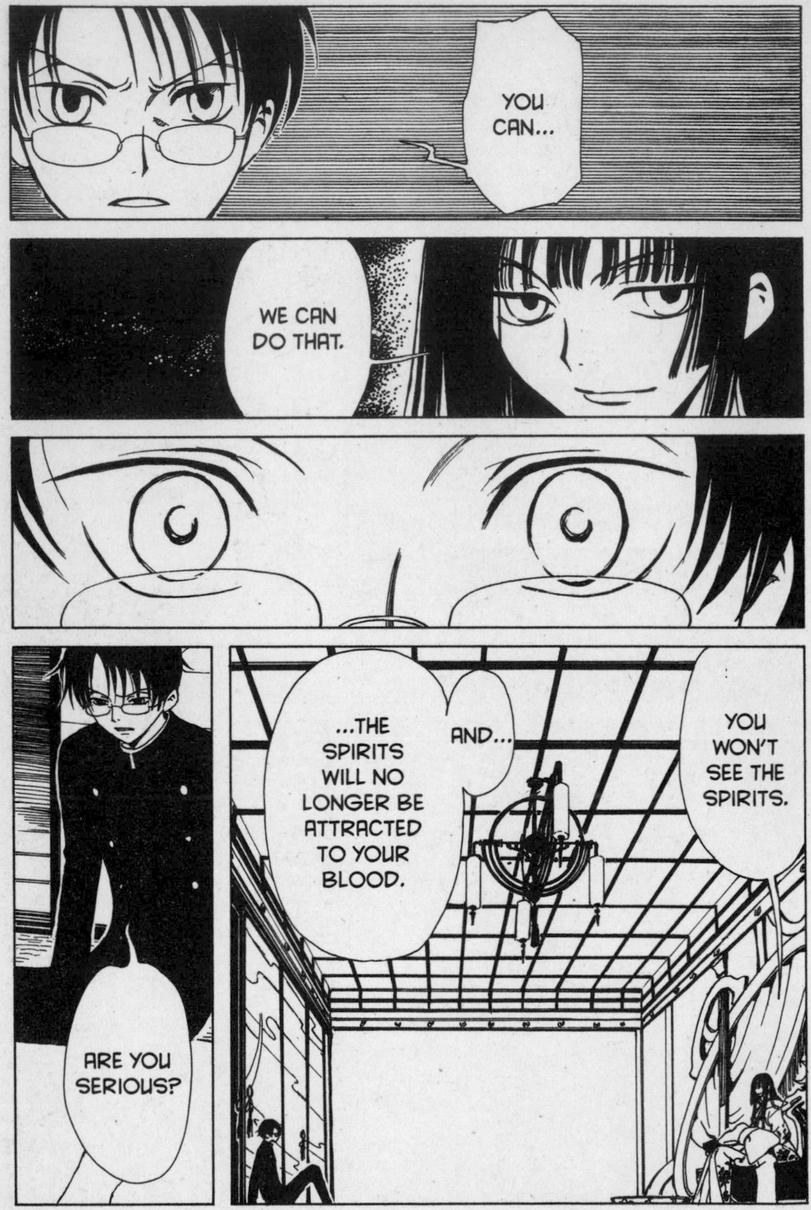
YOU CAN...
WE CAN DO THAT.
YOU WON'T SEE THE SPIRITS.
AND...
...THE SPIRITS WILL NO LONGER BE ATTRACTED TO YOUR BLOOD.
ARE YOU SERIOUS?

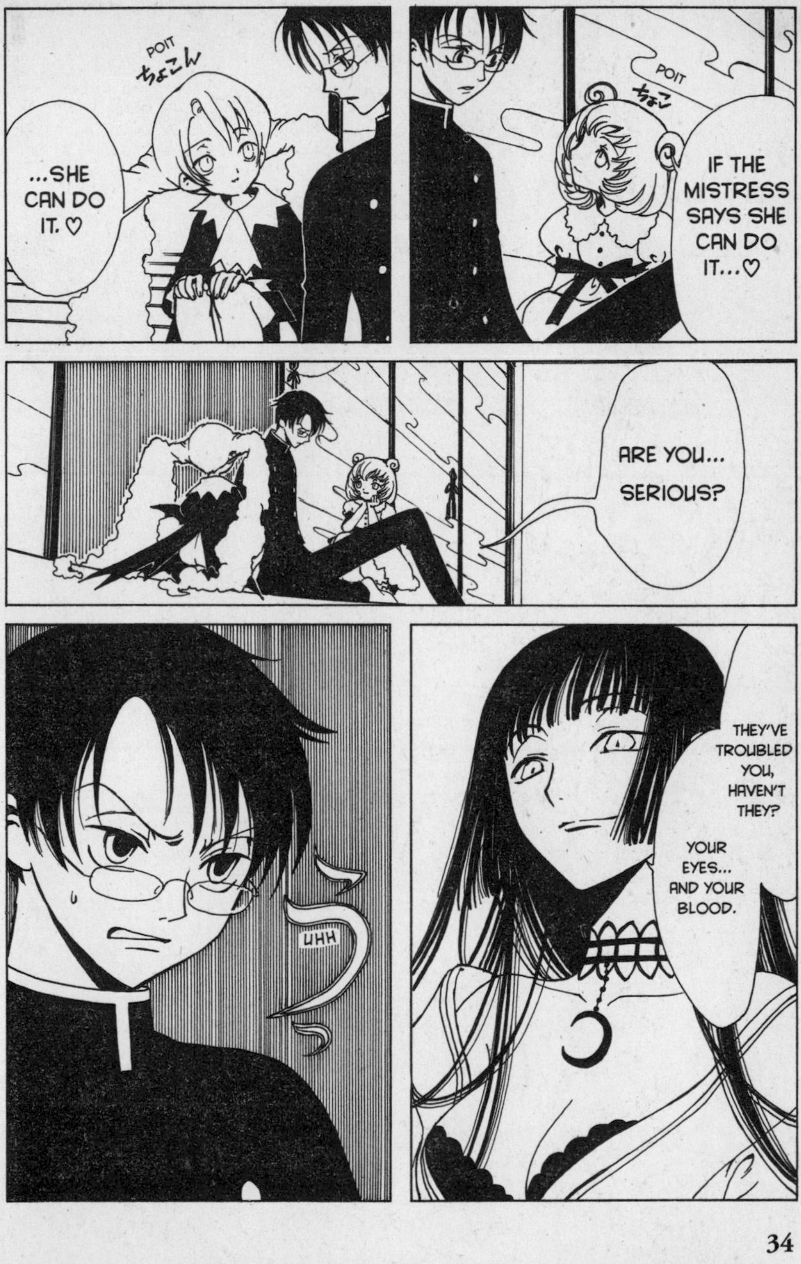
POIT
ちょこ
IF THE MISTRESS SAYS SHE CAN DO IT...♡
POIT
ちょこん
...SHE CAN DO IT. ♡
ARE YOU... SERIOUS?
THEY'VE TROUBLED YOU, HAVEN'T THEY?
YOUR EYES... AND YOUR BLOOD.
UHH

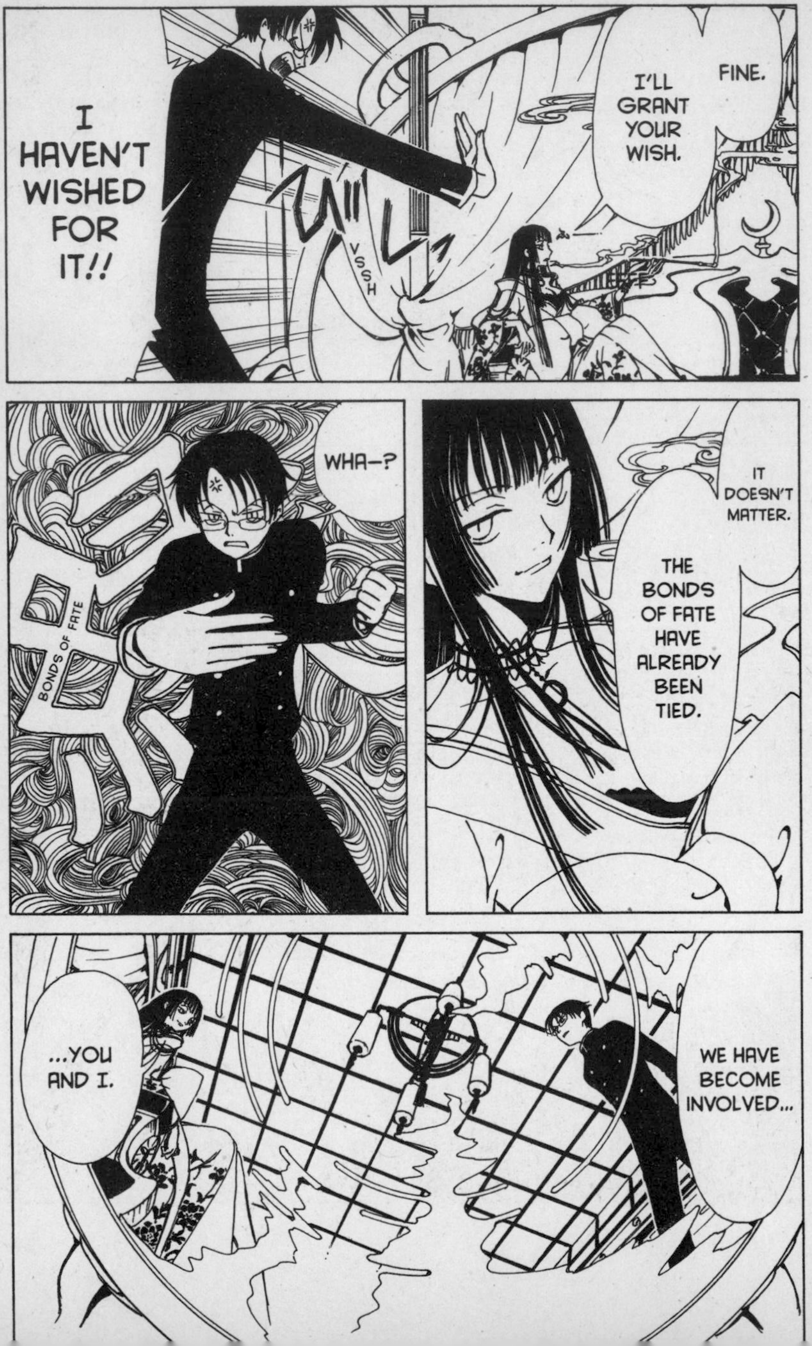
FINE.
I'LL GRANT YOUR WISH.
VSSH
I HAVEN'T WISHED FOR IT!!
IT DOESN'T MATTER.
THE BONDS OF FATE HAVE ALREADY BEEN TIED.
WHA–?
BONDS OF FATE
WE HAVE BECOME INVOLVED...
...YOU AND I.

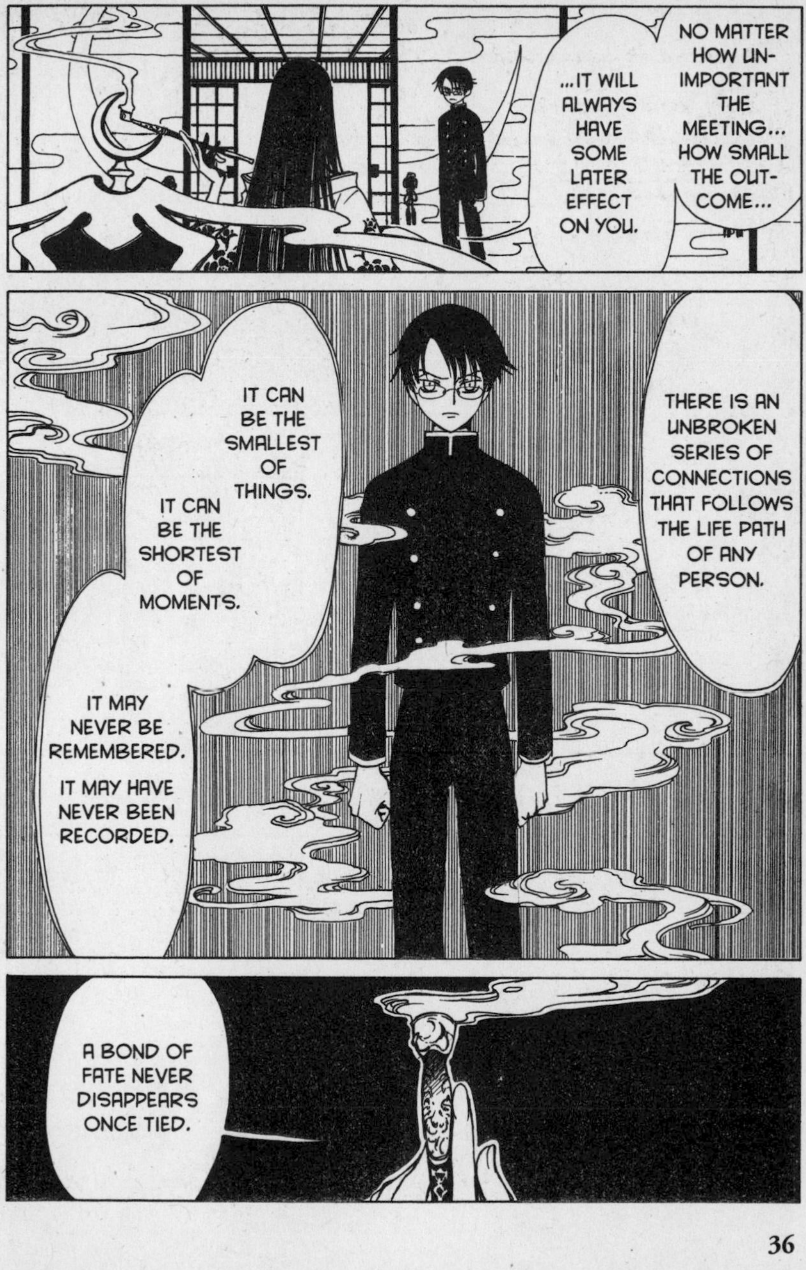
NO MATTER HOW UN-IMPORTANT THE MEETING... HOW SMALL THE OUT-COME...
...IT WILL ALWAYS HAVE SOME LATER EFFECT ON YOU.
THERE IS AN UNBROKEN SERIES OF CONNECTIONS THAT FOLLOWS THE LIFE PATH OF ANY PERSON.
IT CAN BE THE SMALLEST OF THINGS.
IT CAN BE THE SHORTEST OF MOMENTS.
IT MAY NEVER BE REMEMBERED.
IT MAY HAVE NEVER BEEN RECORDED.
A BOND OF FATE NEVER DISAPPEARS ONCE TIED.

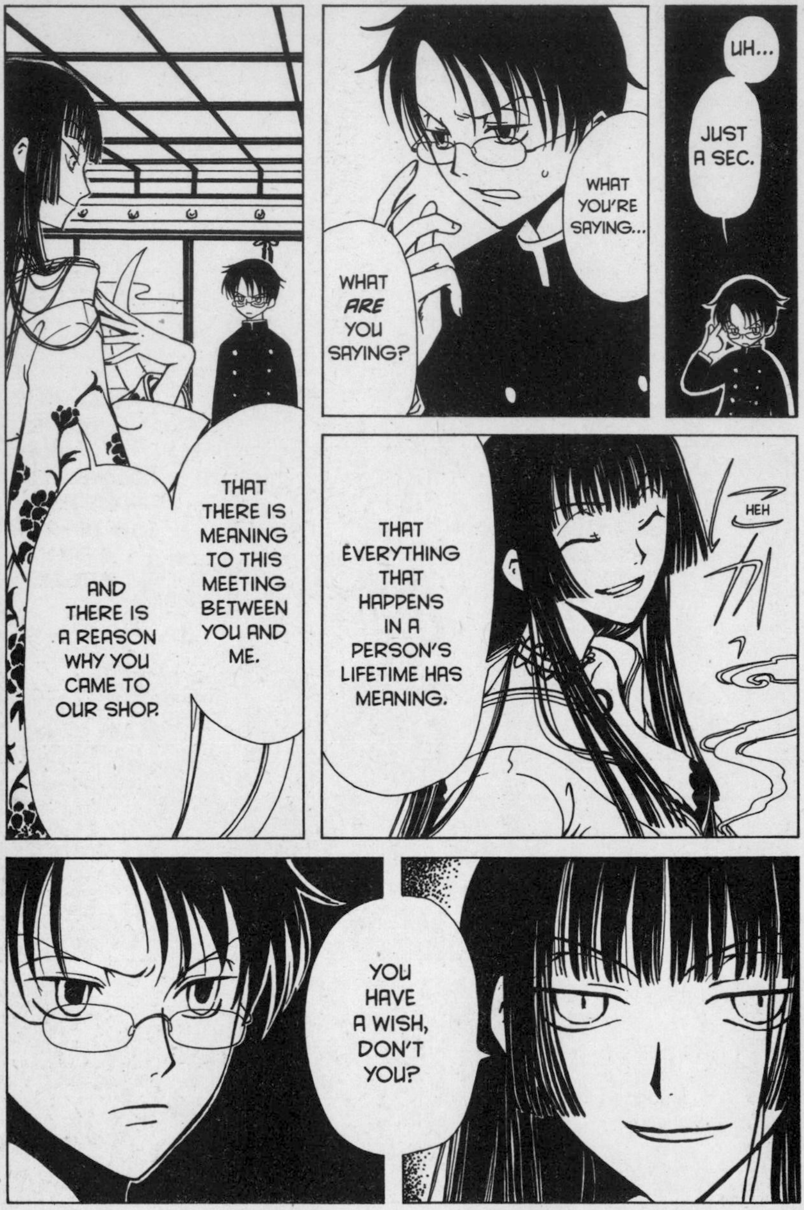
UH...
JUST A SEC.
WHAT YOU'RE SAYING...
WHAT *ARE* YOU SAYING?
HEH
THAT EVERYTHING THAT HAPPENS IN A PERSON'S LIFETIME HAS MEANING.
THAT THERE IS MEANING TO THIS MEETING BETWEEN YOU AND ME.
AND THERE IS A REASON WHY YOU CAME TO OUR SHOP.
YOU HAVE A WISH, DON'T YOU?

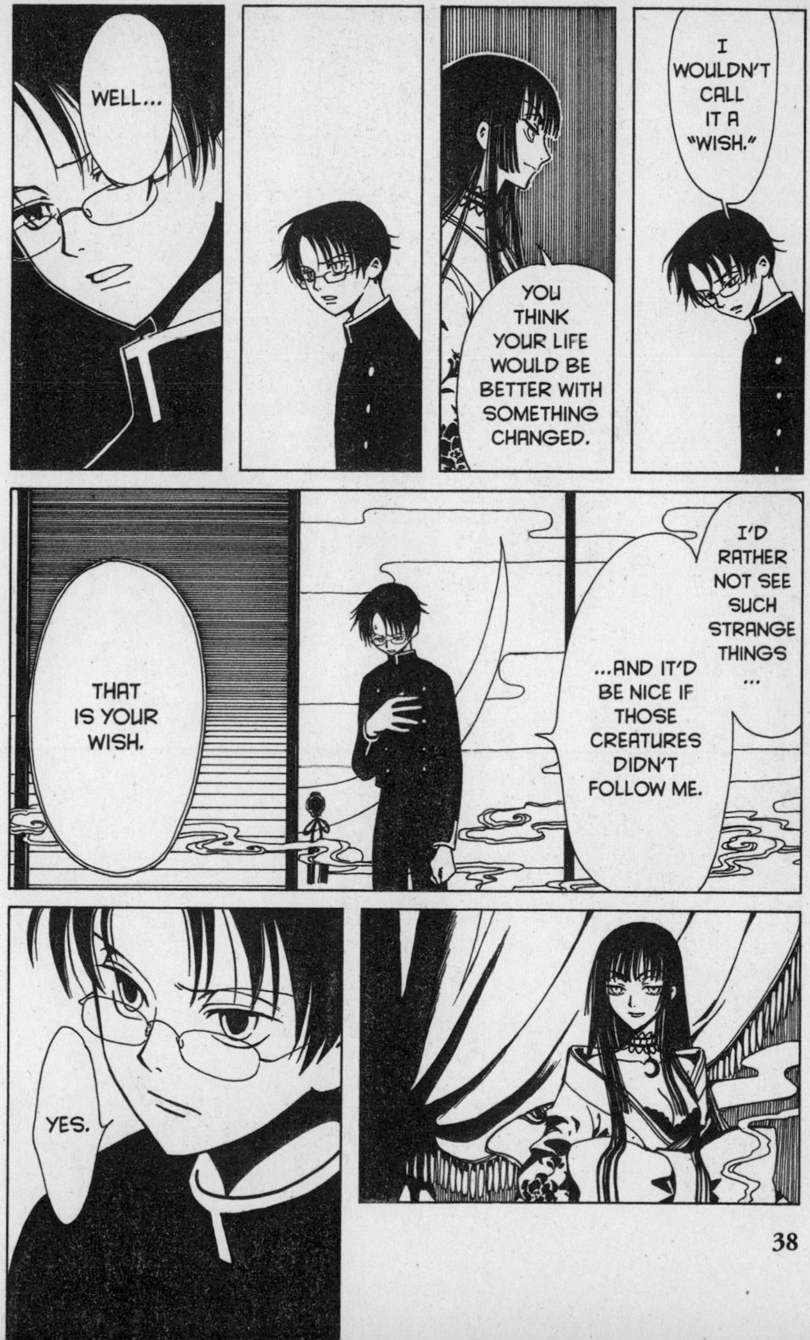
I WOULDN'T CALL IT A "WISH."
YOU THINK YOUR LIFE WOULD BE BETTER WITH SOMETHING CHANGED.
WELL...
I'D RATHER NOT SEE SUCH STRANGE THINGS...
...AND IT'D BE NICE IF THOSE CREATURES DIDN'T FOLLOW ME.
THAT IS YOUR WISH.
YES.

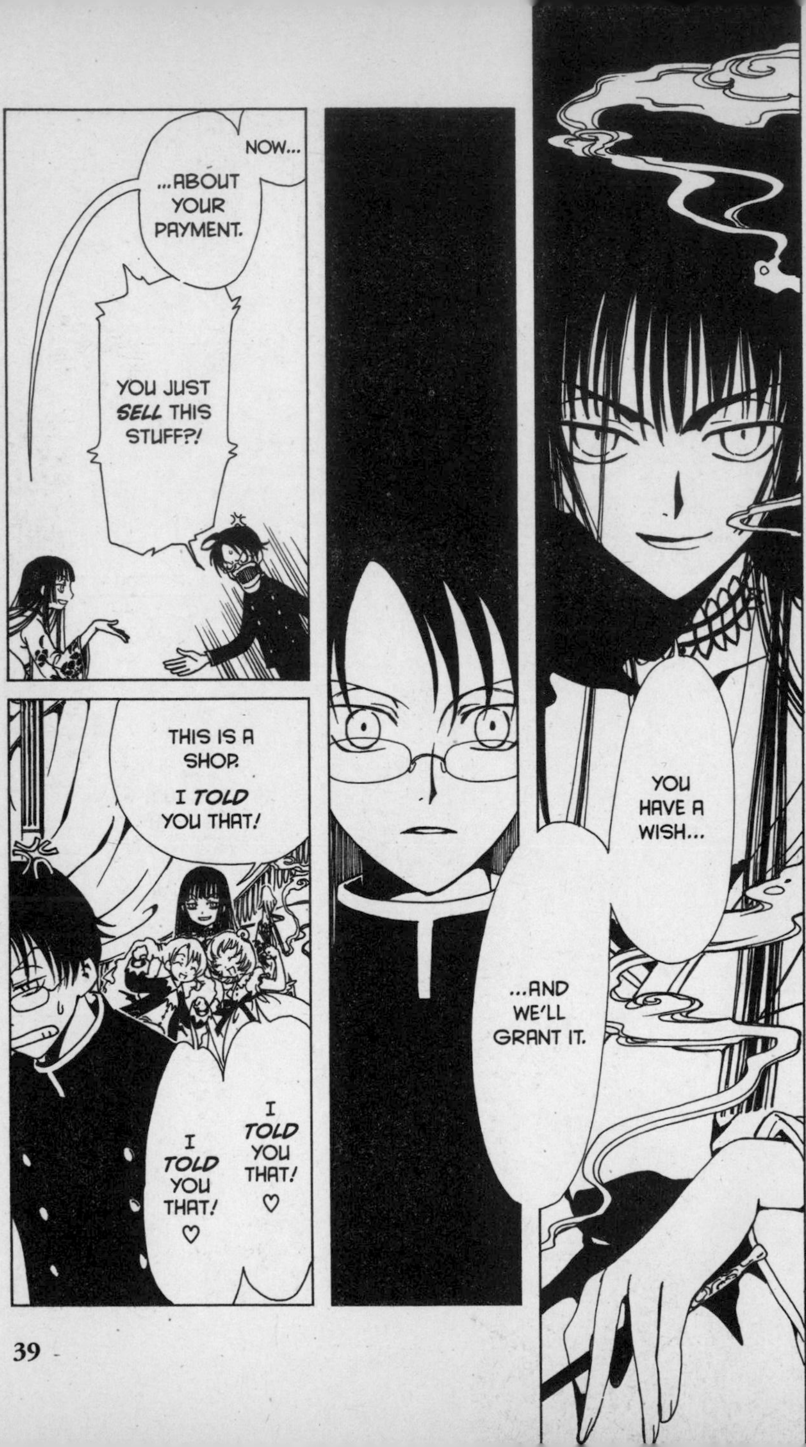
YOU HAVE A WISH...
...AND WE'LL GRANT IT.
NOW...
...ABOUT YOUR PAYMENT.
YOU JUST ***SELL*** THIS STUFF?!
THIS IS A SHOP.
I ***TOLD*** YOU THAT!
I ***TOLD*** YOU THAT! ♡
I ***TOLD*** YOU THAT! ♡

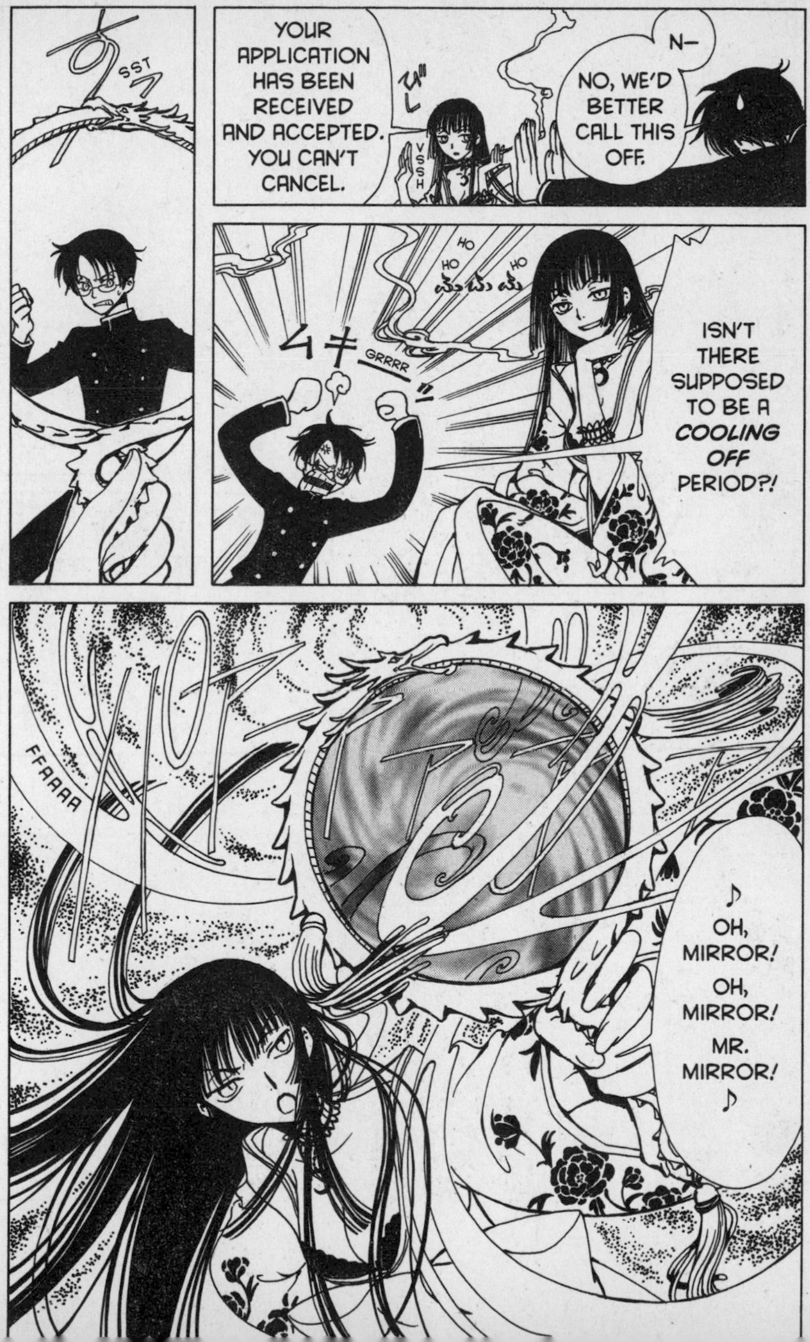
N—
NO, WE'D BETTER CALL THIS OFF.
YOUR APPLICATION HAS BEEN RECEIVED AND ACCEPTED. YOU CAN'T CANCEL.
VSSH
HO HO HO
ISN'T THERE SUPPOSED TO BE A *COOLING OFF* PERIOD?!
GRRRR
SST
♪ OH, MIRROR! OH, MIRROR! MR. MIRROR! ♪
FFAAAA

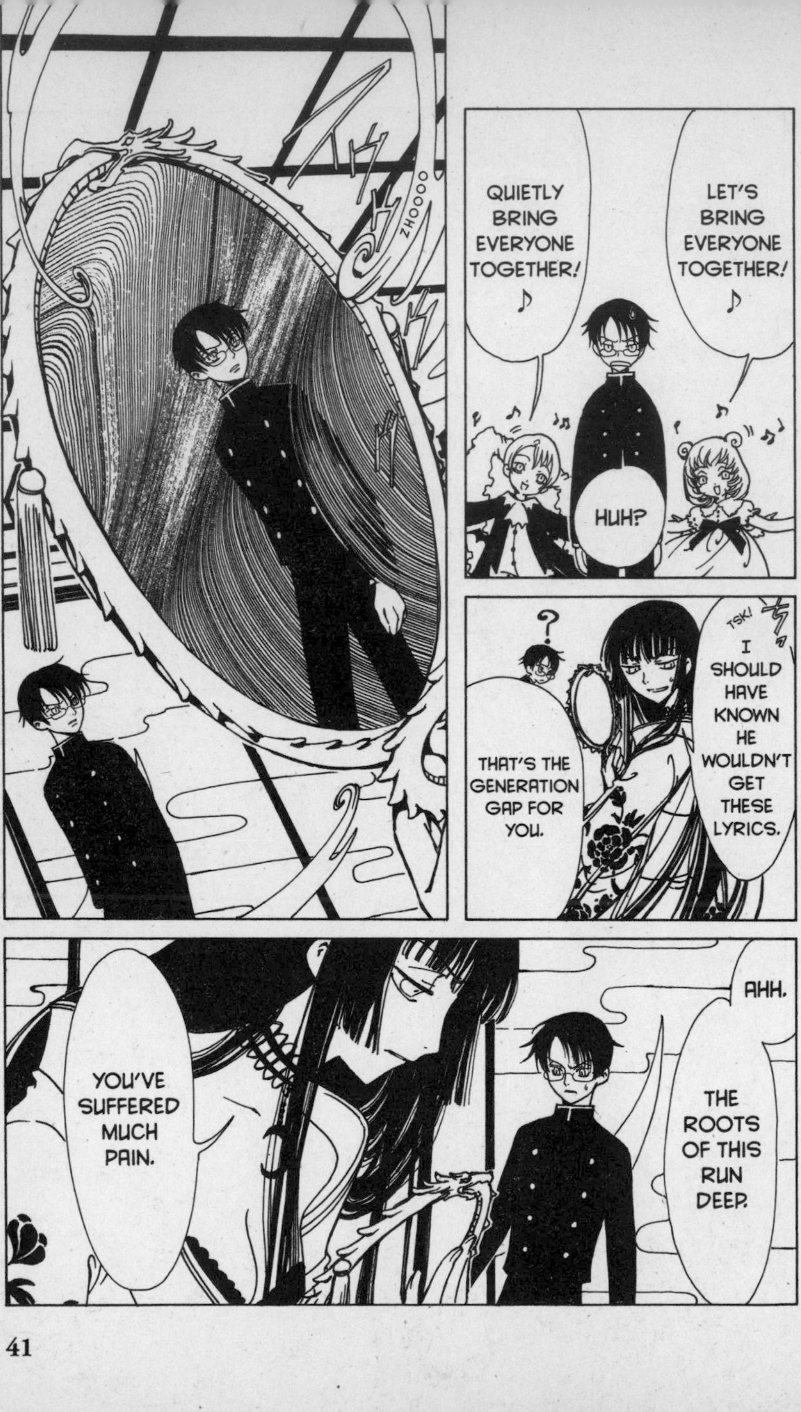
LET'S BRING EVERYONE TOGETHER! ♪
QUIETLY BRING EVERYONE TOGETHER! ♪
HUH?
TSK!
I SHOULD HAVE KNOWN HE WOULDN'T GET THESE LYRICS.
?
THAT'S THE GENERATION GAP FOR YOU.
ZHOOOO
AHH.
THE ROOTS OF THIS RUN DEEP.
YOU'VE SUFFERED MUCH PAIN.

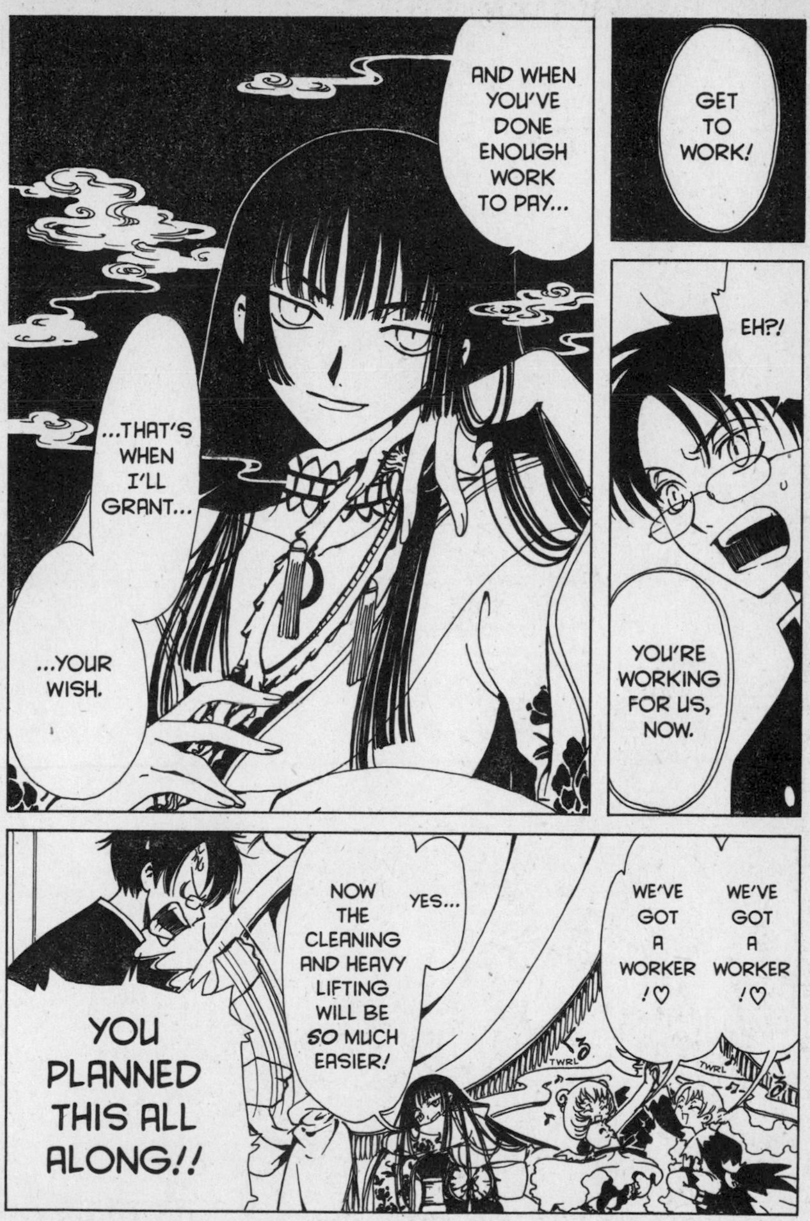
GET TO WORK!
EH?!
YOU'RE WORKING FOR US, NOW.
AND WHEN YOU'VE DONE ENOUGH WORK TO PAY...
...THAT'S WHEN I'LL GRANT...
...YOUR WISH.
WE'VE GOT A WORKER!♡
WE'VE GOT A WORKER!♡
TWRL
TWRL
YES...
NOW THE CLEANING AND HEAVY LIFTING WILL BE SO MUCH EASIER!
YOU PLANNED THIS ALL ALONG!!

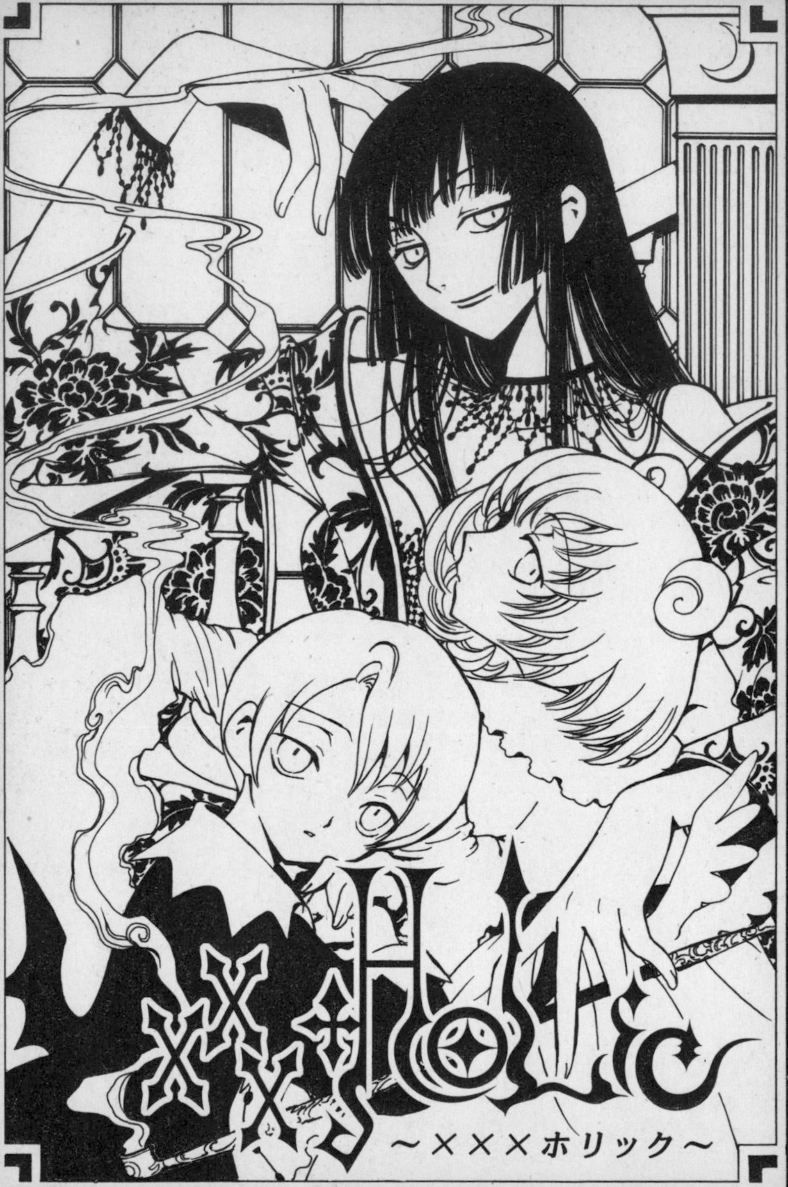
xxxHOLiC
〜×××ホリック〜

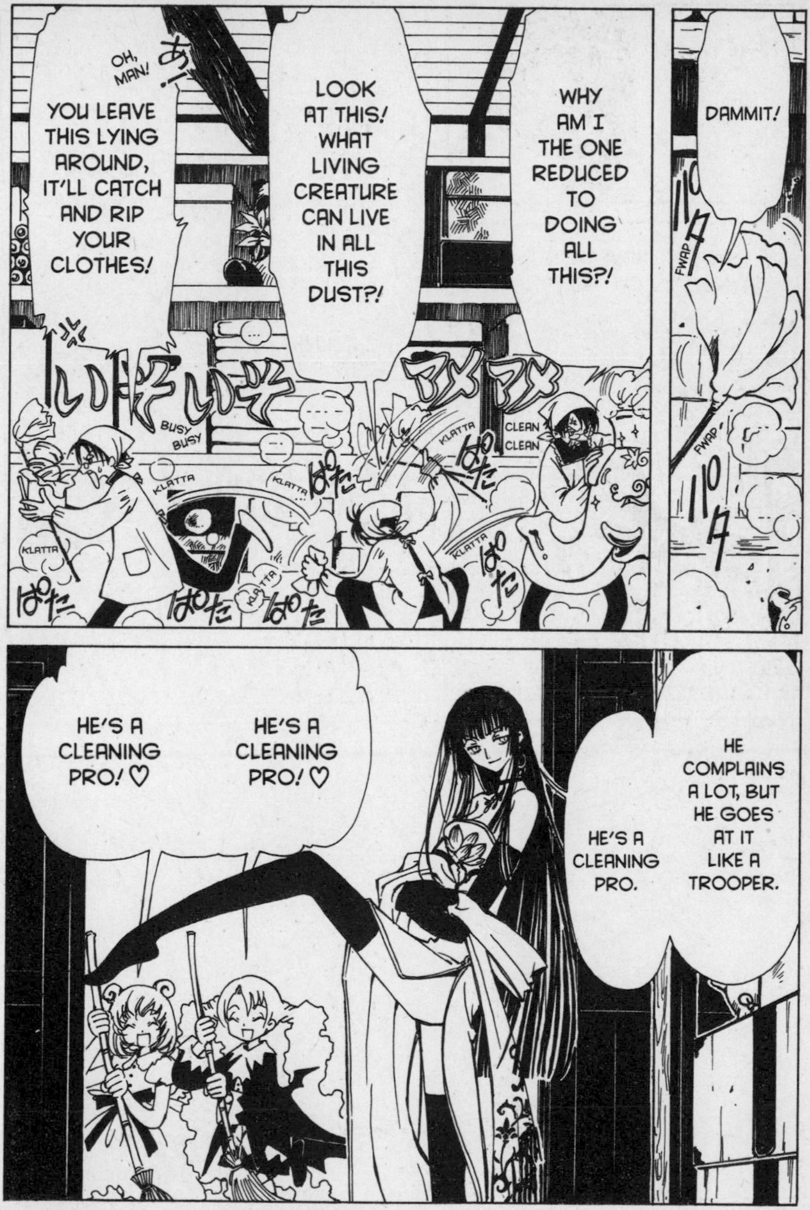
DAMMIT!
FWAP
FWAP
WHY AM I THE ONE REDUCED TO DOING ALL THIS?!
CLEAN CLEAN
LOOK AT THIS! WHAT LIVING CREATURE CAN LIVE IN ALL THIS DUST?!
KLATTA
KLATTA
OH, MAN!
YOU LEAVE THIS LYING AROUND, IT'LL CATCH AND RIP YOUR CLOTHES!
BUSY BUSY
KLATTA
KLATTA
KLATTA
KLATTA
HE COMPLAINS A LOT, BUT HE GOES AT IT LIKE A TROOPER.
HE'S A CLEANING PRO.
HE'S A CLEANING PRO! ♡
HE'S A CLEANING PRO! ♡

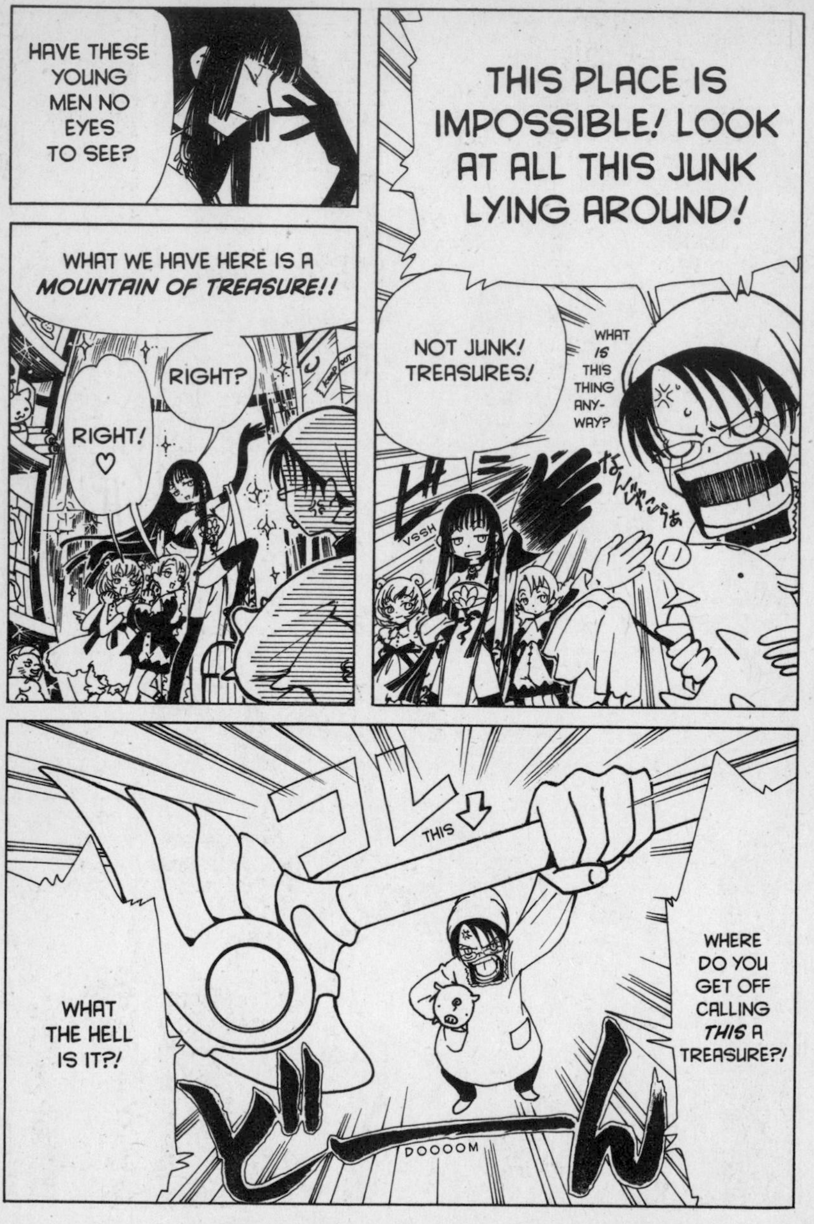
THIS PLACE IS IMPOSSIBLE! LOOK AT ALL THIS JUNK LYING AROUND!
WHAT *IS* THIS THING ANY-WAY?
NOT JUNK! TREASURES!
VSSH
HAVE THESE YOUNG MEN NO EYES TO SEE?
WHAT WE HAVE HERE IS A *MOUNTAIN OF TREASURE!!*
RIGHT?
RIGHT! ♡
WHERE DO YOU GET OFF CALLING *THIS* A TREASURE?!
THIS
WHAT THE HELL IS IT?!
DOOOOM

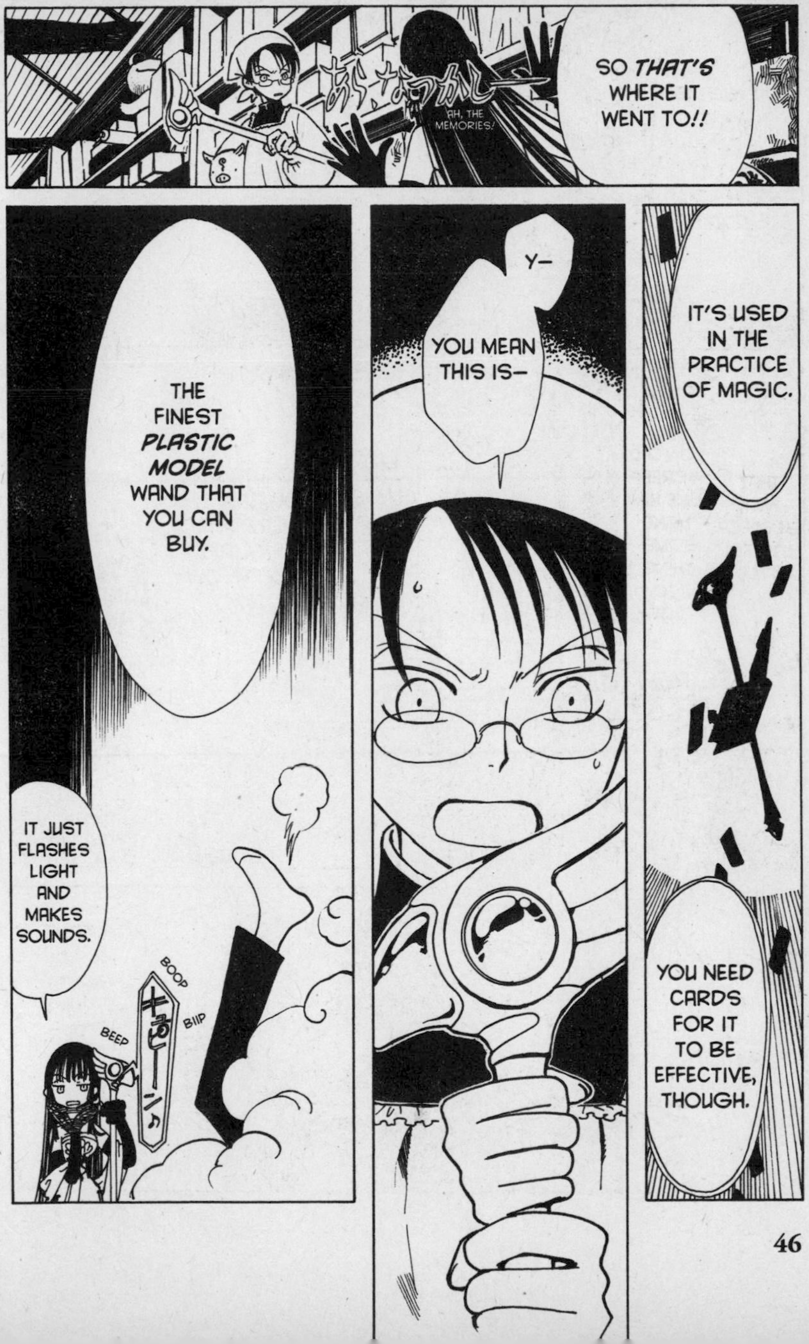
SO *THAT'S* WHERE IT WENT TO!!
AH, THE MEMORIES!
IT'S USED IN THE PRACTICE OF MAGIC.
YOU NEED CARDS FOR IT TO BE EFFECTIVE, THOUGH.
Y—
YOU MEAN THIS IS—
THE FINEST *PLASTIC MODEL* WAND THAT YOU CAN BUY.
IT JUST FLASHES LIGHT AND MAKES SOUNDS.
BOOP
BIIP
BEEP

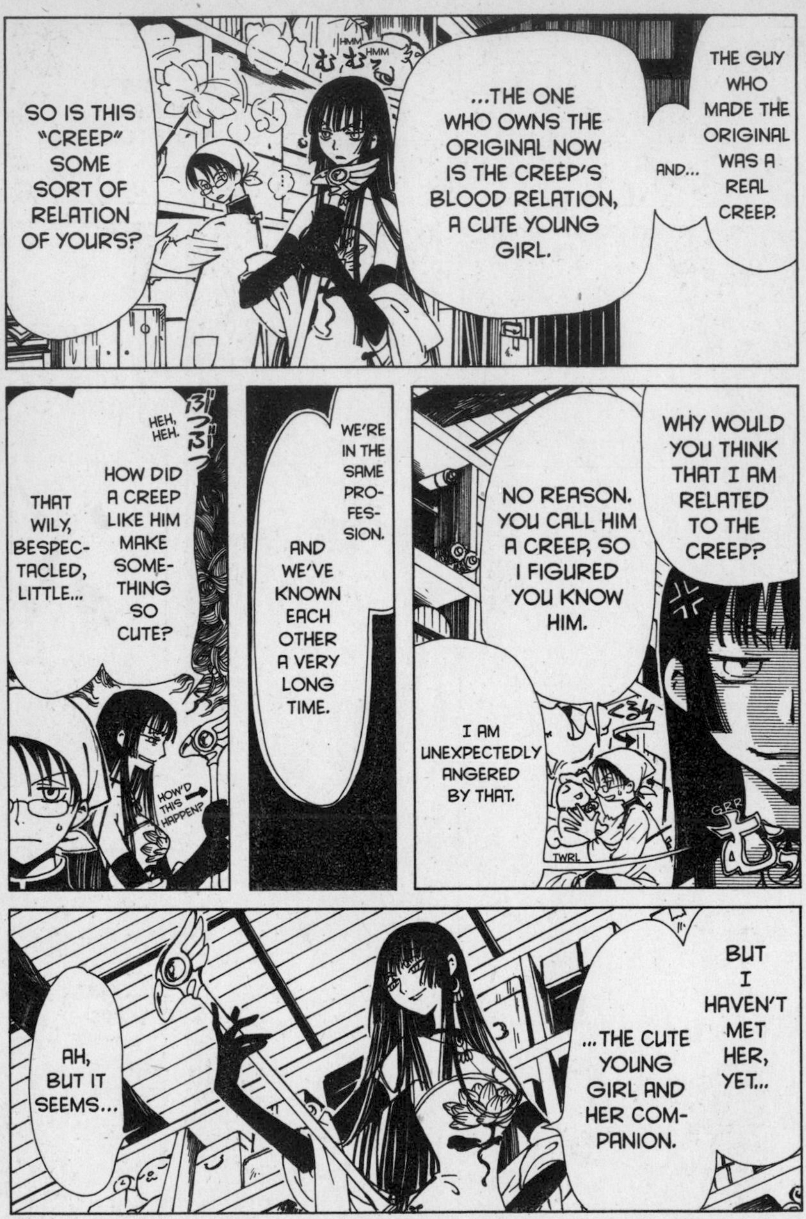
THE GUY WHO MADE THE ORIGINAL WAS A REAL CREEP.
AND...
...THE ONE WHO OWNS THE ORIGINAL NOW IS THE CREEP'S BLOOD RELATION, A CUTE YOUNG GIRL.
HMM HMM
SO IS THIS "CREEP" SOME SORT OF RELATION OF YOURS?
WHY WOULD YOU THINK THAT I AM RELATED TO THE CREEP?
NO REASON. YOU CALL HIM A CREEP, SO I FIGURED YOU KNOW HIM.
I AM UNEXPECTEDLY ANGERED BY THAT.
GRR
TWRL
WE'RE IN THE SAME PRO-FES-SION.
AND WE'VE KNOWN EACH OTHER A VERY LONG TIME.
HEH, HEH.
HOW DID A CREEP LIKE HIM MAKE SOME-THING SO CUTE?
THAT WILY, BESPEC-TACLED, LITTLE...
HOW'D THIS HAPPEN?
BUT I HAVEN'T MET HER, YET...
...THE CUTE YOUNG GIRL AND HER COM-PANION.
AH, BUT IT SEEMS...

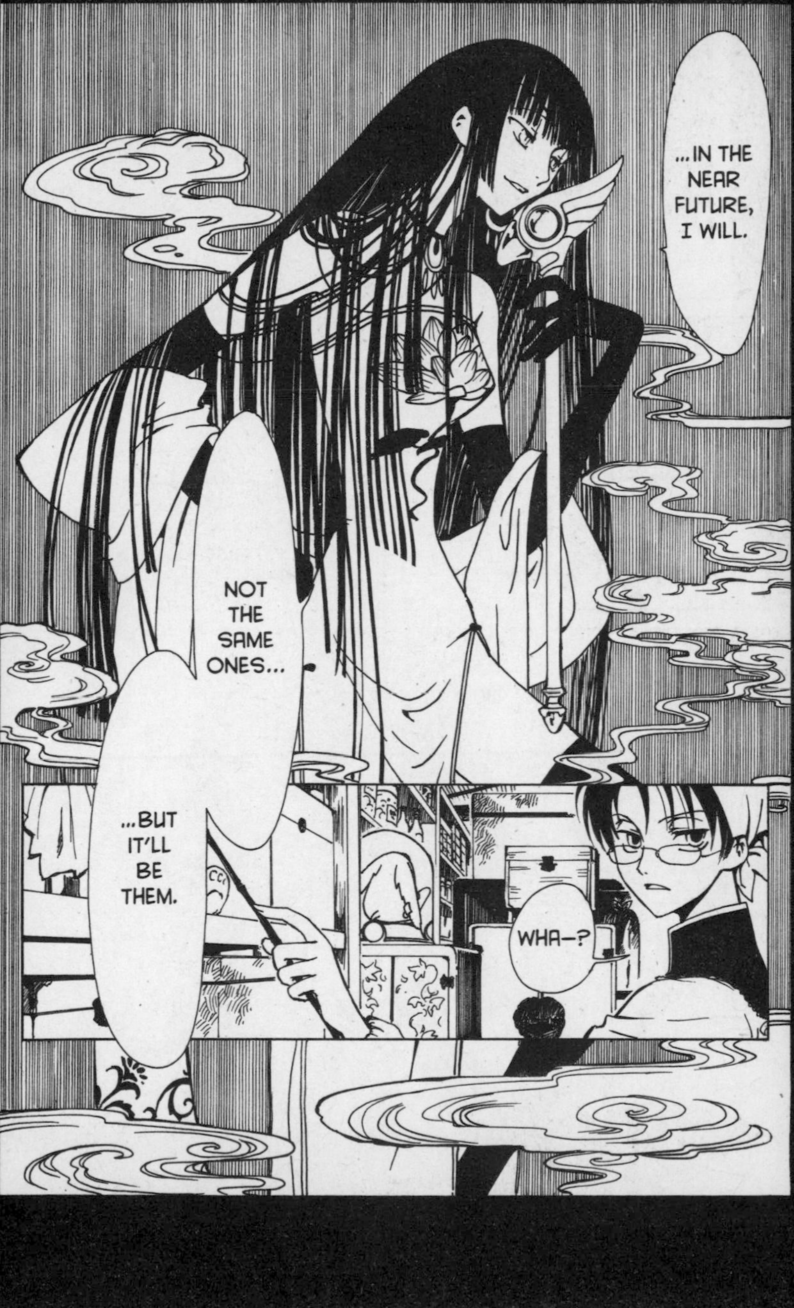
...IN THE NEAR FUTURE, I WILL.
NOT THE SAME ONES...
...BUT IT'LL BE THEM.
WHA–?

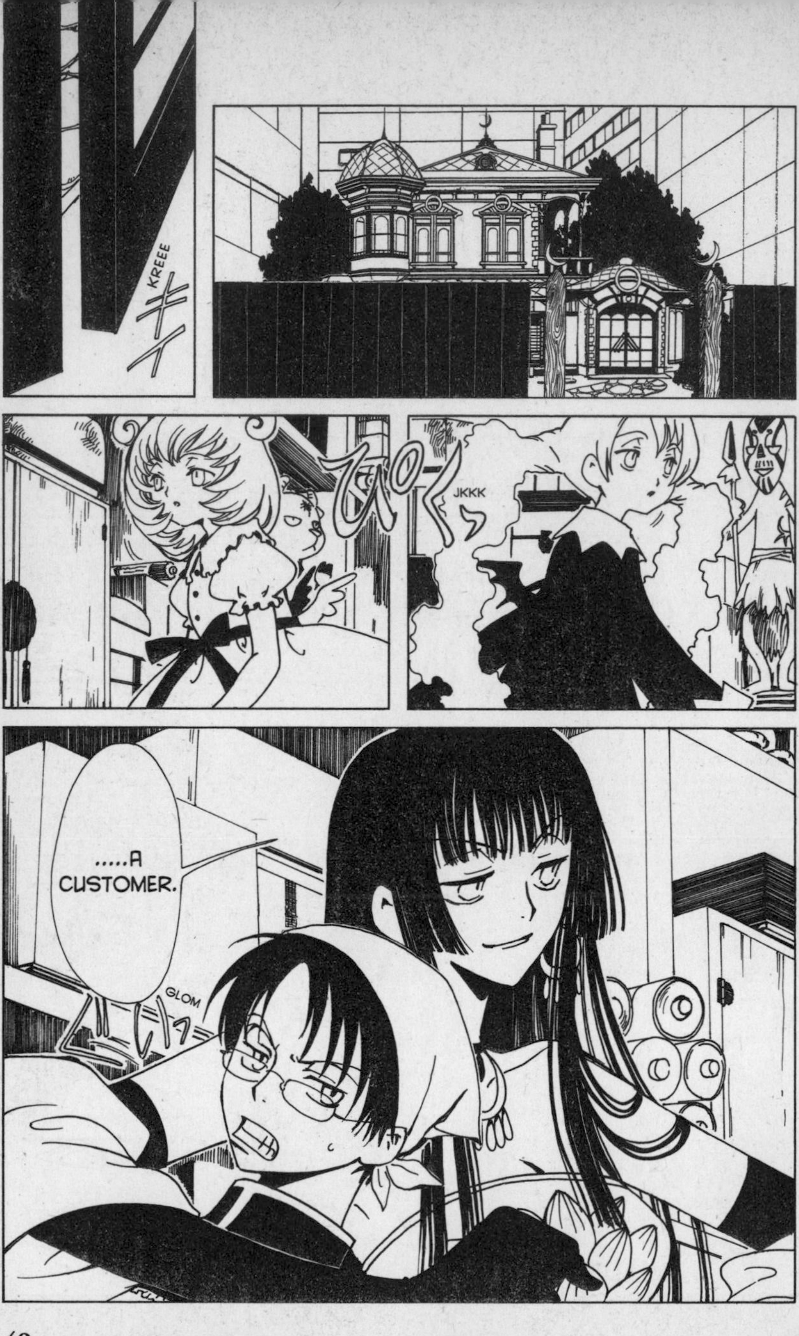
KREEE
JKKK
.....A CUSTOMER.
GLOM

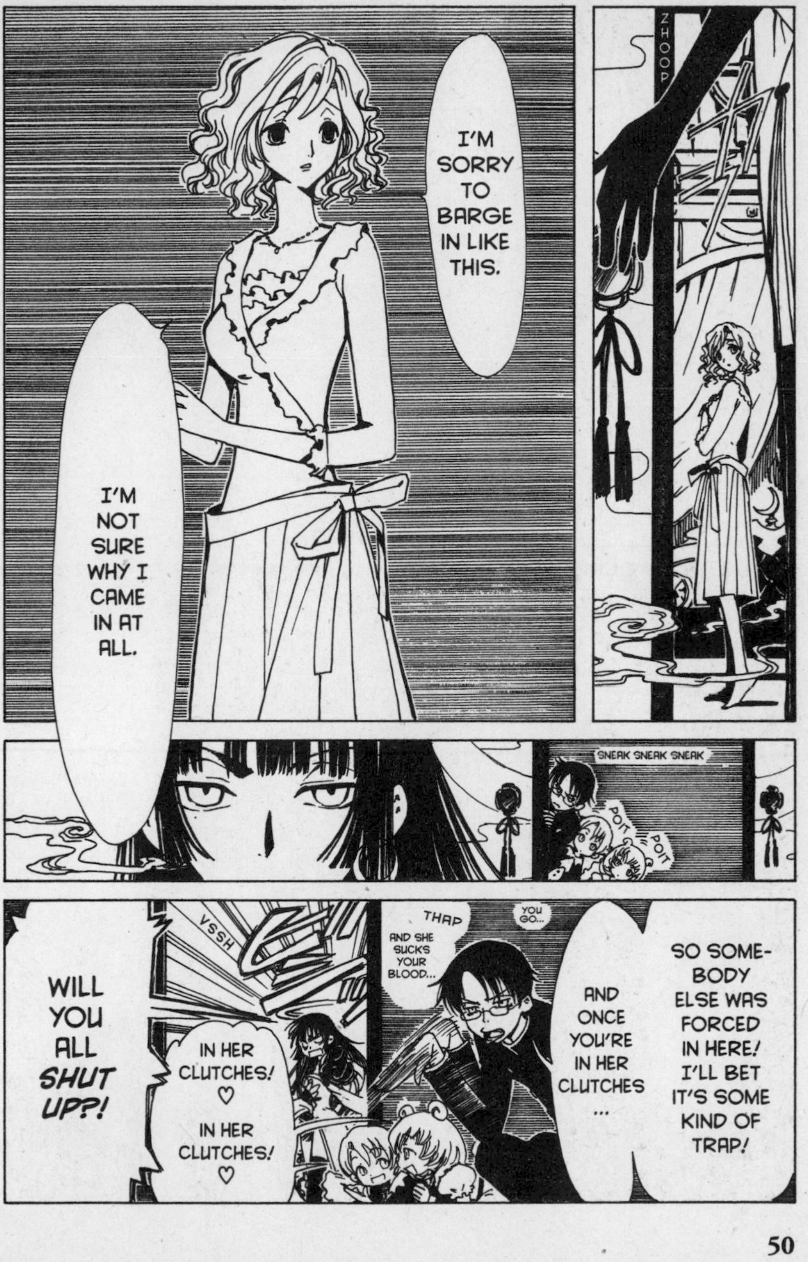
ZHOOP
I'M SORRY TO BARGE IN LIKE THIS.
I'M NOT SURE WHY I CAME IN AT ALL.
SNEAK SNEAK SNEAK
POIT
POIT
SO SOME-BODY ELSE WAS FORCED IN HERE! I'LL BET IT'S SOME KIND OF TRAP!
AND ONCE YOU'RE IN HER CLUTCHES ...
YOU GO...
THAP
AND SHE SUCKS YOUR BLOOD...
IN HER CLUTCHES! ♡
IN HER CLUTCHES! ♡
VSSH
WILL YOU ALL *SHUT UP?!*

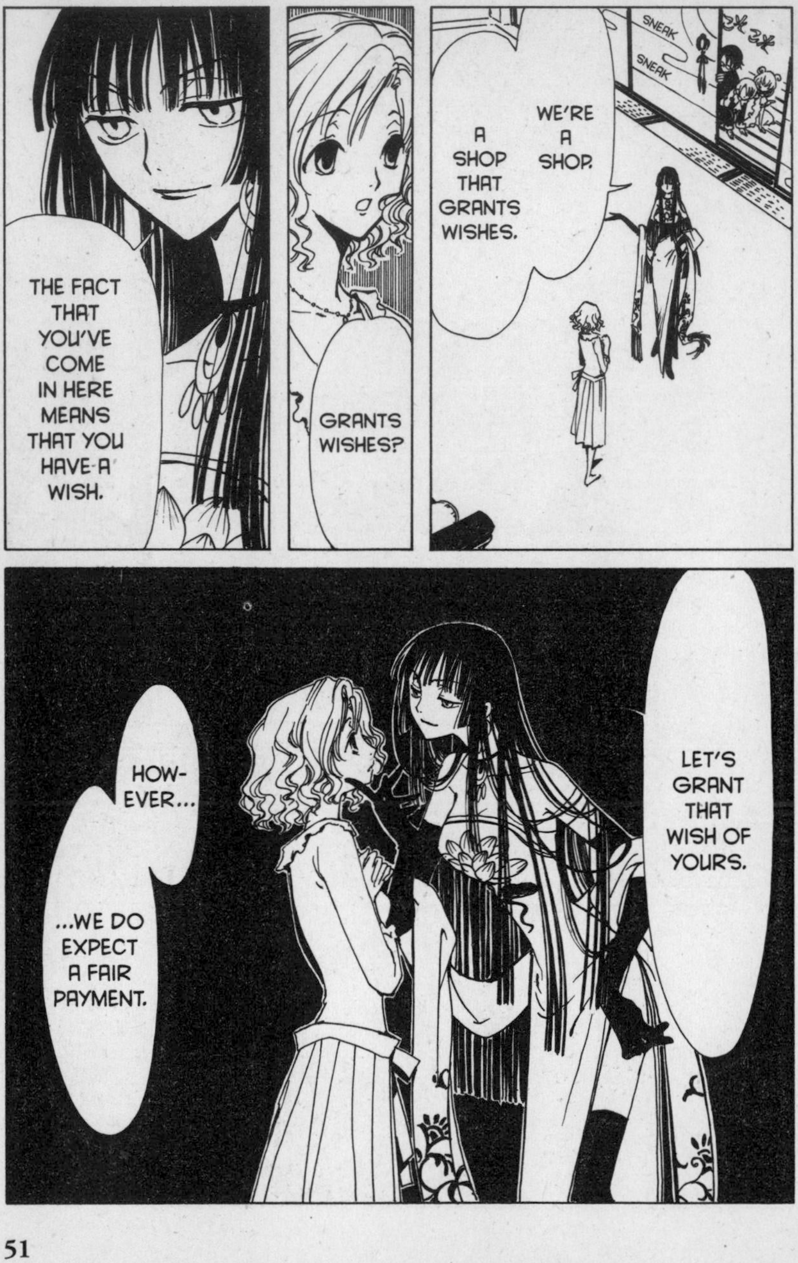
SNEAK
SNEAK
WE'RE A SHOP.
A SHOP THAT GRANTS WISHES.
GRANTS WISHES?
THE FACT THAT YOU'VE COME IN HERE MEANS THAT YOU HAVE A WISH.
LET'S GRANT THAT WISH OF YOURS.
HOW-EVER...
...WE DO EXPECT A FAIR PAYMENT.

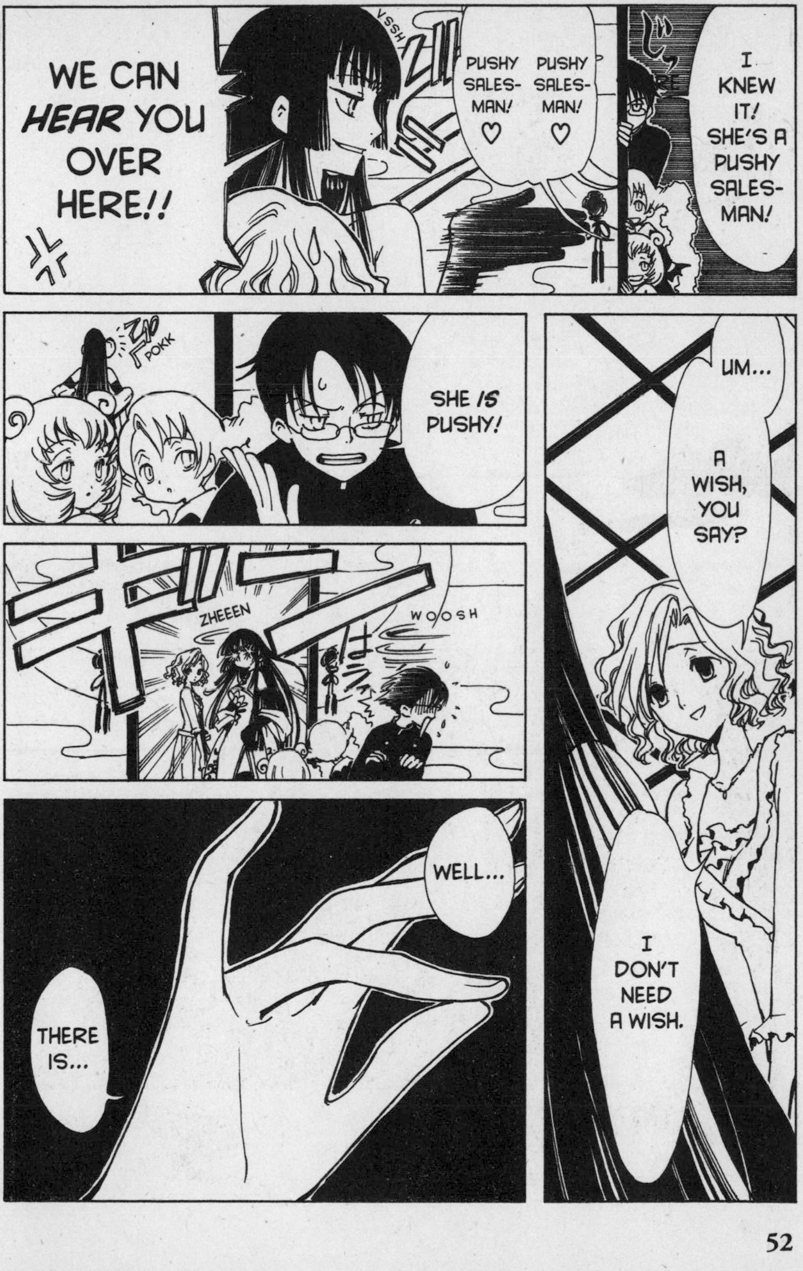

I KNEW IT! SHE'S A PUSHY SALES-MAN!
VSSH
PUSHY SALES-MAN! ♡
PUSHY SALES-MAN! ♡
WE CAN HEAR YOU OVER HERE!!
UM...
A WISH, YOU SAY?
I DON'T NEED A WISH.
SHE IS PUSHY!
POKK
WOOSH
ZHEEEN
WELL...
THERE IS...

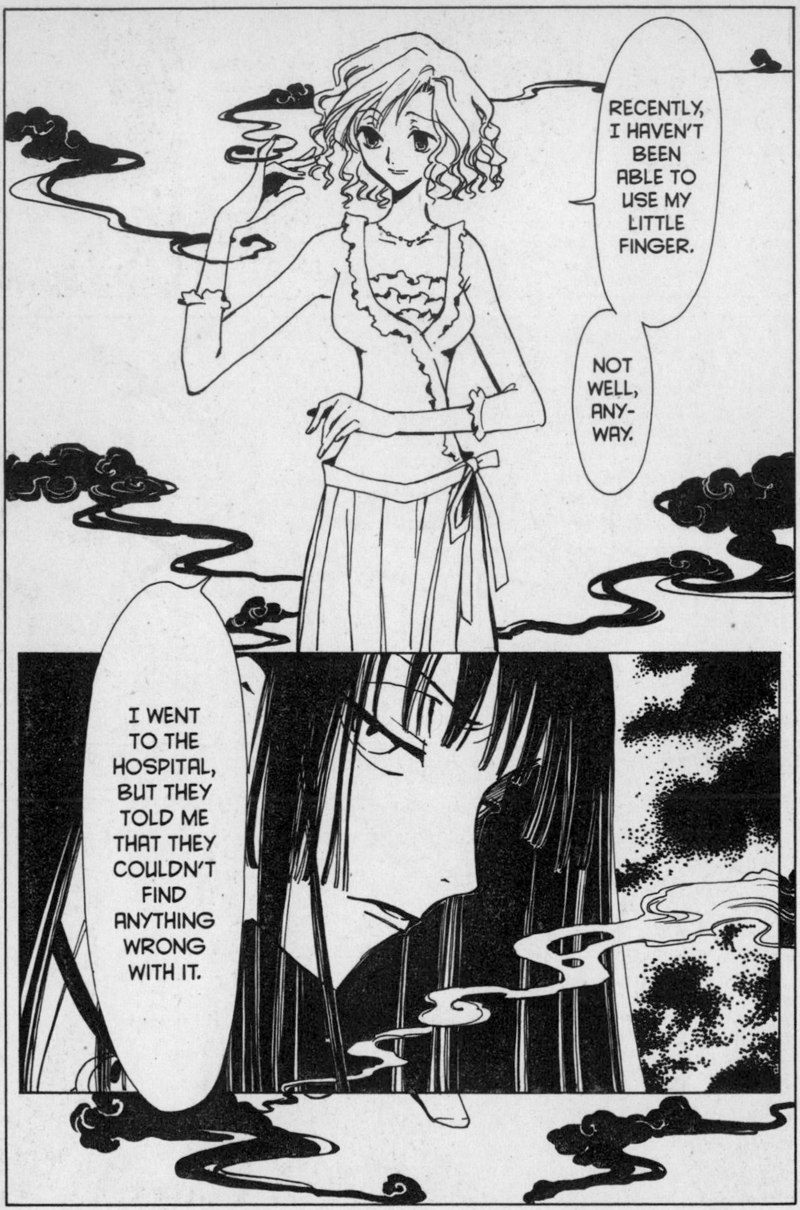
RECENTLY, I HAVEN'T BEEN ABLE TO USE MY LITTLE FINGER.
NOT WELL, ANY-WAY.
I WENT TO THE HOSPITAL, BUT THEY TOLD ME THAT THEY COULDN'T FIND ANYTHING WRONG WITH IT.

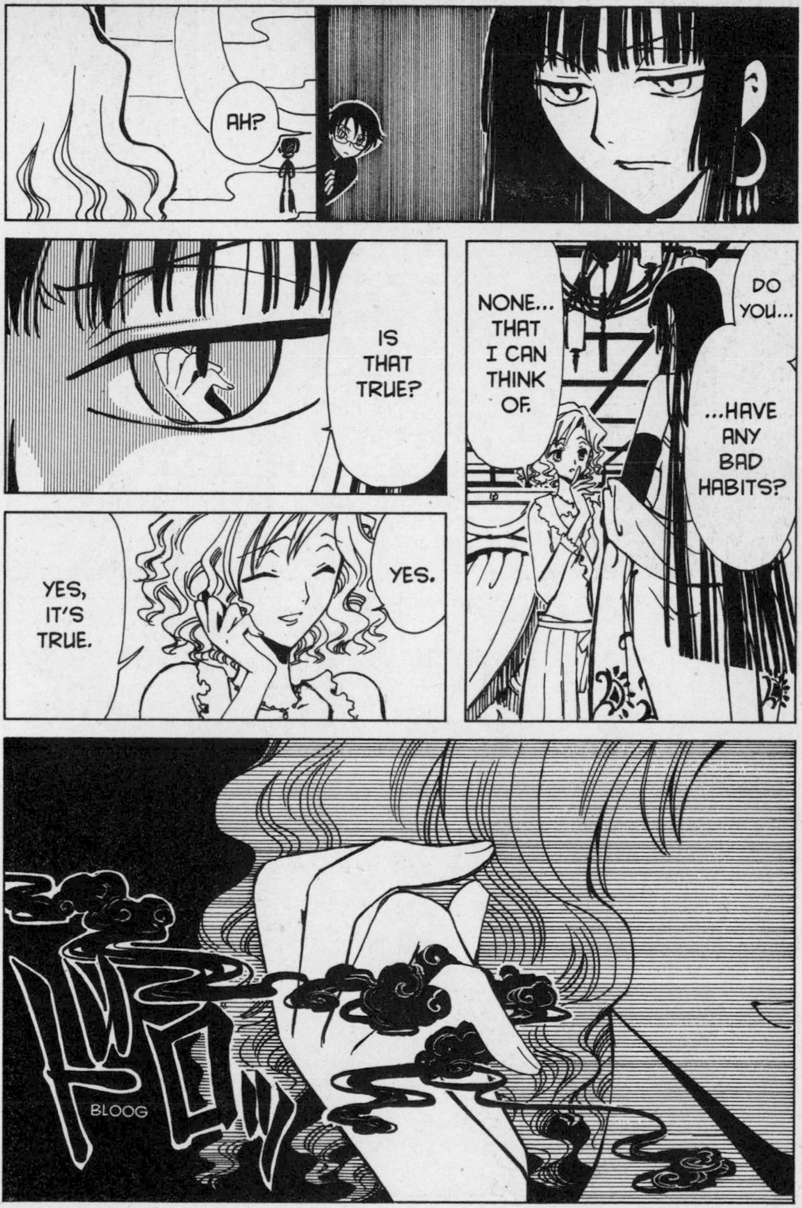
AH?
DO YOU...
...HAVE ANY BAD HABITS?
NONE... THAT I CAN THINK OF.
IS THAT TRUE?
YES.
YES, IT'S TRUE.
BLOOG

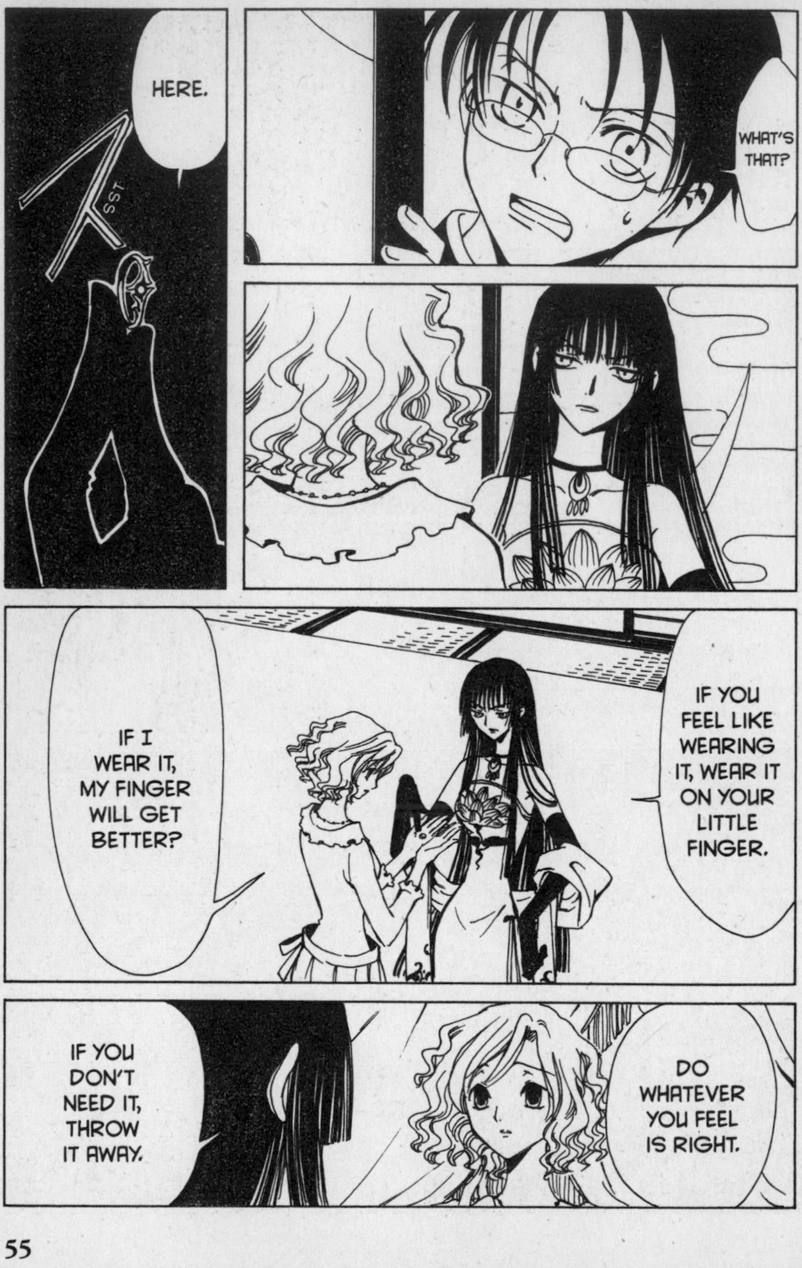
WHAT'S THAT?
HERE.
SST
IF YOU FEEL LIKE WEARING IT, WEAR IT ON YOUR LITTLE FINGER.
IF I WEAR IT, MY FINGER WILL GET BETTER?
DO WHATEVER YOU FEEL IS RIGHT.
IF YOU DON'T NEED IT, THROW IT AWAY.

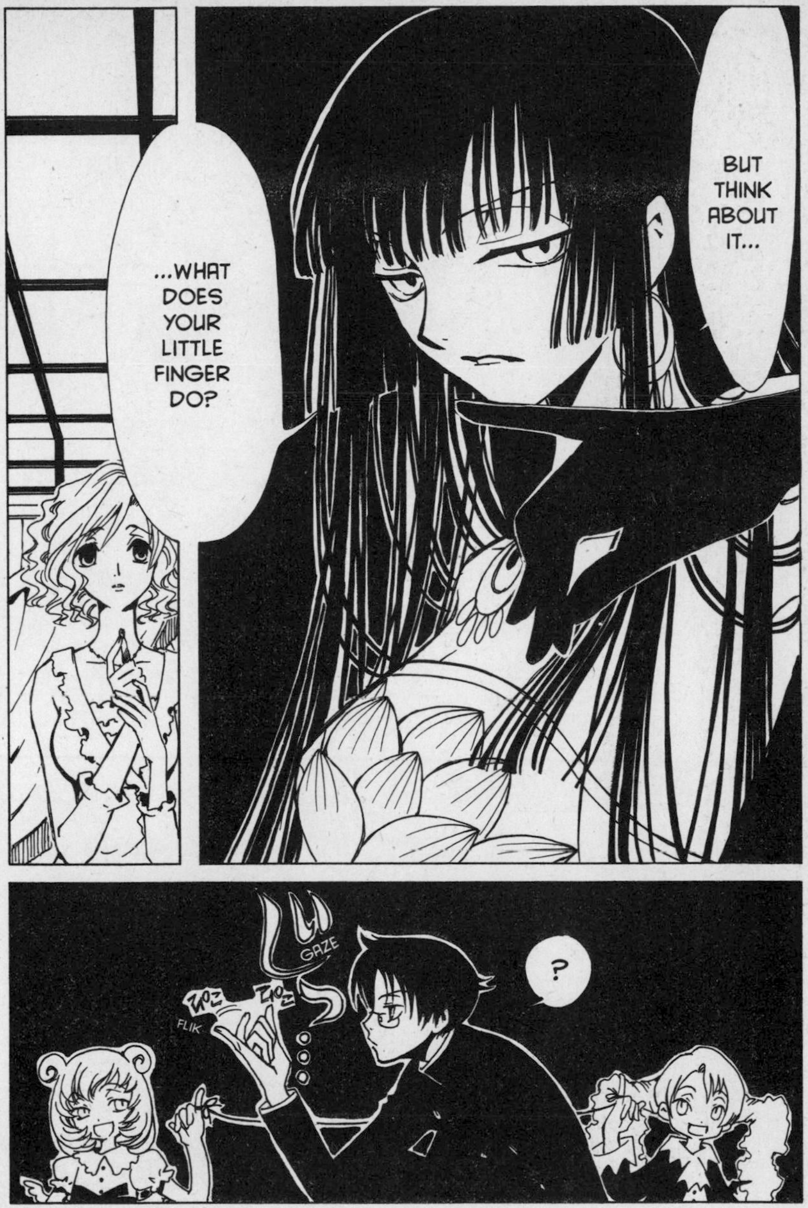
BUT THINK ABOUT IT...
...WHAT DOES YOUR LITTLE FINGER DO?
?
GAZE
FLIK

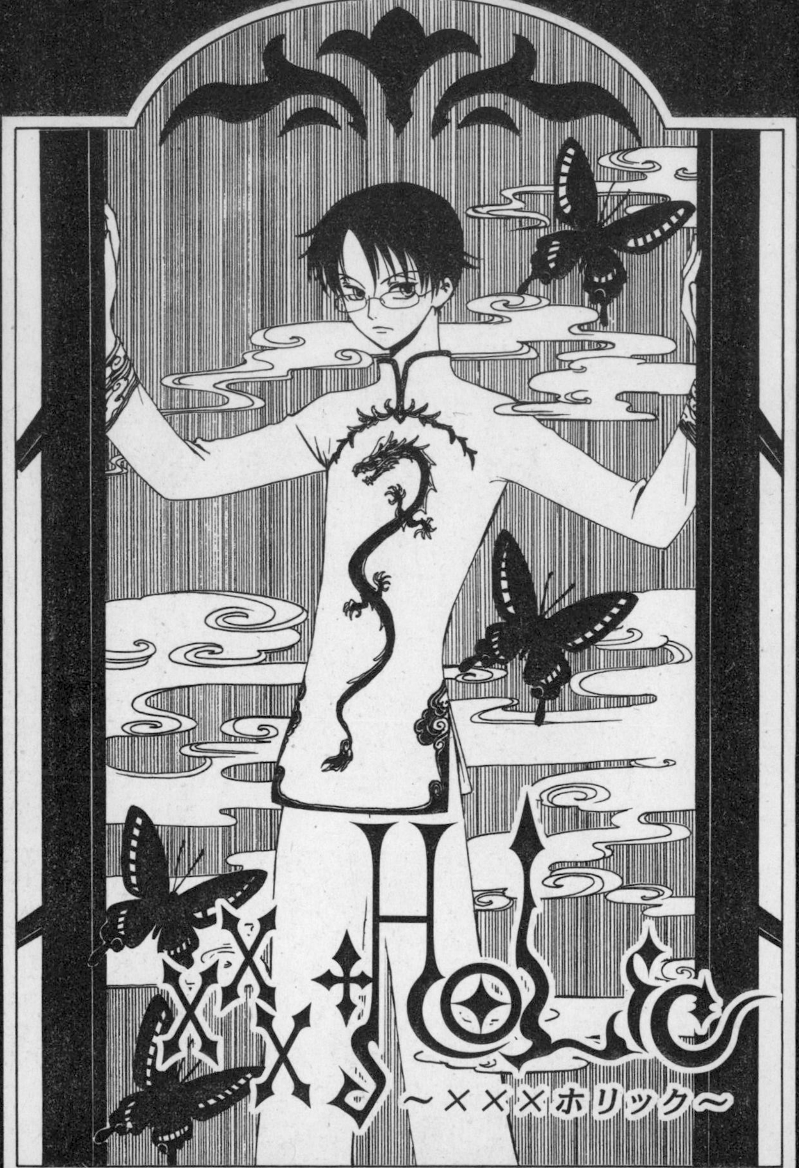
xxxHOLiC
～×××ホリック～

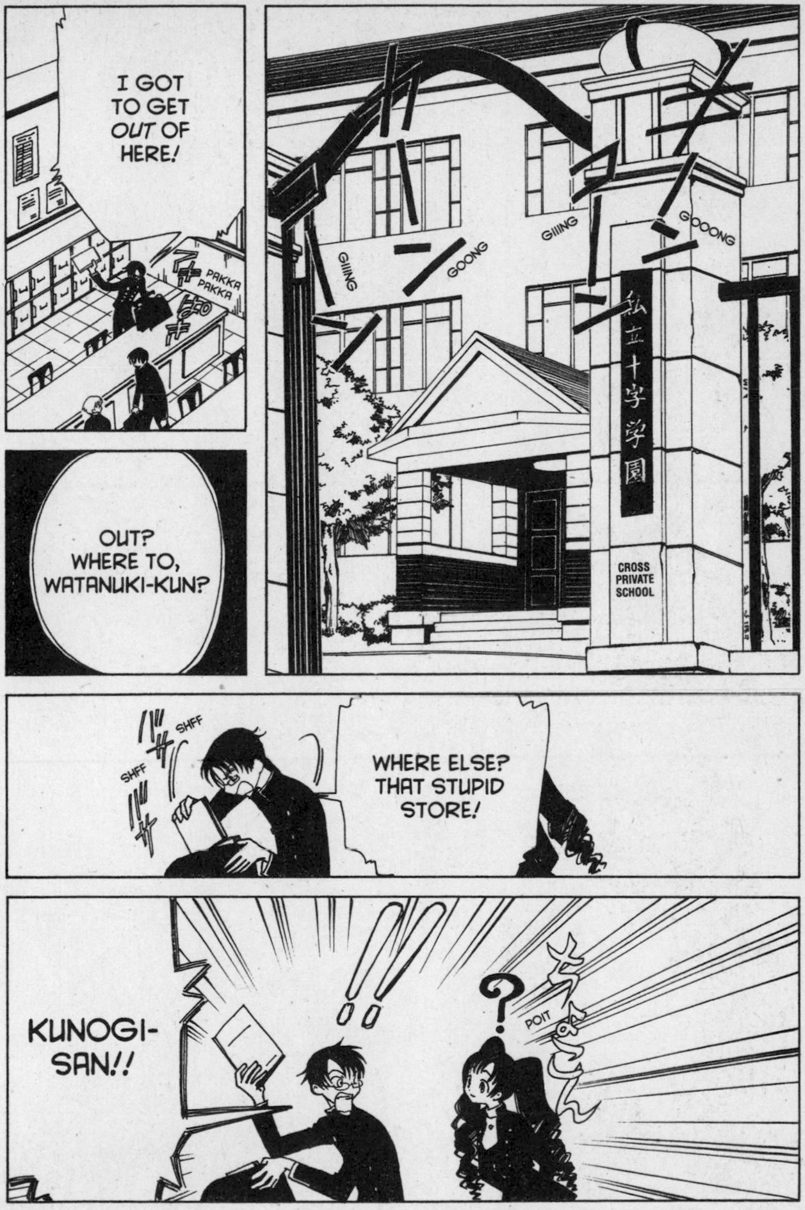
GOOONG
GIIING
GOONG
GIIING
私立十字学園
CROSS PRIVATE SCHOOL
I GOT TO GET *OUT* OF HERE!
PAKKA PAKKA
OUT? WHERE TO, WATANUKI-KUN?
WHERE ELSE? THAT STUPID STORE!
SHFF
SHFF
POIT
KUNOGI-SAN!!

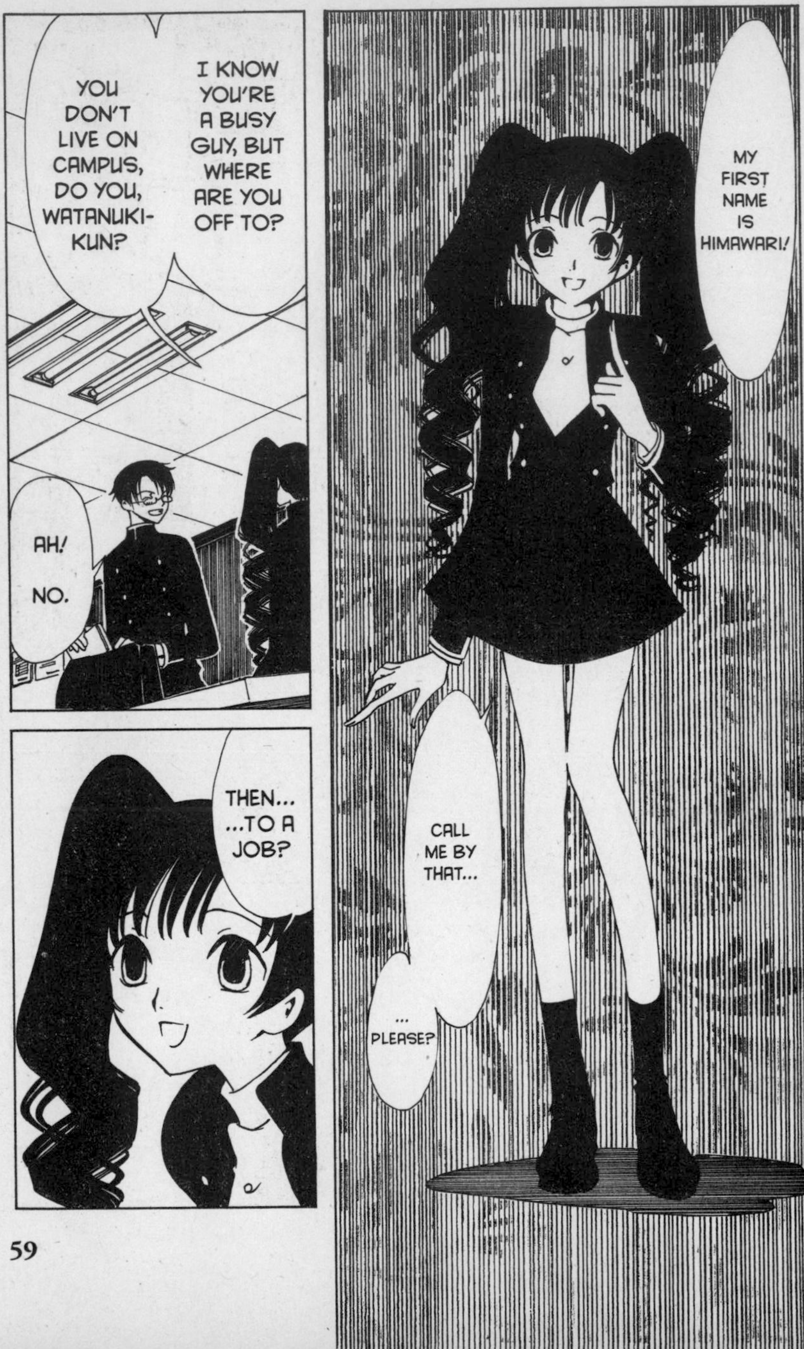
MY FIRST NAME IS HIMAWARI!
CALL ME BY THAT...
...PLEASE?
I KNOW YOU'RE A BUSY GUY, BUT WHERE ARE YOU OFF TO?
YOU DON'T LIVE ON CAMPUS, DO YOU, WATANUKI-KUN?
AH! NO.
THEN... ...TO A JOB?

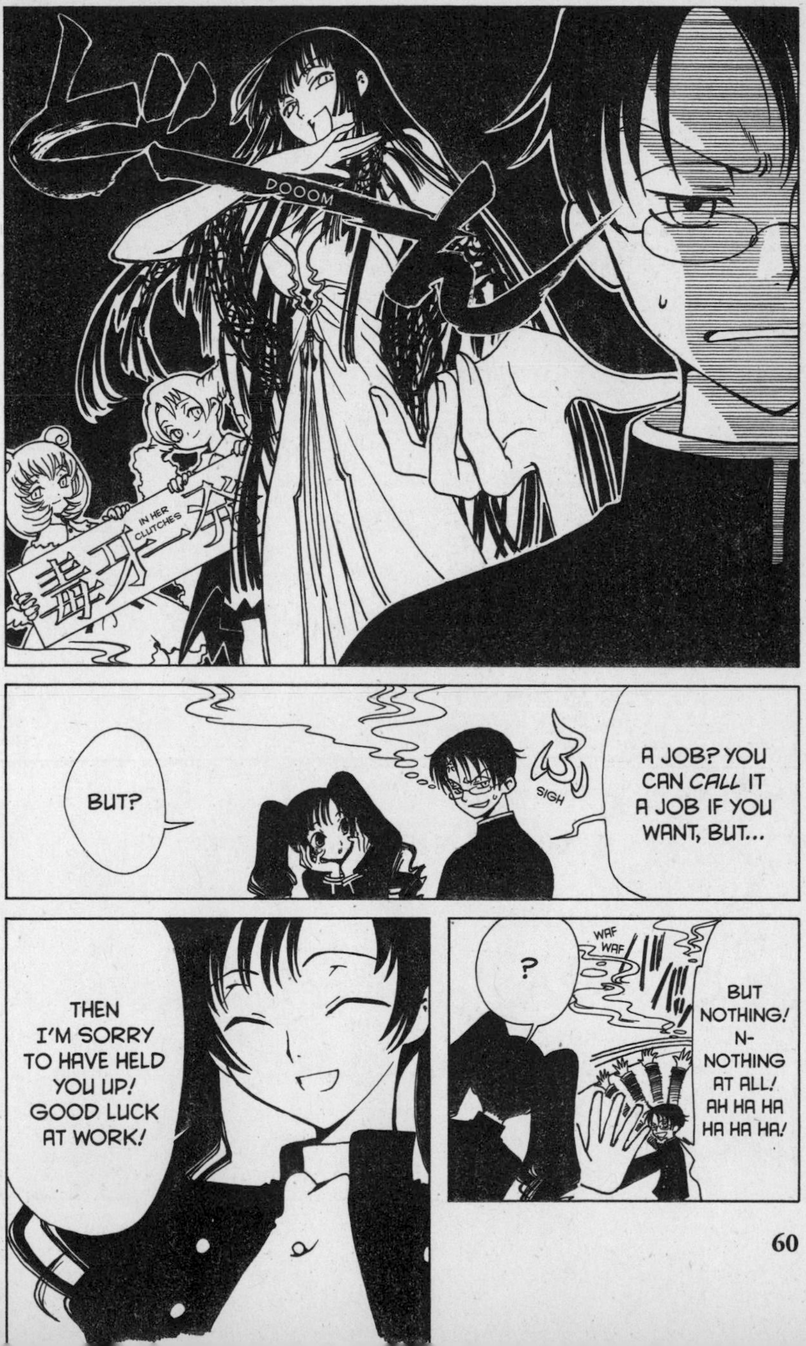
DOOOM
IN HER CLUTCHES
A JOB? YOU CAN *CALL* IT A JOB IF YOU WANT, BUT...
SIGH
BUT?
WAF WAF
BUT NOTHING! N- NOTHING AT ALL! AH HA HA HA HA HA!
?
THEN I'M SORRY TO HAVE HELD YOU UP! GOOD LUCK AT WORK!

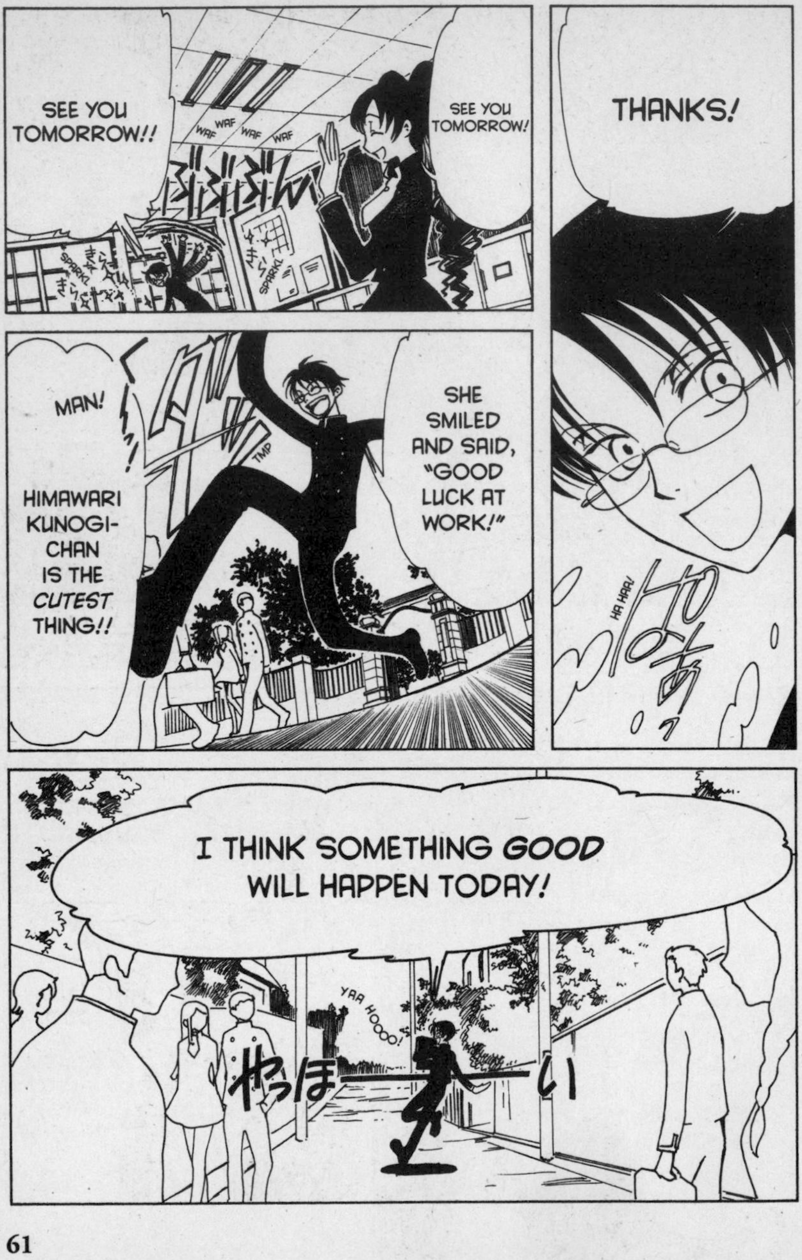
THANKS!
HA HA!
SEE YOU TOMORROW!
WAF WAF WAF WAF
SEE YOU TOMORROW!!
SPARKL SPARKL
SHE SMILED AND SAID, "GOOD LUCK AT WORK!"
TMP
MAN!
HIMAWARI KUNOGI-CHAN IS THE *CUTEST* THING!!
I THINK SOMETHING *GOOD* WILL HAPPEN TODAY!
YAA HOOOO!

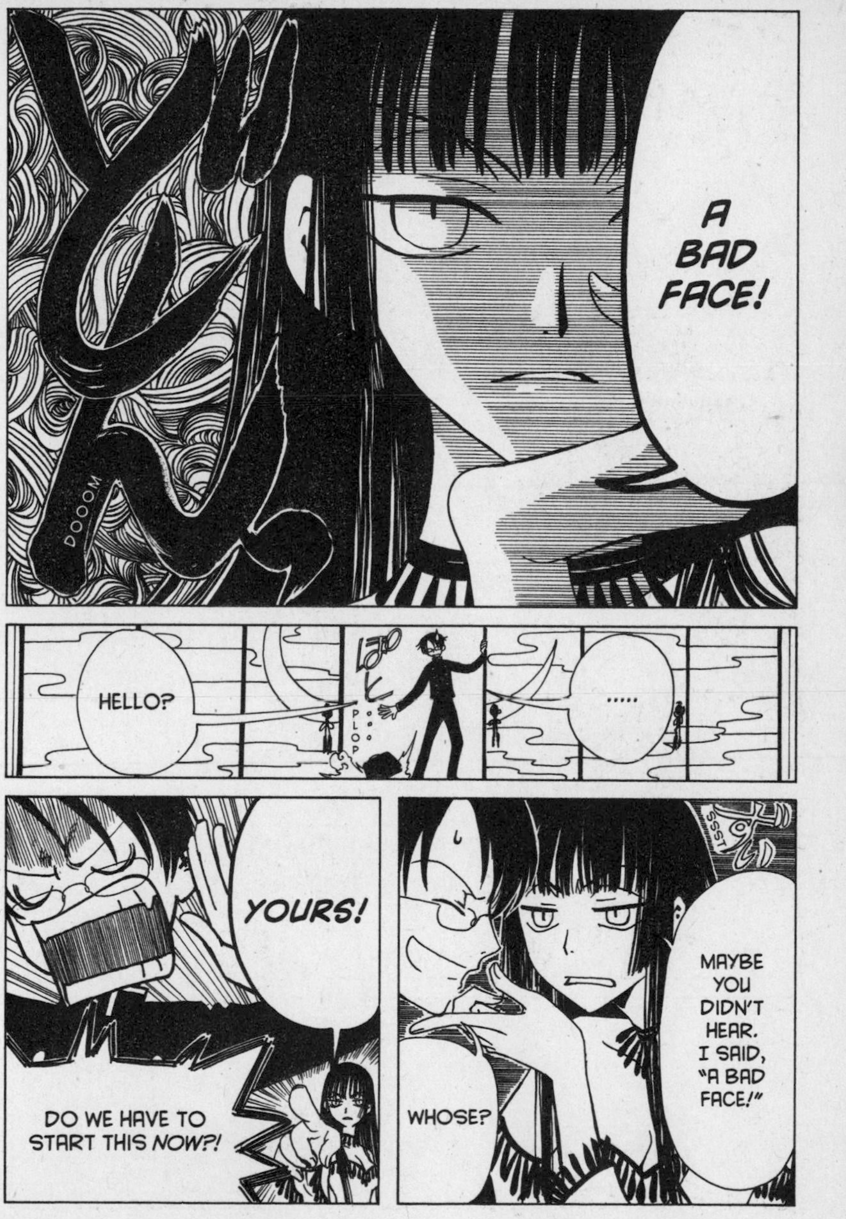
A BAD FACE!
DOOOM
.....
PLOP
HELLO?
SSST
MAYBE YOU DIDN'T HEAR. I SAID, "A BAD FACE!"
WHOSE?
YOURS!
DO WE HAVE TO START THIS NOW?!

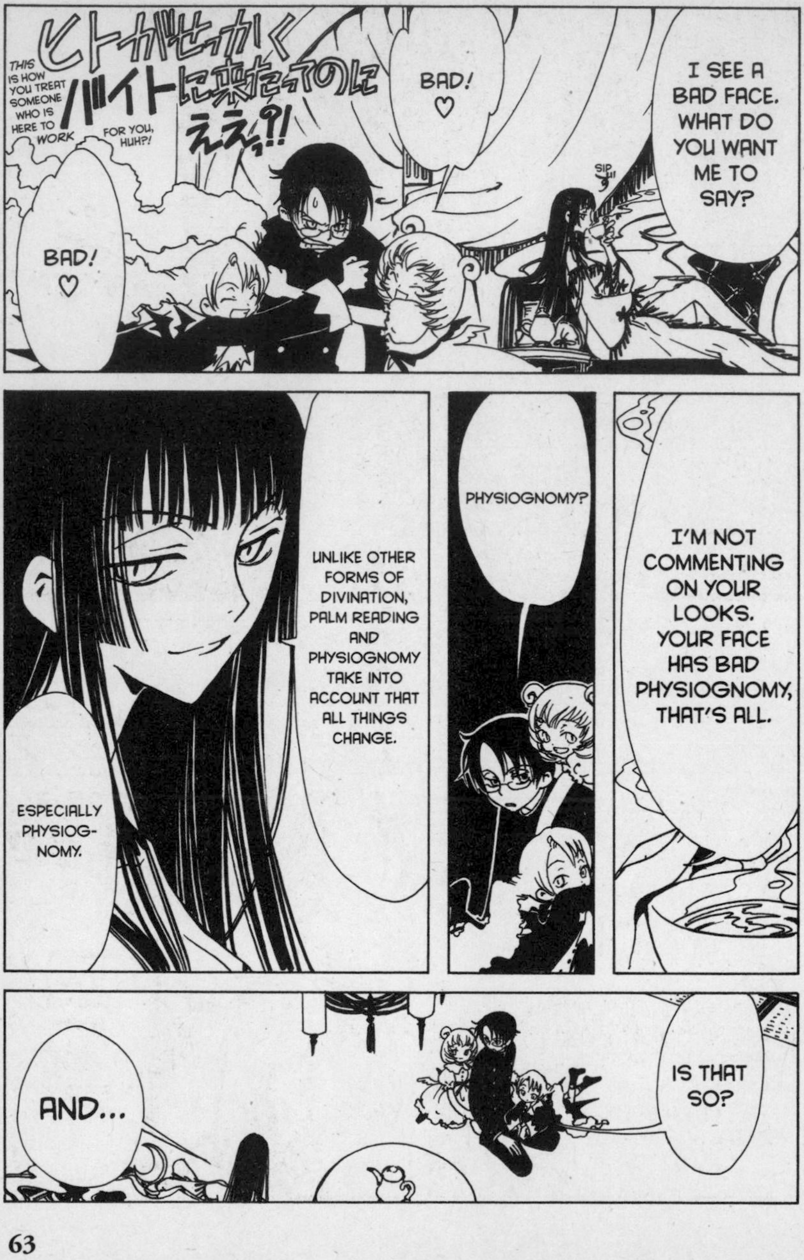
I SEE A BAD FACE. WHAT DO YOU WANT ME TO SAY?
SIP ず
BAD! ♡
ヒトがせっかくバイトに来たってのにええっ?!
THIS IS HOW YOU TREAT SOMEONE WHO IS HERE TO WORK FOR YOU, HUH?!
BAD! ♡
I'M NOT COMMENTING ON YOUR LOOKS. YOUR FACE HAS BAD PHYSIOGNOMY, THAT'S ALL.
PHYSIOGNOMY?
UNLIKE OTHER FORMS OF DIVINATION, PALM READING AND PHYSIOGNOMY TAKE INTO ACCOUNT THAT ALL THINGS CHANGE.
ESPECIALLY PHYSIOG-NOMY.
IS THAT SO?
AND...

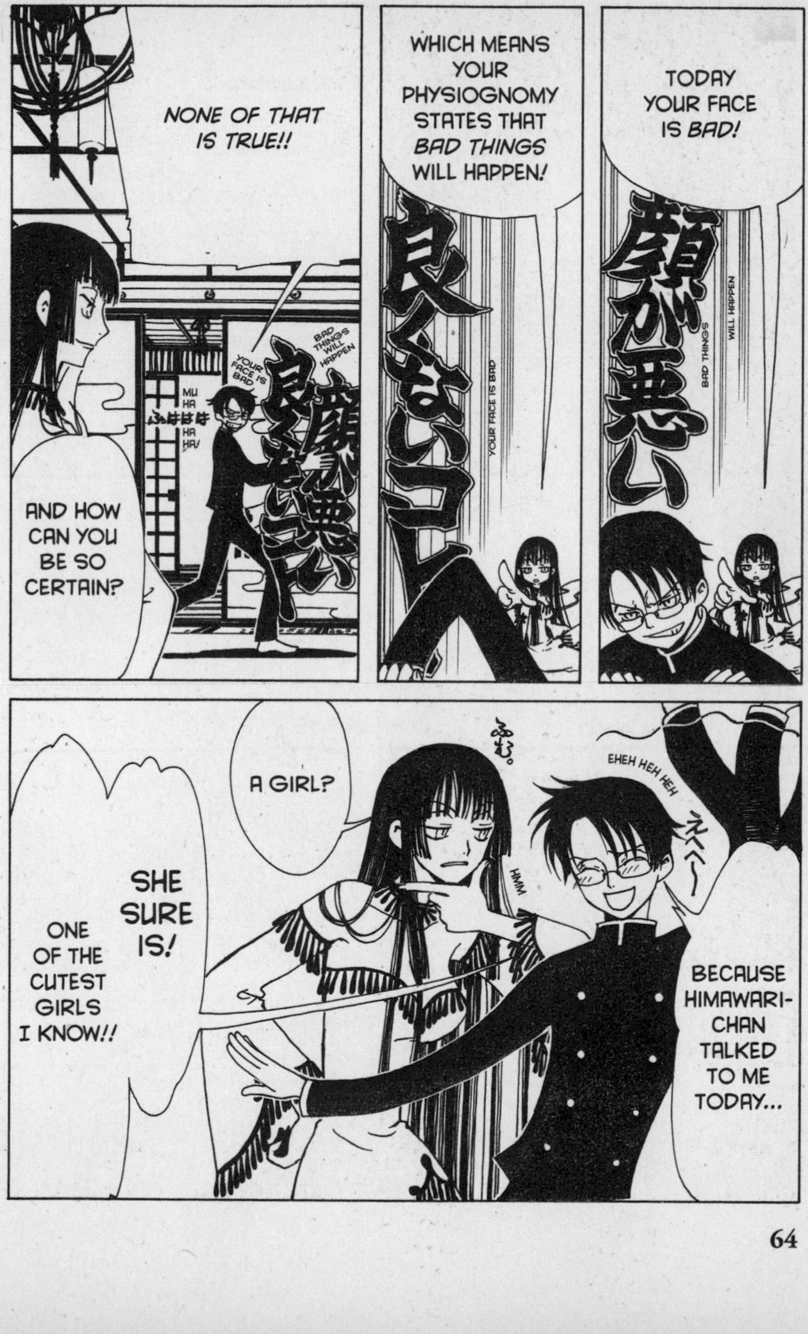
TODAY YOUR FACE IS BAD!
顔が悪い
BAD THINGS
WILL HAPPEN
WHICH MEANS YOUR PHYSIOGNOMY STATES THAT BAD THINGS WILL HAPPEN!
良くないコト
YOUR FACE IS BAD
NONE OF THAT IS TRUE!!
BAD THINGS WILL HAPPEN
YOUR FACE IS BAD
ふははは
MU HA HA HA!
AND HOW CAN YOU BE SO CERTAIN?
BECAUSE HIMAWARI-CHAN TALKED TO ME TODAY...
えへへ~
EHEH HEH HEH
ふむ。
HMM
A GIRL?
SHE SURE IS!
ONE OF THE CUTEST GIRLS I KNOW!!

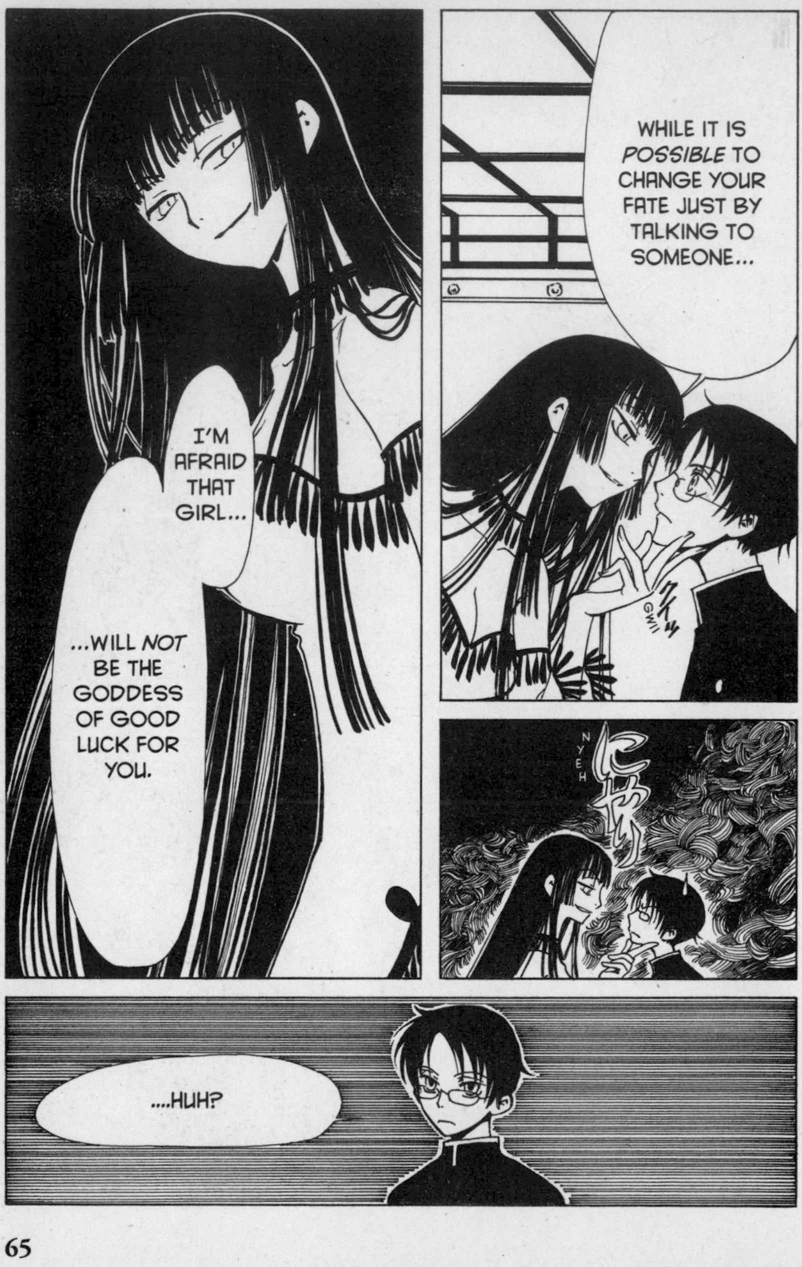
WHILE IT IS *POSSIBLE* TO CHANGE YOUR FATE JUST BY TALKING TO SOMEONE...
GWII
NYEH
I'M AFRAID THAT GIRL...
...WILL *NOT* BE THE GODDESS OF GOOD LUCK FOR YOU.
....HUH?

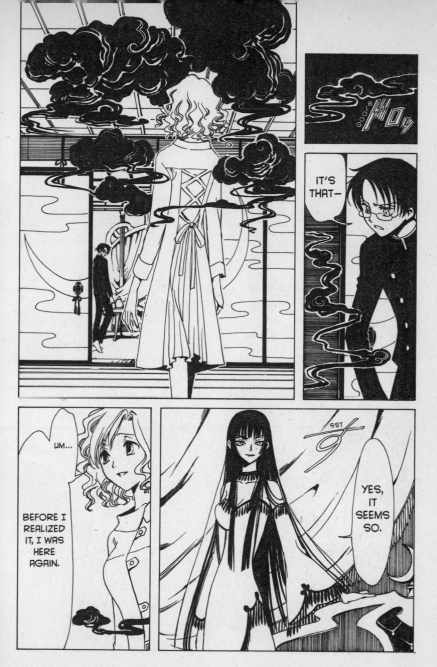

GOOLB
IT'S THAT—
SST
YES, IT SEEMS SO.
UM...
BEFORE I REALIZED IT, I WAS HERE AGAIN.

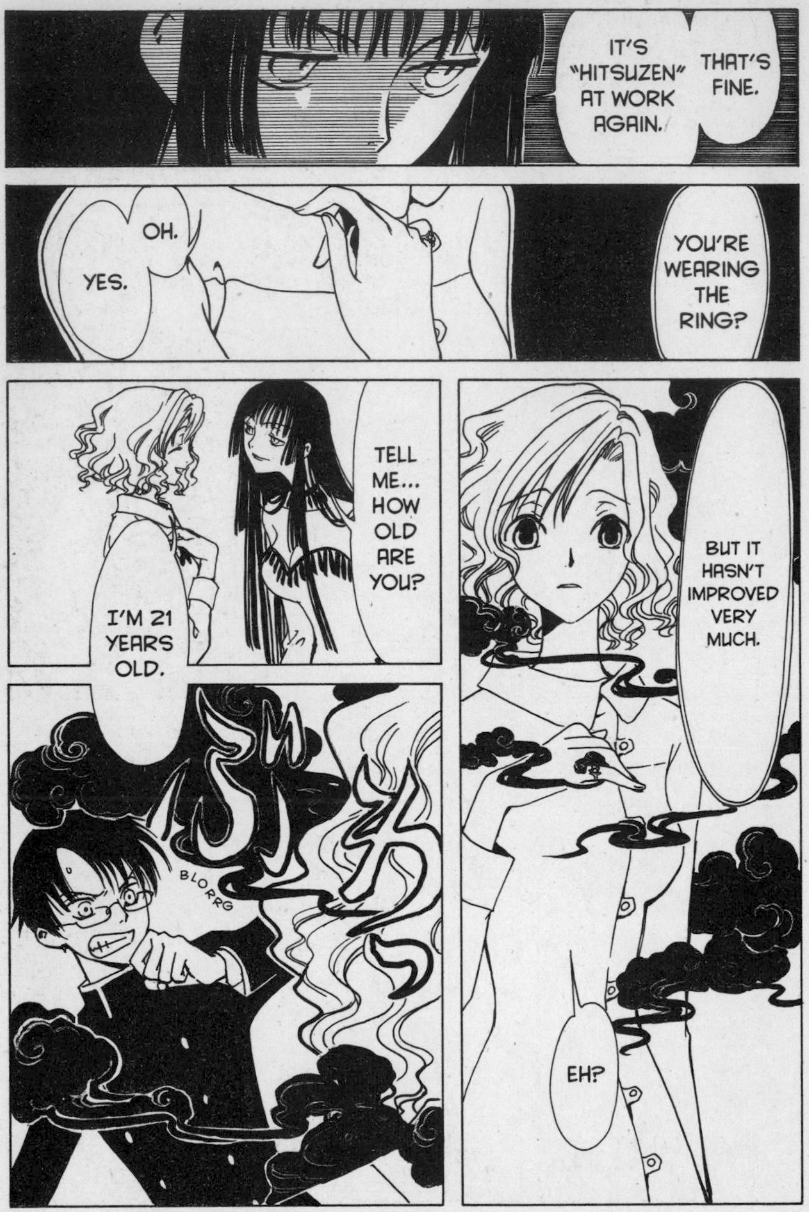
THAT'S FINE.
IT'S "HITSUZEN" AT WORK AGAIN.
YOU'RE WEARING THE RING?
OH.
YES.
BUT IT HASN'T IMPROVED VERY MUCH.
EH?
TELL ME... HOW OLD ARE YOU?
I'M 21 YEARS OLD.
BLORRG

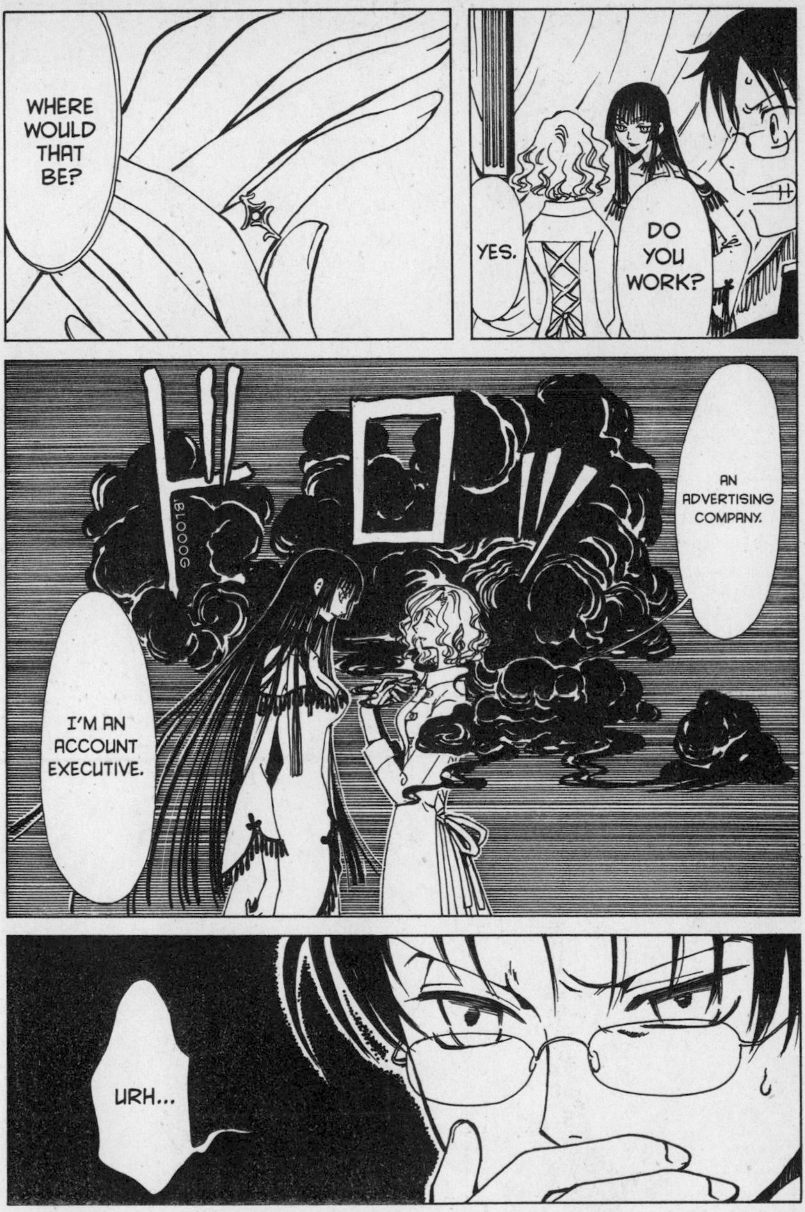
DO YOU WORK?
YES.
WHERE WOULD THAT BE?
AN ADVERTISING COMPANY.
BLOOOG
I'M AN ACCOUNT EXECUTIVE.
URH...

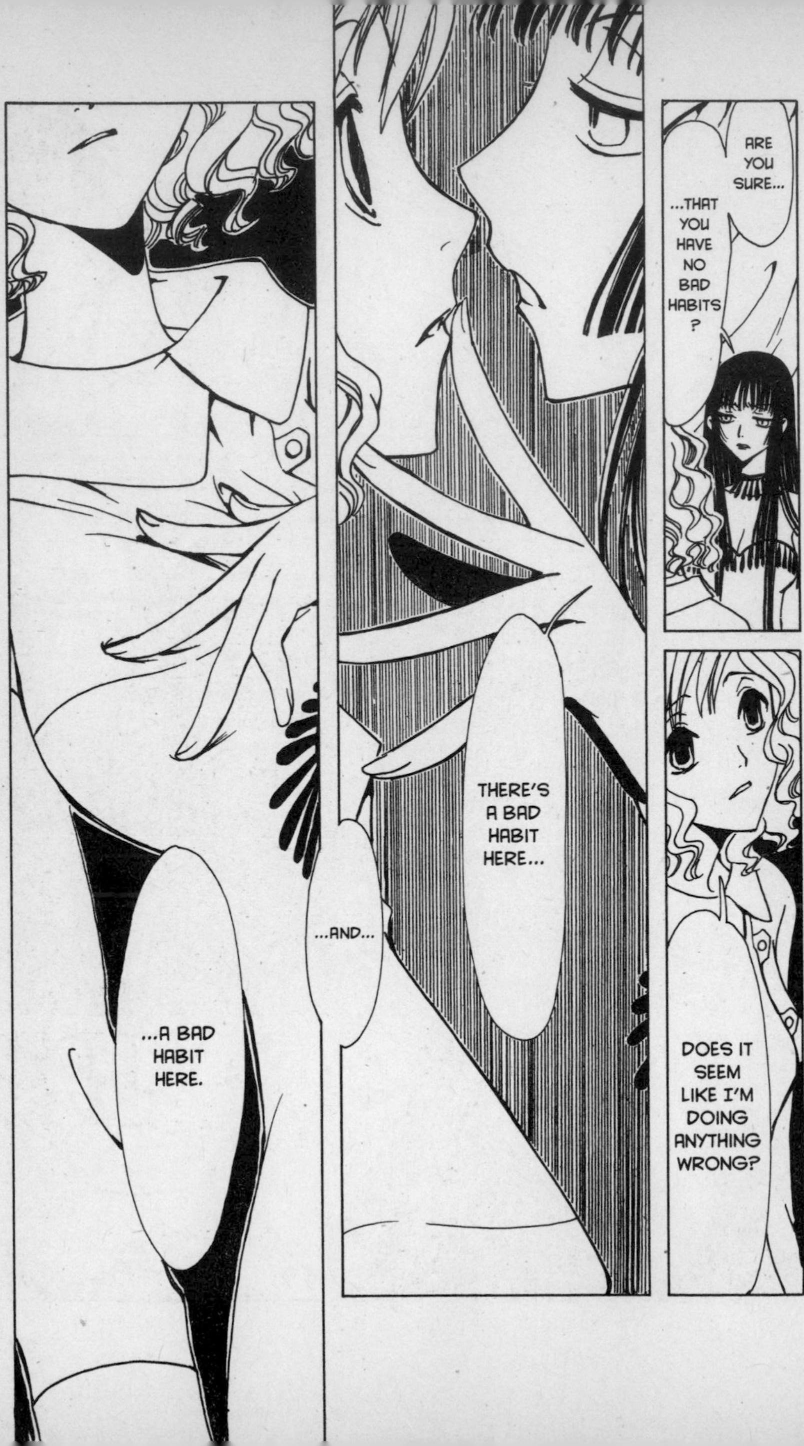
ARE YOU SURE...
...THAT YOU HAVE NO BAD HABITS?
DOES IT SEEM LIKE I'M DOING ANYTHING WRONG?
THERE'S A BAD HABIT HERE...
...AND...
...A BAD HABIT HERE.

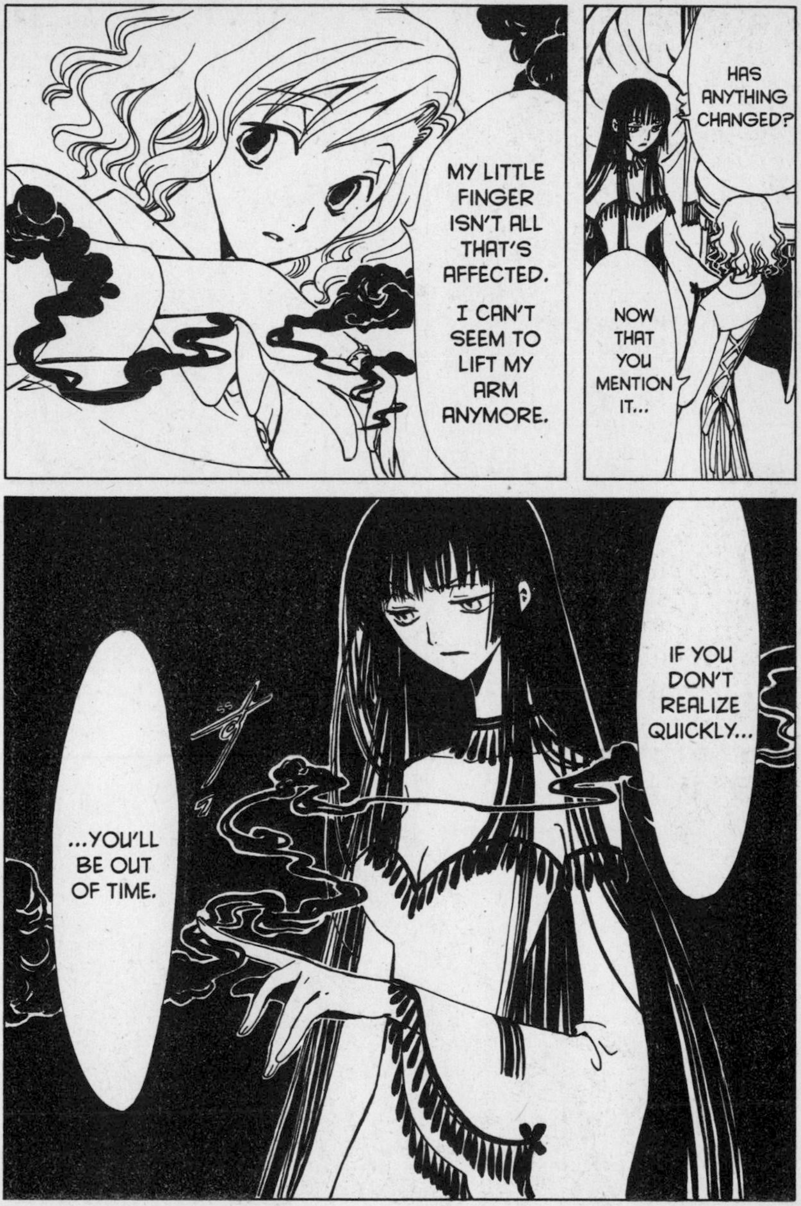
HAS ANYTHING CHANGED?
NOW THAT YOU MENTION IT...
MY LITTLE FINGER ISN'T ALL THAT'S AFFECTED.
I CAN'T SEEM TO LIFT MY ARM ANYMORE.
IF YOU DON'T REALIZE QUICKLY...
...YOU'LL BE OUT OF TIME.

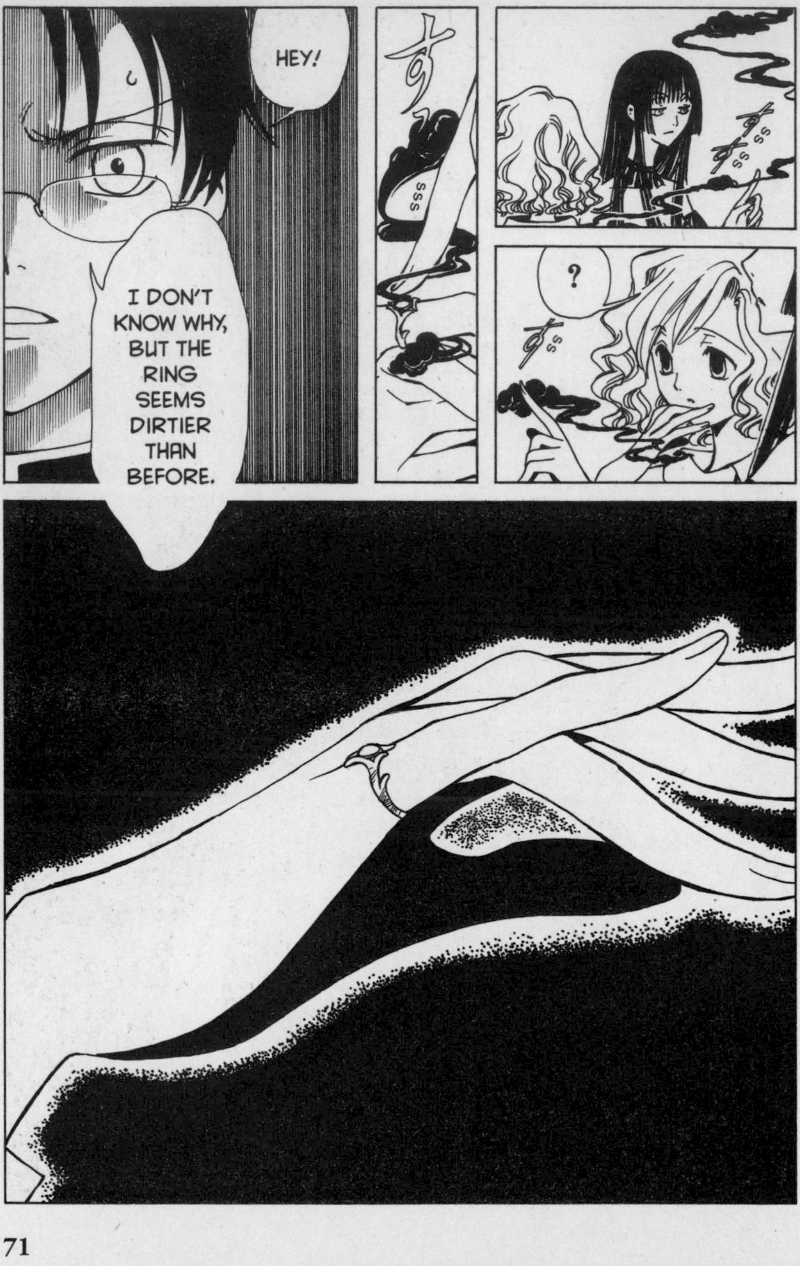
sss
sss
?
ss
sss
HEY!
I DON'T KNOW WHY, BUT THE RING SEEMS DIRTIER THAN BEFORE.

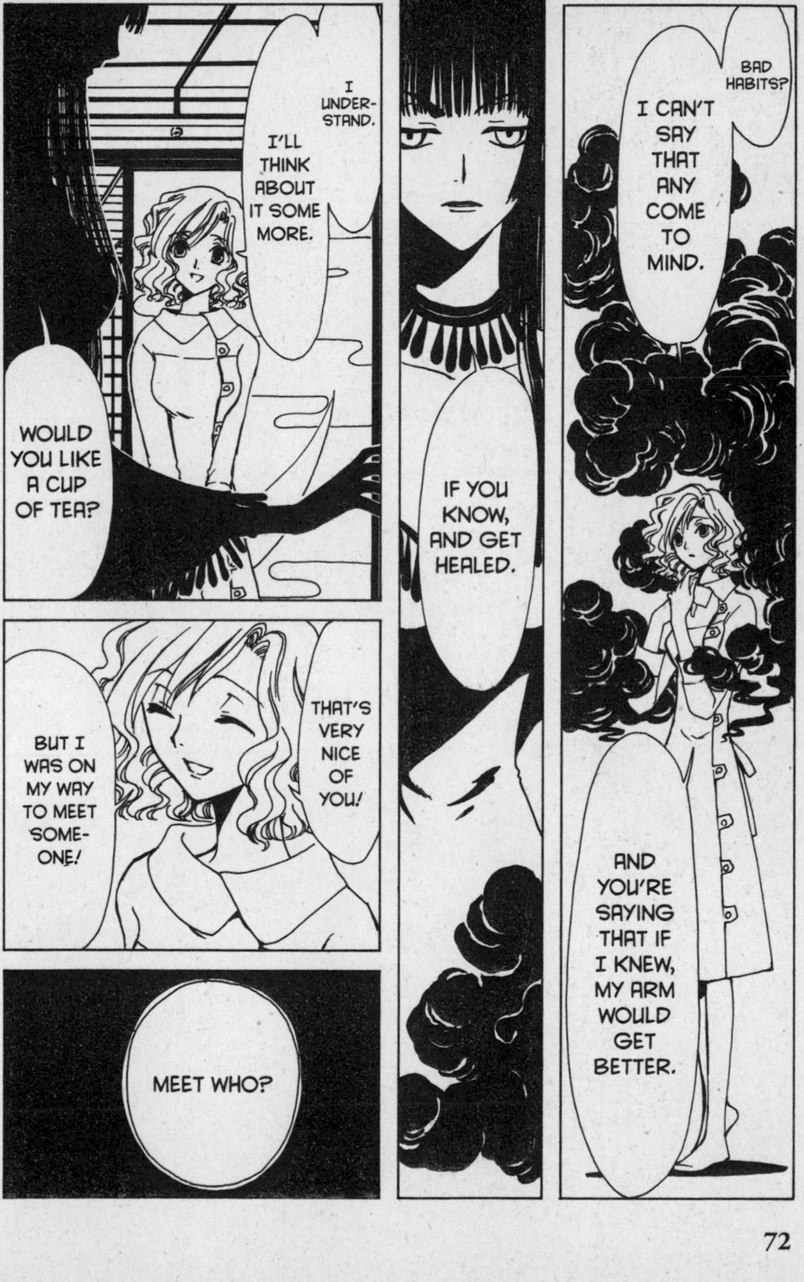
BAD HABITS?
I CAN'T SAY THAT ANY COME TO MIND.
AND YOU'RE SAYING THAT IF I KNEW, MY ARM WOULD GET BETTER.
IF YOU KNOW, AND GET HEALED.
I UNDER-STAND.
I'LL THINK ABOUT IT SOME MORE.
WOULD YOU LIKE A CUP OF TEA?
THAT'S VERY NICE OF YOU!
BUT I WAS ON MY WAY TO MEET SOME-ONE!
MEET WHO?

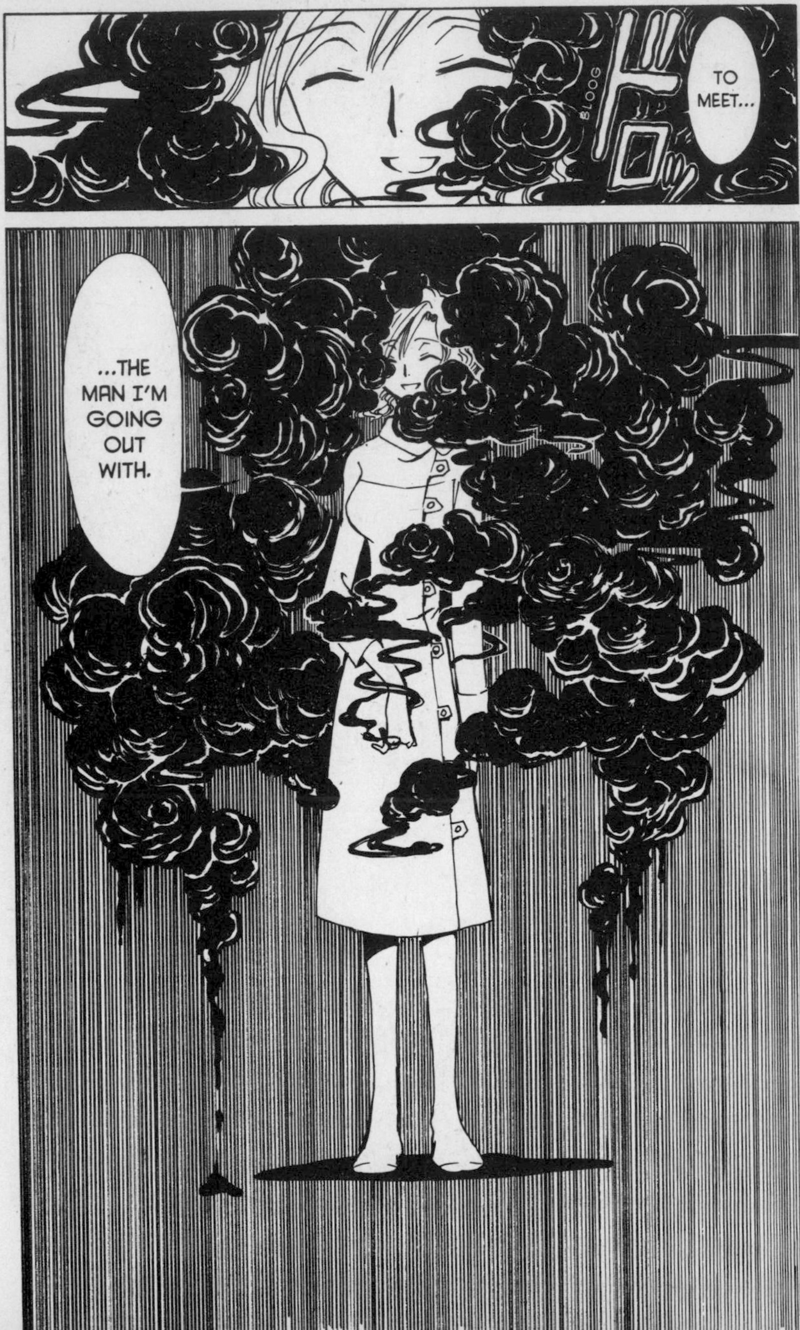
TO MEET...
BLOOG
...THE MAN I'M GOING OUT WITH.

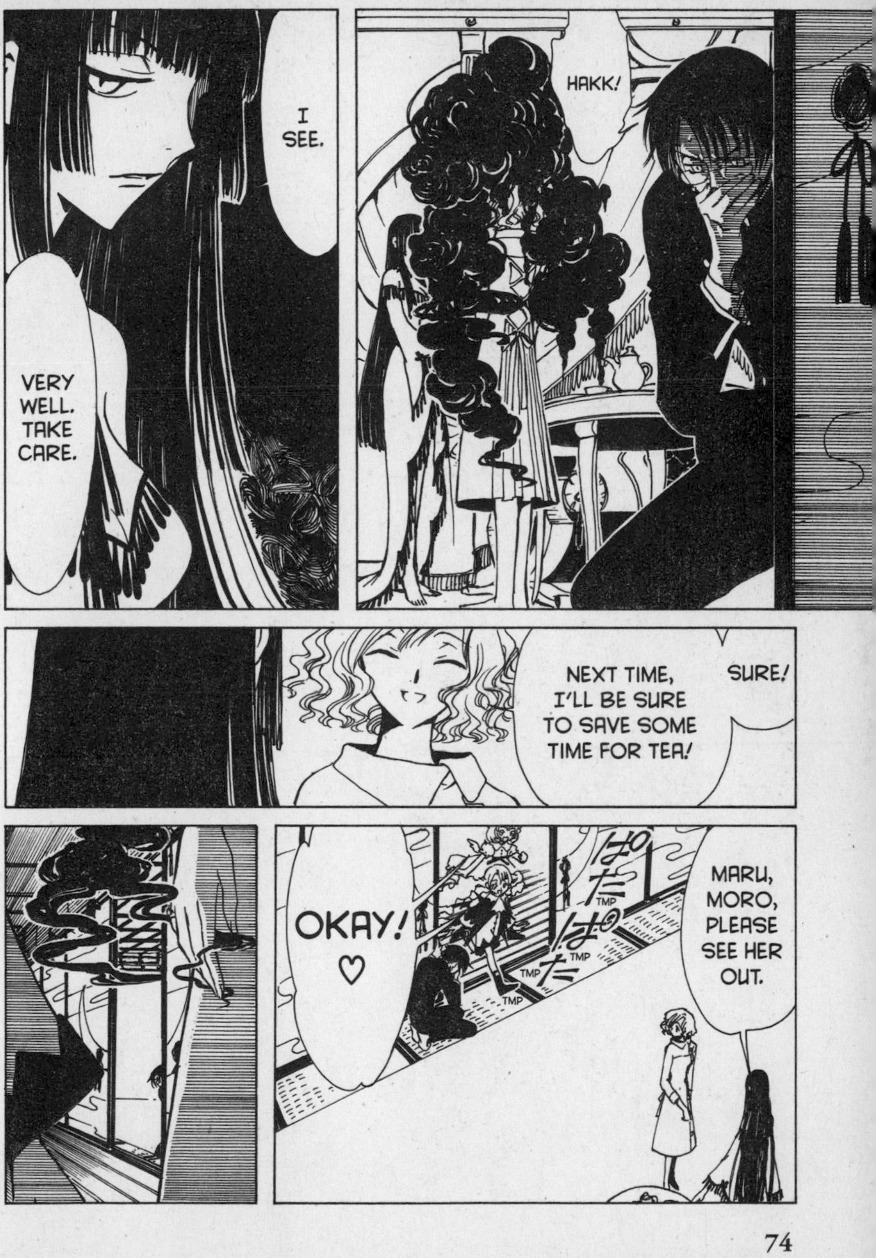
HAKK!
I SEE.
VERY WELL. TAKE CARE.
SURE!
NEXT TIME, I'LL BE SURE TO SAVE SOME TIME FOR TEA!
MARU, MORO, PLEASE SEE HER OUT.
ぱたぱたぱた
TMP TMP TMP TMP
OKAY! ♡

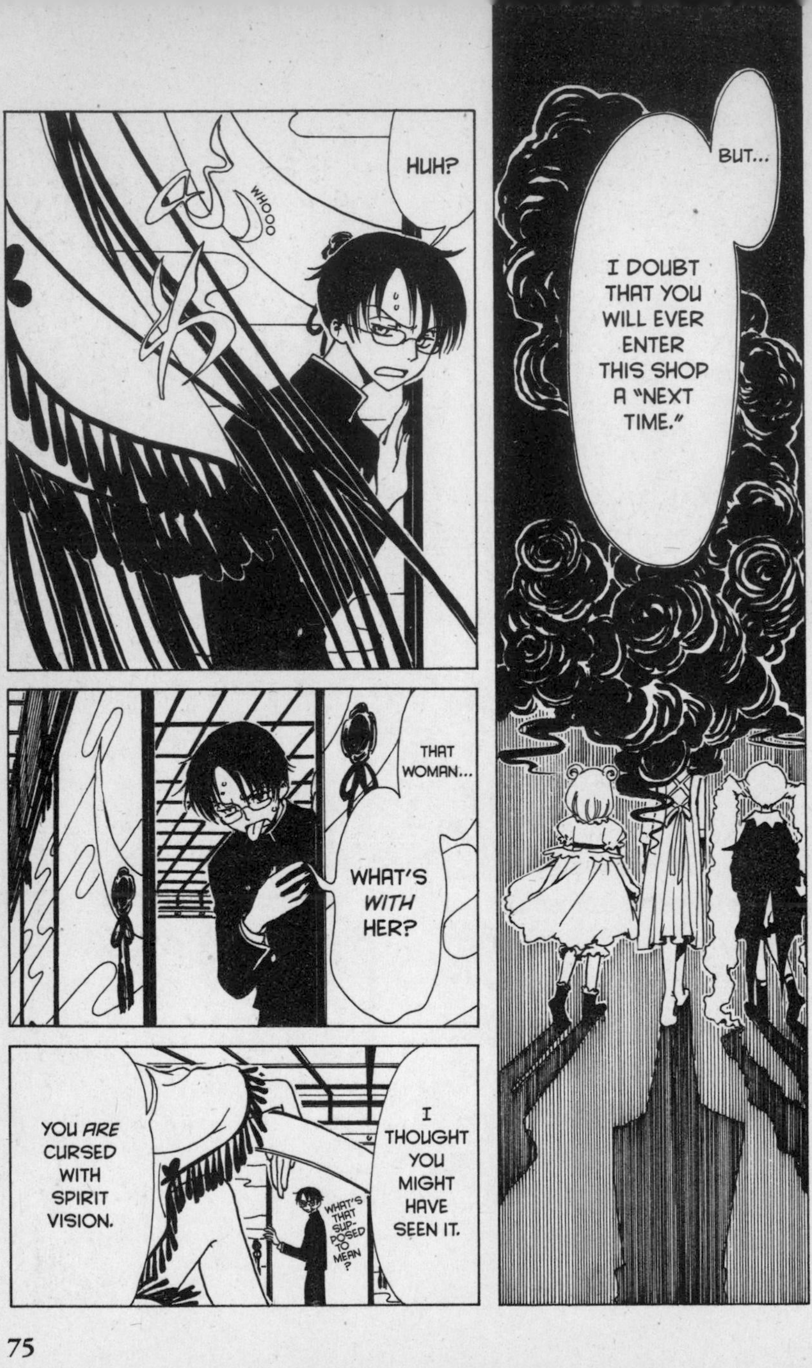
BUT...
I DOUBT THAT YOU WILL EVER ENTER THIS SHOP A "NEXT TIME."
HUH?
WHOOO
THAT WOMAN...
WHAT'S *WITH* HER?
I THOUGHT YOU MIGHT HAVE SEEN IT.
WHAT'S THAT SUP-POSED TO MEAN?
YOU *ARE* CURSED WITH SPIRIT VISION.

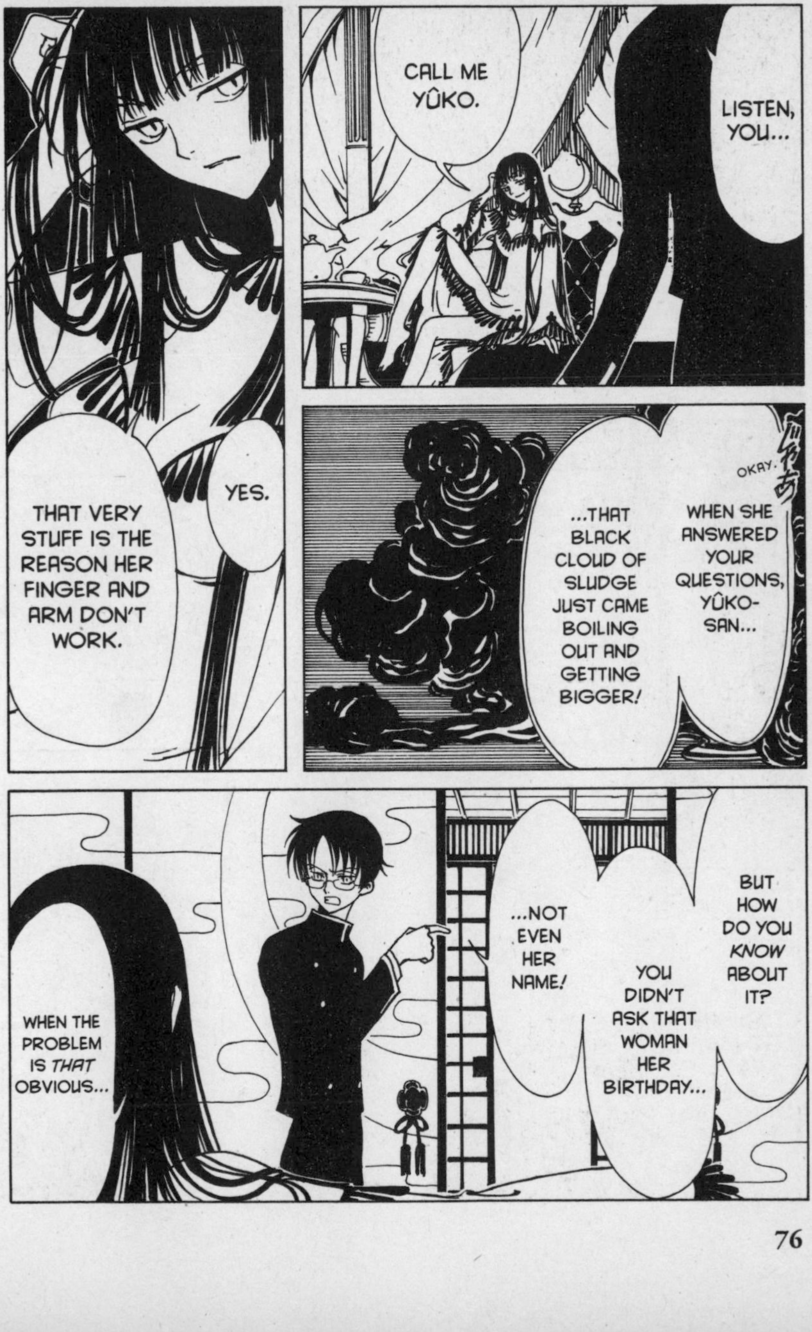
LISTEN, YOU...
CALL ME YÛKO.
OKAY.
WHEN SHE ANSWERED YOUR QUESTIONS, YÛKO-SAN...
...THAT BLACK CLOUD OF SLUDGE JUST CAME BOILING OUT AND GETTING BIGGER!
YES.
THAT VERY STUFF IS THE REASON HER FINGER AND ARM DON'T WORK.
BUT HOW DO YOU *KNOW* ABOUT IT?
YOU DIDN'T ASK THAT WOMAN HER BIRTHDAY...
...NOT EVEN HER NAME!
WHEN THE PROBLEM IS *THAT* OBVIOUS...

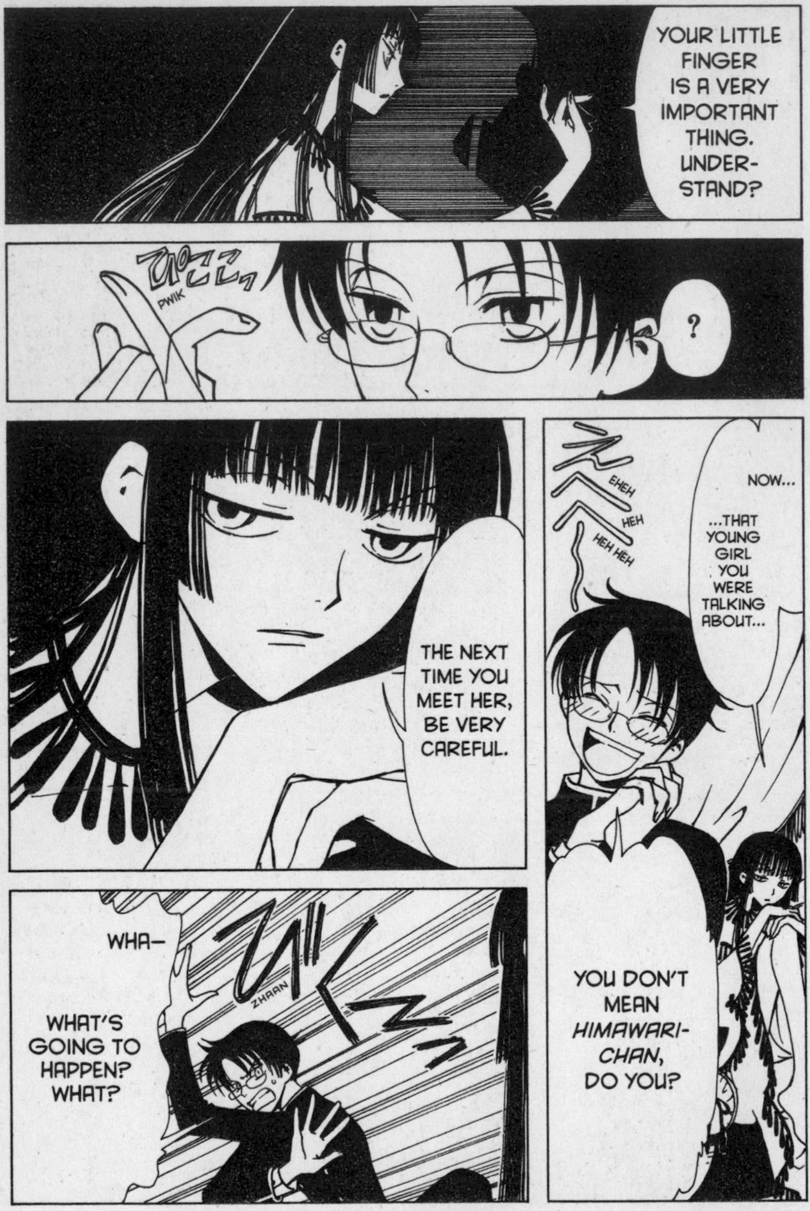
YOUR LITTLE FINGER IS A VERY IMPORTANT THING. UNDER-STAND?
?
PWIK
EHEH HEH HEH HEH
NOW...
...THAT YOUNG GIRL YOU WERE TALKING ABOUT...
YOU DON'T MEAN HIMAWARI-CHAN, DO YOU?
THE NEXT TIME YOU MEET HER, BE VERY CAREFUL.
ZHAAN
WHA-
WHAT'S GOING TO HAPPEN? WHAT?

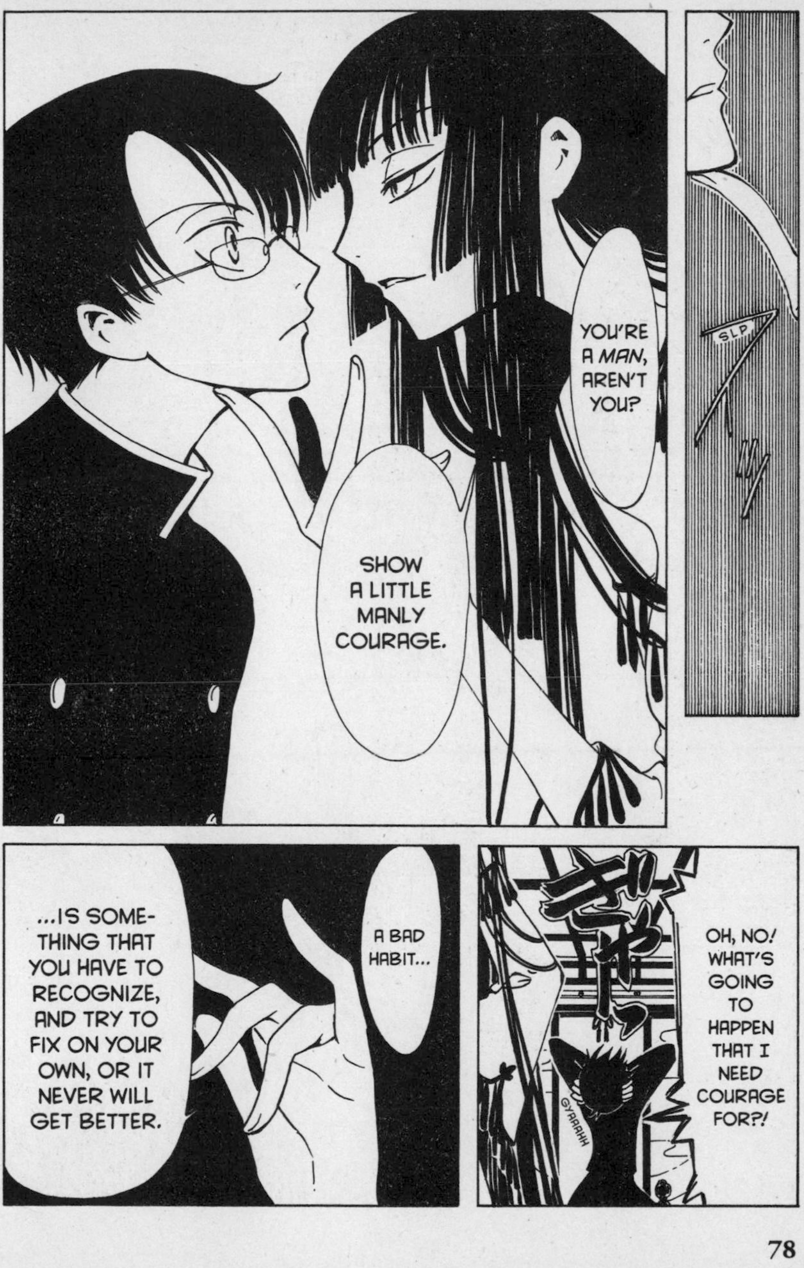
SLP
YOU'RE A *MAN*, AREN'T YOU?
SHOW A LITTLE MANLY COURAGE.
OH, NO! WHAT'S GOING TO HAPPEN THAT I NEED COURAGE FOR?!
GYAAAHH
A BAD HABIT...
...IS SOMETHING THAT YOU HAVE TO RECOGNIZE, AND TRY TO FIX ON YOUR OWN, OR IT NEVER WILL GET BETTER.

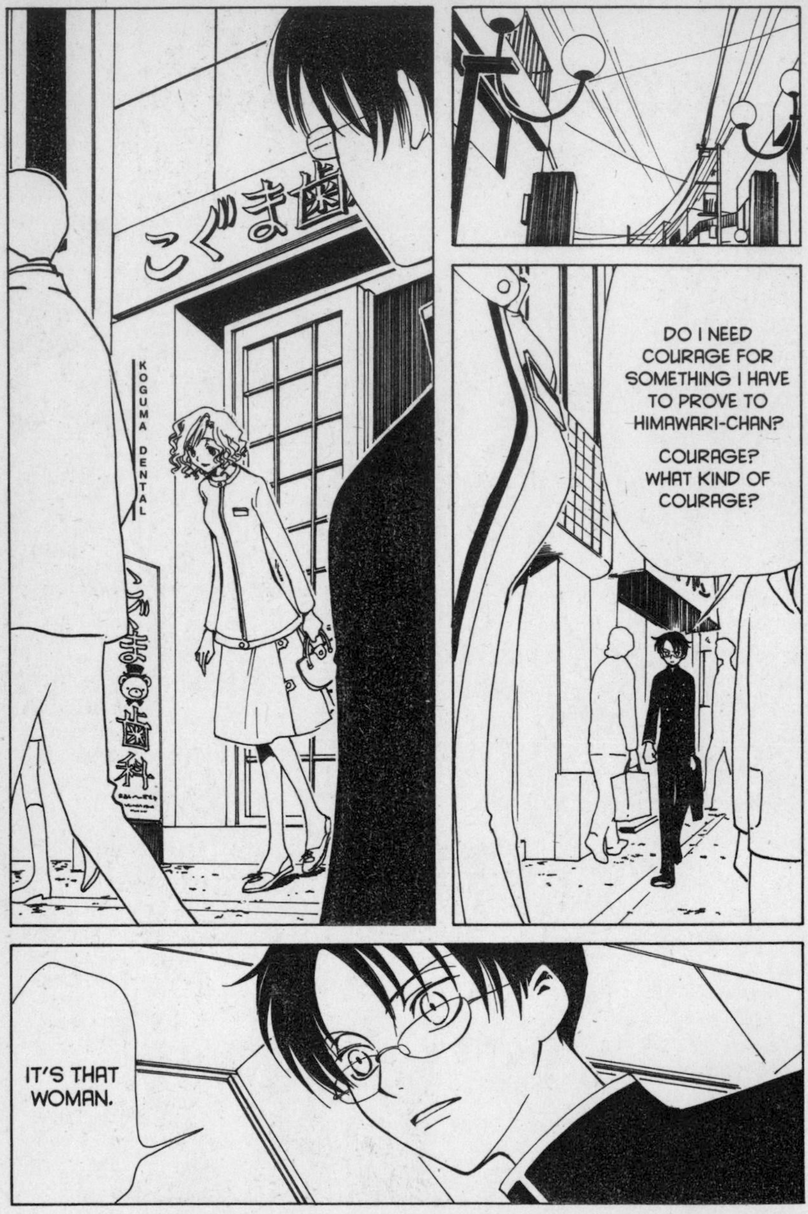
DO I NEED COURAGE FOR SOMETHING I HAVE TO PROVE TO HIMAWARI-CHAN?
COURAGE? WHAT KIND OF COURAGE?
KOGUMA DENTAL
IT'S THAT WOMAN.

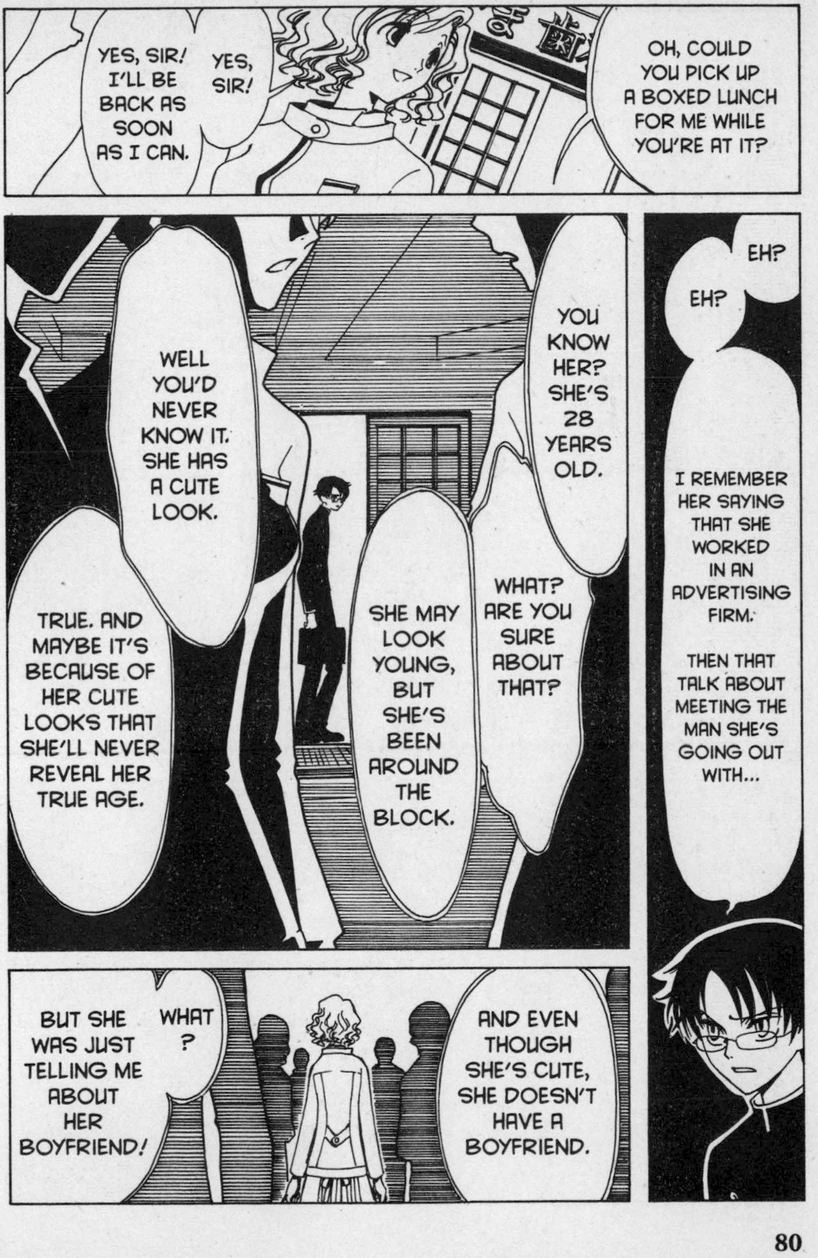
OH, COULD YOU PICK UP A BOXED LUNCH FOR ME WHILE YOU'RE AT IT?
YES, SIR!
YES, SIR! I'LL BE BACK AS SOON AS I CAN.
EH?
EH?
I REMEMBER HER SAYING THAT SHE WORKED IN AN ADVERTISING FIRM.
THEN THAT TALK ABOUT MEETING THE MAN SHE'S GOING OUT WITH...
YOU KNOW HER? SHE'S 28 YEARS OLD.
WELL YOU'D NEVER KNOW IT. SHE HAS A CUTE LOOK.
WHAT? ARE YOU SURE ABOUT THAT?
SHE MAY LOOK YOUNG, BUT SHE'S BEEN AROUND THE BLOCK.
TRUE. AND MAYBE IT'S BECAUSE OF HER CUTE LOOKS THAT SHE'LL NEVER REVEAL HER TRUE AGE.
AND EVEN THOUGH SHE'S CUTE, SHE DOESN'T HAVE A BOYFRIEND.
WHAT?
BUT SHE WAS JUST TELLING ME ABOUT HER BOYFRIEND!

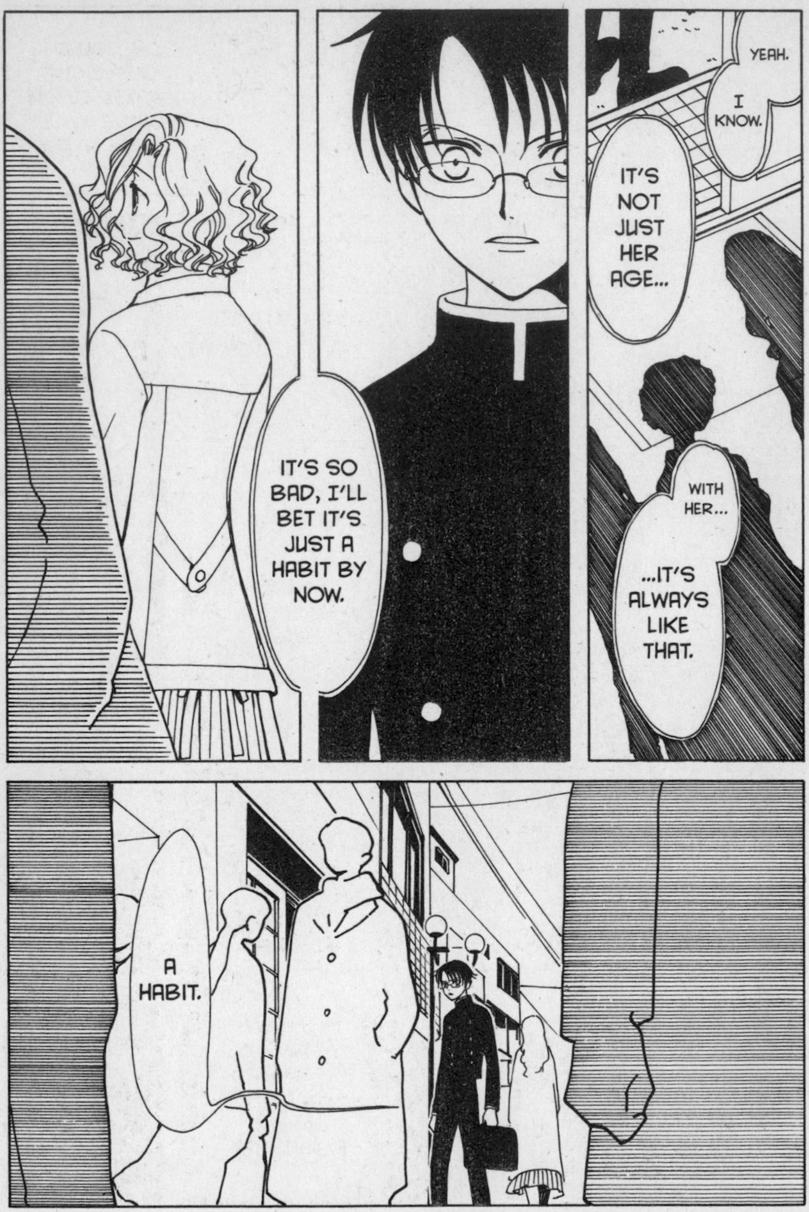
YEAH.
I KNOW.
IT'S NOT JUST HER AGE...
WITH HER...
...IT'S ALWAYS LIKE THAT.
IT'S SO BAD, I'LL BET IT'S JUST A HABIT BY NOW.
A HABIT.

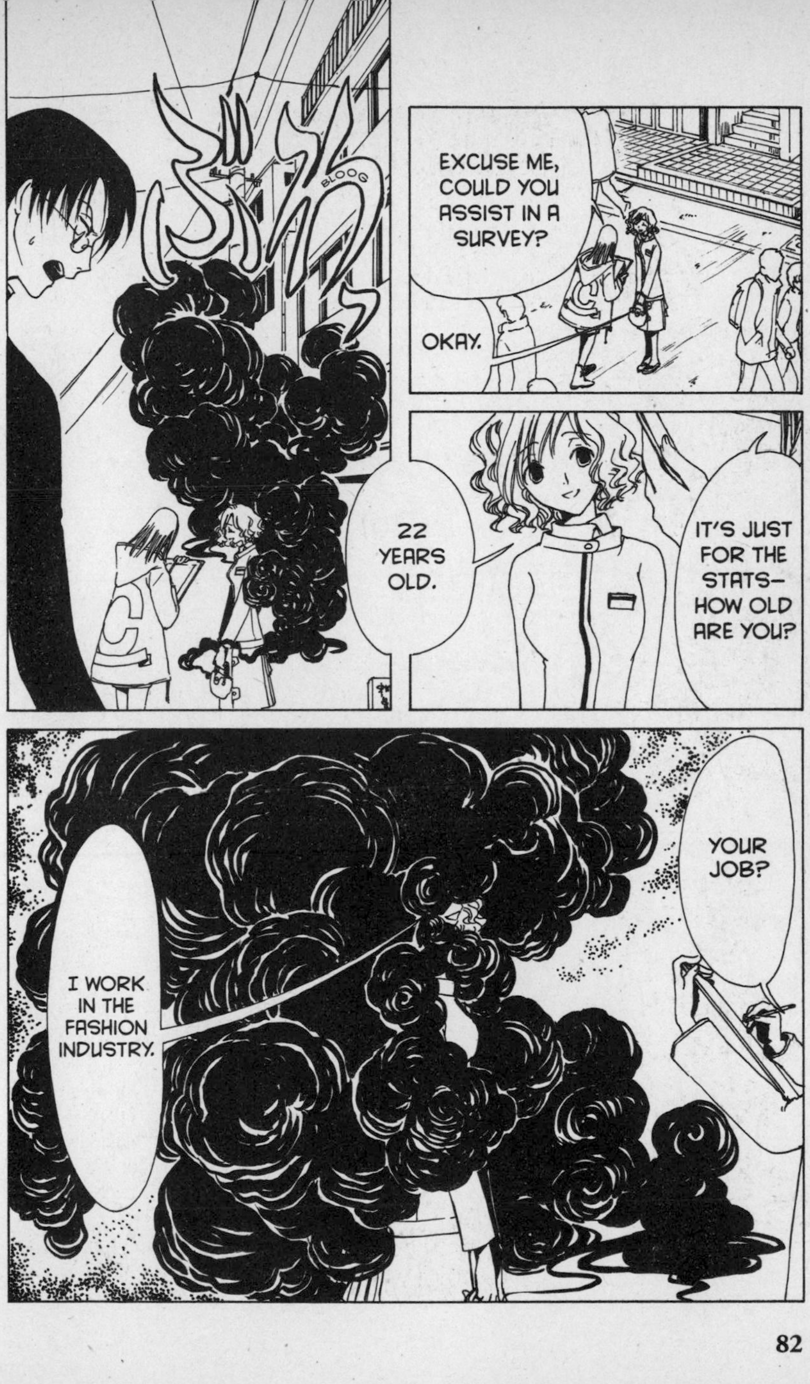
EXCUSE ME, COULD YOU ASSIST IN A SURVEY?
OKAY.
IT'S JUST FOR THE STATS— HOW OLD ARE YOU?
22 YEARS OLD.
BLOOG
YOUR JOB?
I WORK IN THE FASHION INDUSTRY.

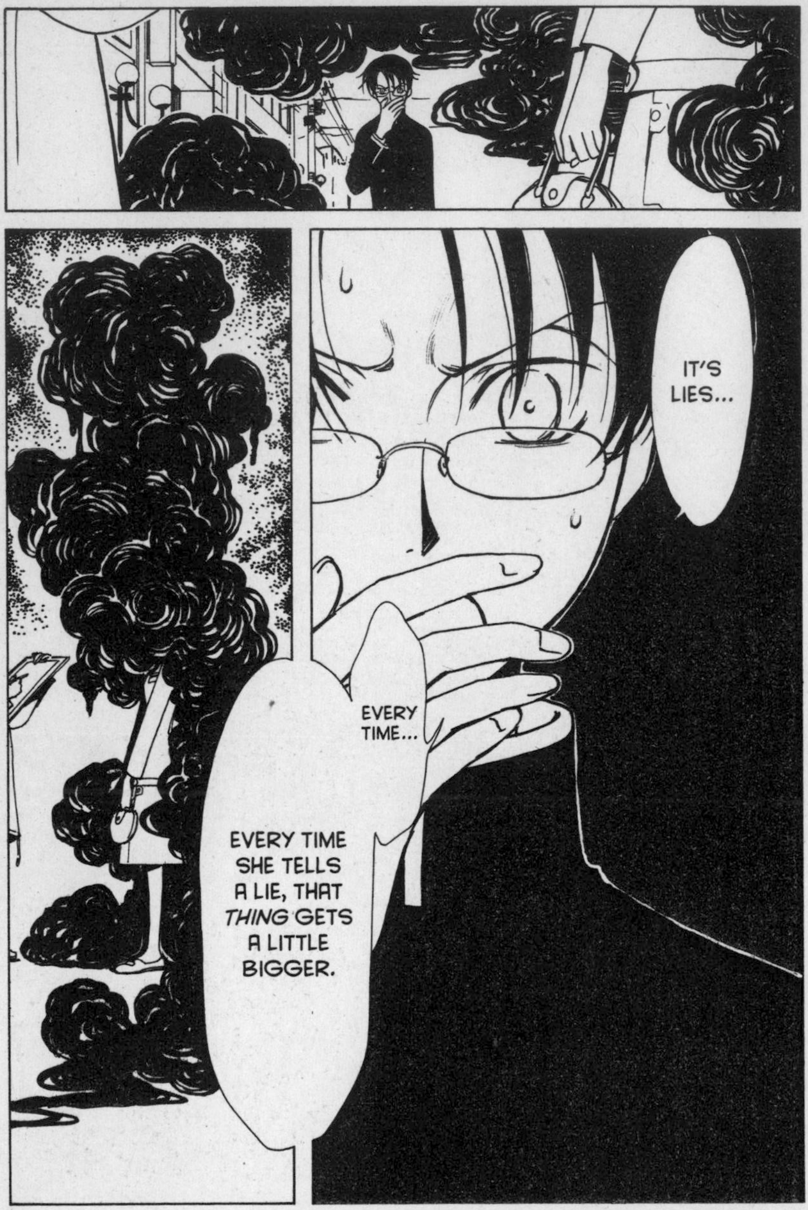
IT'S LIES...
EVERY TIME...
EVERY TIME SHE TELLS A LIE, THAT *THING* GETS A LITTLE BIGGER.

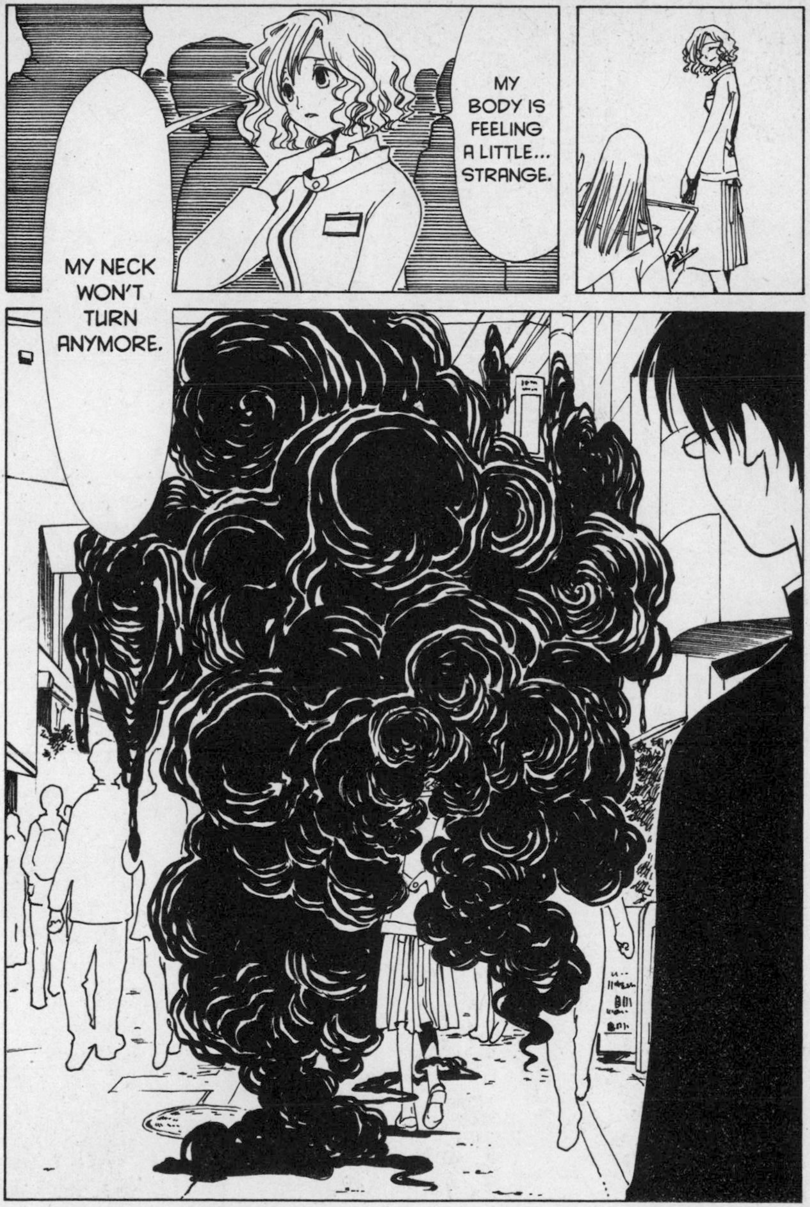
MY BODY IS FEELING A LITTLE... STRANGE.
MY NECK WON'T TURN ANYMORE.

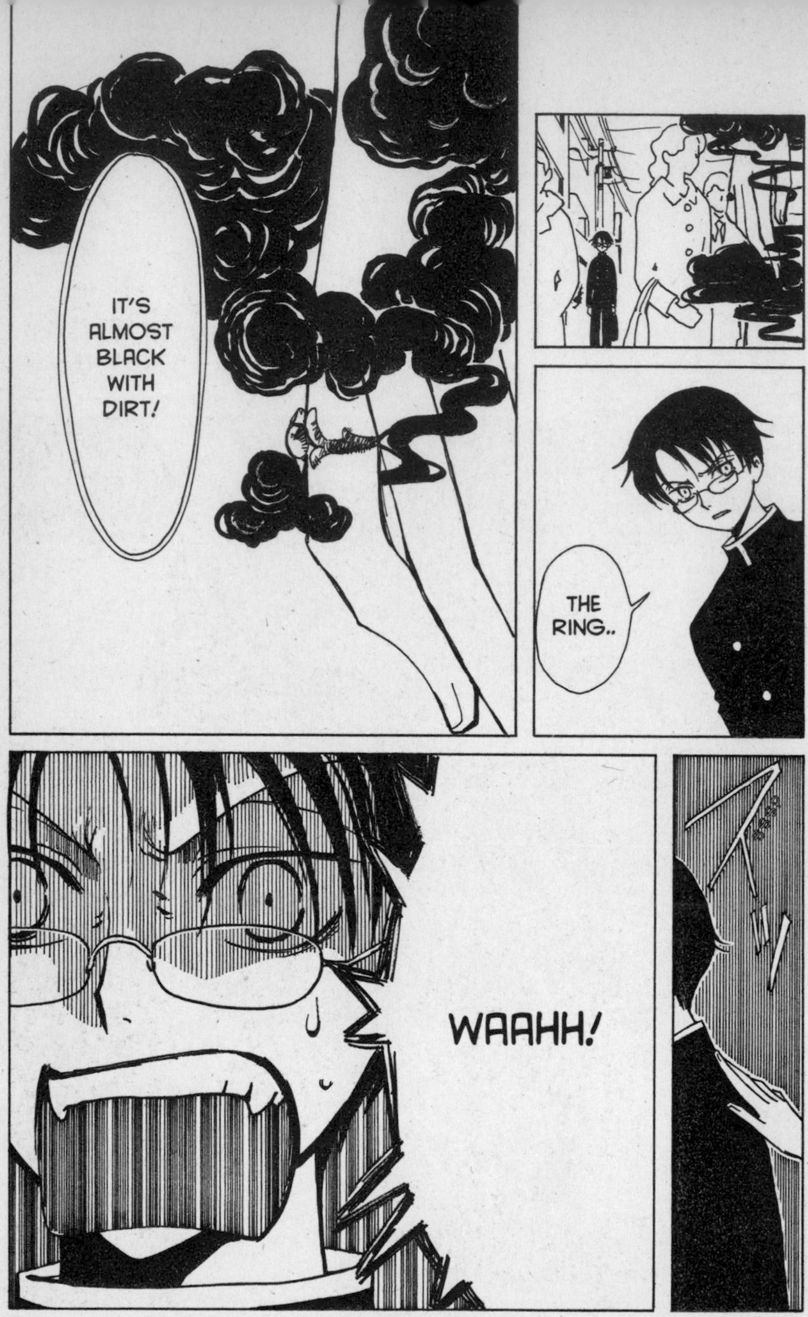
THE RING..
IT'S ALMOST BLACK WITH DIRT!
WAAHH!

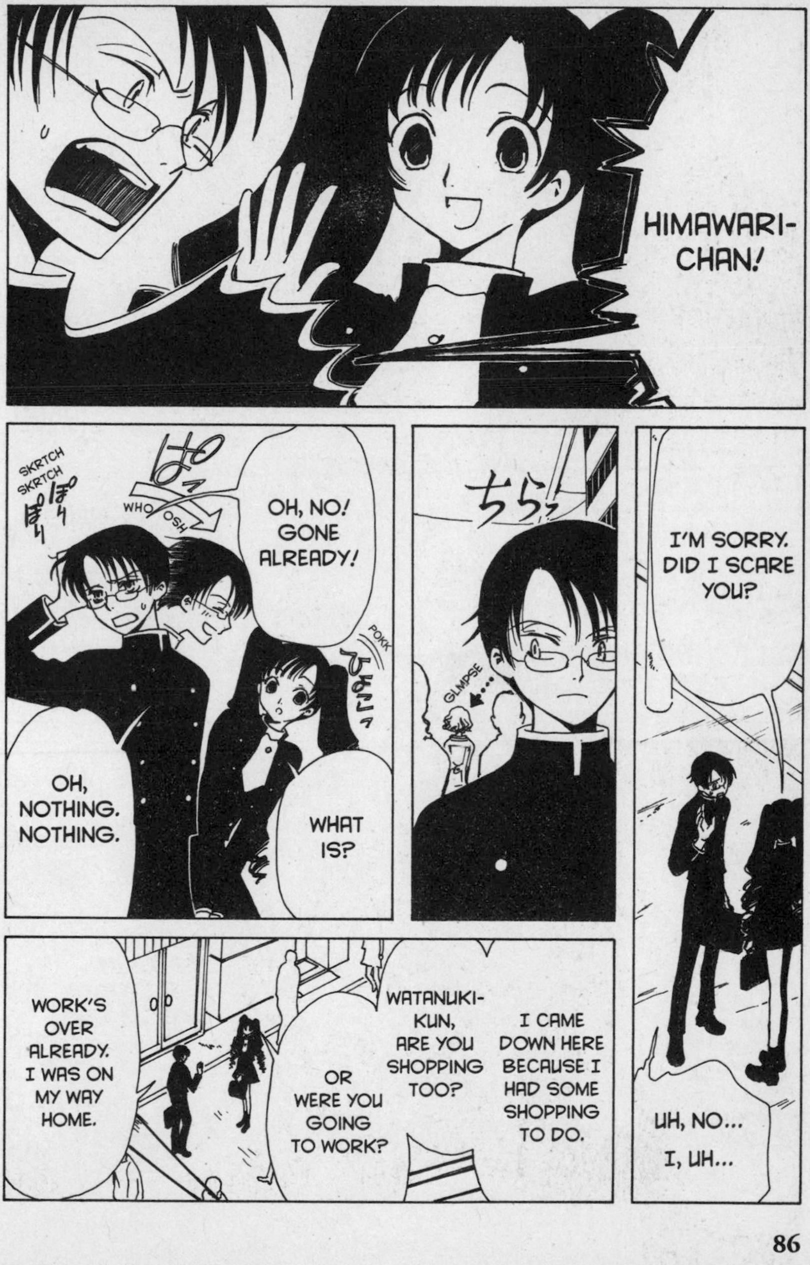
HIMAWARI-CHAN!
I'M SORRY. DID I SCARE YOU?
UH, NO...
I, UH...
ちらっ
GLIMPSE
OH, NO! GONE ALREADY!
WHOOSH
SKRTCH SKRTCH
POKK
WHAT IS?
OH, NOTHING. NOTHING.
I CAME DOWN HERE BECAUSE I HAD SOME SHOPPING TO DO.
WATANUKI-KUN, ARE YOU SHOPPING TOO?
OR WERE YOU GOING TO WORK?
WORK'S OVER ALREADY. I WAS ON MY WAY HOME.

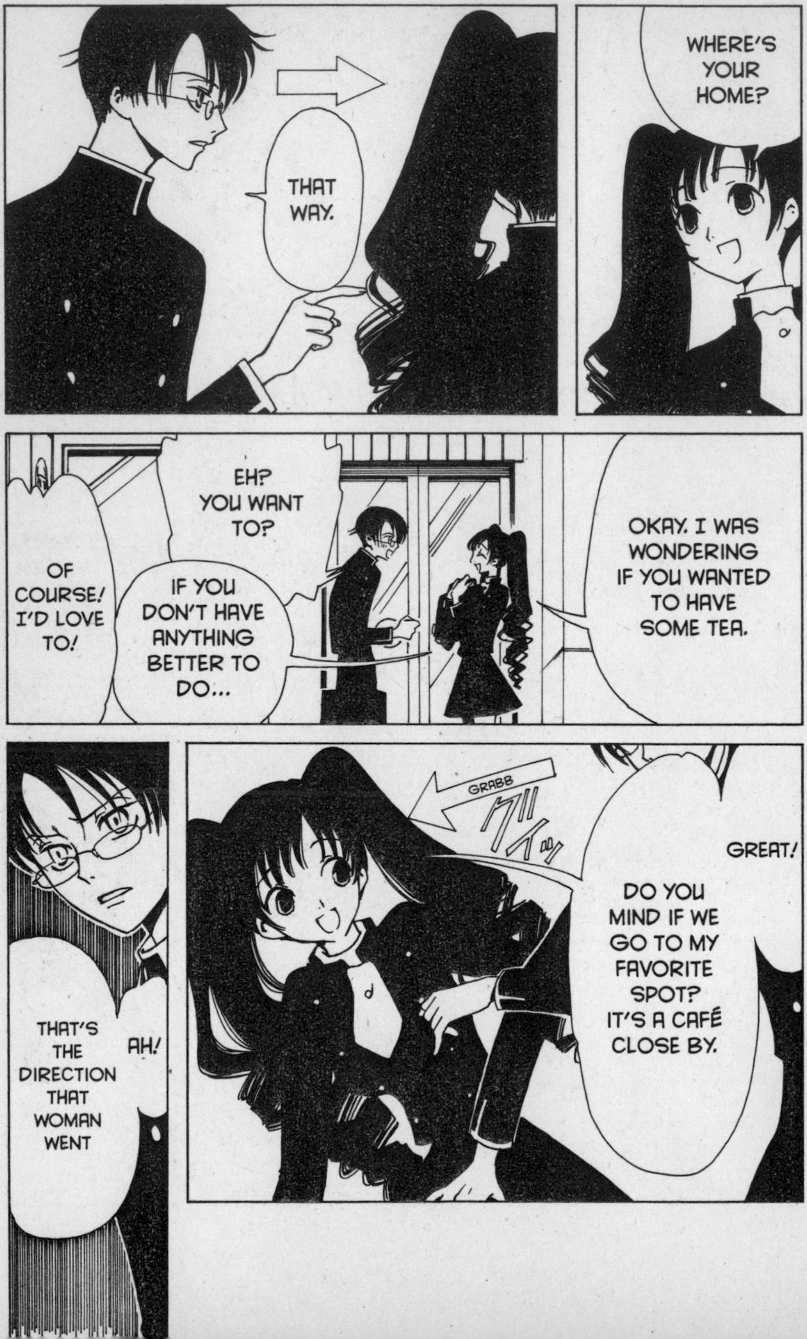
WHERE'S YOUR HOME?
THAT WAY.
OKAY. I WAS WONDERING IF YOU WANTED TO HAVE SOME TEA.
EH? YOU WANT TO?
IF YOU DON'T HAVE ANYTHING BETTER TO DO...
OF COURSE! I'D LOVE TO!
GRABB
GREAT!
DO YOU MIND IF WE GO TO MY FAVORITE SPOT? IT'S A CAFÉ CLOSE BY.
AH!
THAT'S THE DIRECTION THAT WOMAN WENT

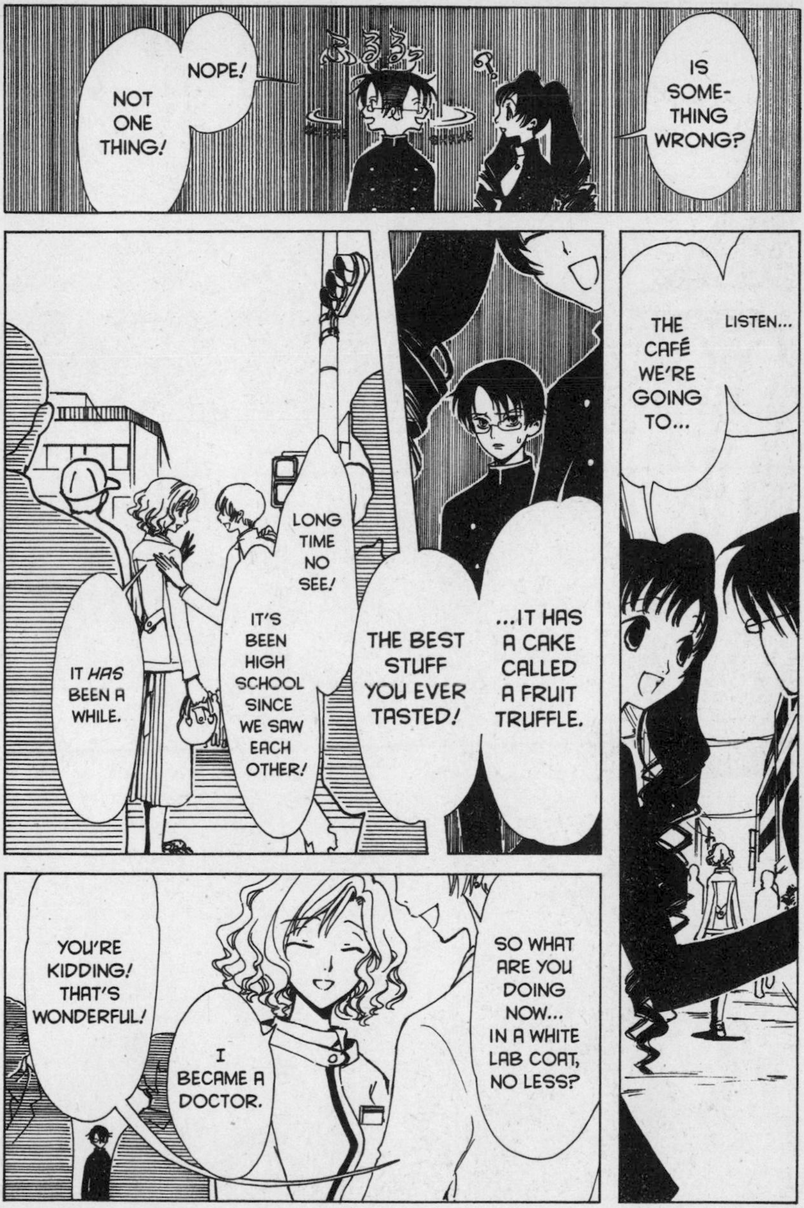
IS SOMETHING WRONG?
NOPE!
NOT ONE THING!
LISTEN...
THE CAFÉ WE'RE GOING TO...
...IT HAS A CAKE CALLED A FRUIT TRUFFLE.
THE BEST STUFF YOU EVER TASTED!
LONG TIME NO SEE!
IT'S BEEN HIGH SCHOOL SINCE WE SAW EACH OTHER!
IT *HAS* BEEN A WHILE.
SO WHAT ARE YOU DOING NOW... IN A WHITE LAB COAT, NO LESS?
I BECAME A DOCTOR.
YOU'RE KIDDING! THAT'S WONDERFUL!

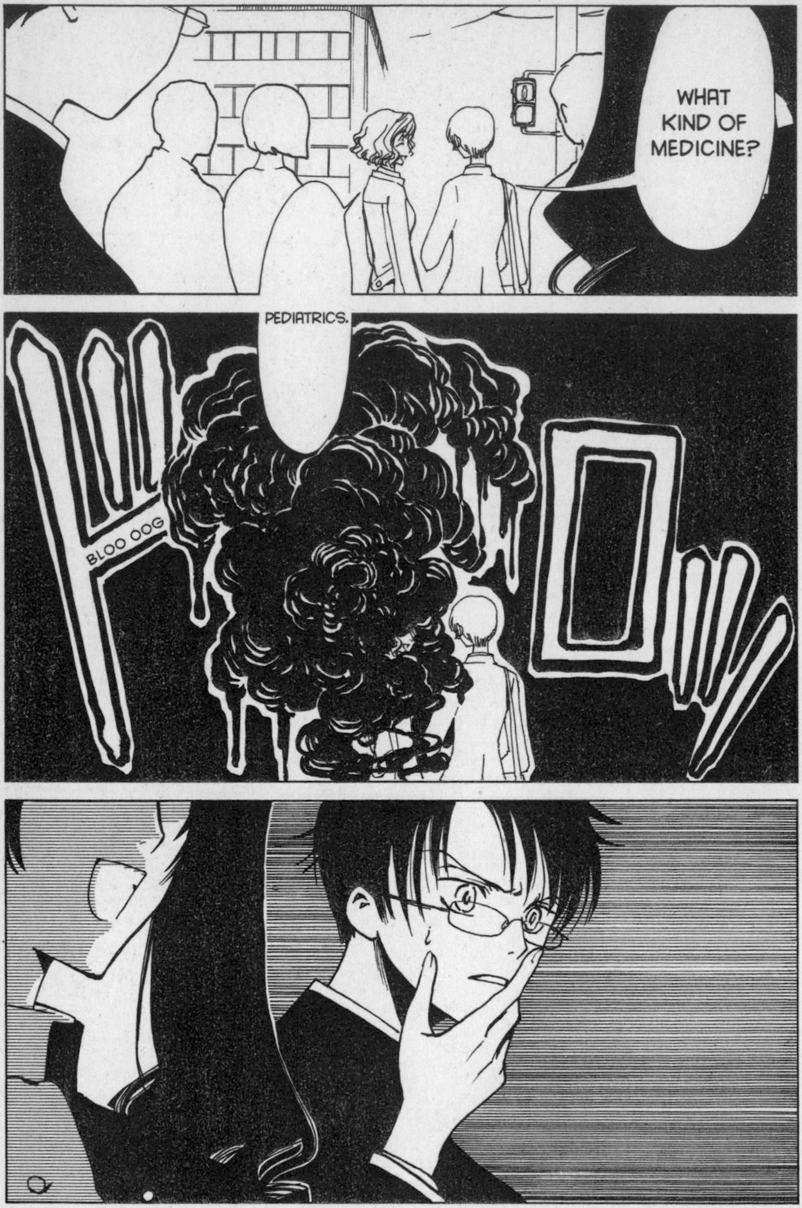
WHAT KIND OF MEDICINE?
PEDIATRICS.
BLOO OOG

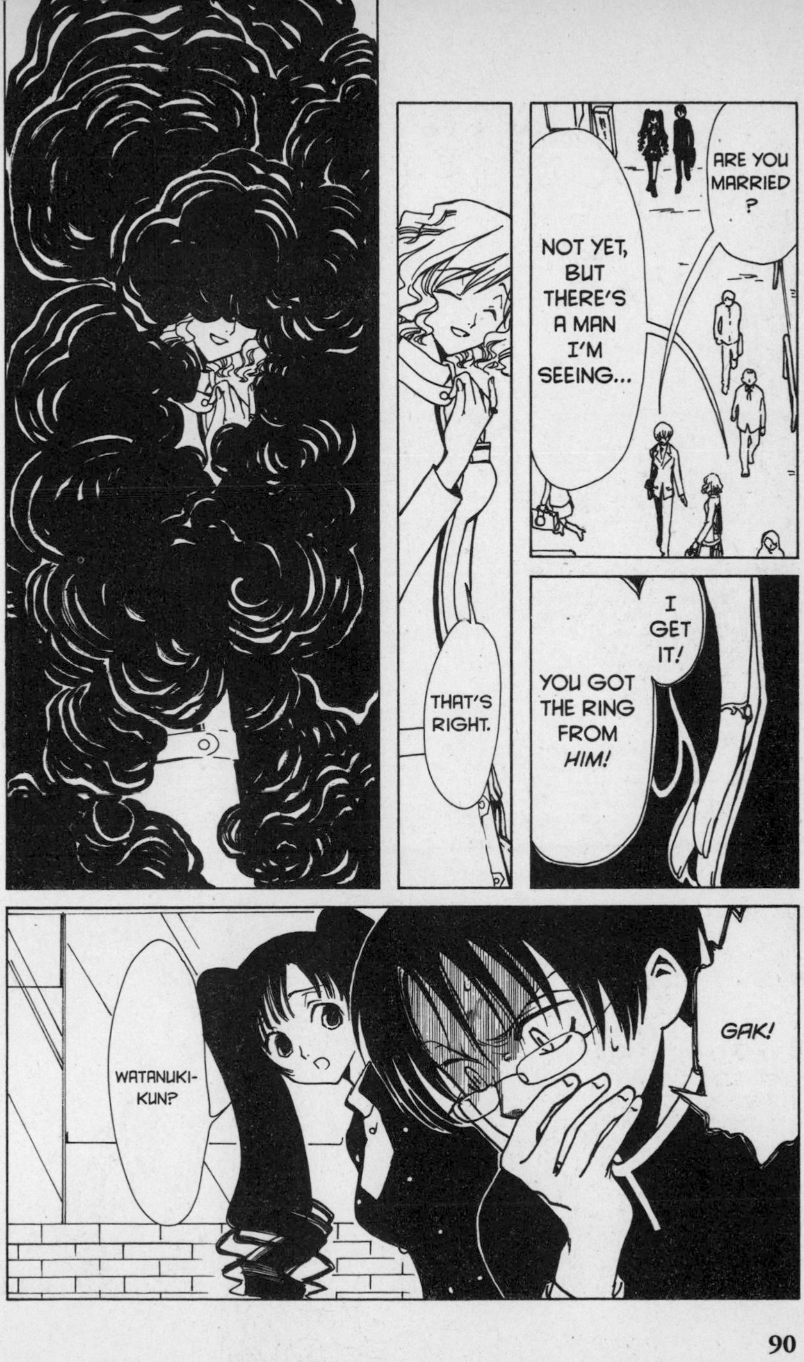
ARE YOU MARRIED?
NOT YET, BUT THERE'S A MAN I'M SEEING...
I GET IT!
YOU GOT THE RING FROM *HIM!*
THAT'S RIGHT.
GAK!
WATANUKI-KUN?

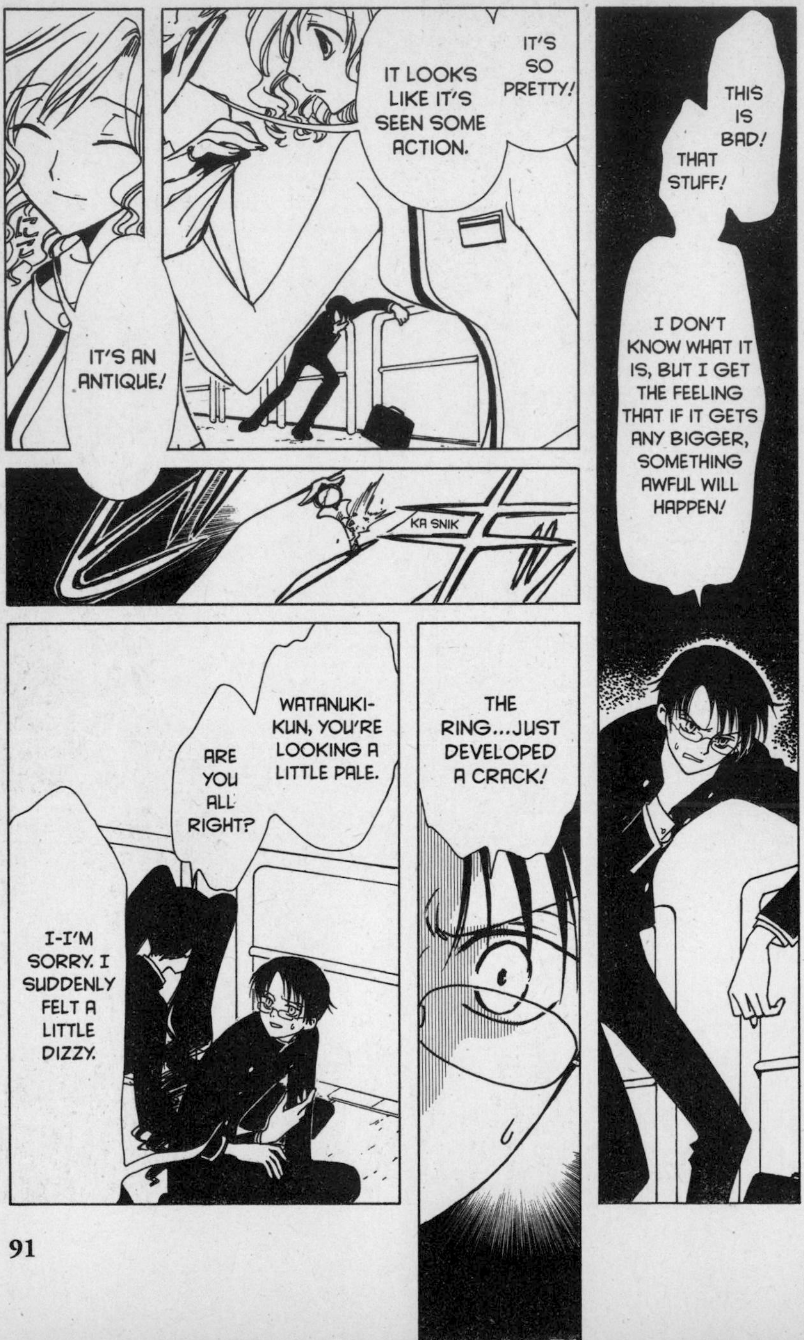
THIS IS BAD! THAT STUFF!
I DON'T KNOW WHAT IT IS, BUT I GET THE FEELING THAT IF IT GETS ANY BIGGER, SOMETHING AWFUL WILL HAPPEN!
IT'S SO PRETTY!
IT LOOKS LIKE IT'S SEEN SOME ACTION.
IT'S AN ANTIQUE!
KA SNIK
THE RING...JUST DEVELOPED A CRACK!
WATANUKI-KUN, YOU'RE LOOKING A LITTLE PALE.
ARE YOU ALL RIGHT?
I-I'M SORRY. I SUDDENLY FELT A LITTLE DIZZY.

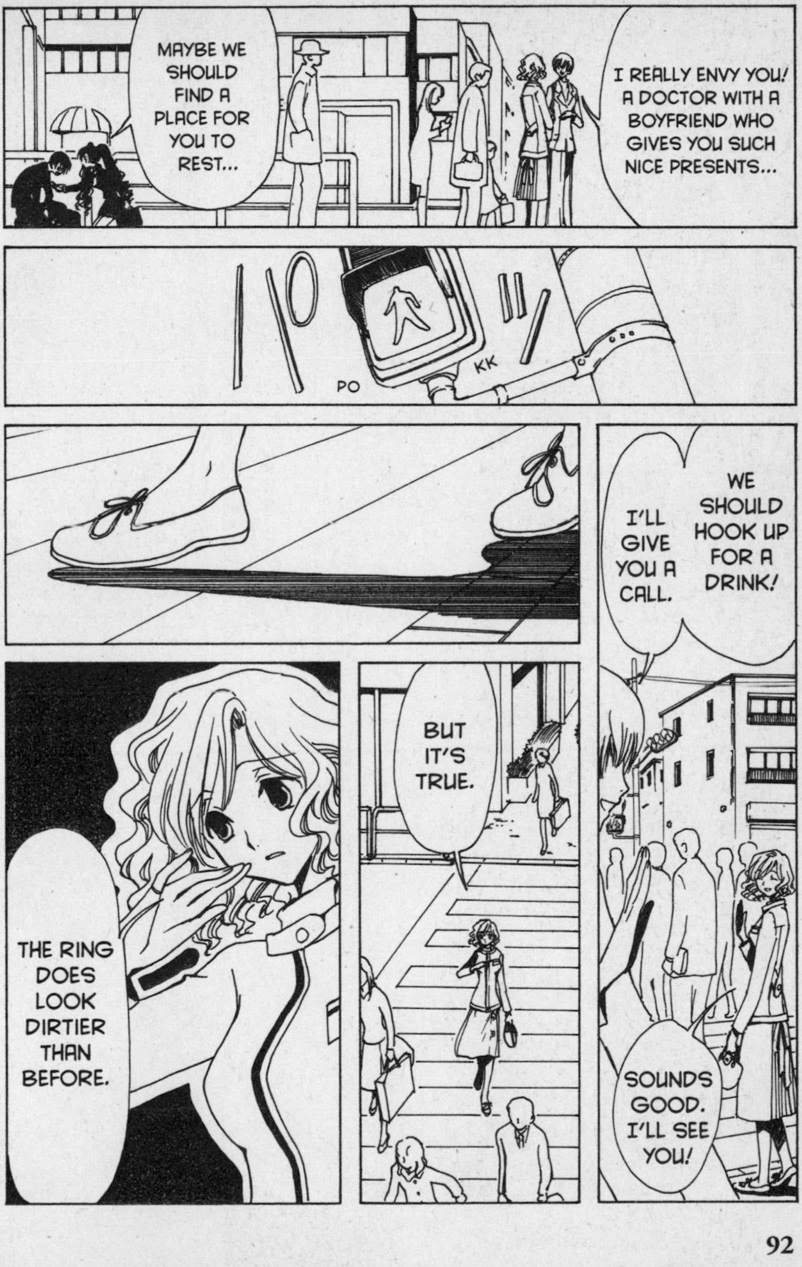

I REALLY ENVY YOU! A DOCTOR WITH A BOYFRIEND WHO GIVES YOU SUCH NICE PRESENTS...
MAYBE WE SHOULD FIND A PLACE FOR YOU TO REST...
PO
KK
WE SHOULD HOOK UP FOR A DRINK!
I'LL GIVE YOU A CALL.
SOUNDS GOOD. I'LL SEE YOU!
BUT IT'S TRUE.
THE RING DOES LOOK DIRTIER THAN BEFORE.

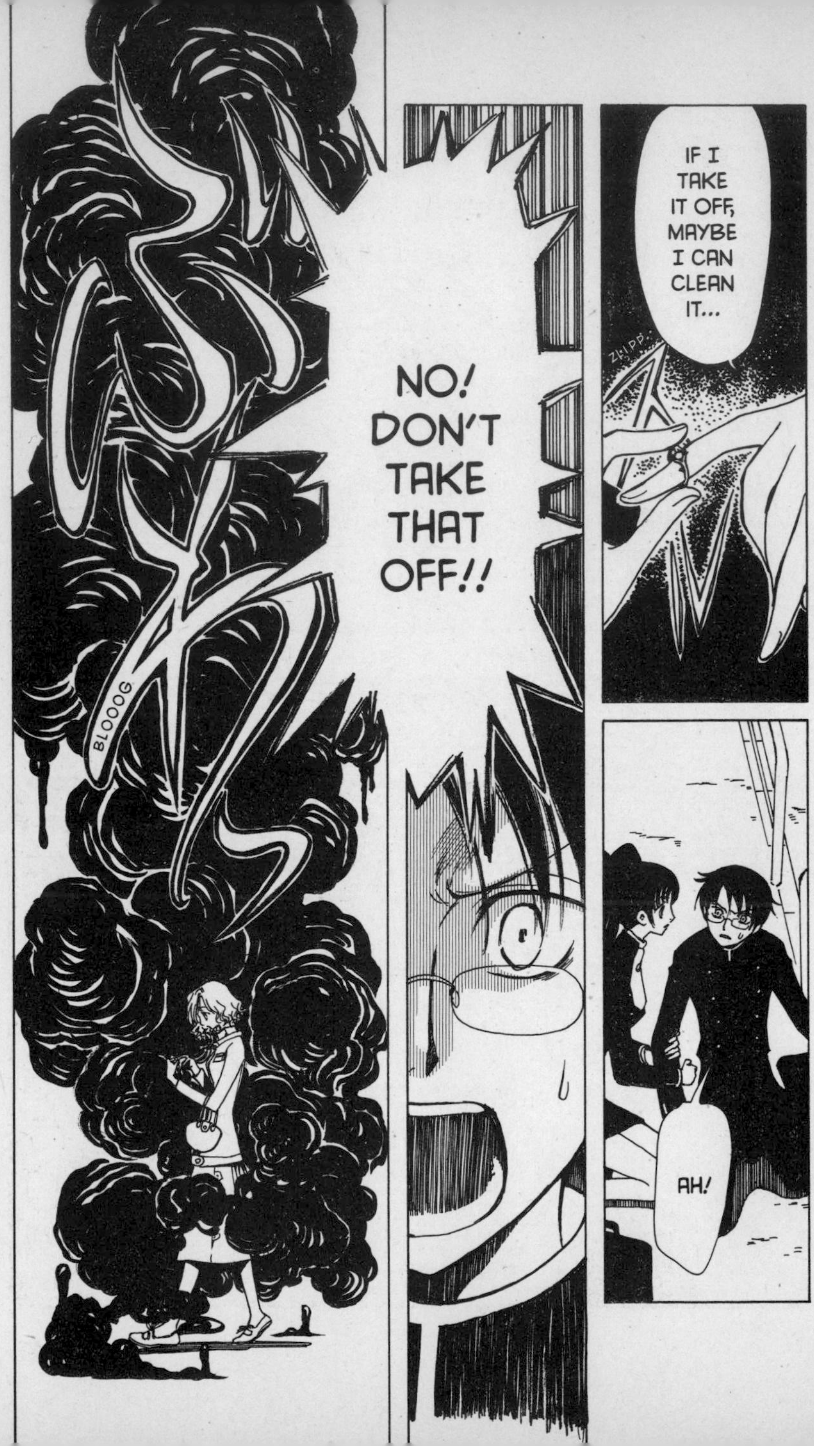
IF I TAKE IT OFF, MAYBE I CAN CLEAN IT...
ZLIPP..
AH!
NO! DON'T TAKE THAT OFF!!
BLOOOG

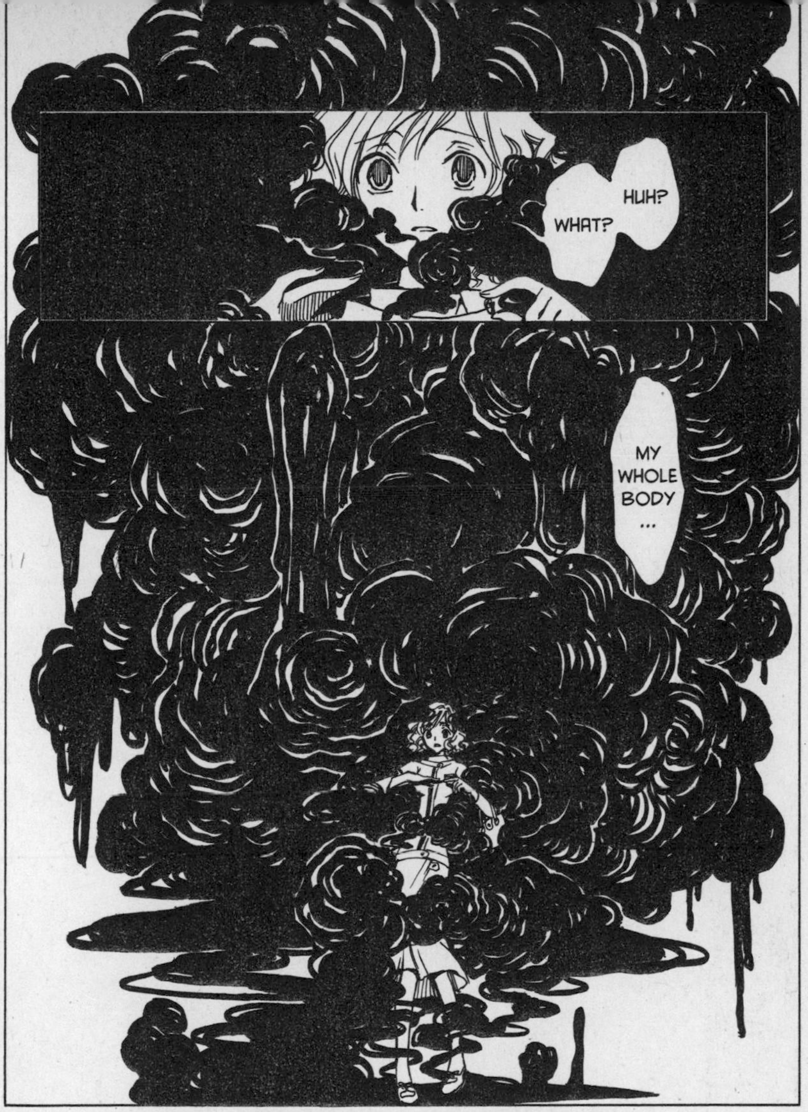
HUH? WHAT?
MY WHOLE BODY ...
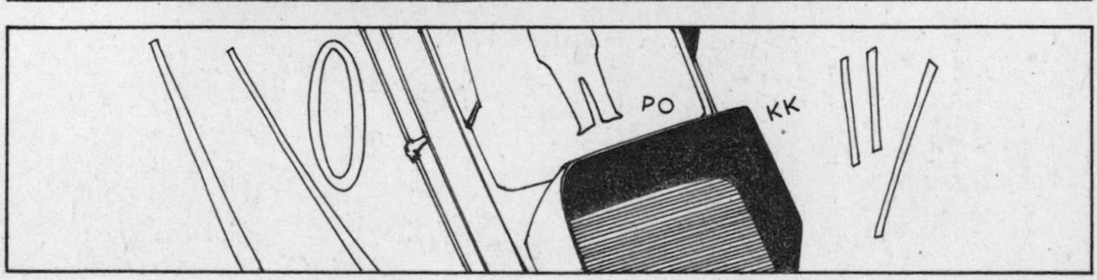
PO KK

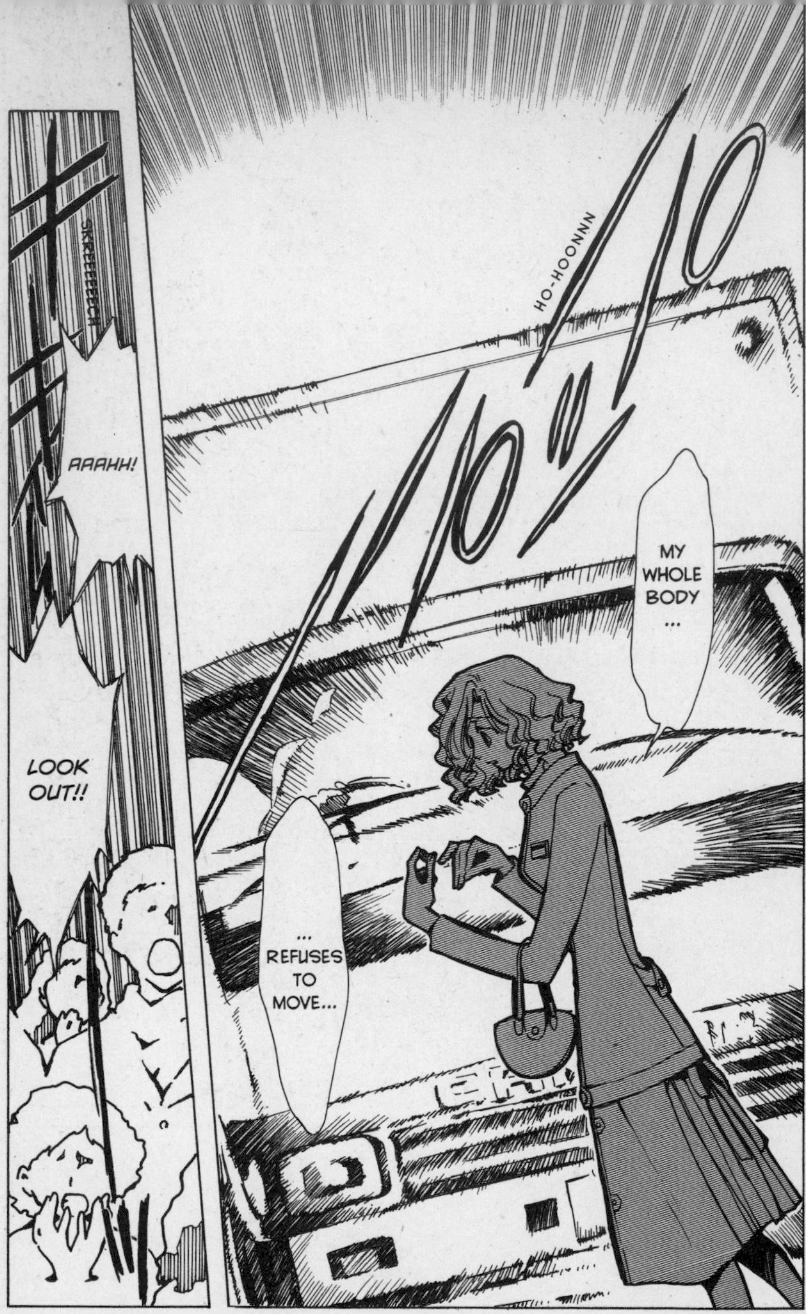
HO-HOONNN
MY WHOLE BODY ...
... REFUSES TO MOVE...
SKREEEEEECH
AAAHH!
LOOK OUT!!

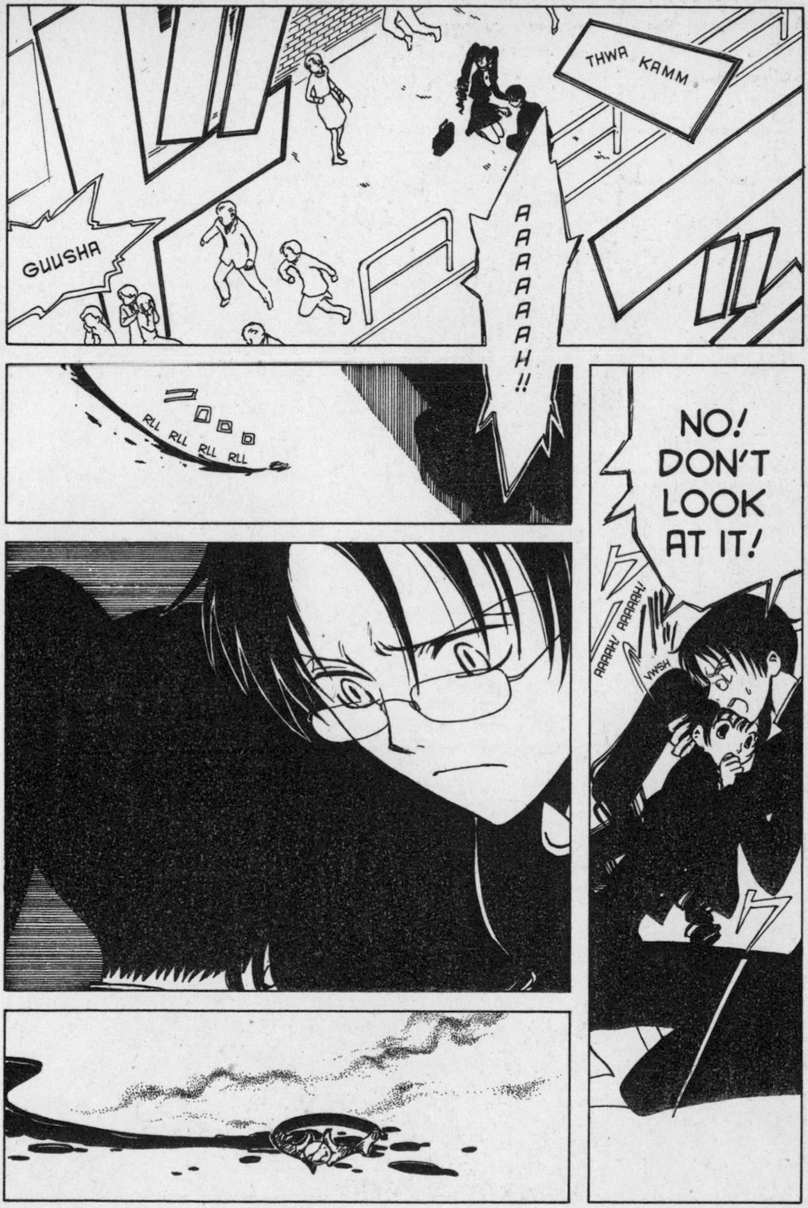
THWA KAMM
AAAAAAAH!!
GUUSHA
NO! DON'T LOOK AT IT!
AAAAH! AAAAAH!
VWSH
RLL RLL RLL RLL

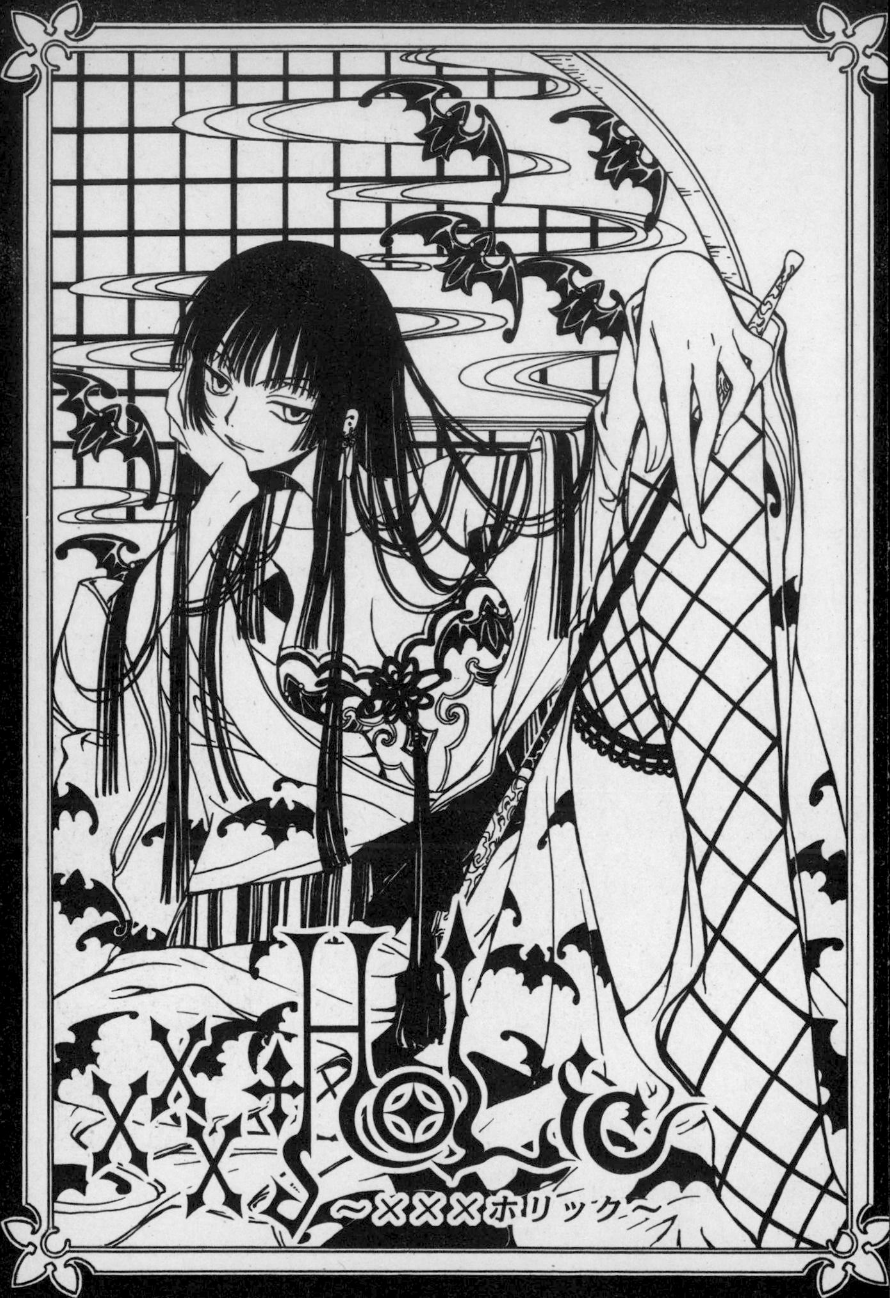
xxxHOLiC
~×××ホリック~

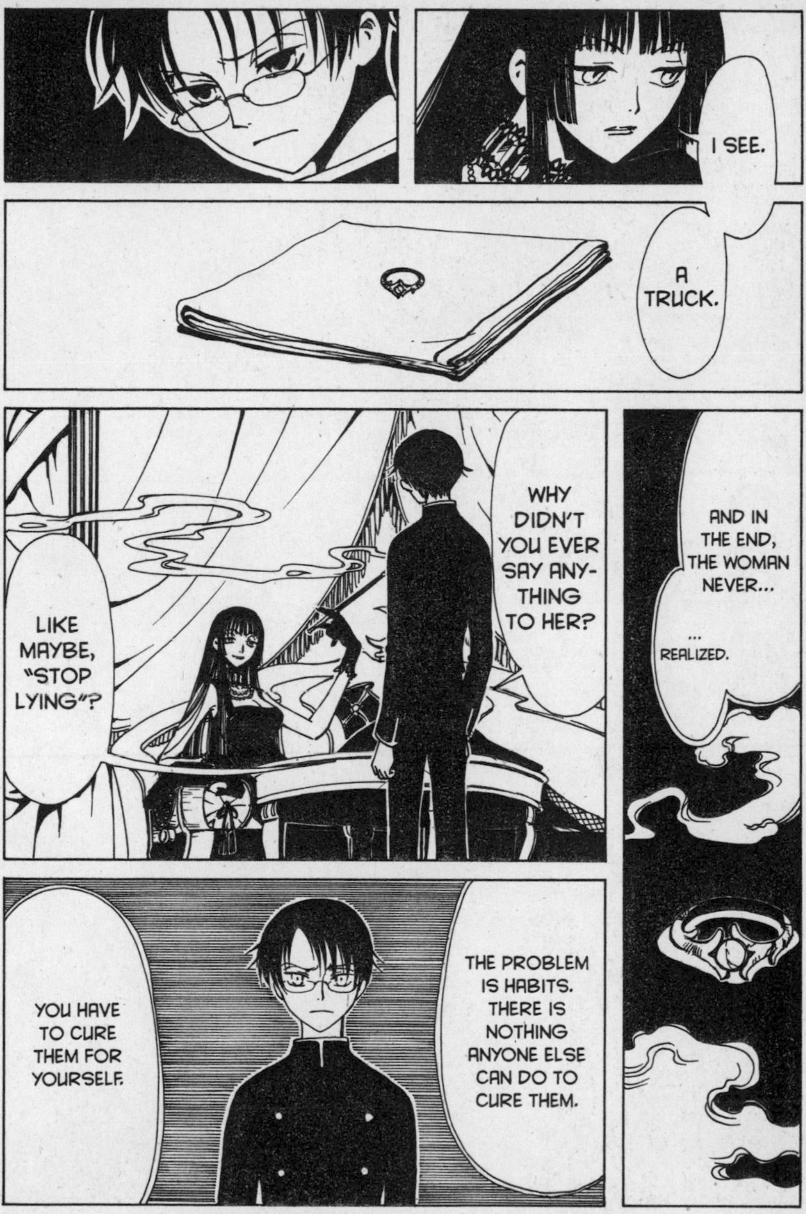
I SEE.
A TRUCK.
AND IN THE END, THE WOMAN NEVER...
...REALIZED.
WHY DIDN'T YOU EVER SAY ANY-THING TO HER?
LIKE MAYBE, "STOP LYING"?
THE PROBLEM IS HABITS. THERE IS NOTHING ANYONE ELSE CAN DO TO CURE THEM.
YOU HAVE TO CURE THEM FOR YOURSELF.

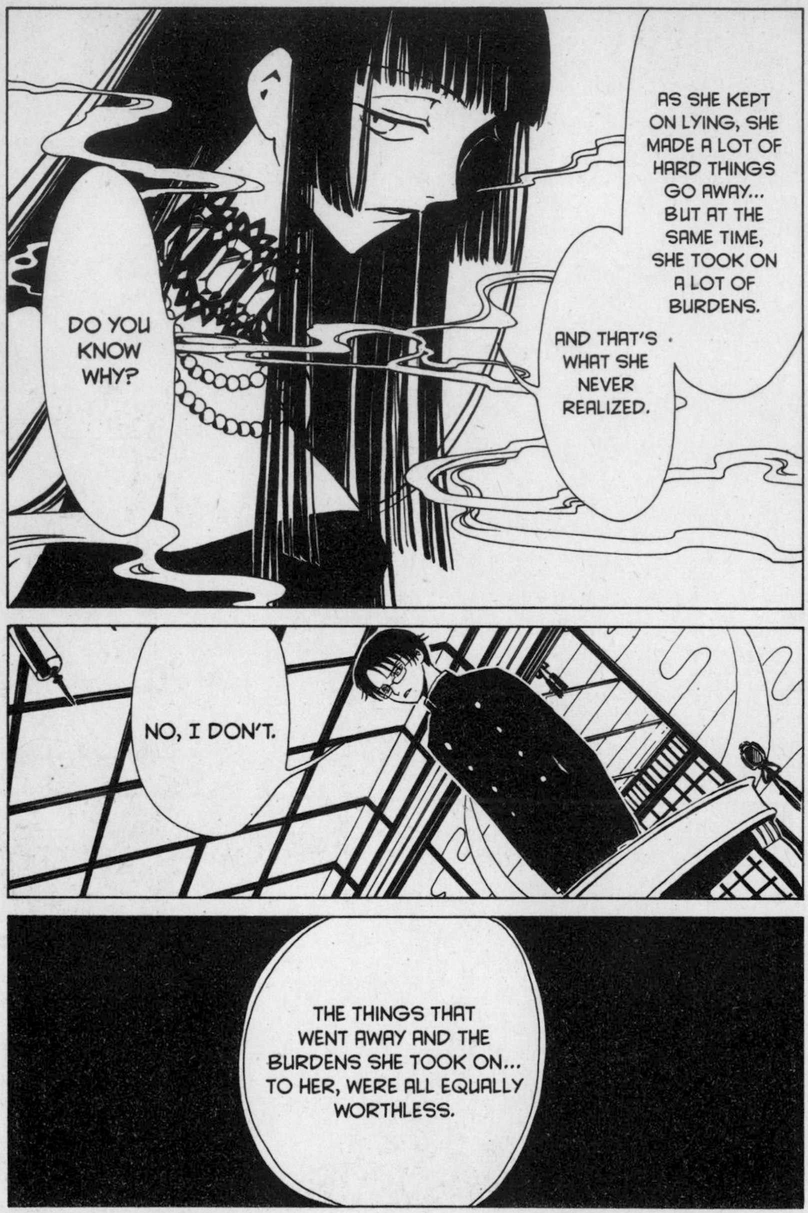
AS SHE KEPT ON LYING, SHE MADE A LOT OF HARD THINGS GO AWAY... BUT AT THE SAME TIME, SHE TOOK ON A LOT OF BURDENS.
AND THAT'S WHAT SHE NEVER REALIZED.
DO YOU KNOW WHY?
NO, I DON'T.
THE THINGS THAT WENT AWAY AND THE BURDENS SHE TOOK ON... TO HER, WERE ALL EQUALLY WORTHLESS.

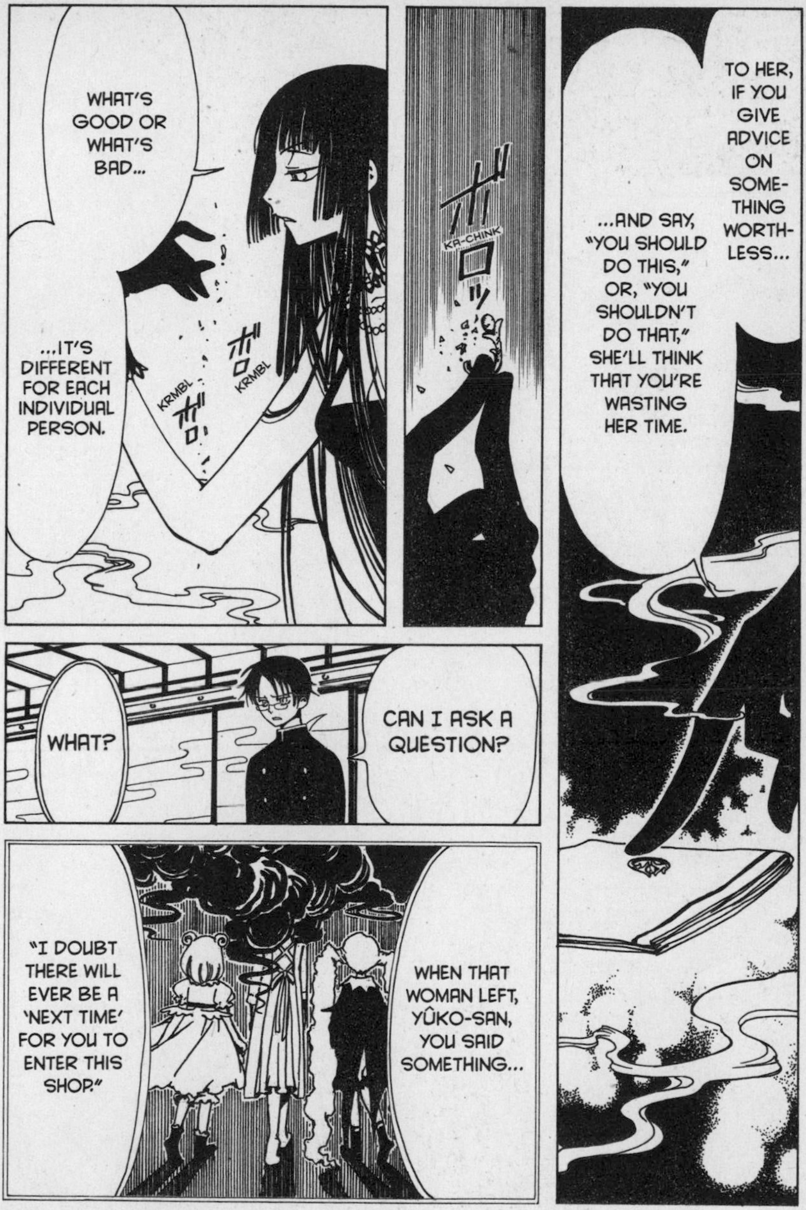
TO HER, IF YOU GIVE ADVICE ON SOMETHING WORTHLESS...
...AND SAY, "YOU SHOULD DO THIS," OR, "YOU SHOULDN'T DO THAT," SHE'LL THINK THAT YOU'RE WASTING HER TIME.
KA-CHINK
WHAT'S GOOD OR WHAT'S BAD...
KRMBL
KRMBL
...IT'S DIFFERENT FOR EACH INDIVIDUAL PERSON.
CAN I ASK A QUESTION?
WHAT?
WHEN THAT WOMAN LEFT, YÛKO-SAN, YOU SAID SOMETHING...
"I DOUBT THERE WILL EVER BE A 'NEXT TIME' FOR YOU TO ENTER THIS SHOP."

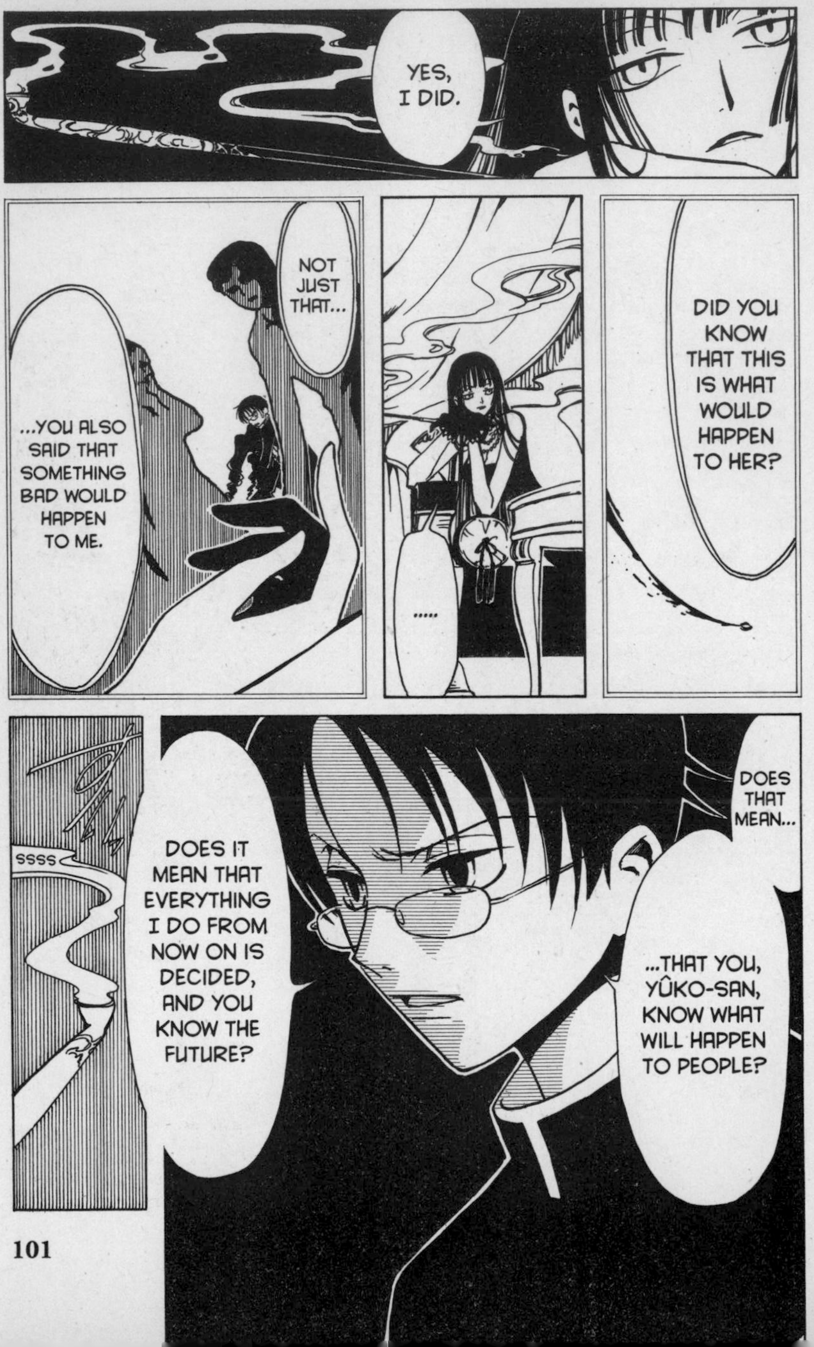
YES, I DID.
DID YOU KNOW THAT THIS IS WHAT WOULD HAPPEN TO HER?
......
NOT JUST THAT...
...YOU ALSO SAID THAT SOMETHING BAD WOULD HAPPEN TO ME.
DOES THAT MEAN...
...THAT YOU, YÛKO-SAN, KNOW WHAT WILL HAPPEN TO PEOPLE?
DOES IT MEAN THAT EVERYTHING I DO FROM NOW ON IS DECIDED, AND YOU KNOW THE FUTURE?
SSSS

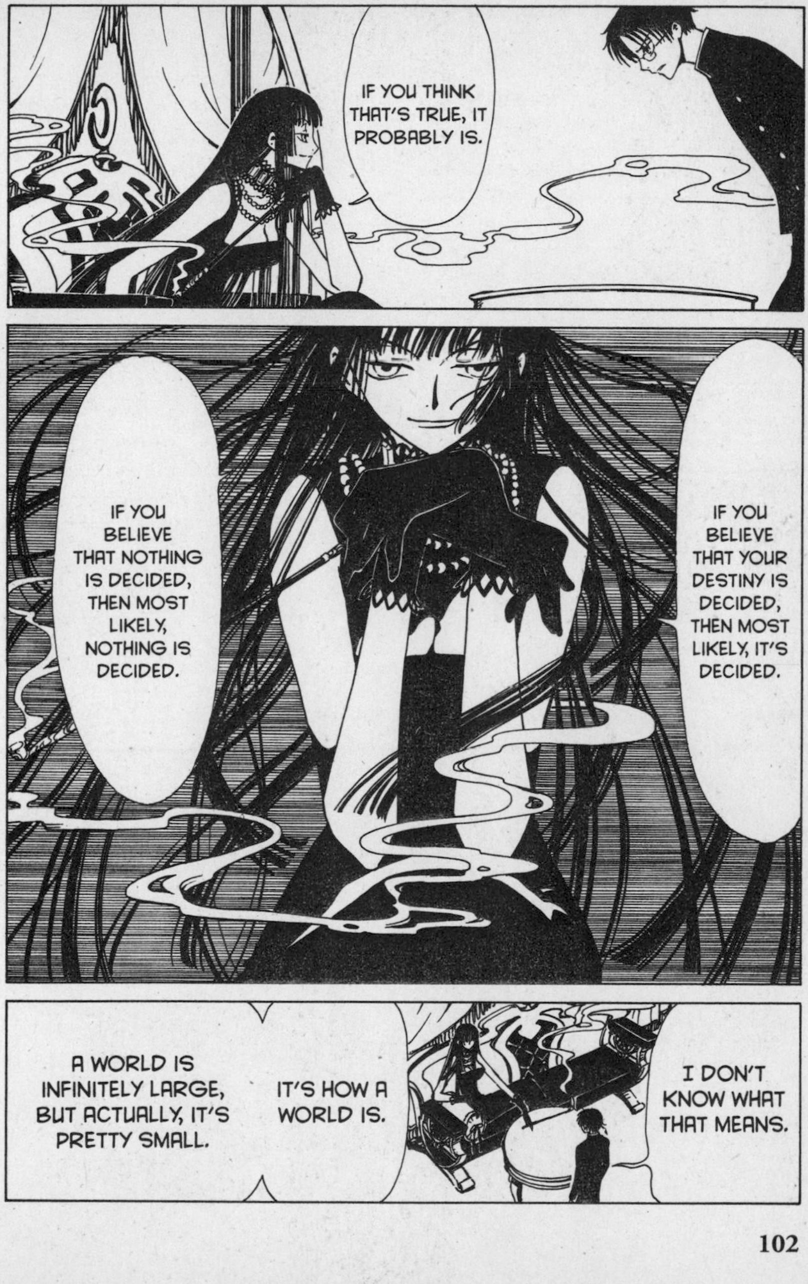
IF YOU THINK THAT'S TRUE, IT PROBABLY IS.
IF YOU BELIEVE THAT YOUR DESTINY IS DECIDED, THEN MOST LIKELY, IT'S DECIDED.
IF YOU BELIEVE THAT NOTHING IS DECIDED, THEN MOST LIKELY, NOTHING IS DECIDED.
I DON'T KNOW WHAT THAT MEANS.
IT'S HOW A WORLD IS.
A WORLD IS INFINITELY LARGE, BUT ACTUALLY, IT'S PRETTY SMALL.

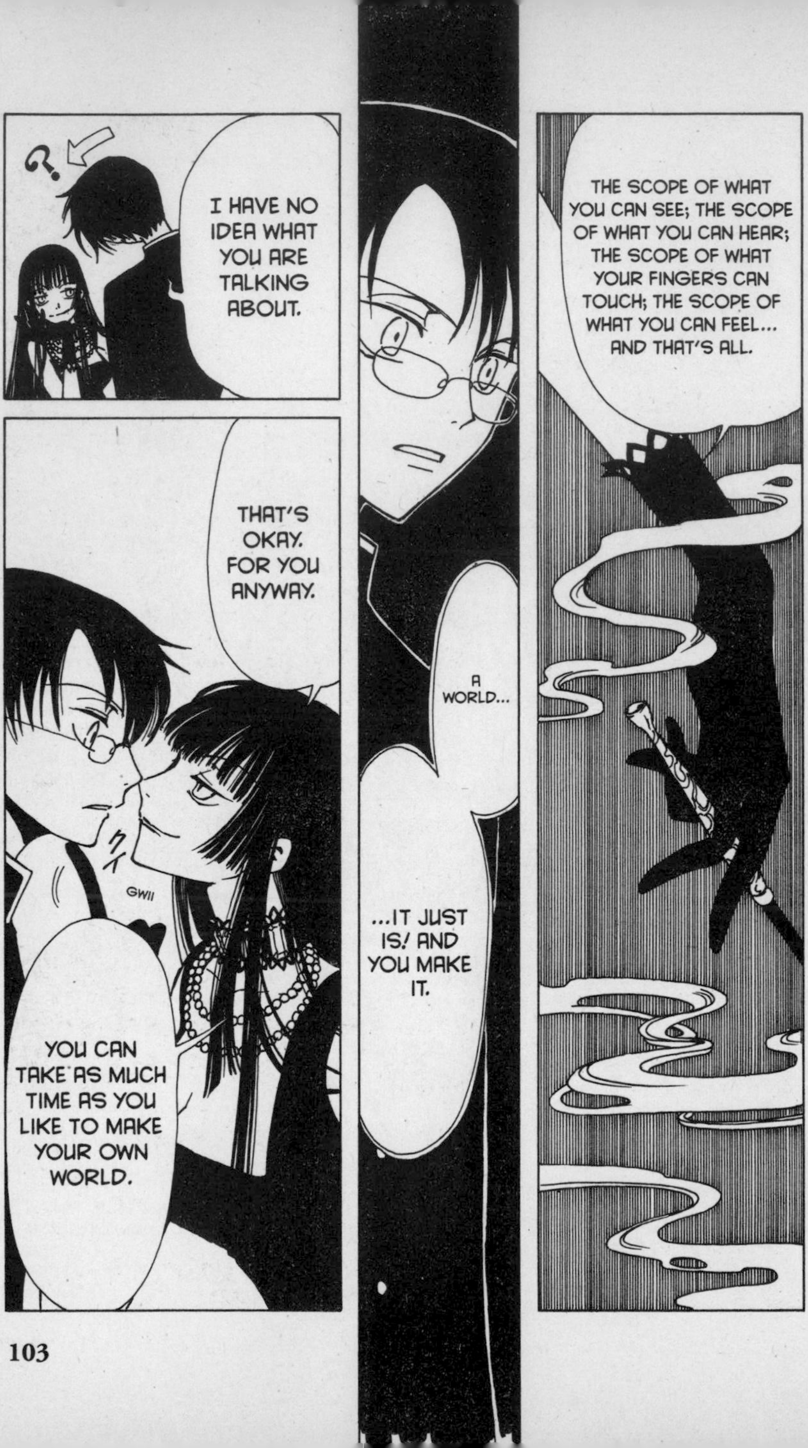
THE SCOPE OF WHAT YOU CAN SEE; THE SCOPE OF WHAT YOU CAN HEAR; THE SCOPE OF WHAT YOUR FINGERS CAN TOUCH; THE SCOPE OF WHAT YOU CAN FEEL... AND THAT'S ALL.
A WORLD...
...IT JUST IS! AND YOU MAKE IT.
I HAVE NO IDEA WHAT YOU ARE TALKING ABOUT.
THAT'S OKAY. FOR YOU ANYWAY.
GWII
YOU CAN TAKE AS MUCH TIME AS YOU LIKE TO MAKE YOUR OWN WORLD.

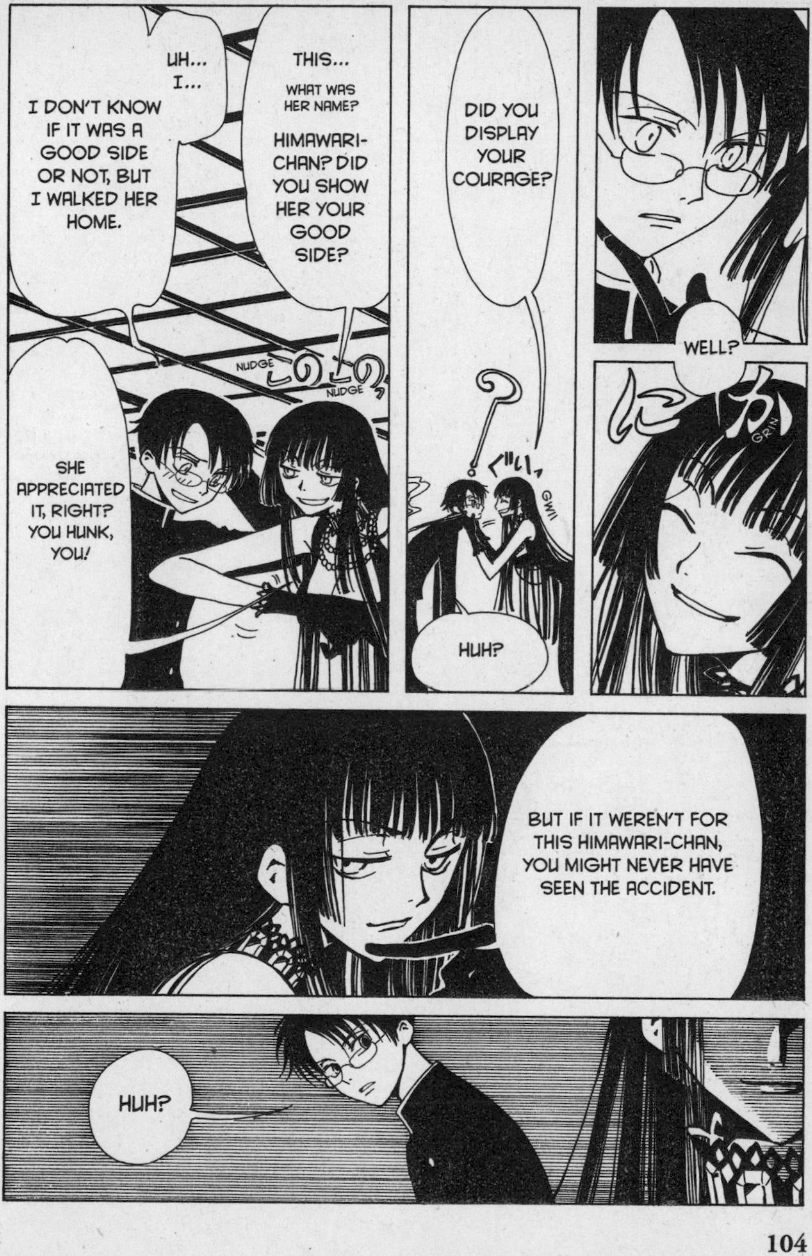
WELL?
GRIN
DID YOU DISPLAY YOUR COURAGE?
GWII
HUH?
THIS...
WHAT WAS HER NAME?
HIMAWARI-CHAN? DID YOU SHOW HER YOUR GOOD SIDE?
UH... I...
I DON'T KNOW IF IT WAS A GOOD SIDE OR NOT, BUT I WALKED HER HOME.
NUDGE
NUDGE
SHE APPRECIATED IT, RIGHT? YOU HUNK, YOU!
BUT IF IT WEREN'T FOR THIS HIMAWARI-CHAN, YOU MIGHT NEVER HAVE SEEN THE ACCIDENT.
HUH?

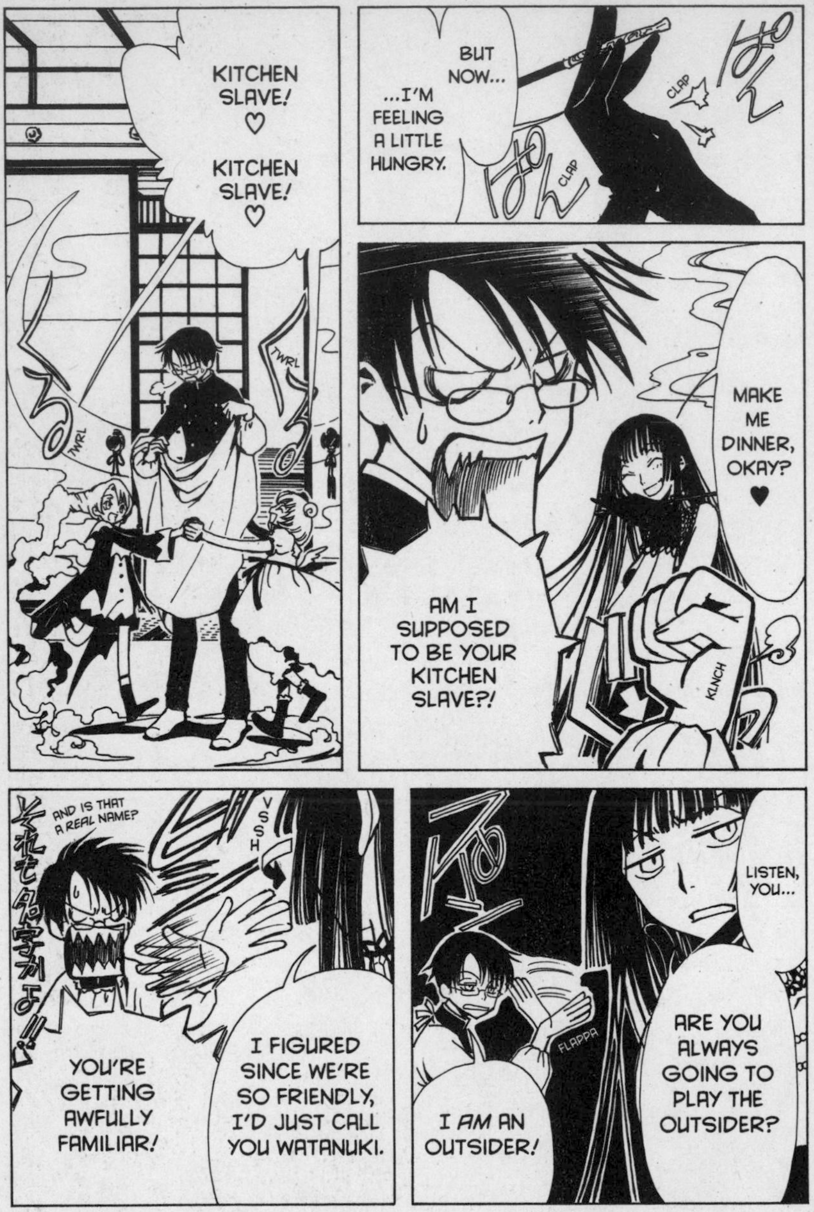
CLAP
CLAP
BUT NOW...
...I'M FEELING A LITTLE HUNGRY.
MAKE ME DINNER, OKAY? ♥
KLNCH
AM I SUPPOSED TO BE YOUR KITCHEN SLAVE?!
KITCHEN SLAVE! ♡
KITCHEN SLAVE! ♡
TWRL
TWRL
LISTEN, YOU...
ARE YOU ALWAYS GOING TO PLAY THE OUTSIDER?
FLAPPA
I *AM* AN OUTSIDER!
VSSH
I FIGURED SINCE WE'RE SO FRIENDLY, I'D JUST CALL YOU WATANUKI.
AND IS THAT A REAL NAME?
YOU'RE GETTING AWFULLY FAMILIAR!

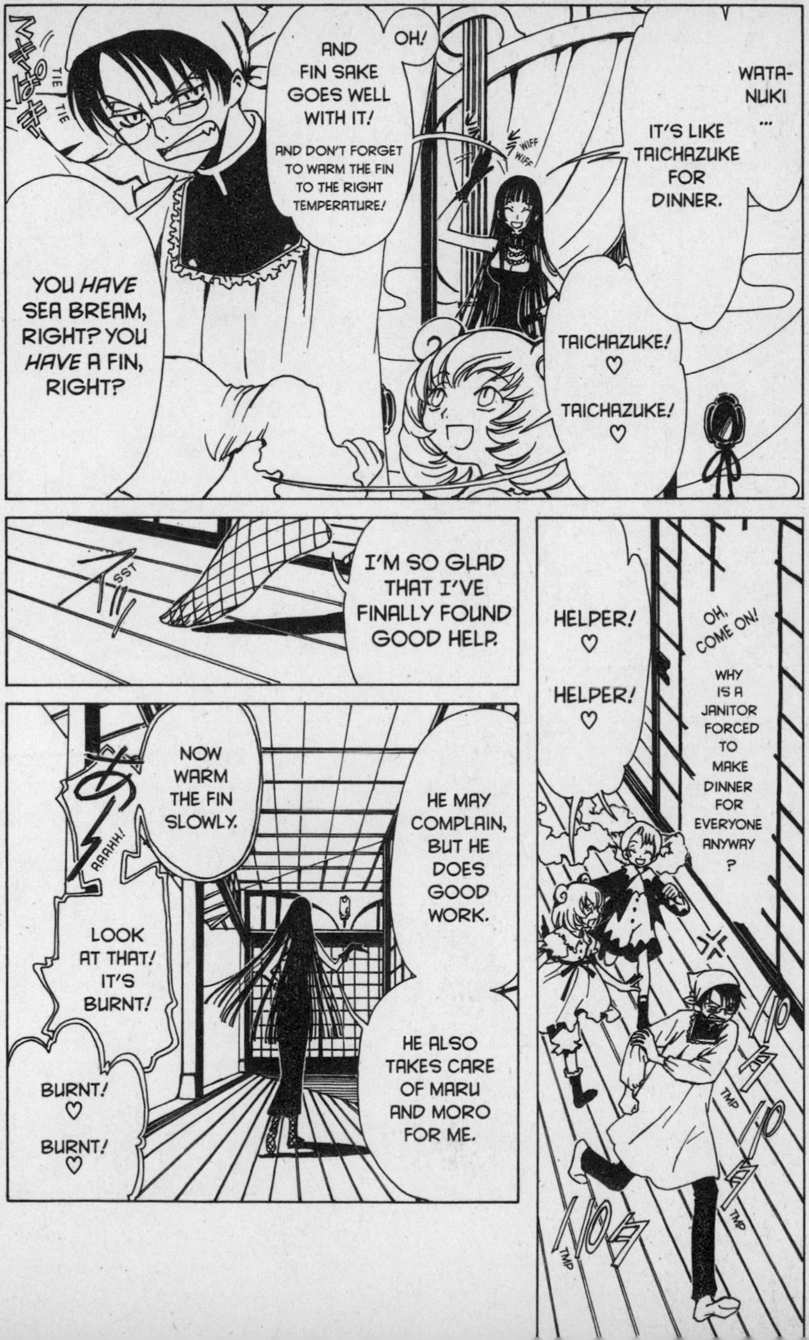
WATA-NUKI ...
IT'S LIKE TAICHAZUKE FOR DINNER.
OH!
AND FIN SAKE GOES WELL WITH IT!
AND DON'T FORGET TO WARM THE FIN TO THE RIGHT TEMPERATURE!
WIFF WIFF
TAICHAZUKE! ♡
TAICHAZUKE! ♡
TIE TIE
YOU *HAVE* SEA BREAM, RIGHT? YOU *HAVE* A FIN, RIGHT?
OH, COME ON!
WHY IS A JANITOR FORCED TO MAKE DINNER FOR EVERYONE ANYWAY ?
HELPER! ♡
HELPER! ♡
TMP
TMP
TMP
I'M SO GLAD THAT I'VE FINALLY FOUND GOOD HELP.
SST
HE MAY COMPLAIN, BUT HE DOES GOOD WORK.
HE ALSO TAKES CARE OF MARU AND MORO FOR ME.
NOW WARM THE FIN SLOWLY.
AAAHH!
LOOK AT THAT! IT'S BURNT!
BURNT! ♡
BURNT! ♡

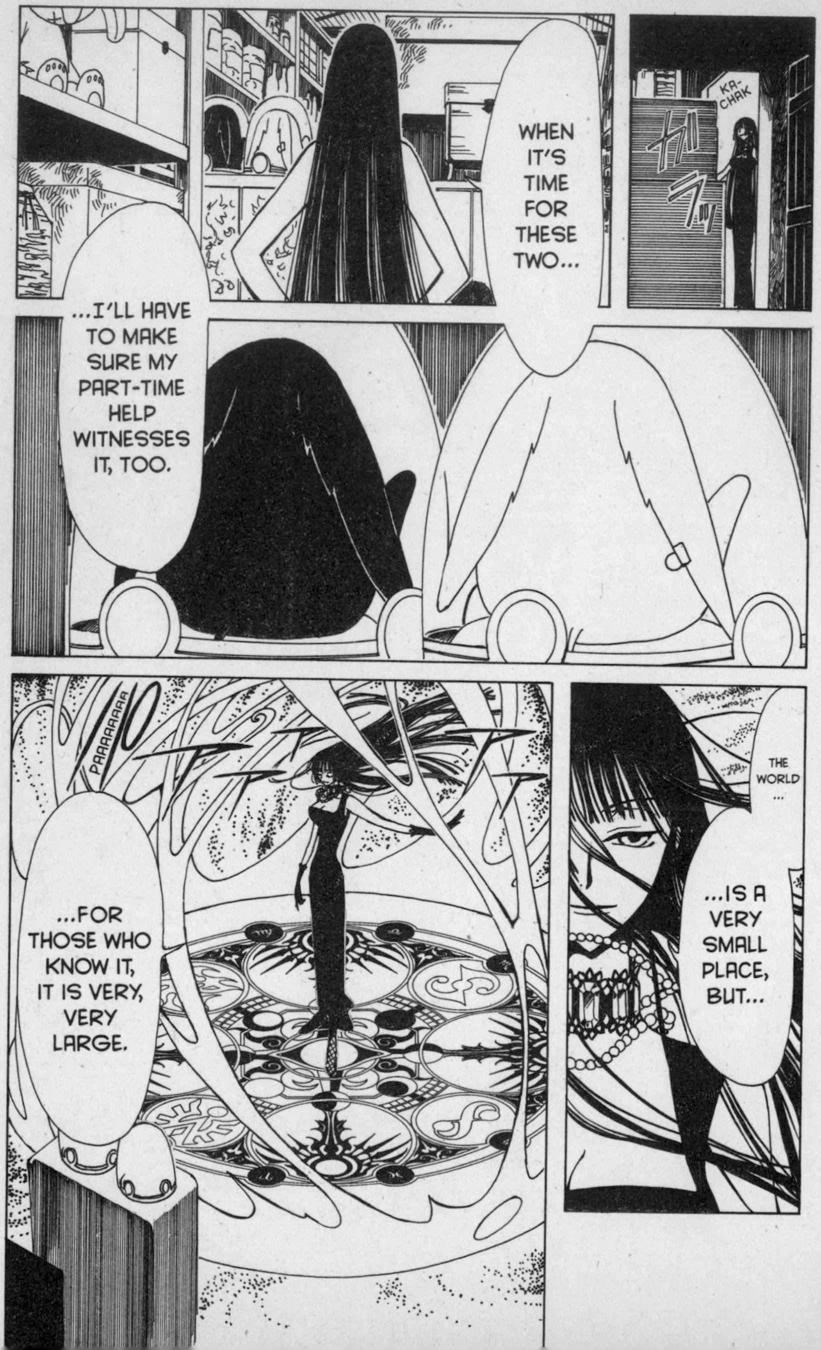
KA-CHAK
WHEN IT'S TIME FOR THESE TWO...
...I'LL HAVE TO MAKE SURE MY PART-TIME HELP WITNESSES IT, TOO.
THE WORLD ...
...IS A VERY SMALL PLACE, BUT...
PAAAAAAAA
...FOR THOSE WHO KNOW IT, IT IS VERY, VERY LARGE.

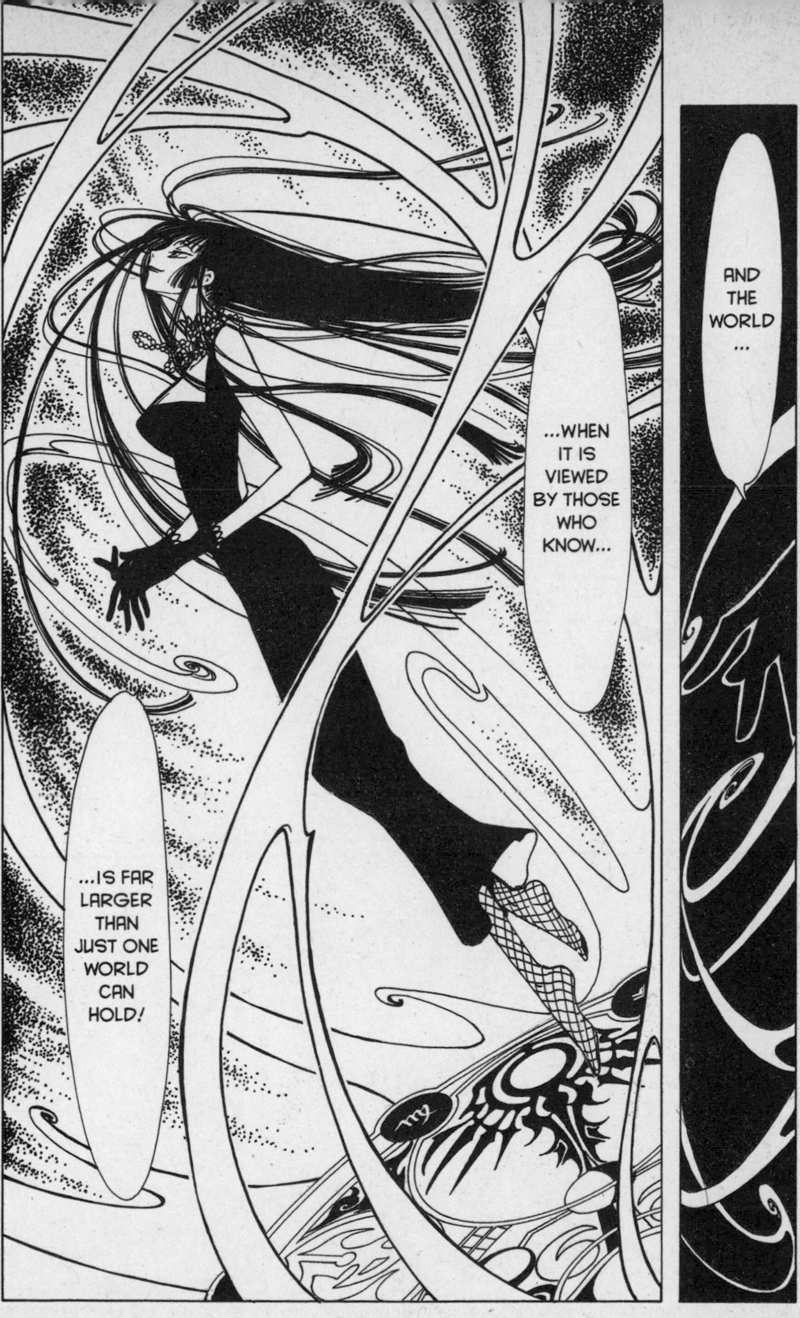
AND THE WORLD ...
...WHEN IT IS VIEWED BY THOSE WHO KNOW...
...IS FAR LARGER THAN JUST ONE WORLD CAN HOLD!

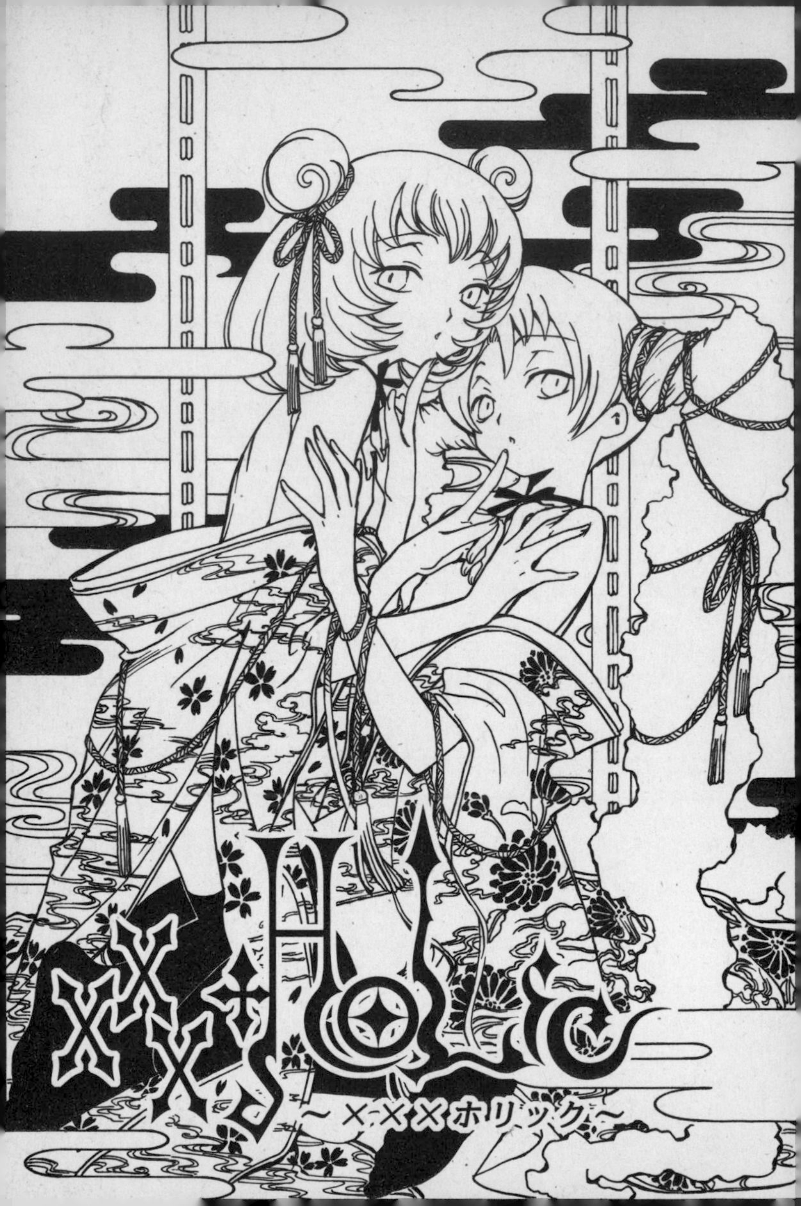
xxxHOLiC
〜×××ホリック〜

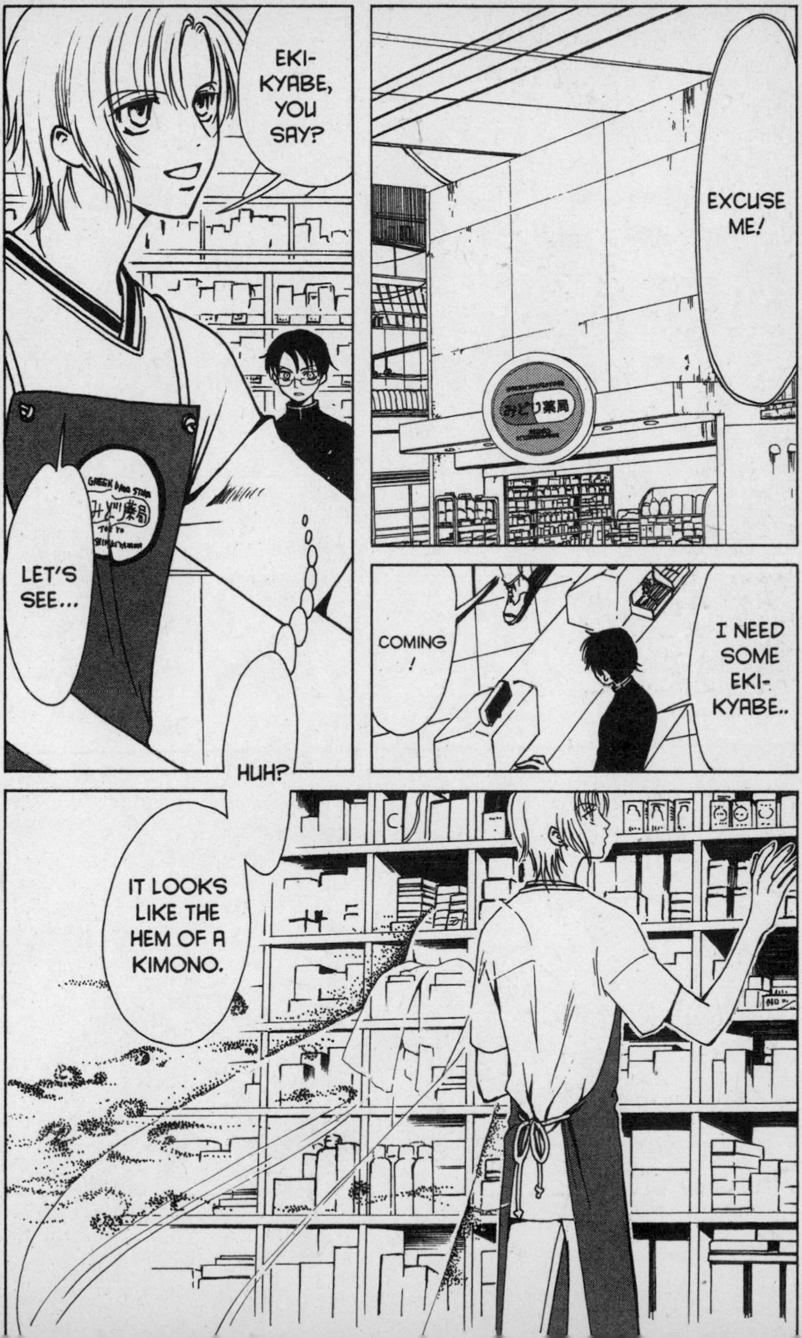
EXCUSE ME!
I NEED SOME EKI-KYABE..
COMING!
EKI-KYABE, YOU SAY?
LET'S SEE...
HUH?
IT LOOKS LIKE THE HEM OF A KIMONO.

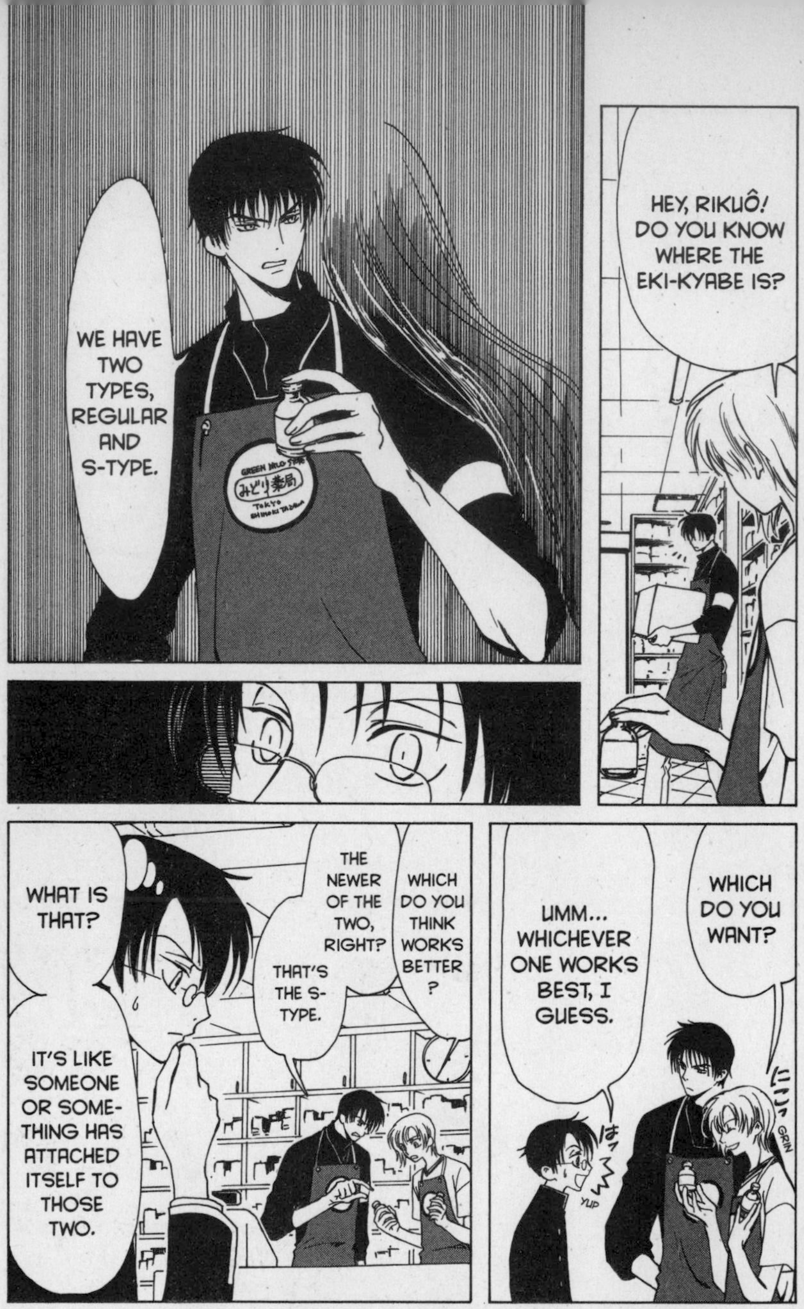
HEY, RIKUÔ! DO YOU KNOW WHERE THE EKI-KYABE IS?
WE HAVE TWO TYPES, REGULAR AND S-TYPE.
みどり薬局
WHICH DO YOU WANT?
UMM... WHICHEVER ONE WORKS BEST, I GUESS.
YUP
GRIN
WHICH DO YOU THINK WORKS BETTER?
THE NEWER OF THE TWO, RIGHT?
THAT'S THE S-TYPE.
WHAT IS THAT?
IT'S LIKE SOMEONE OR SOMETHING HAS ATTACHED ITSELF TO THOSE TWO.

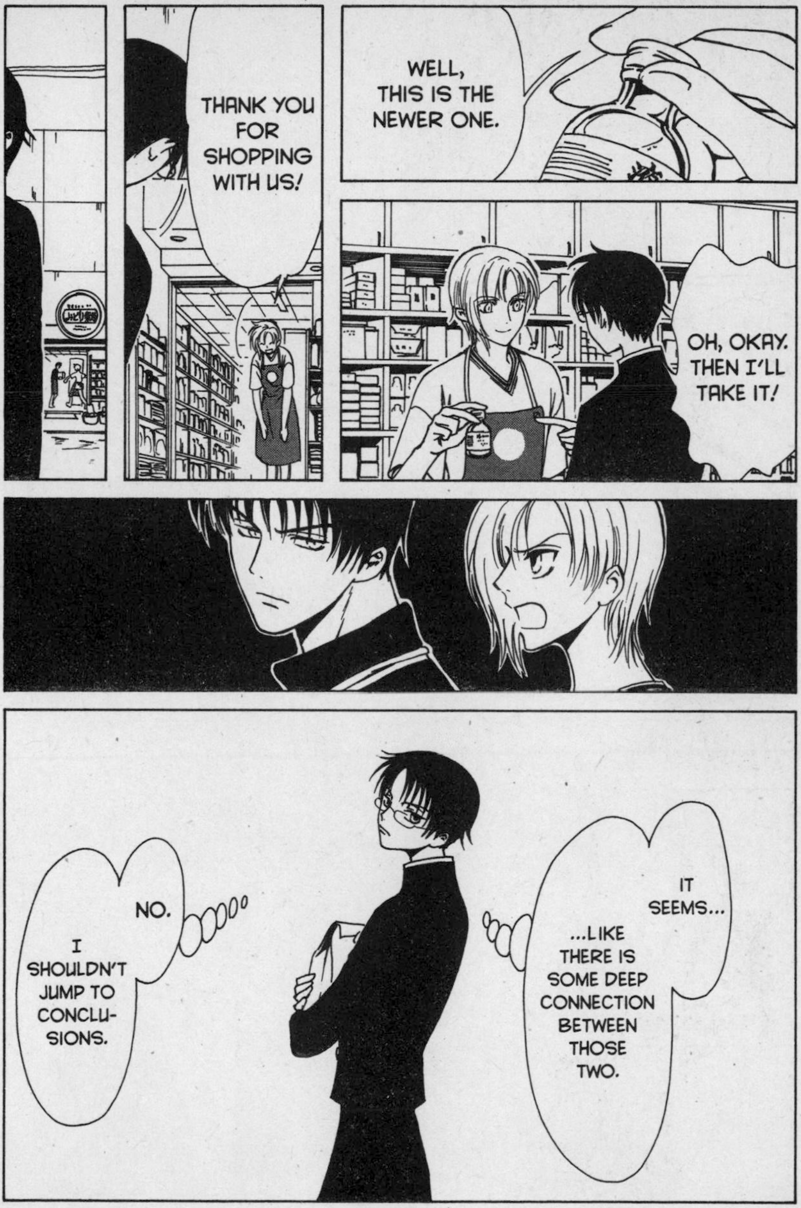
WELL, THIS IS THE NEWER ONE.
OH, OKAY. THEN I'LL TAKE IT!
THANK YOU FOR SHOPPING WITH US!
IT SEEMS...
...LIKE THERE IS SOME DEEP CONNECTION BETWEEN THOSE TWO.
NO.
I SHOULDN'T JUMP TO CONCLUSIONS.

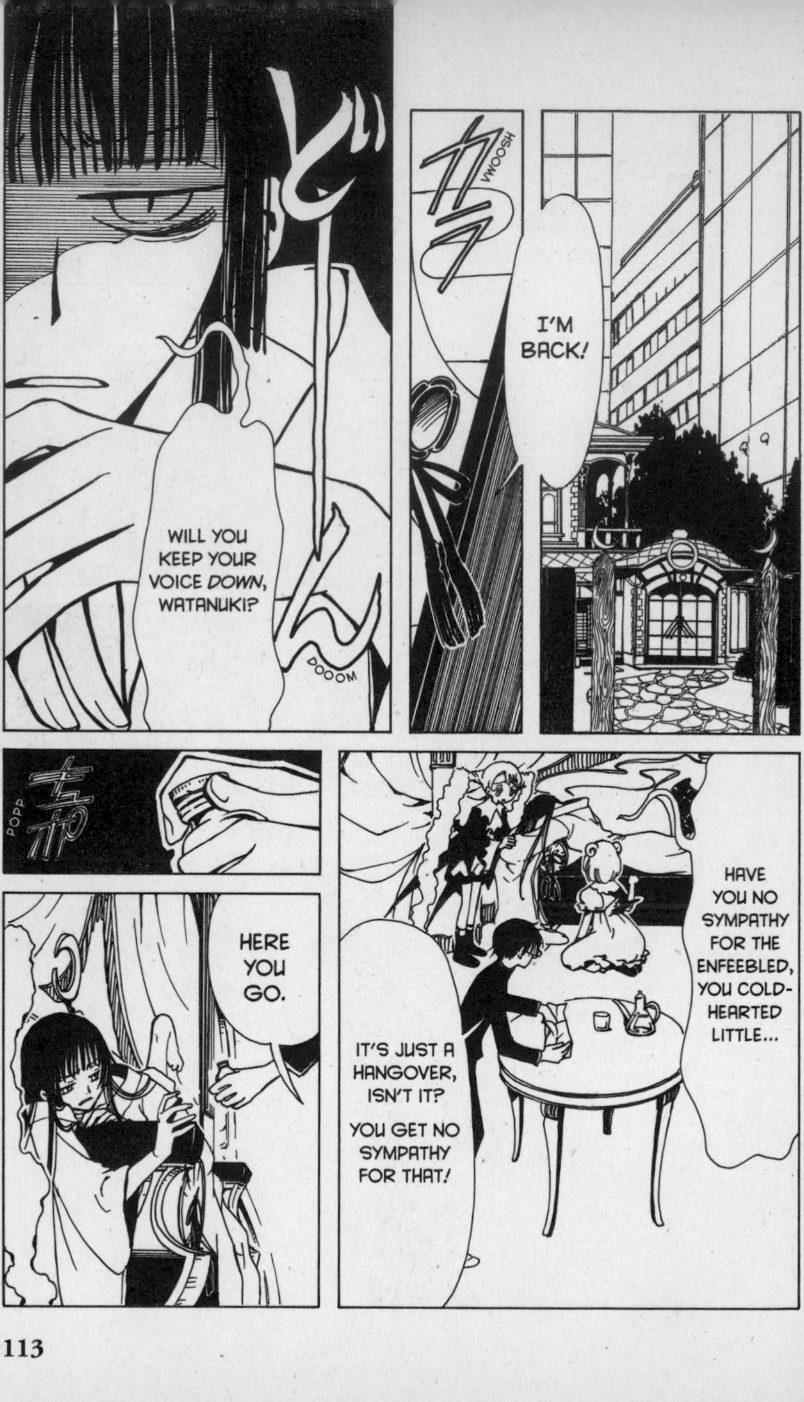
VWOOSH
I'M BACK!
WILL YOU KEEP YOUR VOICE *DOWN*, WATANUKI?
DOOOM
HAVE YOU NO SYMPATHY FOR THE ENFEEBLED, YOU COLD-HEARTED LITTLE...
IT'S JUST A HANGOVER, ISN'T IT?
YOU GET NO SYMPATHY FOR THAT!
POPP
HERE YOU GO.

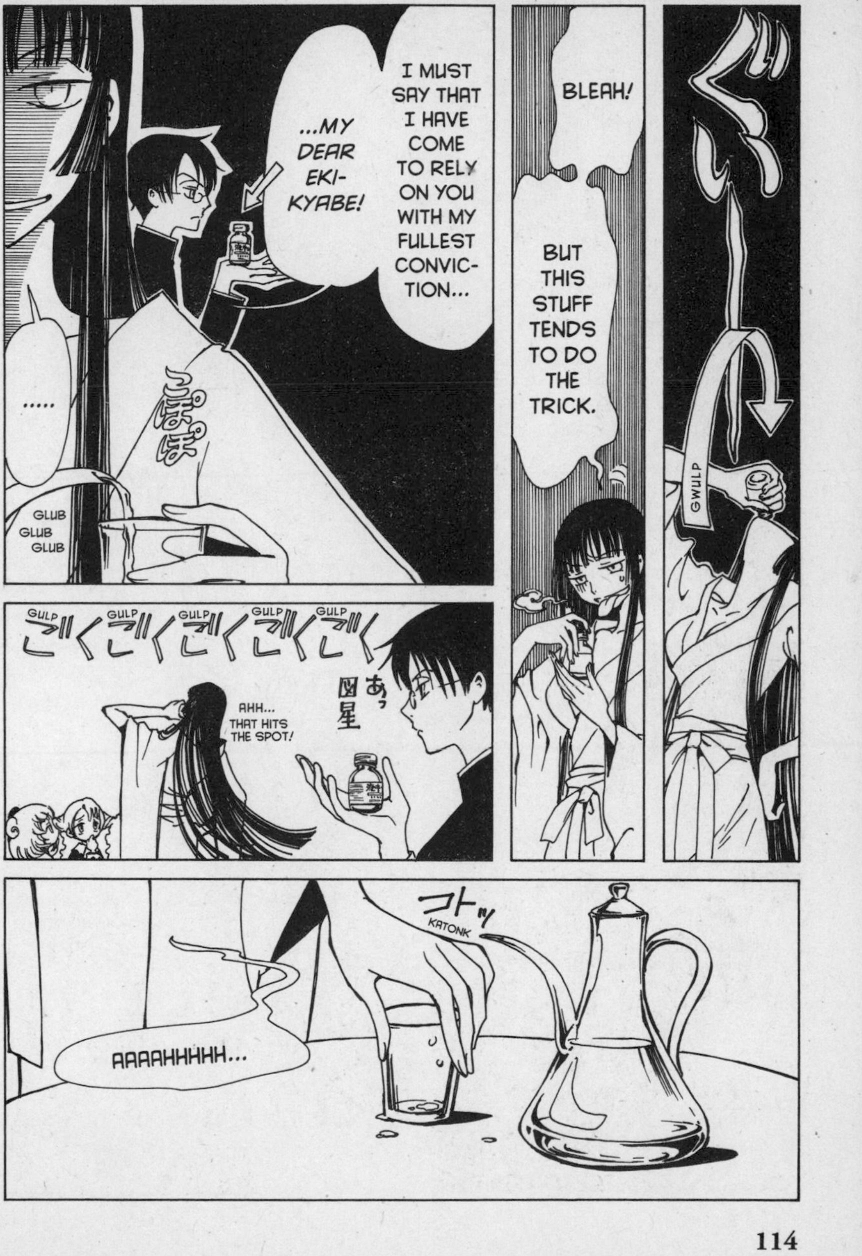
GWULP
BLEAH!
BUT THIS STUFF TENDS TO DO THE TRICK.
I MUST SAY THAT I HAVE COME TO RELY ON YOU WITH MY FULLEST CONVICTION...
...MY DEAR EKI-KYABE!
.....
こぽぽ
GLUB GLUB GLUB
GULP GULP GULP GULP GULP
ごくごくごくごくごく
あっ 図星
AHHH... THAT HITS THE SPOT!
コトッ
KATONK
AAAAHHHHH...

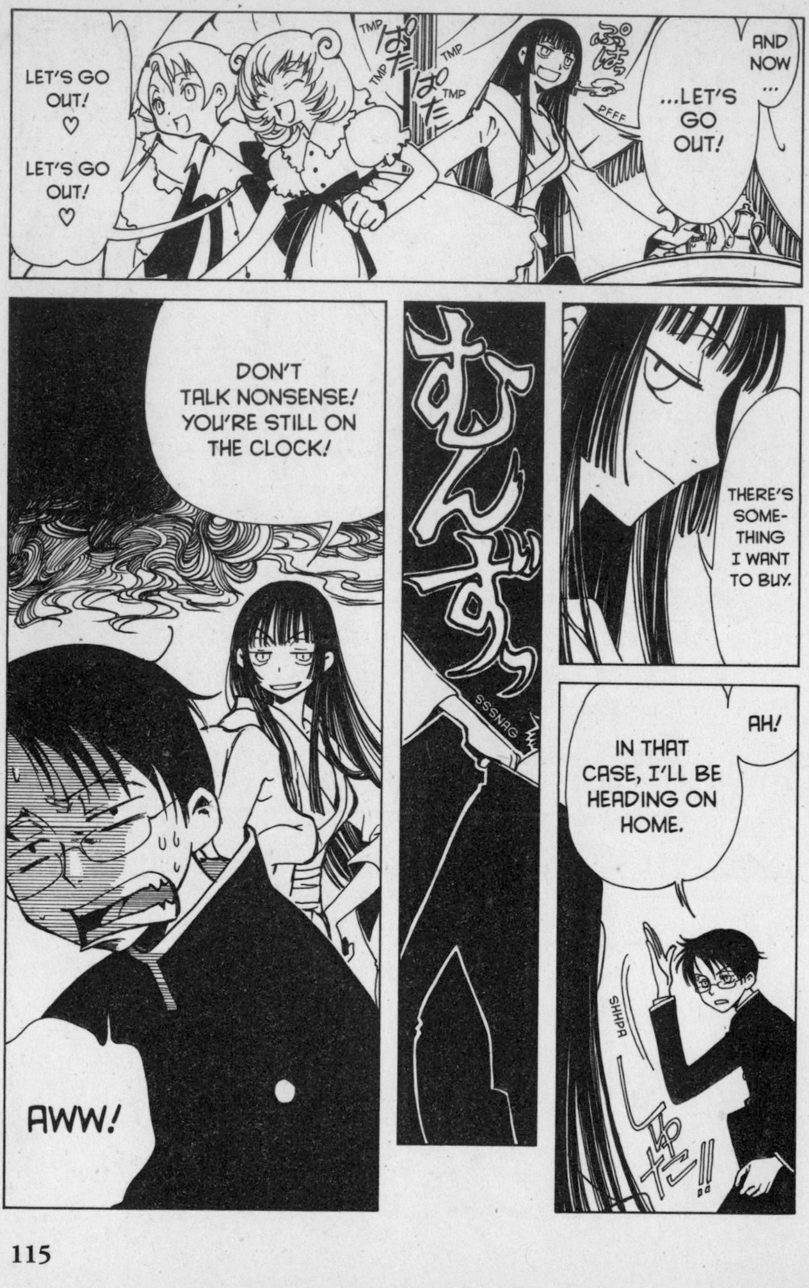
AND NOW ...
...LET'S GO OUT!
PFFF
ぷはっ
TMP TMP TMP TMP
ぱたぱた
LET'S GO OUT! ♡
LET'S GO OUT! ♡
THERE'S SOMETHING I WANT TO BUY.
AH!
IN THAT CASE, I'LL BE HEADING ON HOME.
SHHPA
しゅた!!
むんず
SSSNAG
DON'T TALK NONSENSE! YOU'RE STILL ON THE CLOCK!
AWW!

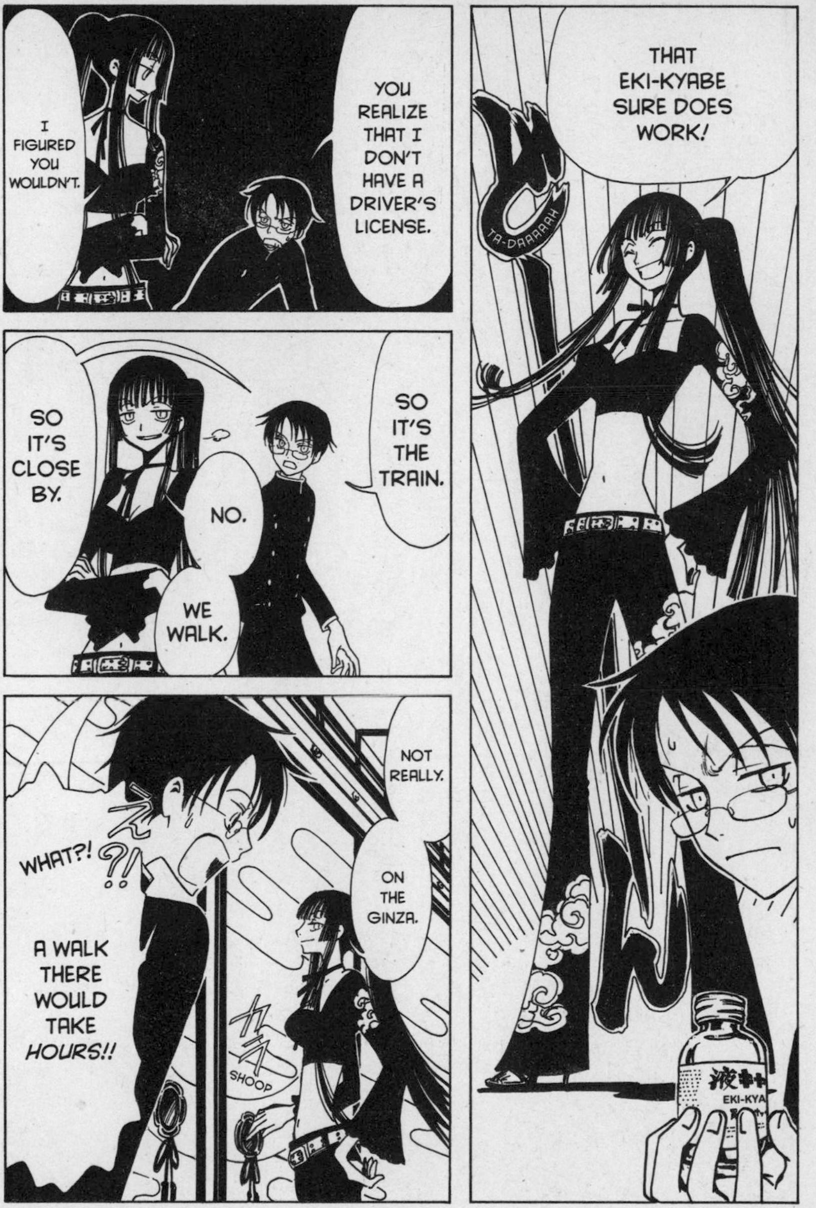
THAT EKI-KYABE SURE DOES WORK!
TA-DAAAAAH
EKI-KYA
YOU REALIZE THAT I DON'T HAVE A DRIVER'S LICENSE.
I FIGURED YOU WOULDN'T.
SO IT'S THE TRAIN.
NO.
WE WALK.
SO IT'S CLOSE BY.
NOT REALLY.
ON THE GINZA.
WHAT?! ?!
A WALK THERE WOULD TAKE *HOURS!!*
SHOOP

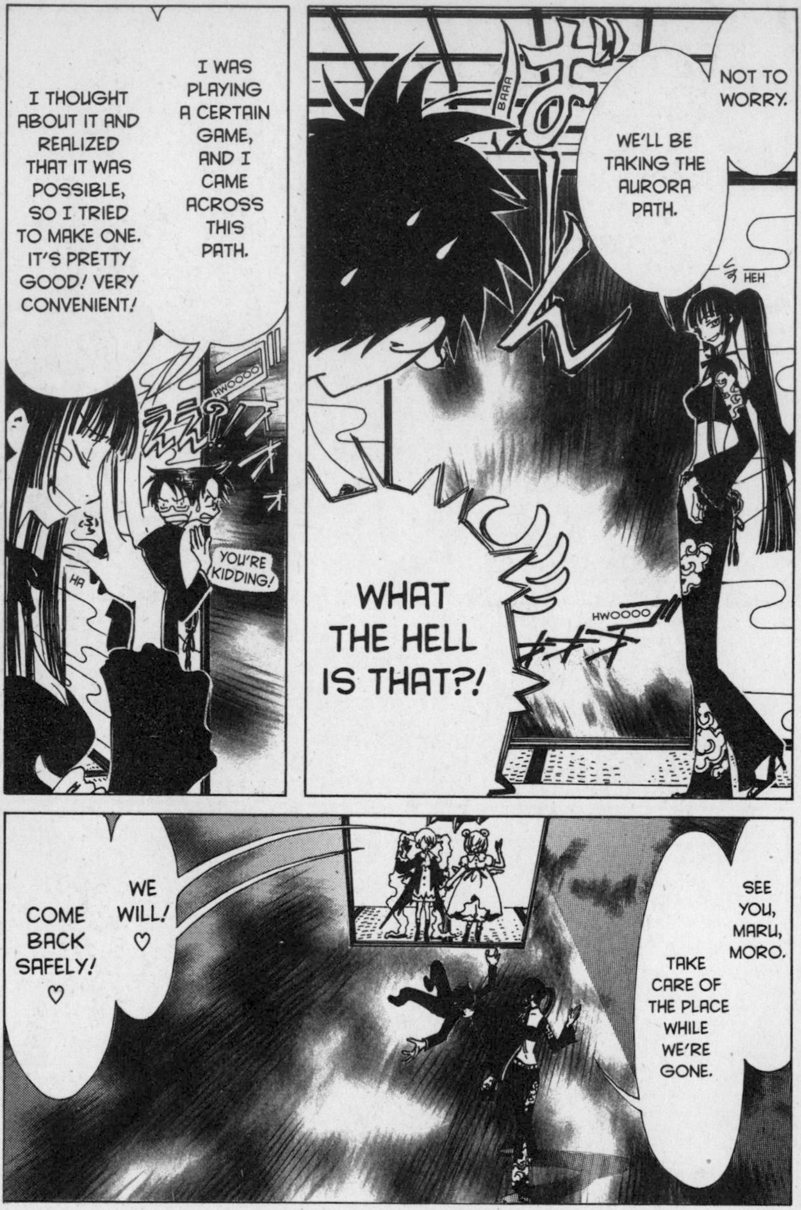
BAAA
NOT TO WORRY.
WE'LL BE TAKING THE AURORA PATH.
HEH
WHAT THE HELL IS THAT?!
HWOOOO
I WAS PLAYING A CERTAIN GAME, AND I CAME ACROSS THIS PATH.
I THOUGHT ABOUT IT AND REALIZED THAT IT WAS POSSIBLE, SO I TRIED TO MAKE ONE. IT'S PRETTY GOOD! VERY CONVENIENT!
HWOOOO
YOU'RE KIDDING!
HA
SEE YOU, MARU, MORO.
TAKE CARE OF THE PLACE WHILE WE'RE GONE.
WE WILL! ♡
COME BACK SAFELY! ♡

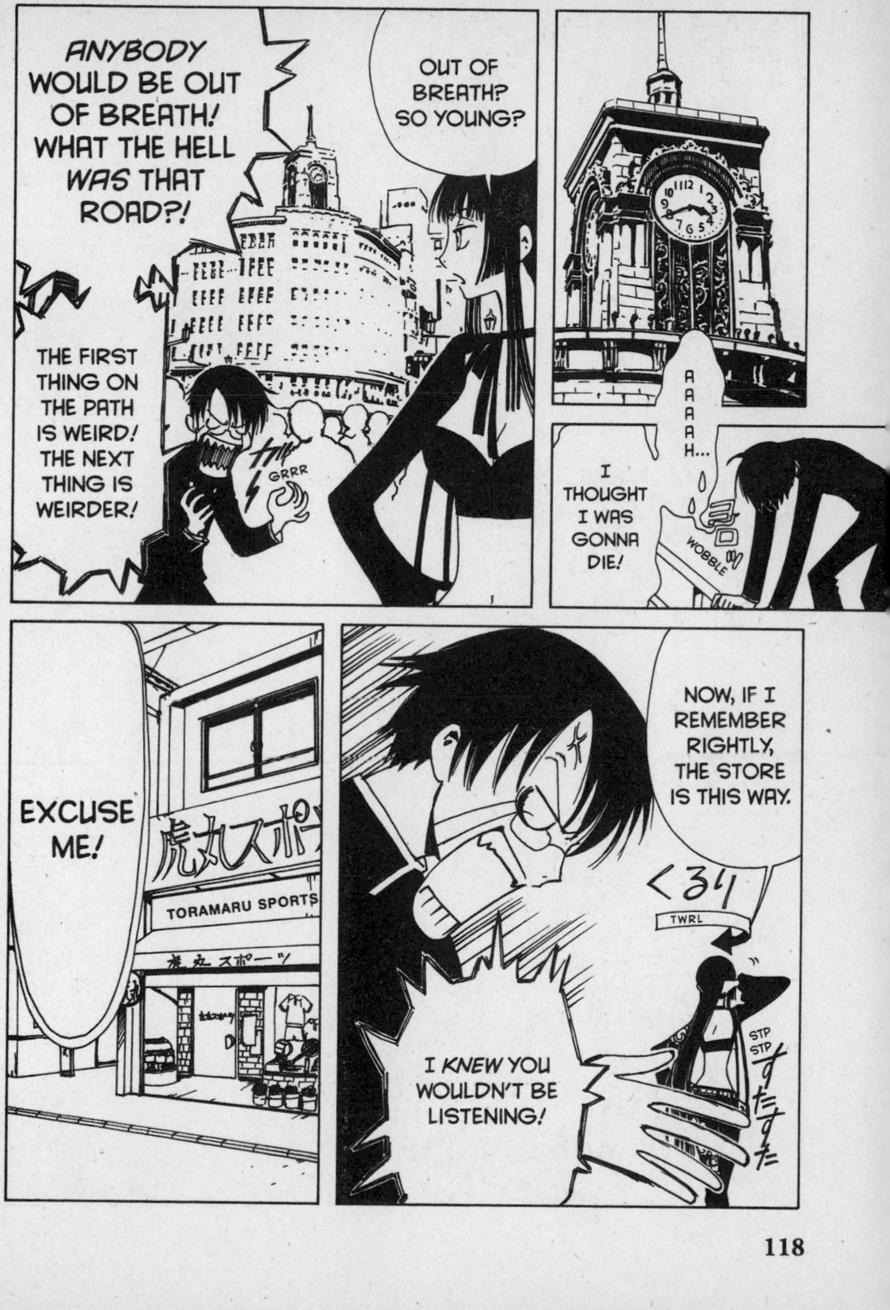
AAAAH...
I THOUGHT I WAS GONNA DIE!
WOBBLE
OUT OF BREATH? SO YOUNG?
ANYBODY WOULD BE OUT OF BREATH! WHAT THE HELL WAS THAT ROAD?!
THE FIRST THING ON THE PATH IS WEIRD! THE NEXT THING IS WEIRDER!
GRRR
NOW, IF I REMEMBER RIGHTLY, THE STORE IS THIS WAY.
くるり
TWRL
STP STP
すたすた
I KNEW YOU WOULDN'T BE LISTENING!
EXCUSE ME!
TORAMARU SPORTS

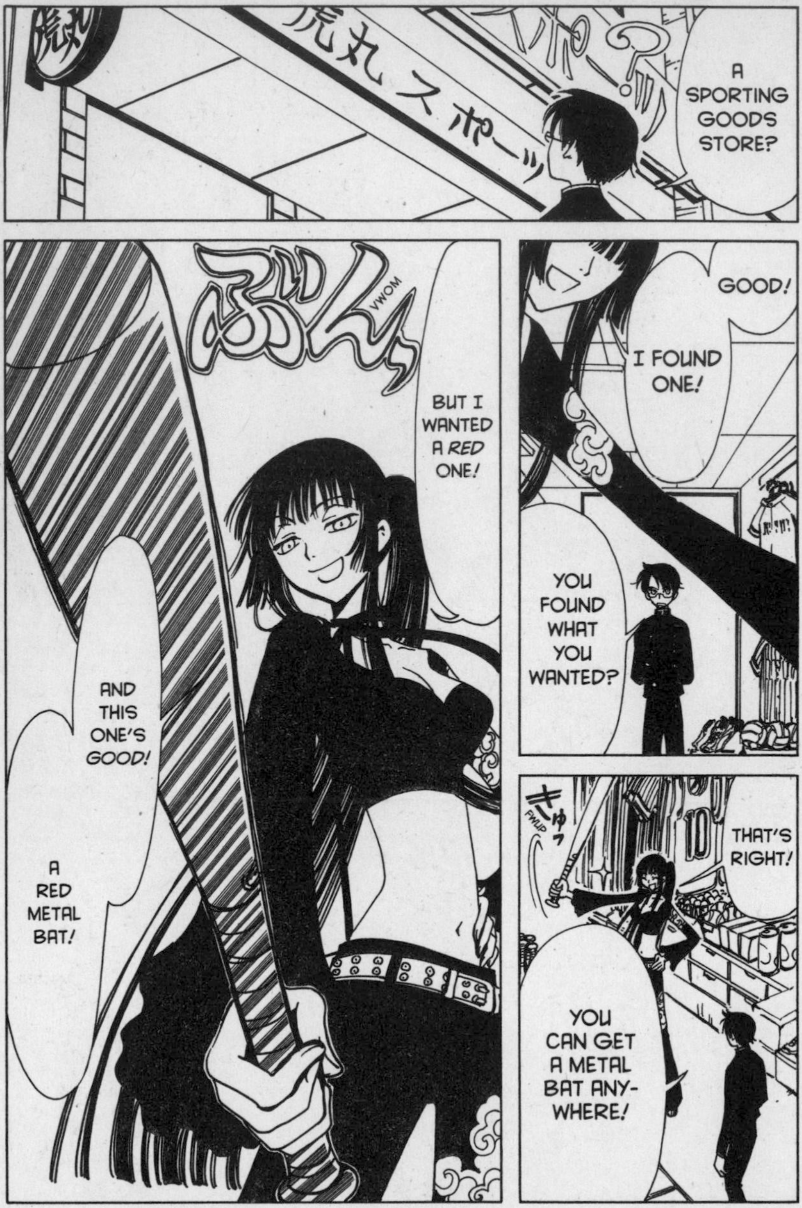
虎丸
虎丸スポーツ
A SPORTING GOODS STORE?
GOOD!
I FOUND ONE!
YOU FOUND WHAT YOU WANTED?
THAT'S RIGHT!
きゅっ
FWIP
YOU CAN GET A METAL BAT ANY-WHERE!
ぶん
VWOM
BUT I WANTED A *RED* ONE!
AND THIS ONE'S *GOOD!*
A RED METAL BAT!

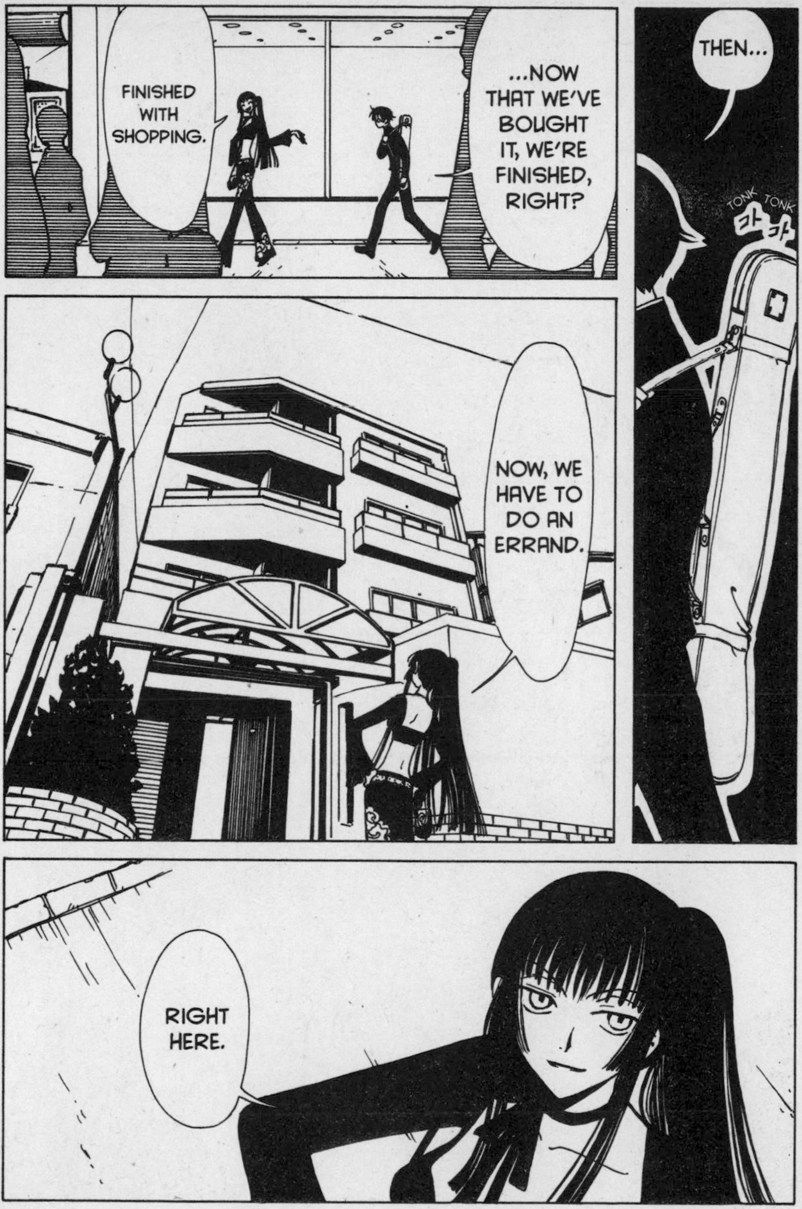
THEN...
TONK TONK
...NOW THAT WE'VE BOUGHT IT, WE'RE FINISHED, RIGHT?
FINISHED WITH SHOPPING.
NOW, WE HAVE TO DO AN ERRAND.
RIGHT HERE.

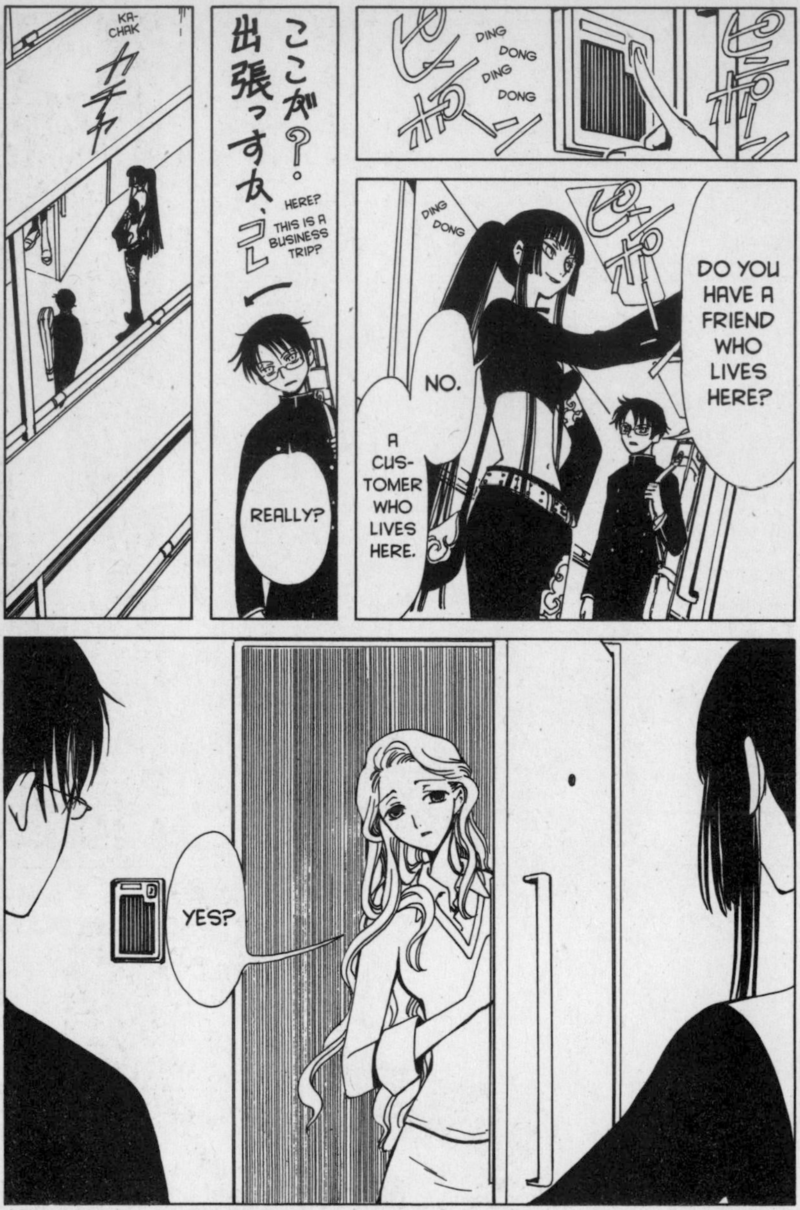
DING DONG DING DONG
DING DONG
DO YOU HAVE A FRIEND WHO LIVES HERE?
NO.
A CUSTOMER WHO LIVES HERE.
ここが？。出張っすか、コレ
HERE? THIS IS A BUSINESS TRIP?
REALLY?
KA-CHAK
YES?

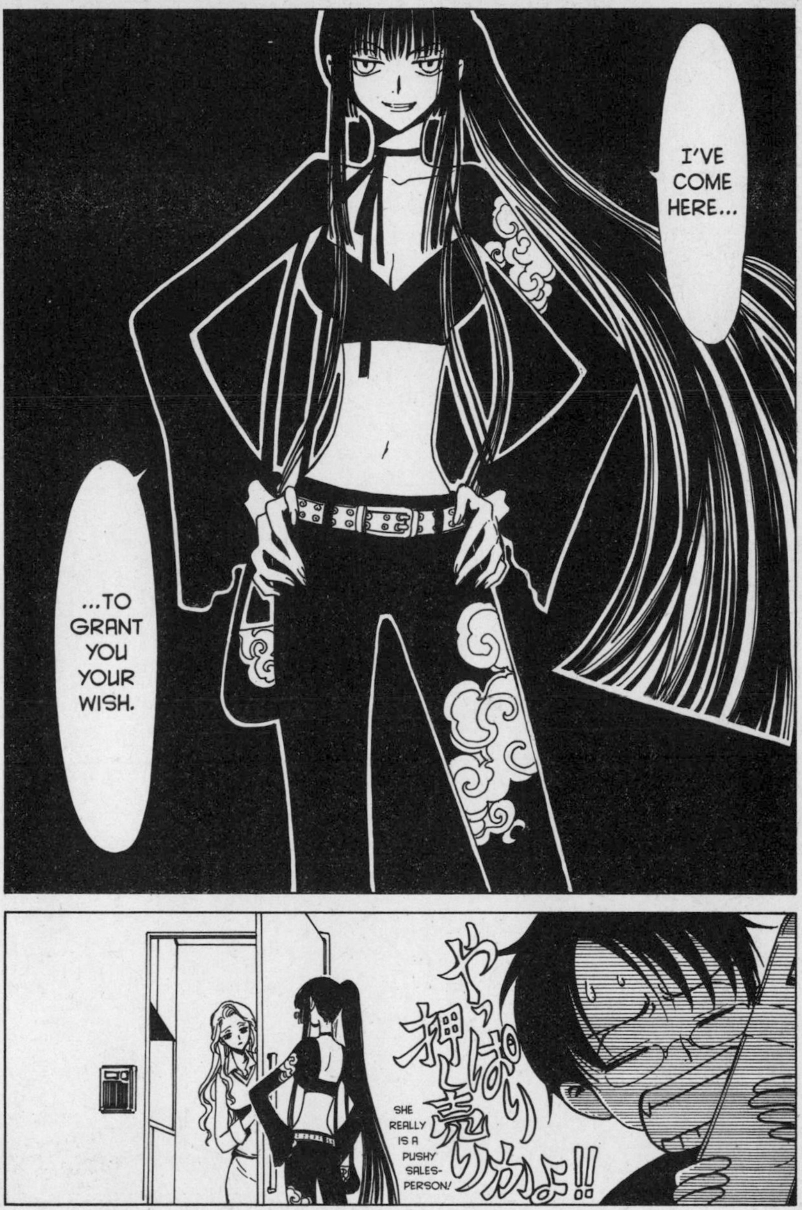
I'VE COME HERE...
...TO GRANT YOU YOUR WISH.
やっぱり押し売りかよ!!
SHE REALLY IS A PUSHY SALES-PERSON!

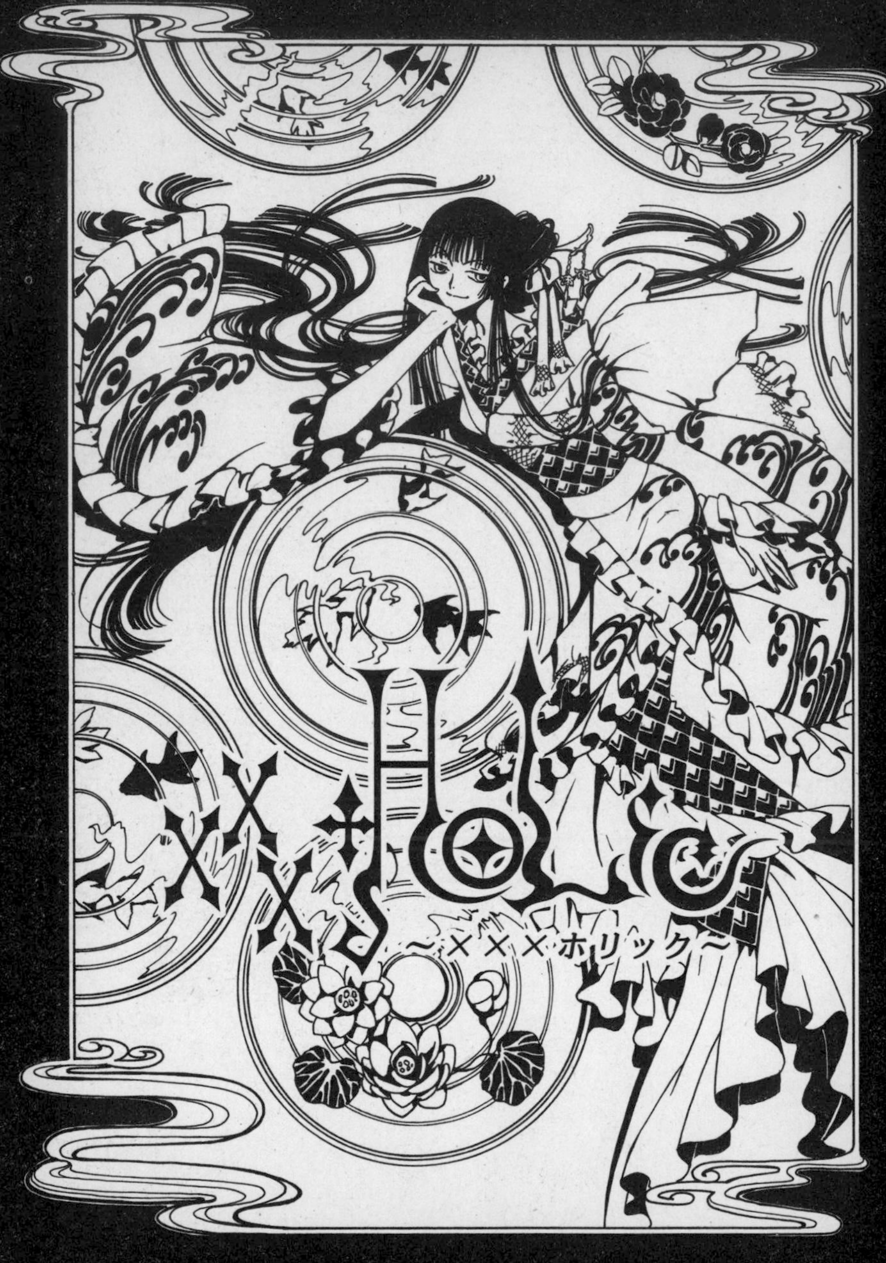
xxxHOLiC
~×××ホリック~

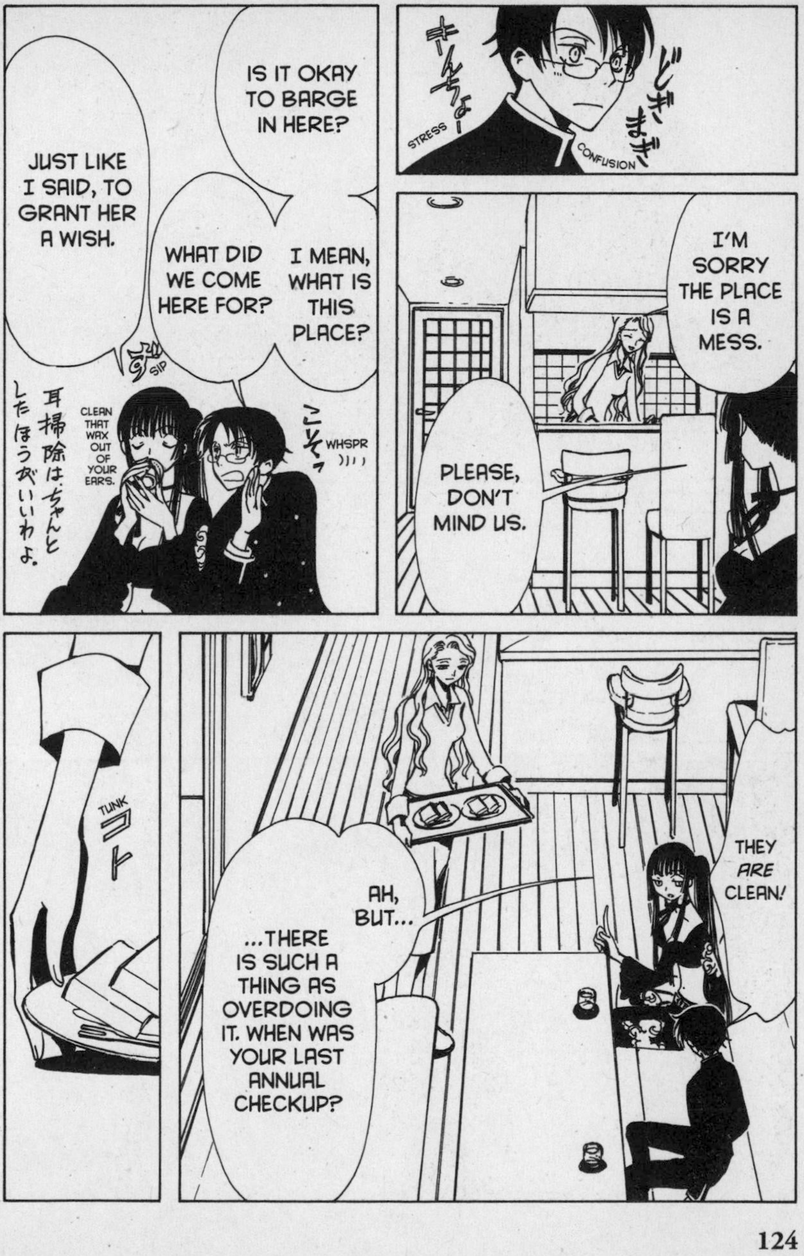
STRESS
どぎまぎ
CONFUSION
I'M SORRY THE PLACE IS A MESS.
PLEASE, DON'T MIND US.
IS IT OKAY TO BARGE IN HERE?
I MEAN, WHAT IS THIS PLACE?
WHAT DID WE COME HERE FOR?
WHSPR
JUST LIKE I SAID, TO GRANT HER A WISH.
SIP
耳掃除は、ちゃんとしたほうがいいわよ。
CLEAN THAT WAX OUT OF YOUR EARS.
THEY ARE CLEAN!
AH, BUT...
...THERE IS SUCH A THING AS OVERDOING IT. WHEN WAS YOUR LAST ANNUAL CHECKUP?
TUNK
コト

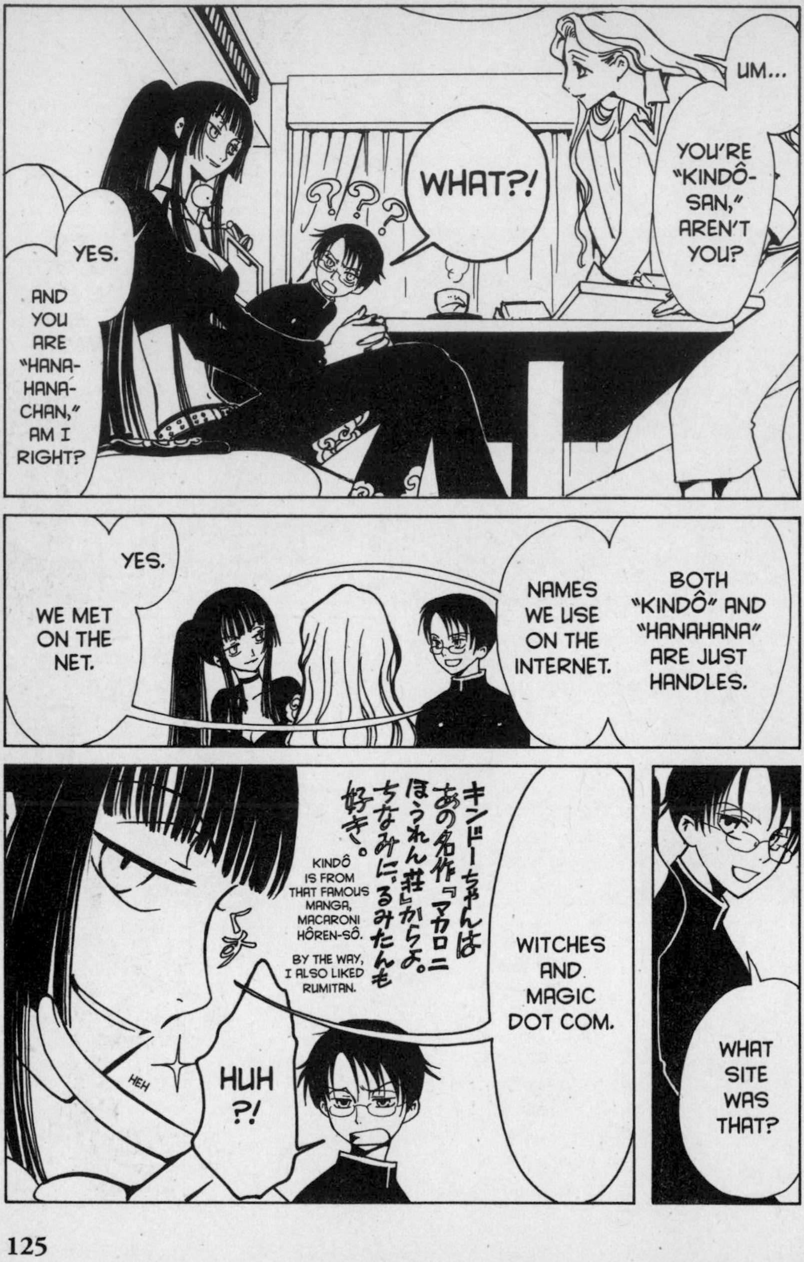
UM...
YOU'RE "KINDÔ-SAN," AREN'T YOU?
WHAT?!
???
YES.
AND YOU ARE "HANA-HANA-CHAN," AM I RIGHT?
BOTH "KINDÔ" AND "HANAHANA" ARE JUST HANDLES.
NAMES WE USE ON THE INTERNET.
YES.
WE MET ON THE NET.
WHAT SITE WAS THAT?
WITCHES AND MAGIC DOT COM.
キンドーちゃんはあの名作『マカロニほうれん荘』からよ。ちなみに、るみたんも好き。
KINDÔ IS FROM THAT FAMOUS MANGA, MACARONI HÔREN-SÔ.
BY THE WAY, I ALSO LIKED RUMITAN.
HUH?!
HEH

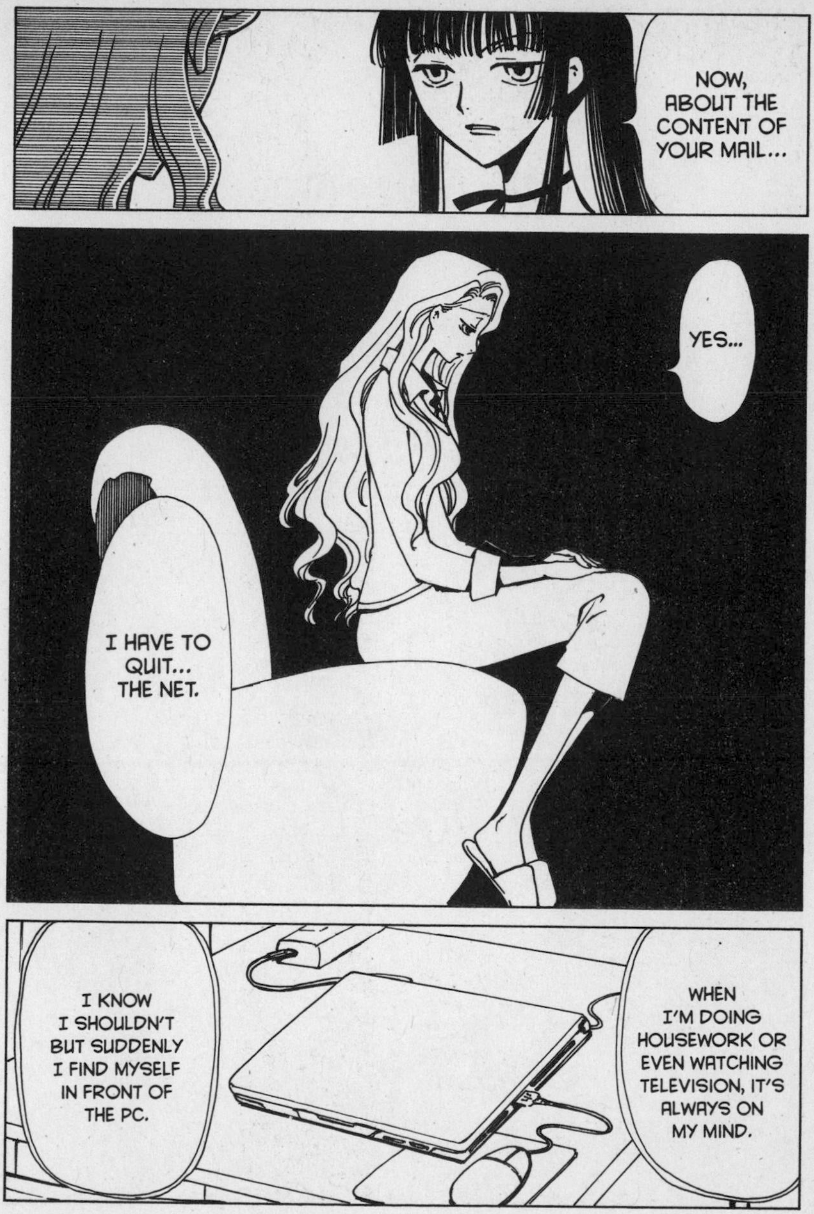
NOW, ABOUT THE CONTENT OF YOUR MAIL...
YES...
I HAVE TO QUIT... THE NET.
WHEN I'M DOING HOUSEWORK OR EVEN WATCHING TELEVISION, IT'S ALWAYS ON MY MIND.
I KNOW I SHOULDN'T BUT SUDDENLY I FIND MYSELF IN FRONT OF THE PC.

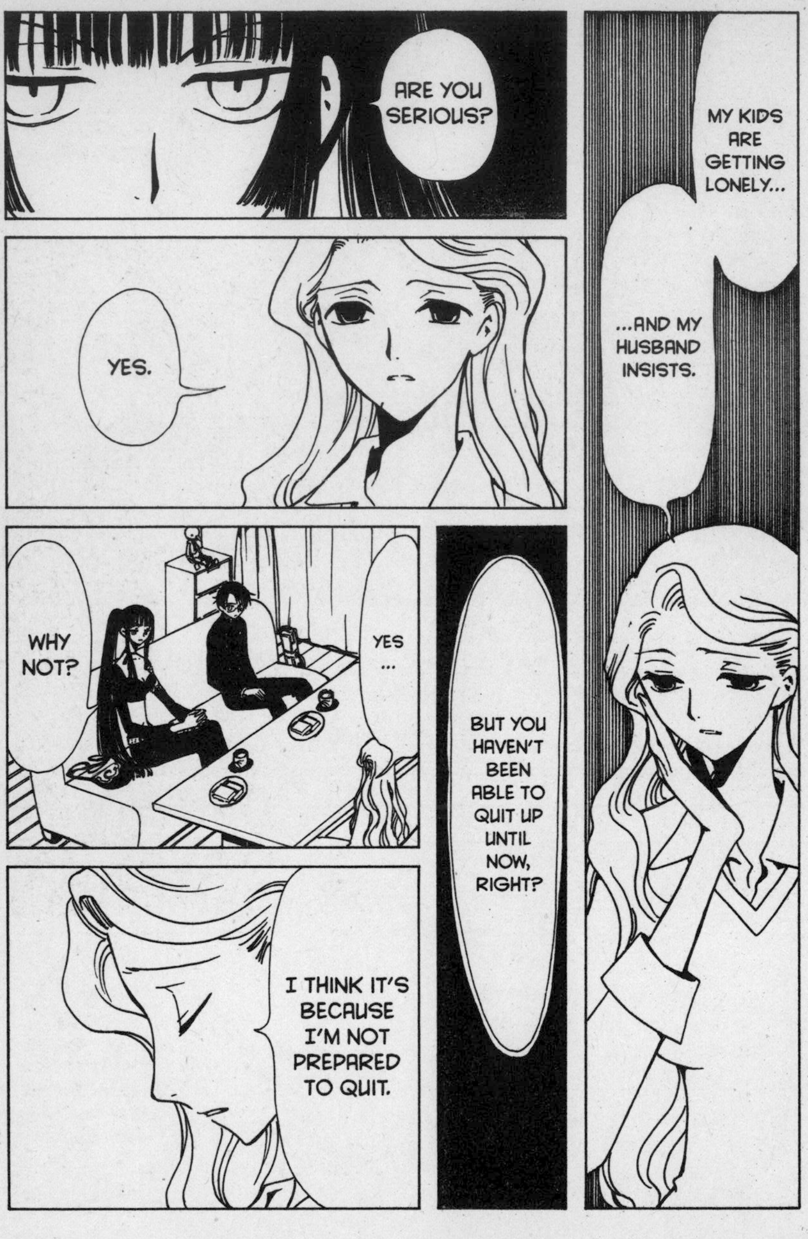
MY KIDS ARE GETTING LONELY...
...AND MY HUSBAND INSISTS.
ARE YOU SERIOUS?
YES.
BUT YOU HAVEN'T BEEN ABLE TO QUIT UP UNTIL NOW, RIGHT?
YES ...
WHY NOT?
I THINK IT'S BECAUSE I'M NOT PREPARED TO QUIT.

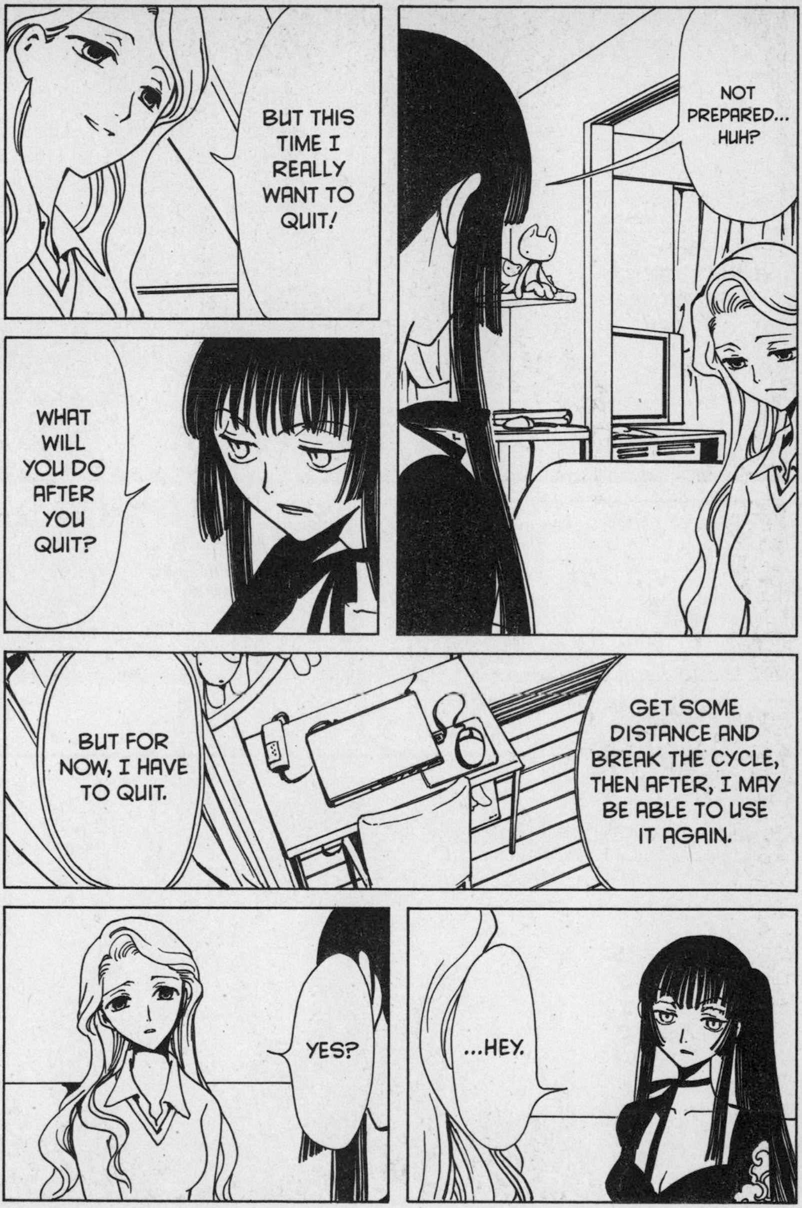
NOT PREPARED... HUH?
BUT THIS TIME I REALLY WANT TO QUIT!
WHAT WILL YOU DO AFTER YOU QUIT?
GET SOME DISTANCE AND BREAK THE CYCLE, THEN AFTER, I MAY BE ABLE TO USE IT AGAIN.
BUT FOR NOW, I HAVE TO QUIT.
...HEY.
YES?

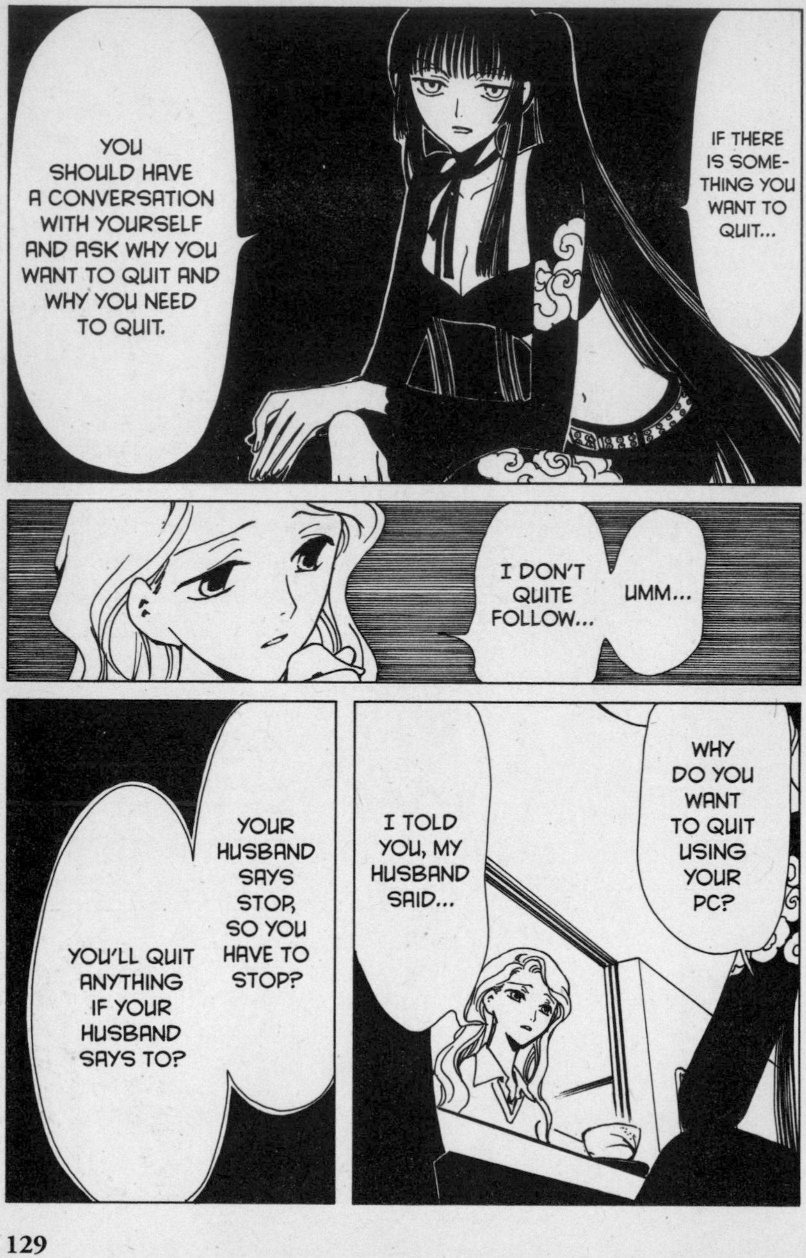
IF THERE IS SOME-THING YOU WANT TO QUIT...
YOU SHOULD HAVE A CONVERSATION WITH YOURSELF AND ASK WHY YOU WANT TO QUIT AND WHY YOU NEED TO QUIT.
UMM...
I DON'T QUITE FOLLOW...
WHY DO YOU WANT TO QUIT USING YOUR PC?
I TOLD YOU, MY HUSBAND SAID...
YOUR HUSBAND SAYS STOP, SO YOU HAVE TO STOP?
YOU'LL QUIT ANYTHING IF YOUR HUSBAND SAYS TO?

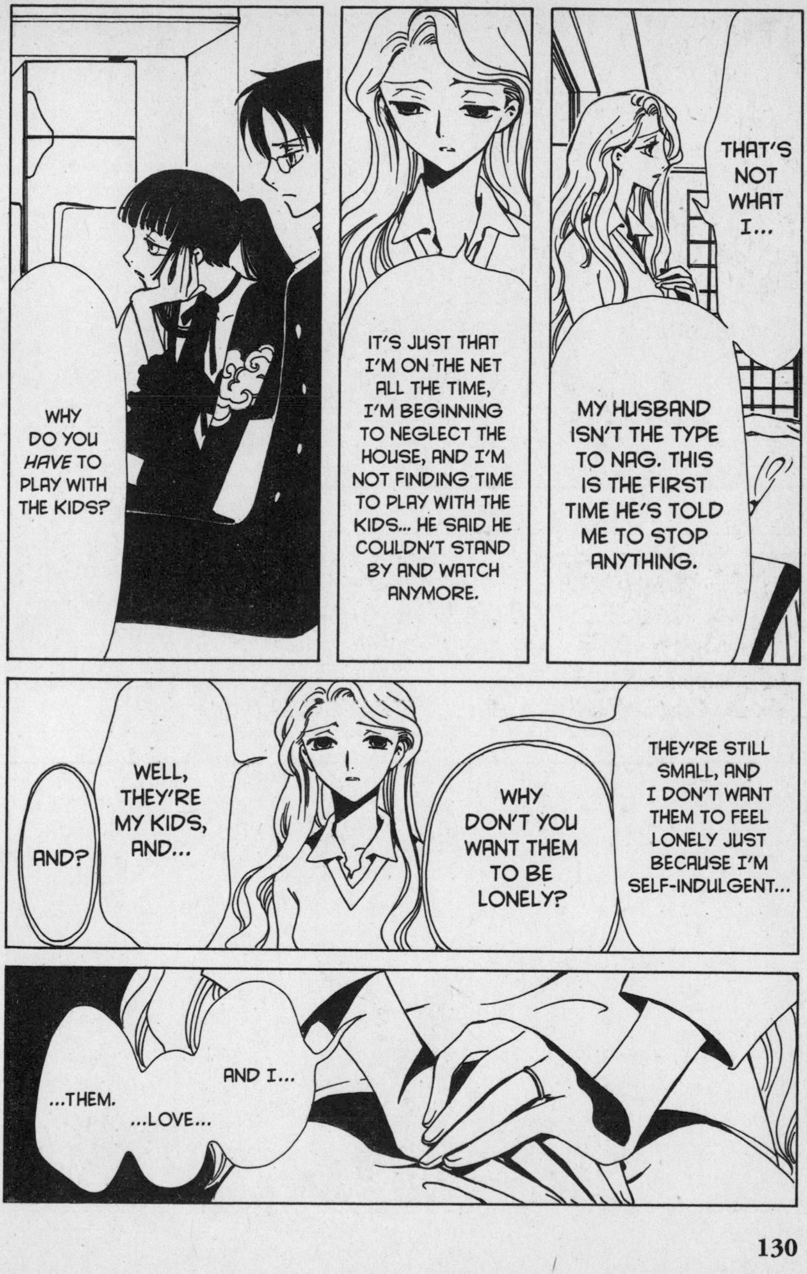

THAT'S NOT WHAT I...
MY HUSBAND ISN'T THE TYPE TO NAG. THIS IS THE FIRST TIME HE'S TOLD ME TO STOP ANYTHING.
IT'S JUST THAT I'M ON THE NET ALL THE TIME, I'M BEGINNING TO NEGLECT THE HOUSE, AND I'M NOT FINDING TIME TO PLAY WITH THE KIDS... HE SAID HE COULDN'T STAND BY AND WATCH ANYMORE.
WHY DO YOU *HAVE* TO PLAY WITH THE KIDS?
THEY'RE STILL SMALL, AND I DON'T WANT THEM TO FEEL LONELY JUST BECAUSE I'M SELF-INDULGENT...
WHY DON'T YOU WANT THEM TO BE LONELY?
WELL, THEY'RE MY KIDS, AND...
AND?
AND I...
...LOVE...
...THEM.

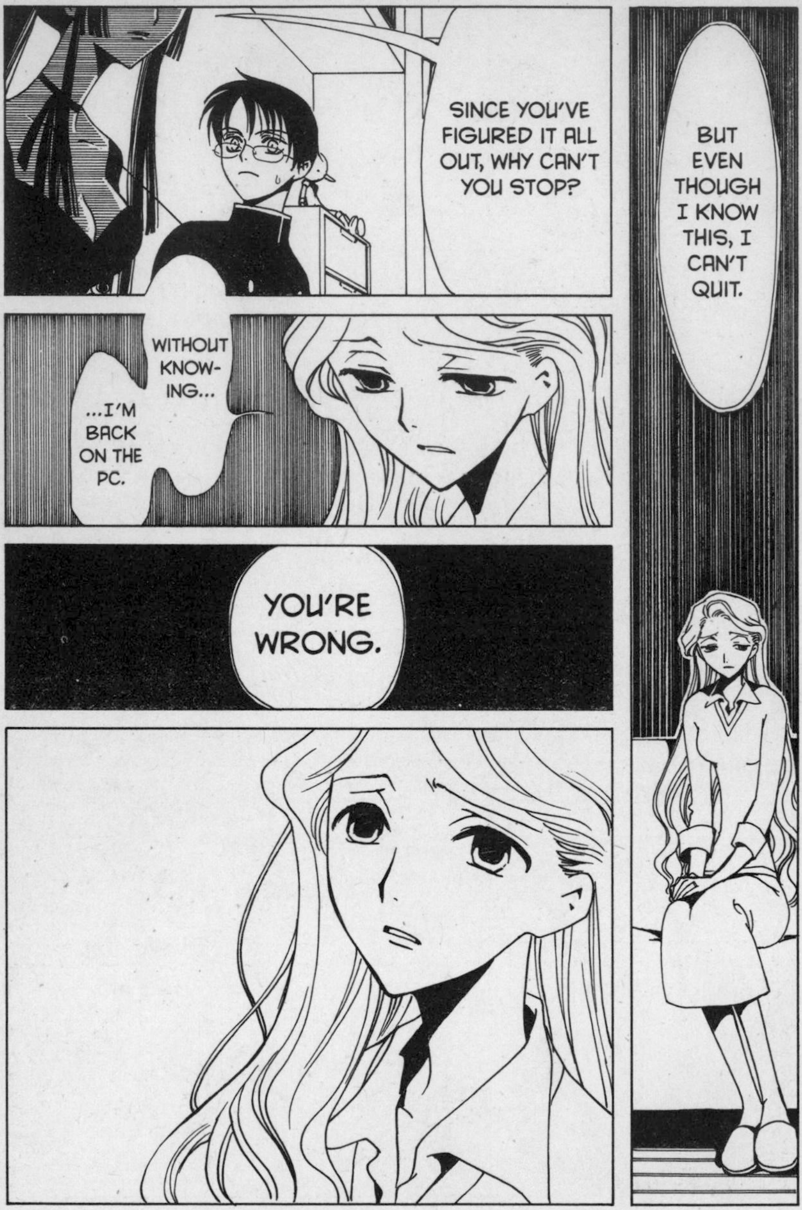
BUT EVEN THOUGH I KNOW THIS, I CAN'T QUIT.
SINCE YOU'VE FIGURED IT ALL OUT, WHY CAN'T YOU STOP?
WITHOUT KNOWING...
...I'M BACK ON THE PC.
YOU'RE WRONG.

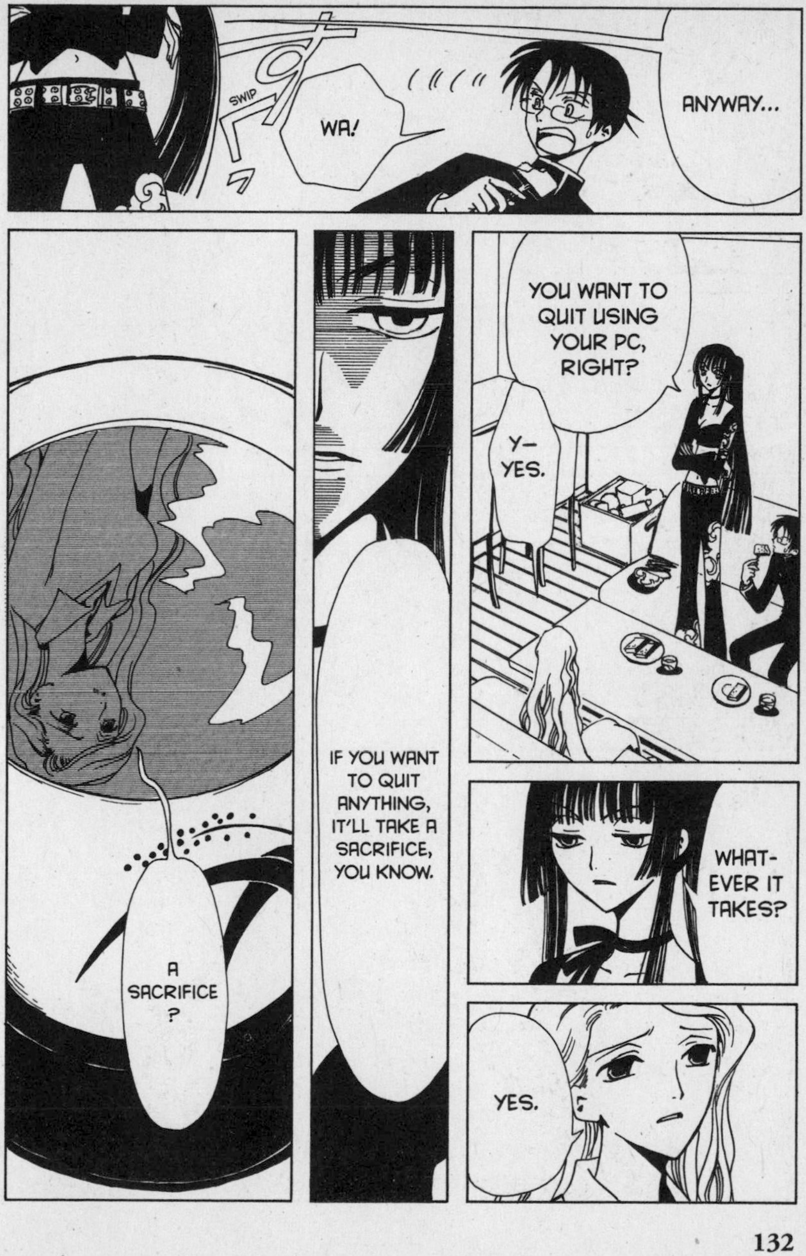

ANYWAY...
WA!
SWIP
YOU WANT TO QUIT USING YOUR PC, RIGHT?
Y— YES.
WHAT-EVER IT TAKES?
YES.
IF YOU WANT TO QUIT ANYTHING, IT'LL TAKE A SACRIFICE, YOU KNOW.
A SACRIFICE ?

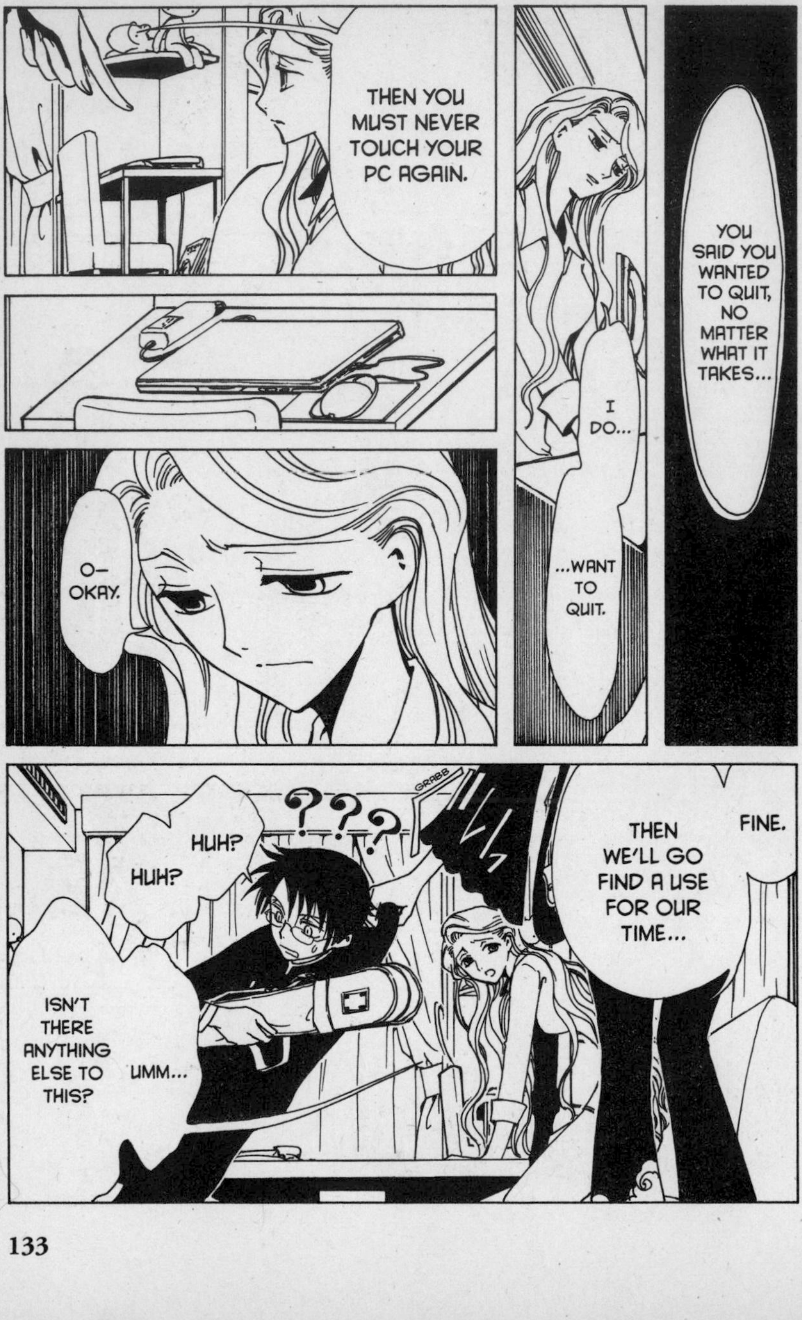
YOU SAID YOU WANTED TO QUIT, NO MATTER WHAT IT TAKES...
I DO...
...WANT TO QUIT.
THEN YOU MUST NEVER TOUCH YOUR PC AGAIN.
O-OKAY.
FINE.
THEN WE'LL GO FIND A USE FOR OUR TIME...
GRABB
???
HUH?
HUH?
UMM...
ISN'T THERE ANYTHING ELSE TO THIS?

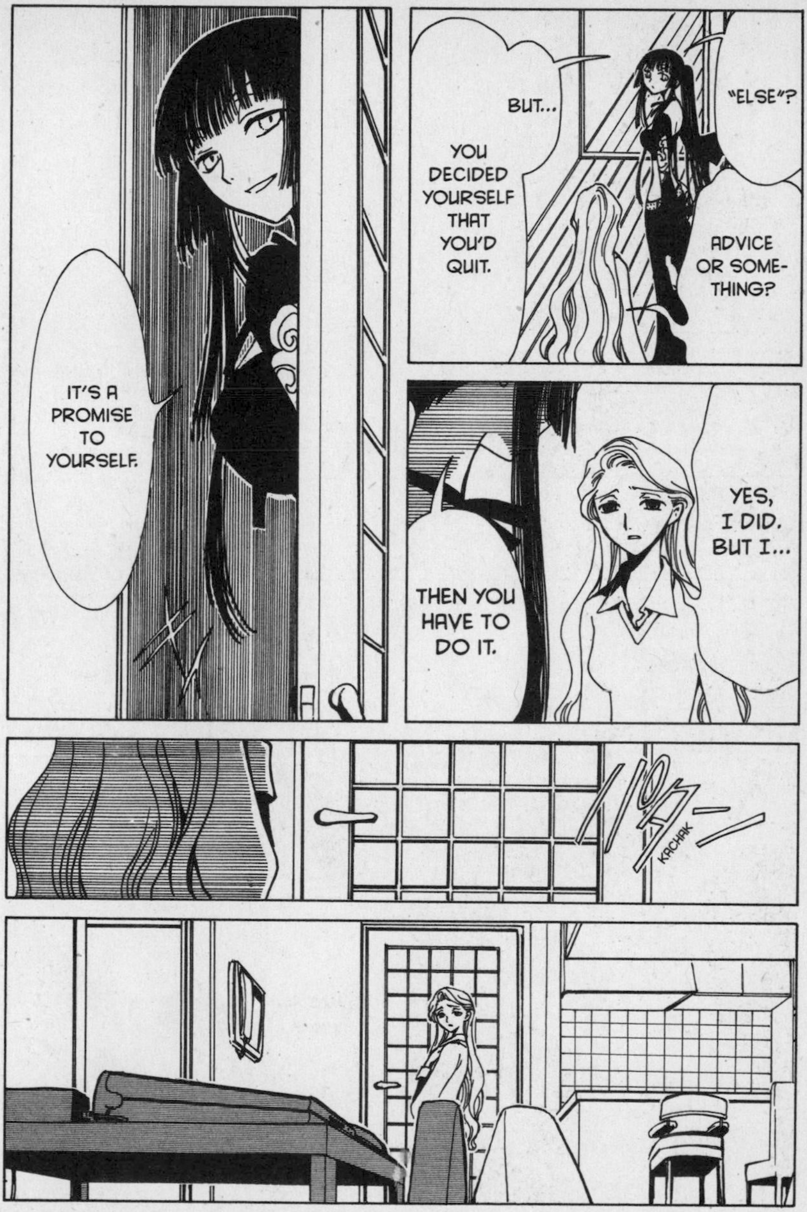
"ELSE"?
ADVICE OR SOME-THING?
BUT...
YOU DECIDED YOURSELF THAT YOU'D QUIT.
YES, I DID. BUT I...
THEN YOU HAVE TO DO IT.
IT'S A PROMISE TO YOURSELF.
KACHAK

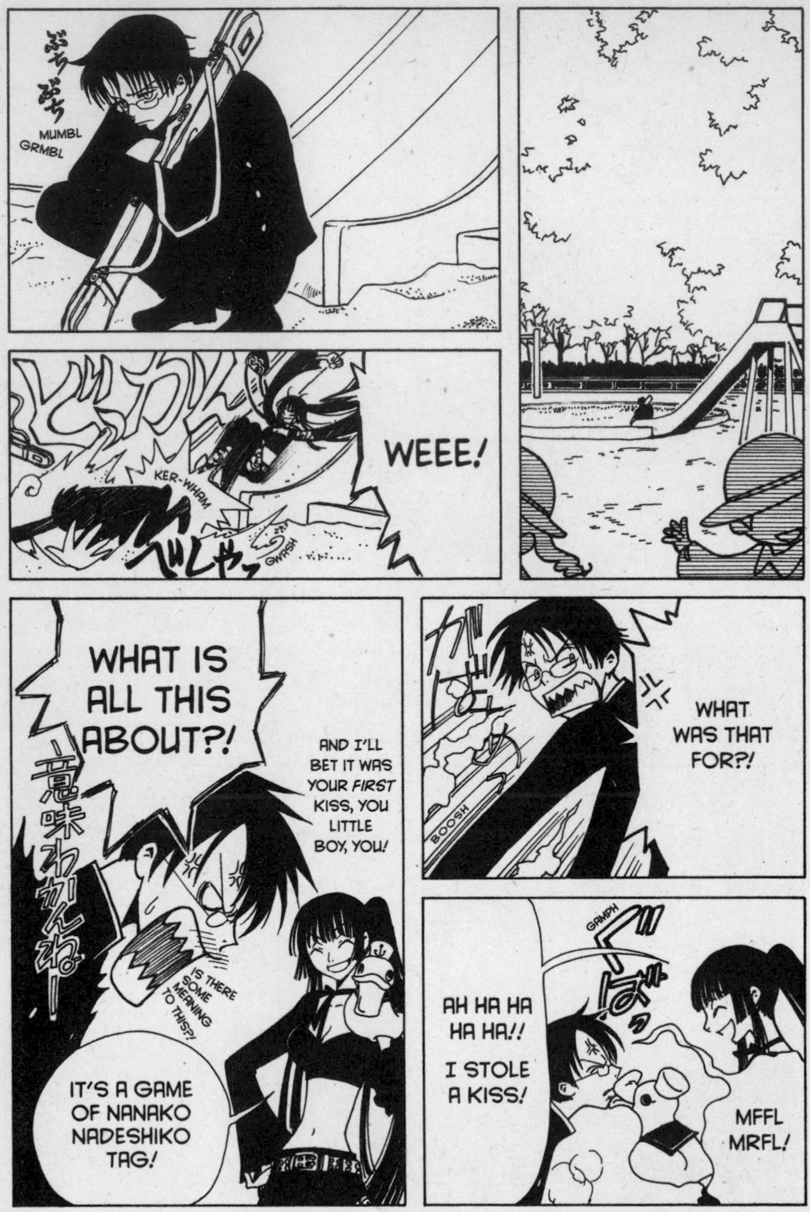
MUMBL
GRMBL
WEEE!
KER-WHAM
GWASH
WHAT WAS THAT FOR?!
BOOSH
GAMPH
AH HA HA HA HA!!
I STOLE A KISS!
MFFL MRFL!
WHAT IS ALL THIS ABOUT?!
AND I'LL BET IT WAS YOUR *FIRST* KISS, YOU LITTLE BOY, YOU!
意味わかんね!
IS THERE SOME MEANING TO THIS?!
IT'S A GAME OF NANAKO NADESHIKO TAG!

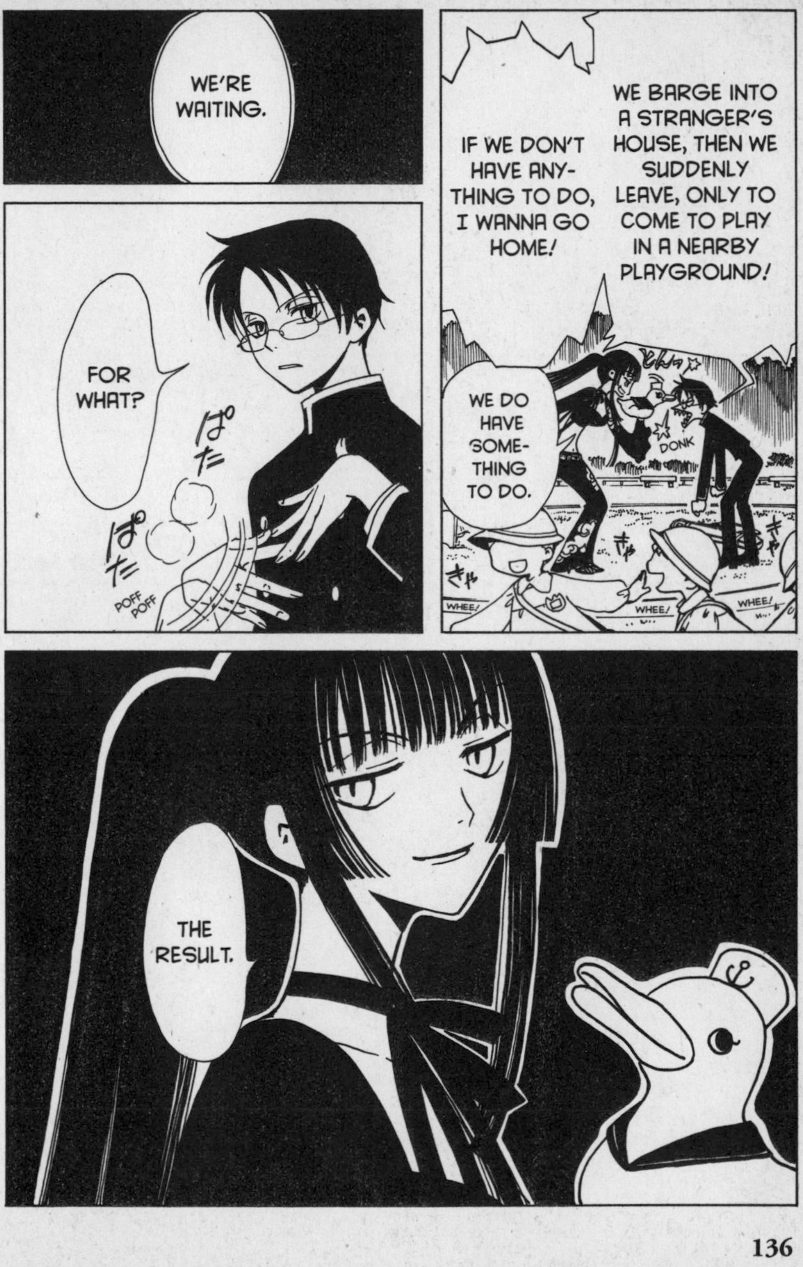
WE BARGE INTO A STRANGER'S HOUSE, THEN WE SUDDENLY LEAVE, ONLY TO COME TO PLAY IN A NEARBY PLAYGROUND!
IF WE DON'T HAVE ANY-THING TO DO, I WANNA GO HOME!
DONK
WE DO HAVE SOME-THING TO DO.
WHEE!
WHEE!
WHEE!
WE'RE WAITING.
FOR WHAT?
POFF POFF
THE RESULT.

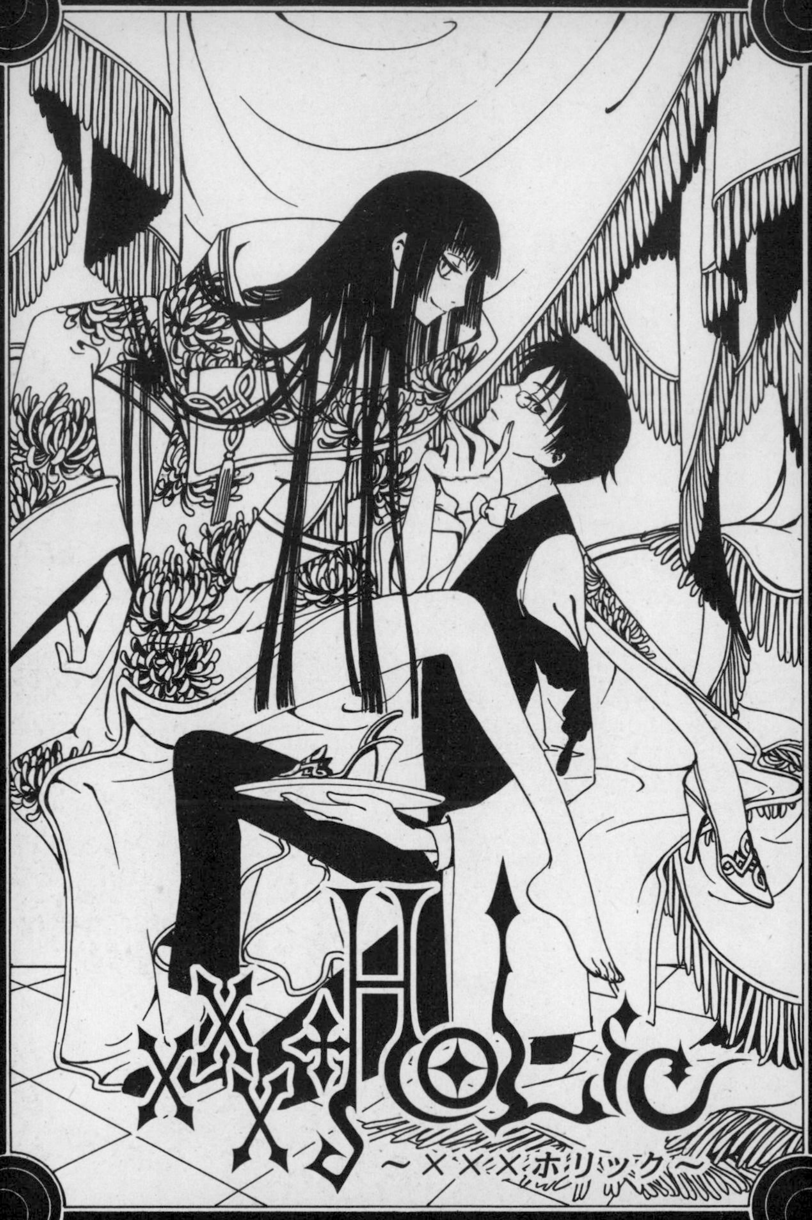
xxxHOLiC
〜×××ホリック〜

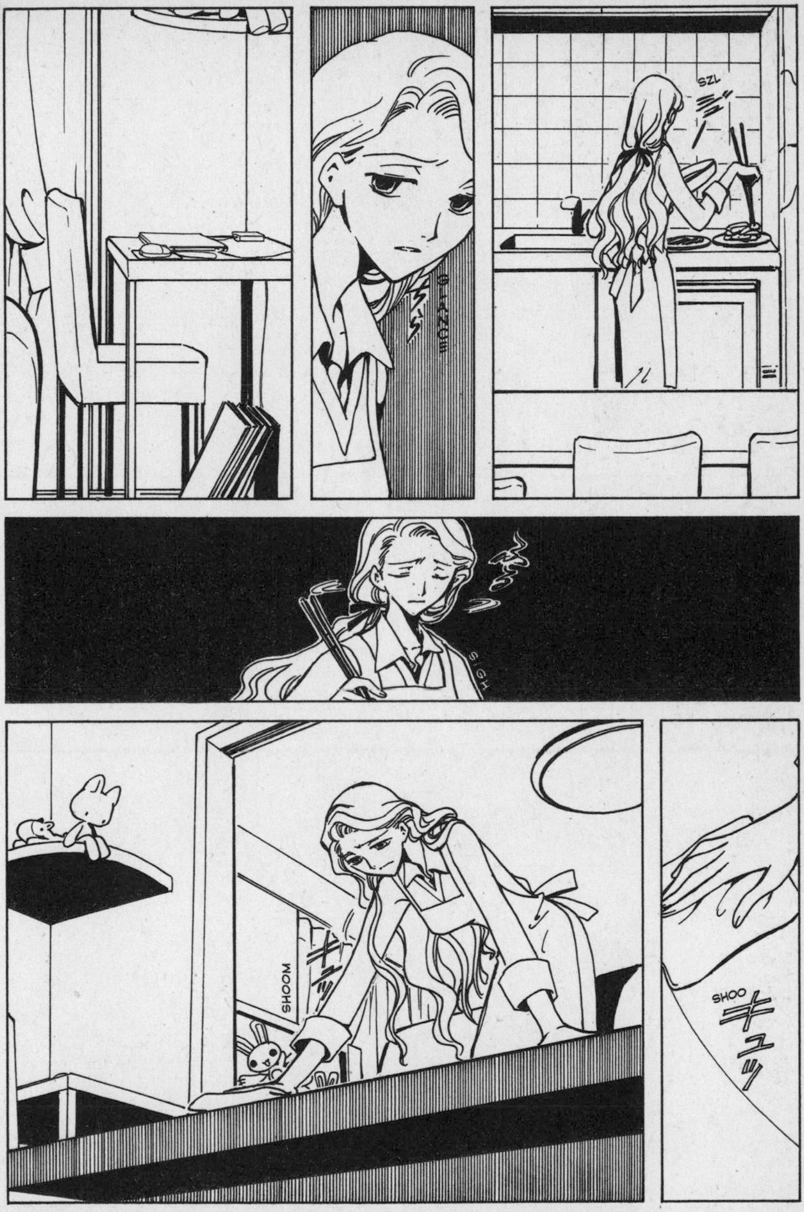
SZL
GLANCE
SIGH
SHOO
SHOOM

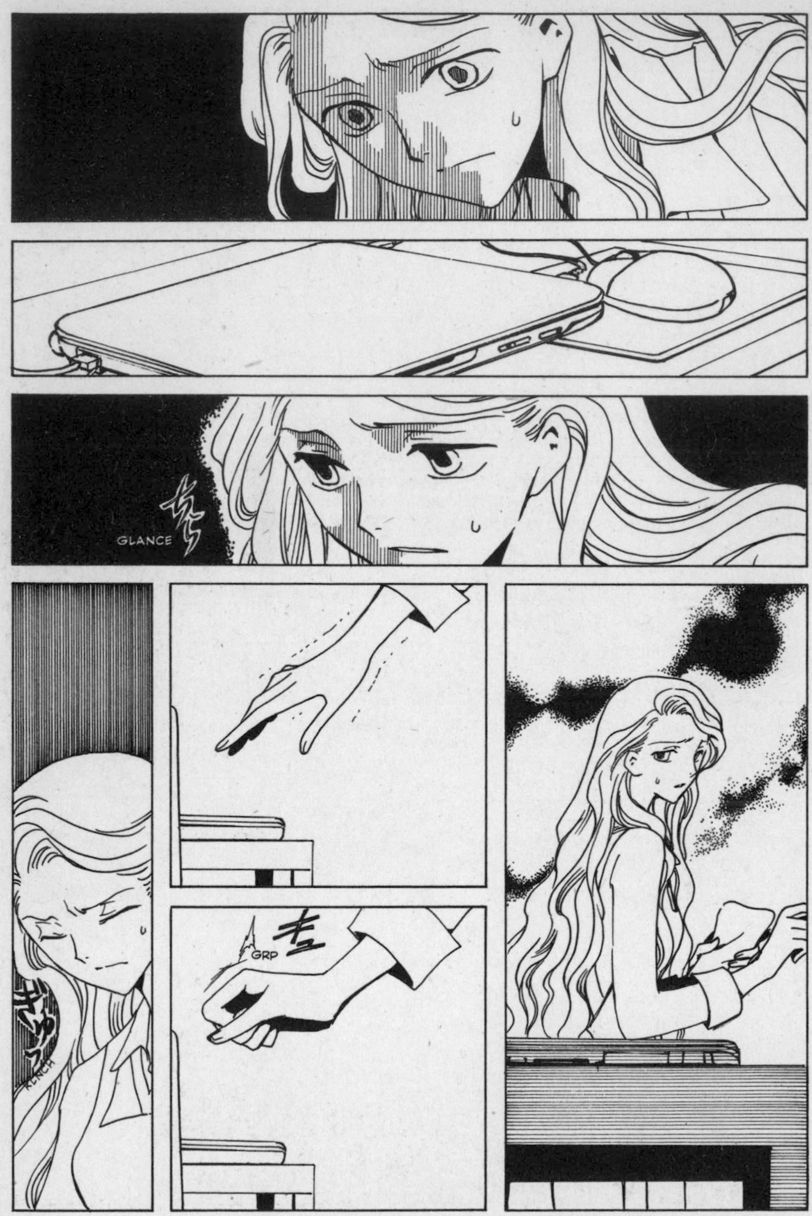
GLANCE
GRP
KLNCH

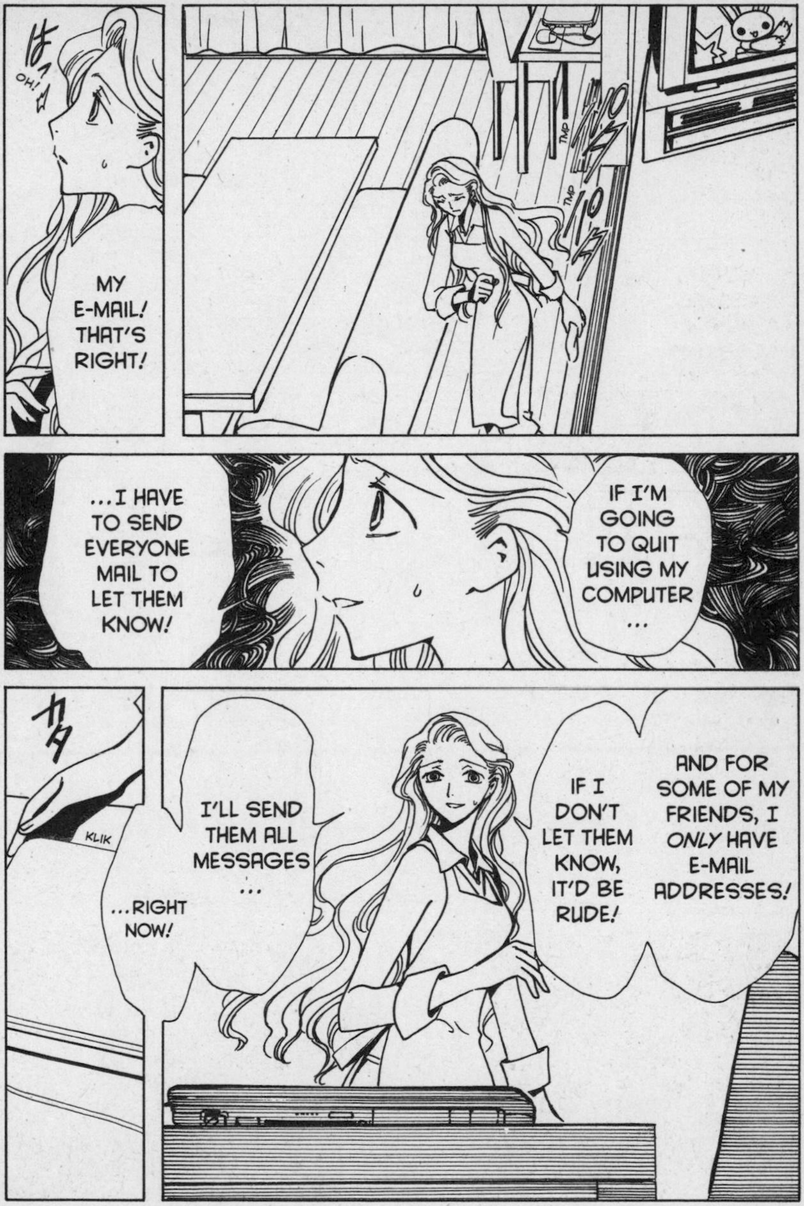
TMP
TMP
OH!
MY E-MAIL! THAT'S RIGHT!
IF I'M GOING TO QUIT USING MY COMPUTER ...
...I HAVE TO SEND EVERYONE MAIL TO LET THEM KNOW!
AND FOR SOME OF MY FRIENDS, I *ONLY* HAVE E-MAIL ADDRESSES!
IF I DON'T LET THEM KNOW, IT'D BE RUDE!
I'LL SEND THEM ALL MESSAGES ...
...RIGHT NOW!
KLIK

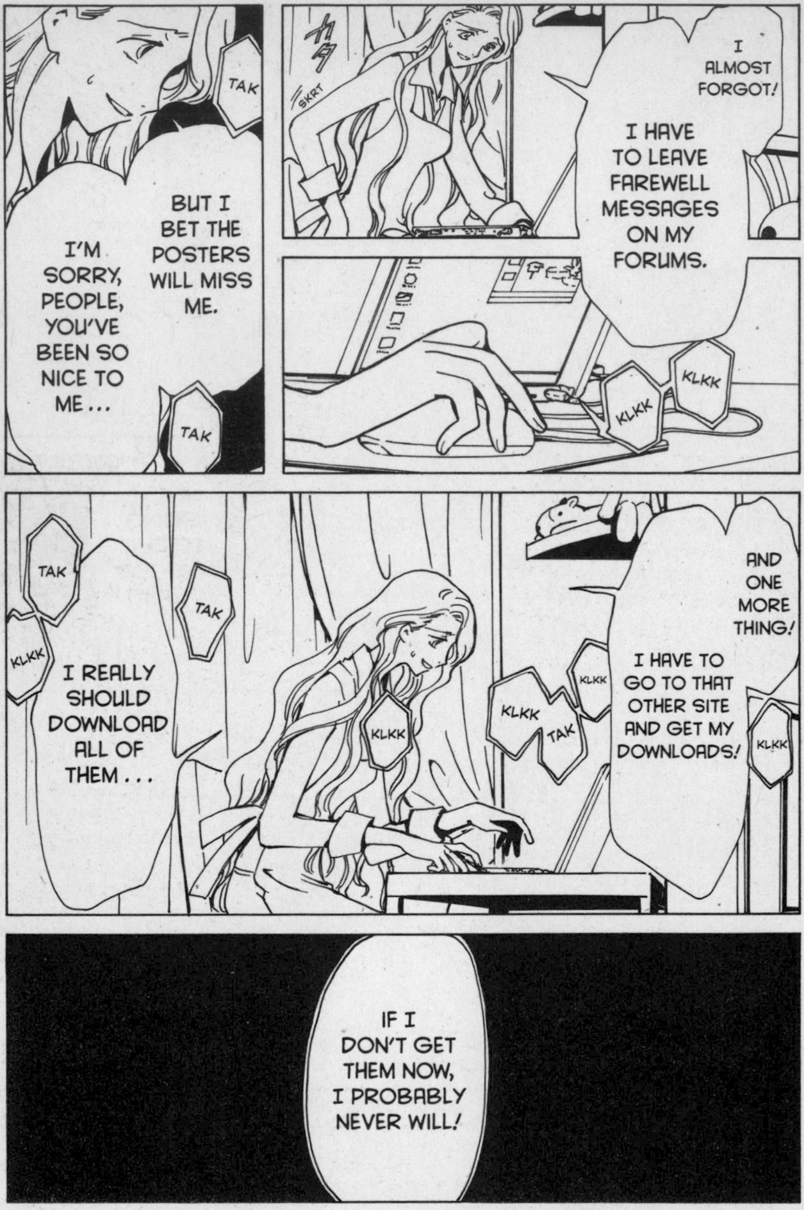
カタ
SKRT
I ALMOST FORGOT!
I HAVE TO LEAVE FAREWELL MESSAGES ON MY FORUMS.
KLKK
KLKK
TAK
BUT I BET THE POSTERS WILL MISS ME.
I'M SORRY, PEOPLE, YOU'VE BEEN SO NICE TO ME...
TAK
AND ONE MORE THING!
I HAVE TO GO TO THAT OTHER SITE AND GET MY DOWNLOADS!
KLKK
KLKK
KLKK
TAK
KLKK
TAK
TAK
KLKK
I REALLY SHOULD DOWNLOAD ALL OF THEM . . .
IF I DON'T GET THEM NOW, I PROBABLY NEVER WILL!

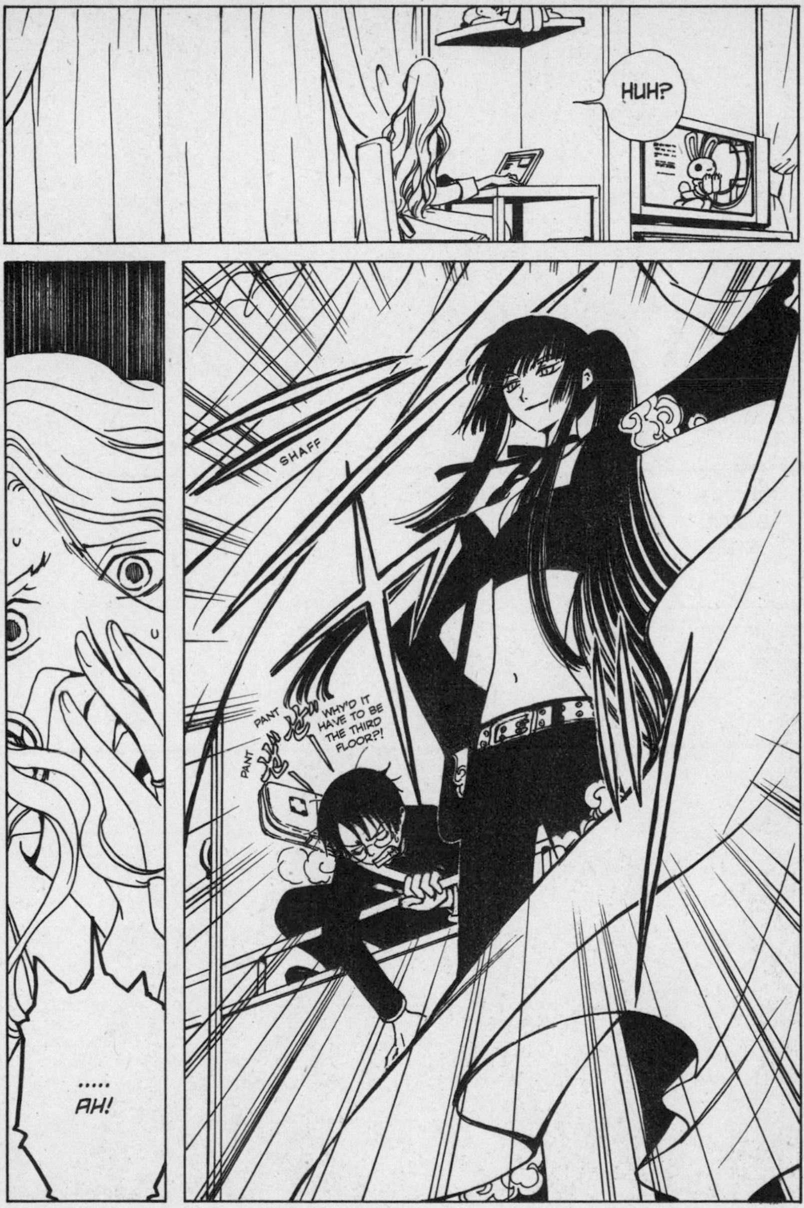
HUH?
SHAFF
PANT
PANT
WHY'D IT HAVE TO BE THE THIRD FLOOR?!
.....
AH!

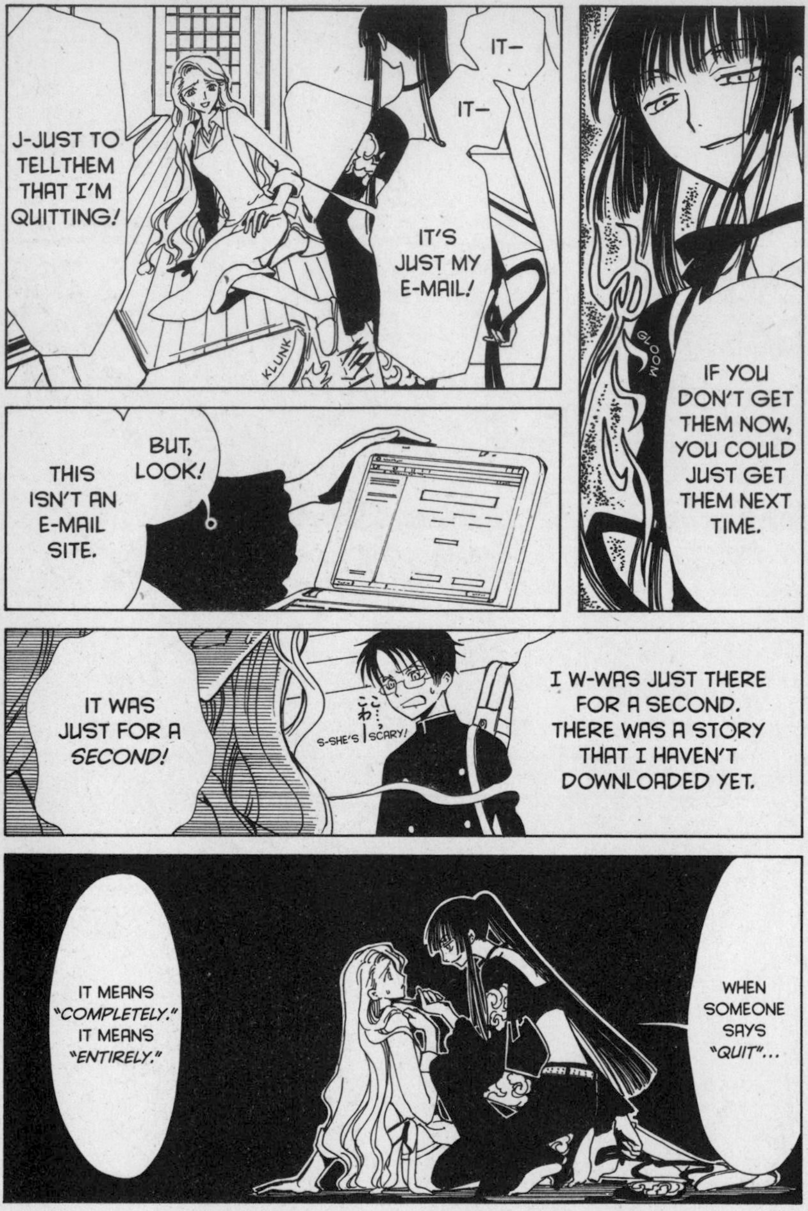

IF YOU DON'T GET THEM NOW, YOU COULD JUST GET THEM NEXT TIME.
GLOOM
IT—
IT—
IT'S JUST MY E-MAIL!
J-JUST TO TELLTHEM THAT I'M QUITTING!
KLUNK
BUT, LOOK!
THIS ISN'T AN E-MAIL SITE.
I W-WAS JUST THERE FOR A SECOND. THERE WAS A STORY THAT I HAVEN'T DOWNLOADED YET.
こわ…
S-SHE'S SCARY!
IT WAS JUST FOR A *SECOND!*
WHEN SOMEONE SAYS *"QUIT"*...
IT MEANS *"COMPLETELY."* IT MEANS *"ENTIRELY."*

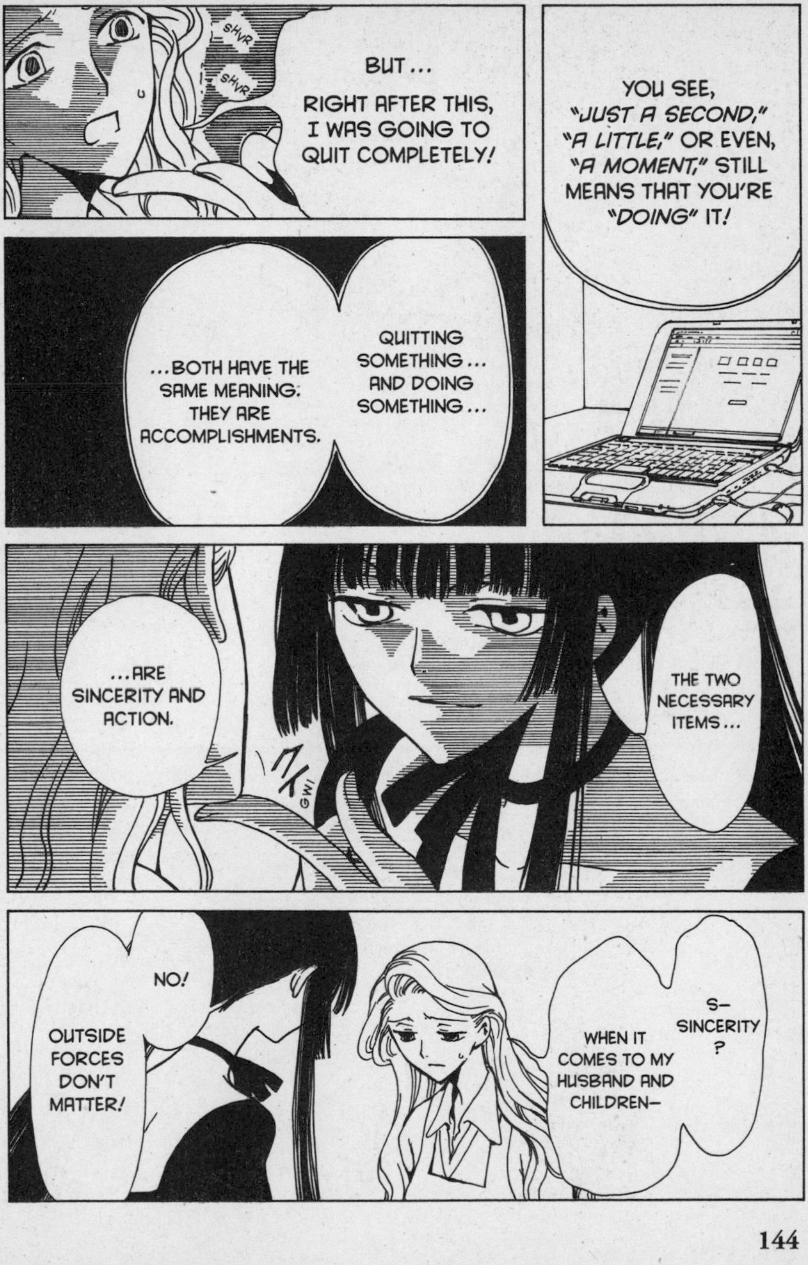
YOU SEE, "JUST A SECOND," "A LITTLE," OR EVEN, "A MOMENT," STILL MEANS THAT YOU'RE "DOING" IT!
SHVR
SHVR
BUT...
RIGHT AFTER THIS, I WAS GOING TO QUIT COMPLETELY!
QUITTING SOMETHING... AND DOING SOMETHING...
...BOTH HAVE THE SAME MEANING: THEY ARE ACCOMPLISHMENTS.
THE TWO NECESSARY ITEMS...
GWI
...ARE SINCERITY AND ACTION.
S— SINCERITY?
WHEN IT COMES TO MY HUSBAND AND CHILDREN—
NO!
OUTSIDE FORCES DON'T MATTER!

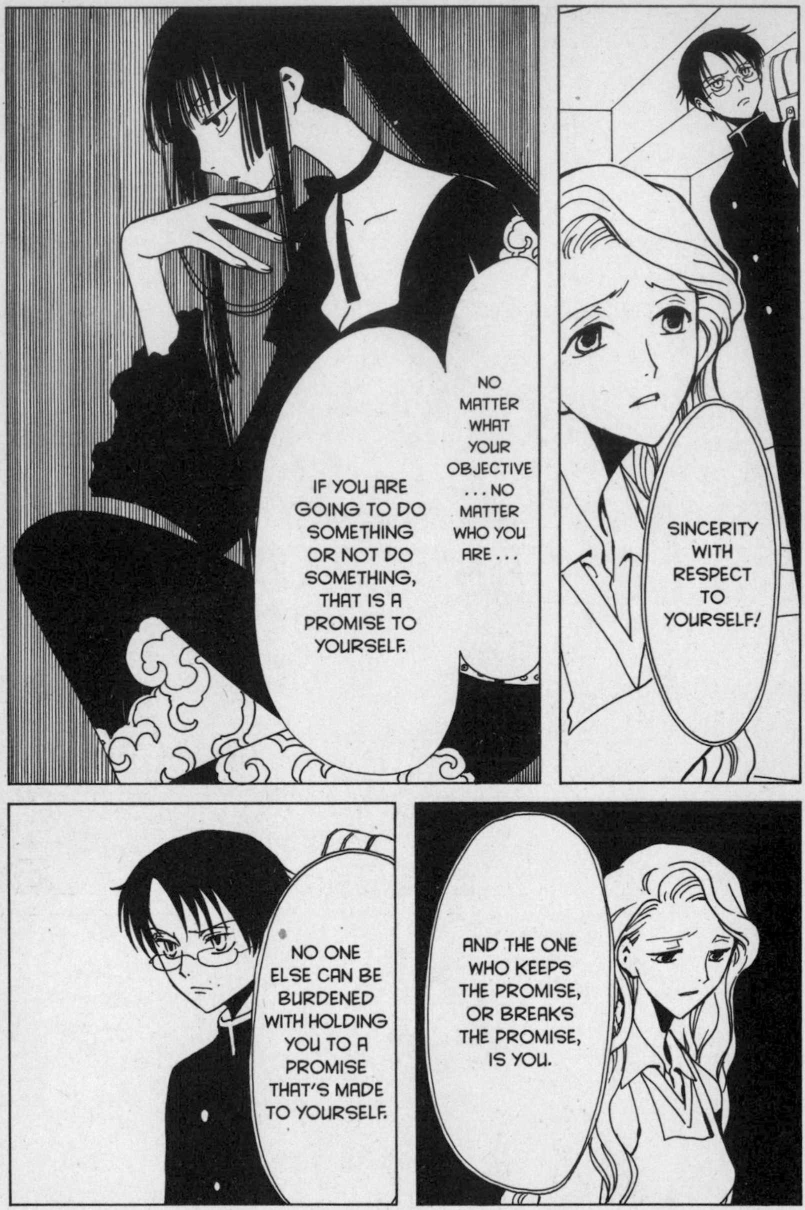
SINCERITY WITH RESPECT TO YOURSELF!
NO MATTER WHAT YOUR OBJECTIVE . . . NO MATTER WHO YOU ARE . . .
IF YOU ARE GOING TO DO SOMETHING OR NOT DO SOMETHING, THAT IS A PROMISE TO YOURSELF.
AND THE ONE WHO KEEPS THE PROMISE, OR BREAKS THE PROMISE, IS YOU.
NO ONE ELSE CAN BE BURDENED WITH HOLDING YOU TO A PROMISE THAT'S MADE TO YOURSELF.

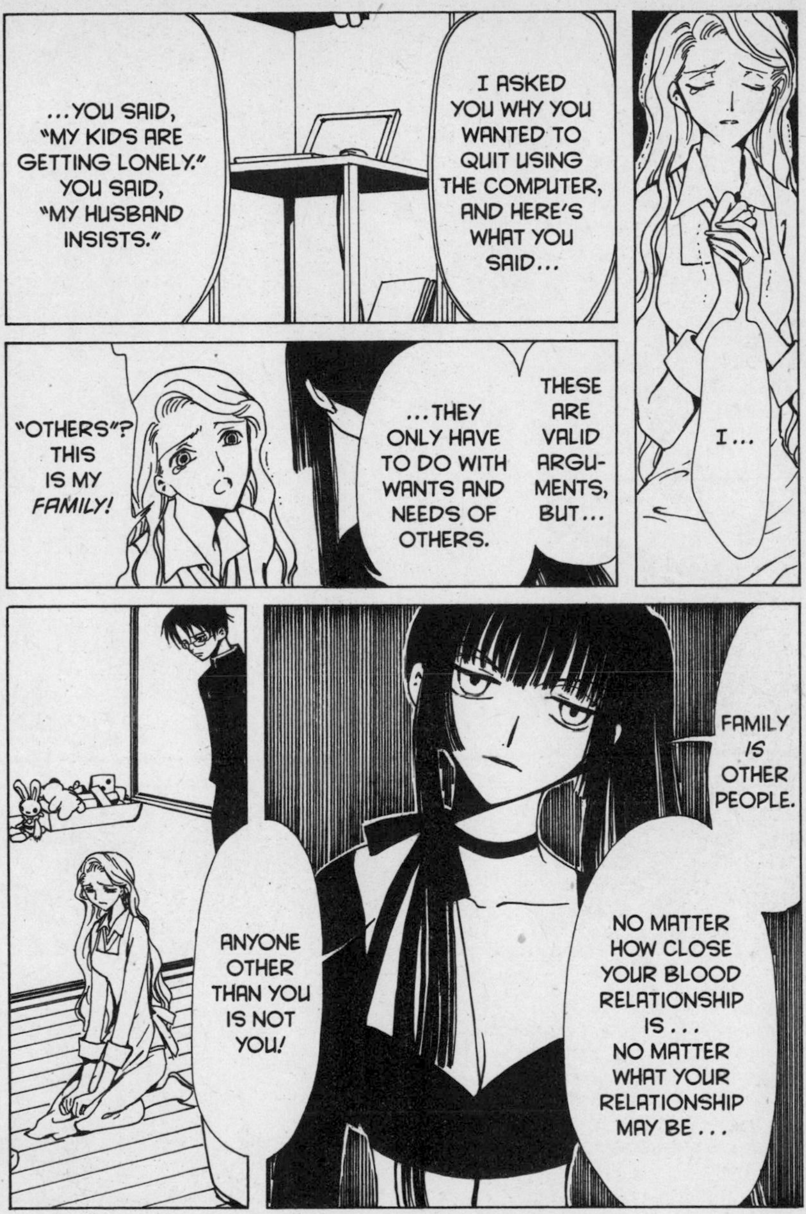
I...
I ASKED YOU WHY YOU WANTED TO QUIT USING THE COMPUTER, AND HERE'S WHAT YOU SAID...
...YOU SAID, "MY KIDS ARE GETTING LONELY." YOU SAID, "MY HUSBAND INSISTS."
THESE ARE VALID ARGU- MENTS, BUT...
...THEY ONLY HAVE TO DO WITH WANTS AND NEEDS OF OTHERS.
"OTHERS"? THIS IS MY *FAMILY!*
FAMILY *IS* OTHER PEOPLE.
NO MATTER HOW CLOSE YOUR BLOOD RELATIONSHIP IS... NO MATTER WHAT YOUR RELATIONSHIP MAY BE...
ANYONE OTHER THAN YOU IS NOT YOU!

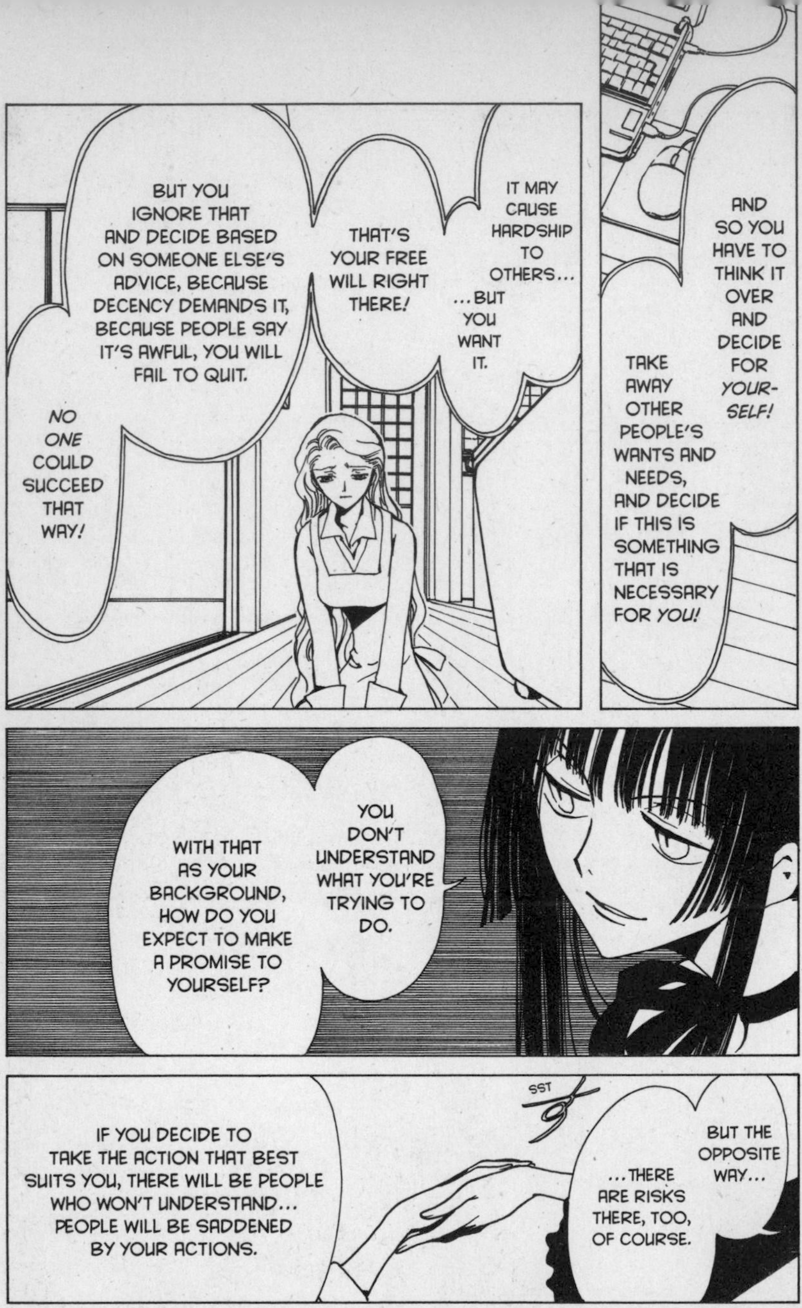
AND SO YOU HAVE TO THINK IT OVER AND DECIDE FOR *YOURSELF!*
TAKE AWAY OTHER PEOPLE'S WANTS AND NEEDS, AND DECIDE IF THIS IS SOMETHING THAT IS NECESSARY FOR *YOU!*
IT MAY CAUSE HARDSHIP TO OTHERS...
...BUT YOU WANT IT.
THAT'S YOUR FREE WILL RIGHT THERE!
BUT YOU IGNORE THAT AND DECIDE BASED ON SOMEONE ELSE'S ADVICE, BECAUSE DECENCY DEMANDS IT, BECAUSE PEOPLE SAY IT'S AWFUL, YOU WILL FAIL TO QUIT.
NO ONE COULD SUCCEED THAT WAY!
YOU DON'T UNDERSTAND WHAT YOU'RE TRYING TO DO.
WITH THAT AS YOUR BACKGROUND, HOW DO YOU EXPECT TO MAKE A PROMISE TO YOURSELF?
SST
BUT THE OPPOSITE WAY...
...THERE ARE RISKS THERE, TOO, OF COURSE.
IF YOU DECIDE TO TAKE THE ACTION THAT BEST SUITS YOU, THERE WILL BE PEOPLE WHO WON'T UNDERSTAND... PEOPLE WILL BE SADDENED BY YOUR ACTIONS.

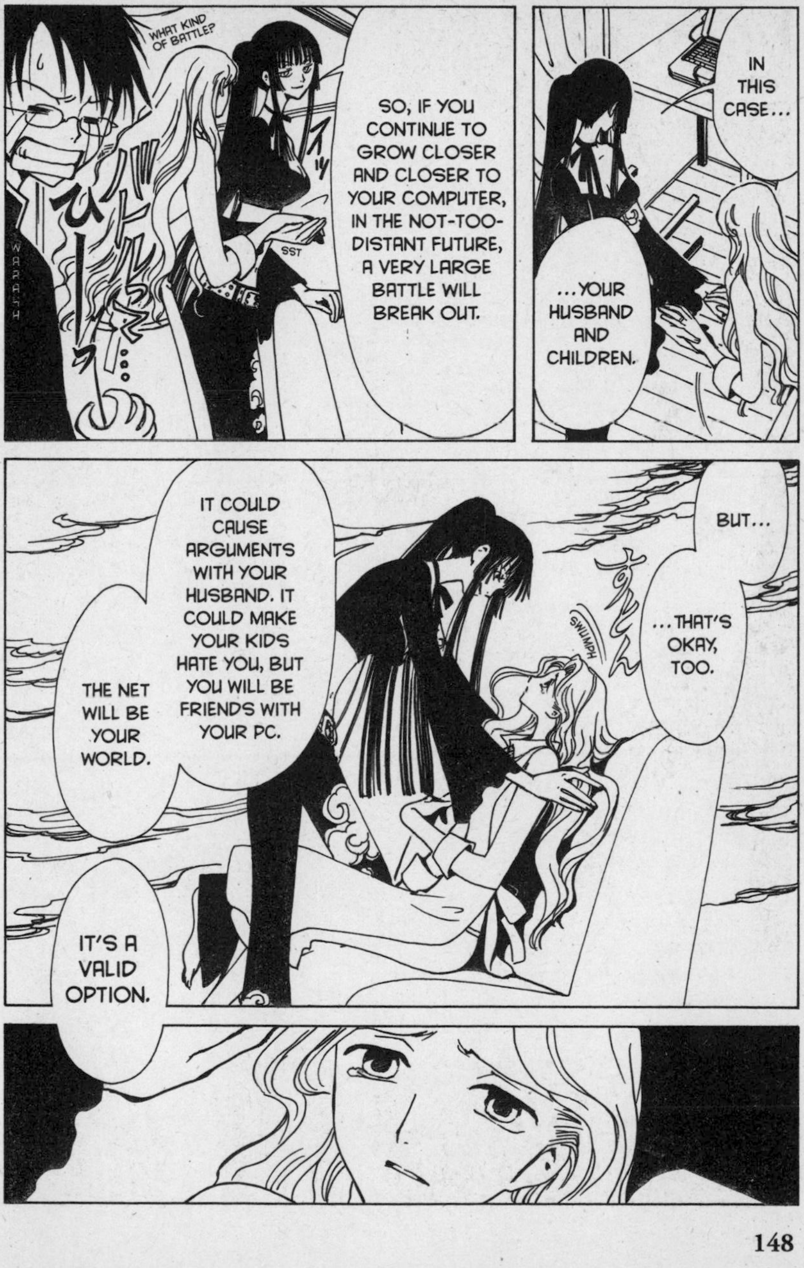
IN THIS CASE...
...YOUR HUSBAND AND CHILDREN.
SO, IF YOU CONTINUE TO GROW CLOSER AND CLOSER TO YOUR COMPUTER, IN THE NOT-TOO-DISTANT FUTURE, A VERY LARGE BATTLE WILL BREAK OUT.
SST
WHAT KIND OF BATTLE?
WARASH
BUT...
...THAT'S OKAY, TOO.
SWUMPH
IT COULD CAUSE ARGUMENTS WITH YOUR HUSBAND. IT COULD MAKE YOUR KIDS HATE YOU, BUT YOU WILL BE FRIENDS WITH YOUR PC.
THE NET WILL BE YOUR WORLD.
IT'S A VALID OPTION.

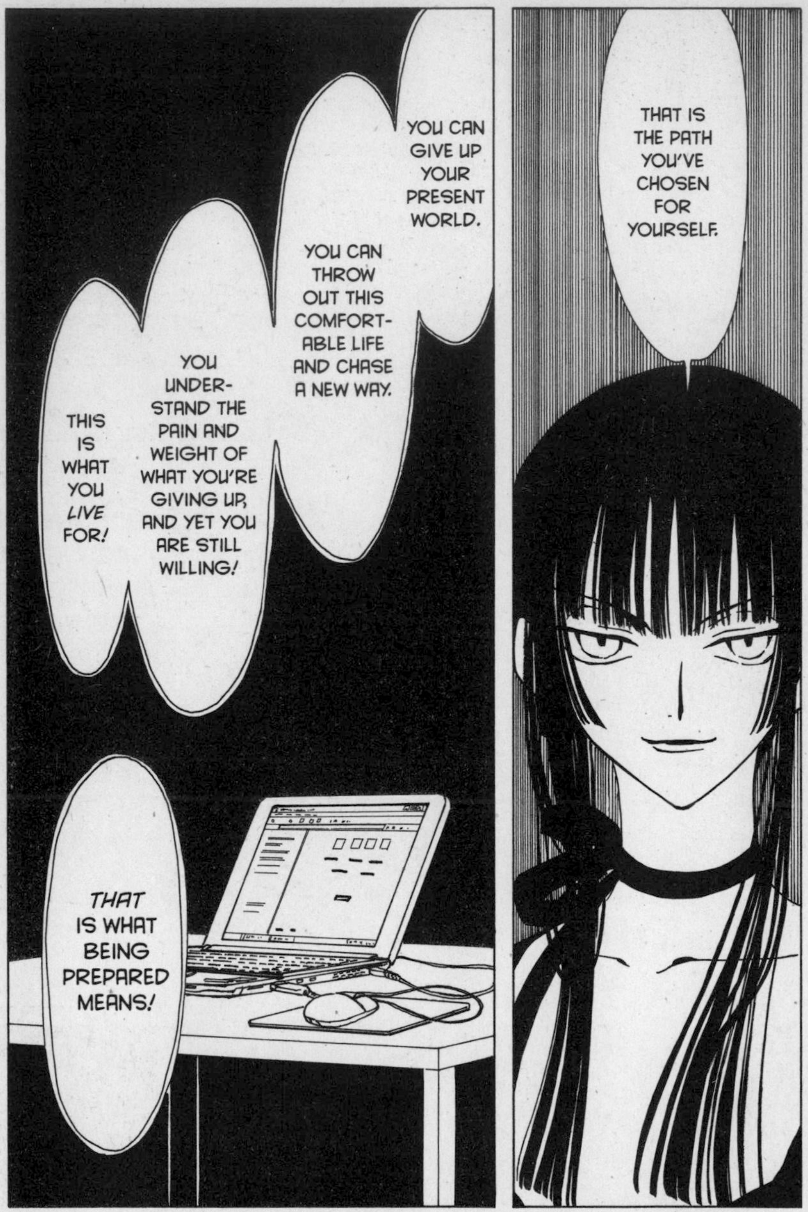
THAT IS THE PATH YOU'VE CHOSEN FOR YOURSELF.
YOU CAN GIVE UP YOUR PRESENT WORLD.
YOU CAN THROW OUT THIS COMFORT-ABLE LIFE AND CHASE A NEW WAY.
YOU UNDER-STAND THE PAIN AND WEIGHT OF WHAT YOU'RE GIVING UP, AND YET YOU ARE STILL WILLING!
THIS IS WHAT YOU *LIVE* FOR!
THAT IS WHAT BEING PREPARED MEANS!

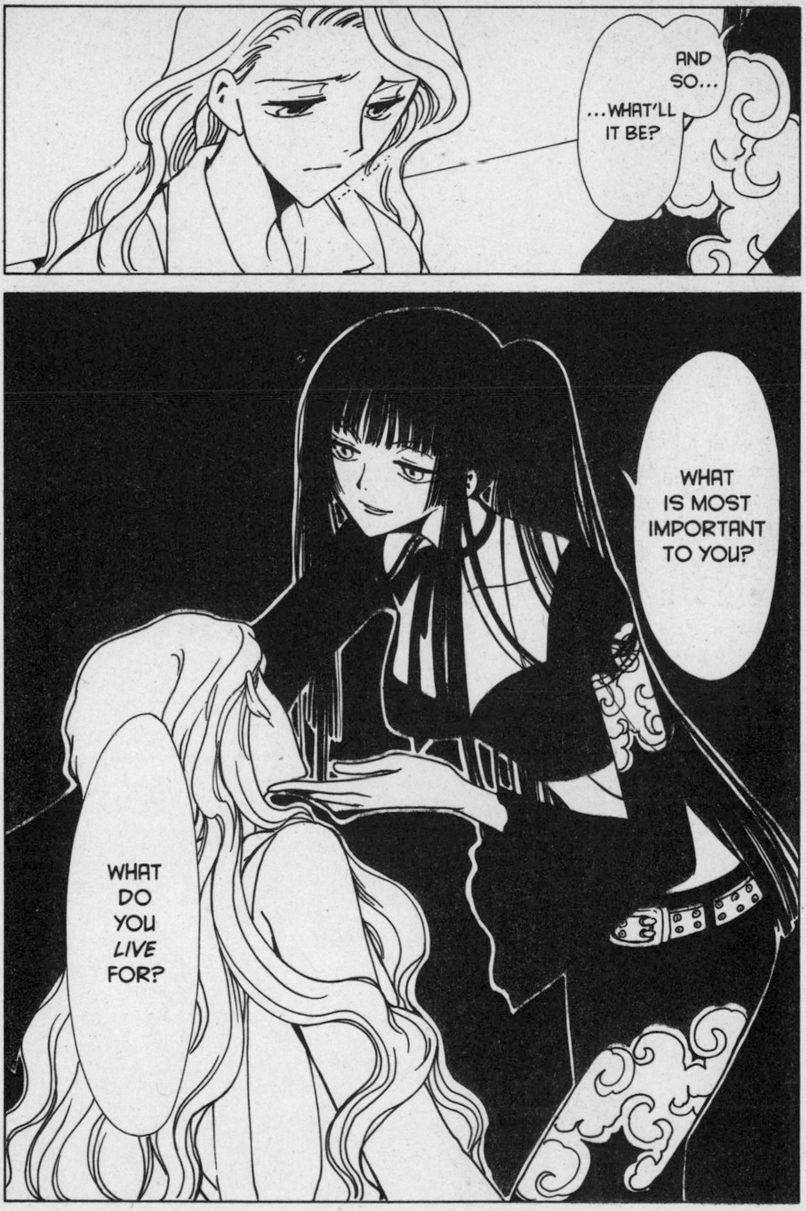
AND SO...
...WHAT'LL IT BE?
WHAT IS MOST IMPORTANT TO YOU?
WHAT DO YOU *LIVE* FOR?

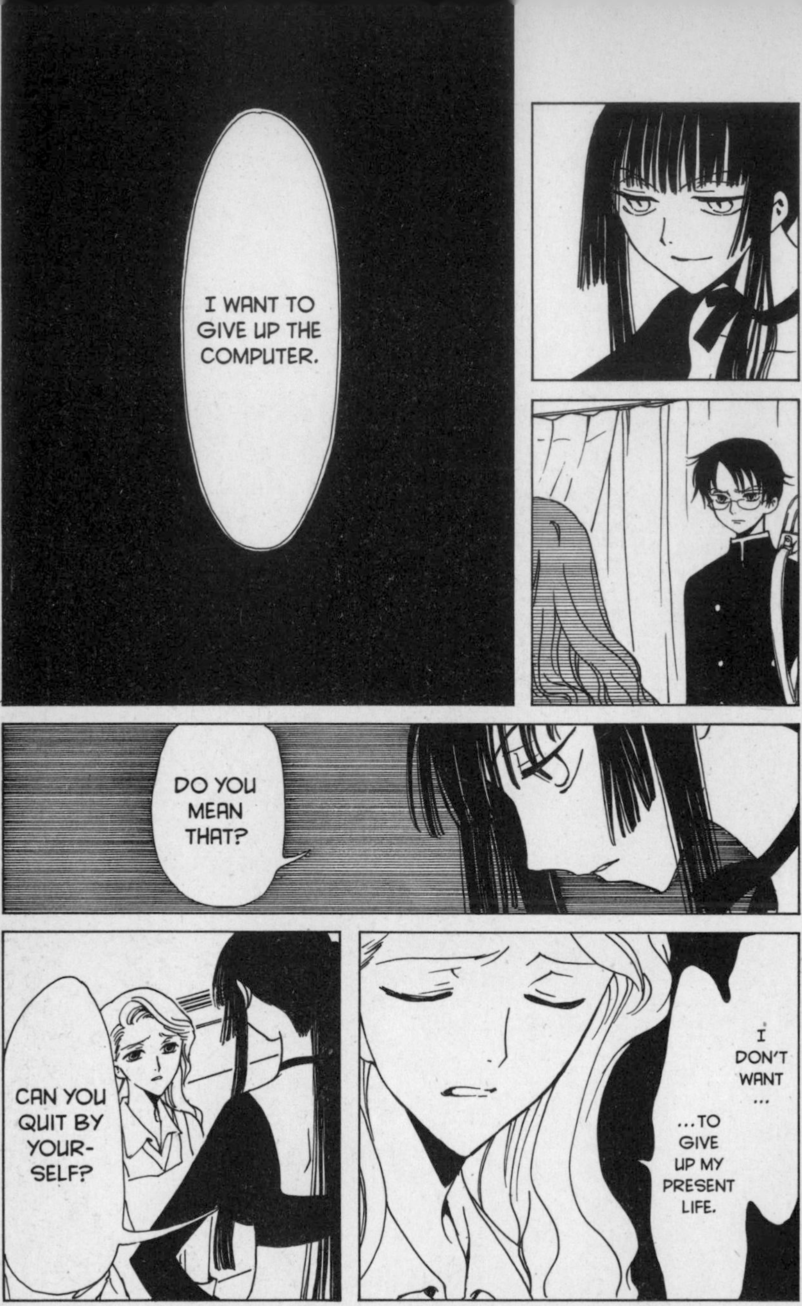
I WANT TO GIVE UP THE COMPUTER.
DO YOU MEAN THAT?
I DON'T WANT ...
...TO GIVE UP MY PRESENT LIFE.
CAN YOU QUIT BY YOUR-SELF?

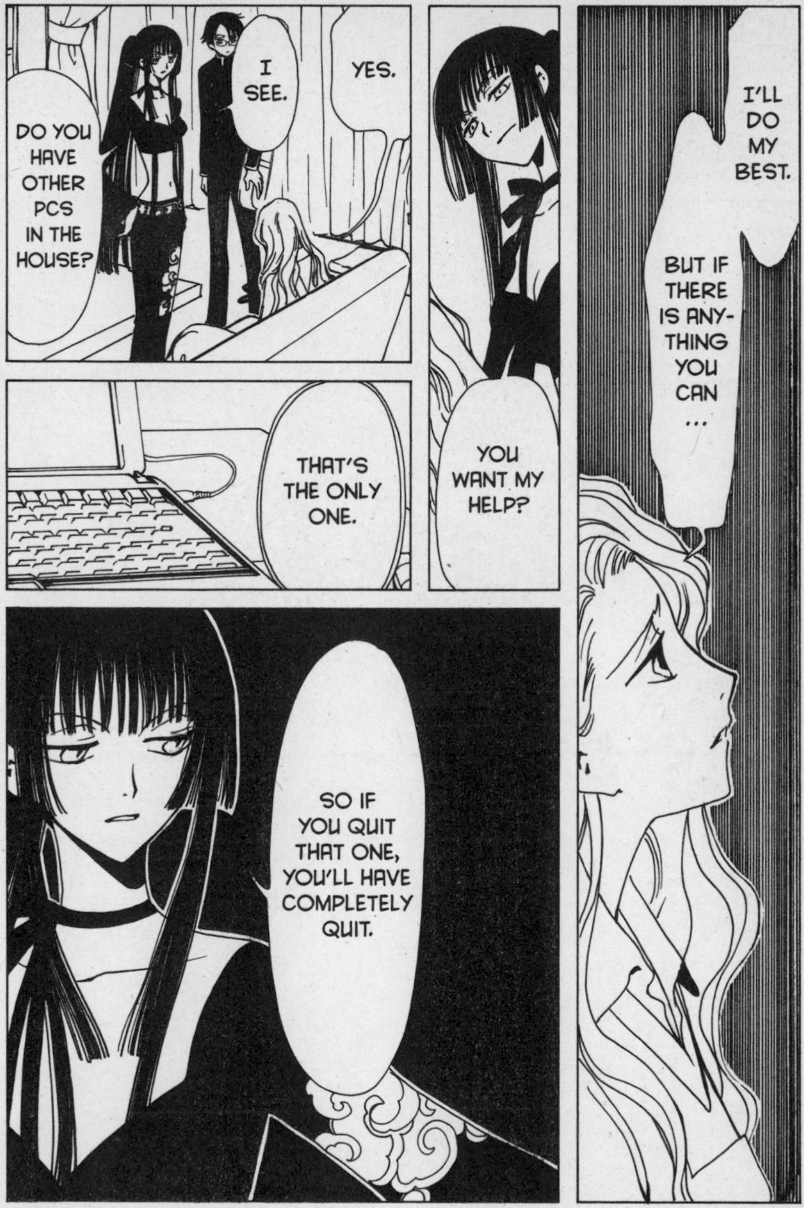
I'LL DO MY BEST.
BUT IF THERE IS ANY-THING YOU CAN ...
YOU WANT MY HELP?
YES.
I SEE.
DO YOU HAVE OTHER PCS IN THE HOUSE?
THAT'S THE ONLY ONE.
SO IF YOU QUIT THAT ONE, YOU'LL HAVE COMPLETELY QUIT.

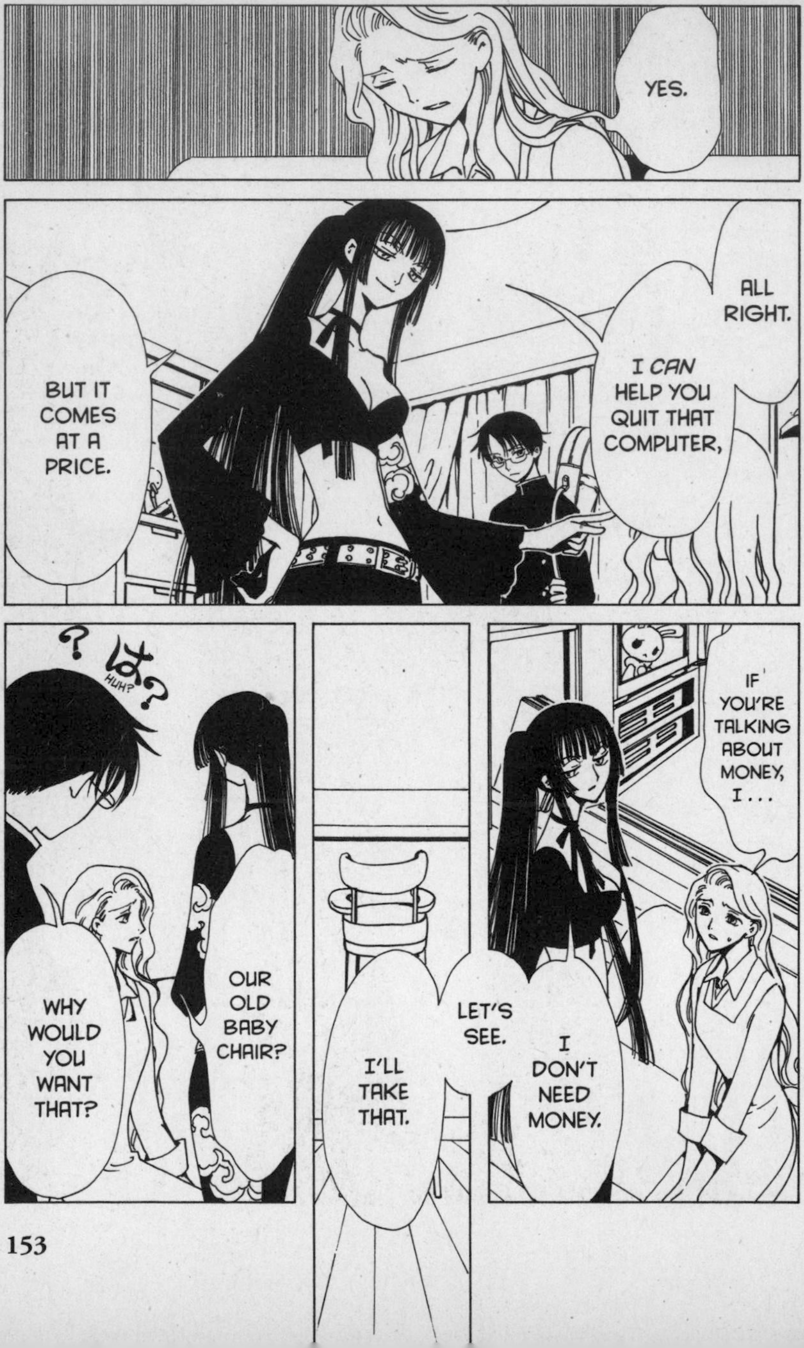
YES.
ALL RIGHT.
I *CAN* HELP YOU QUIT THAT COMPUTER,
BUT IT COMES AT A PRICE.
IF YOU'RE TALKING ABOUT MONEY, I . . .
I DON'T NEED MONEY.
LET'S SEE.
I'LL TAKE THAT.
? は? ?
HUH?
OUR OLD BABY CHAIR?
WHY WOULD YOU WANT THAT?

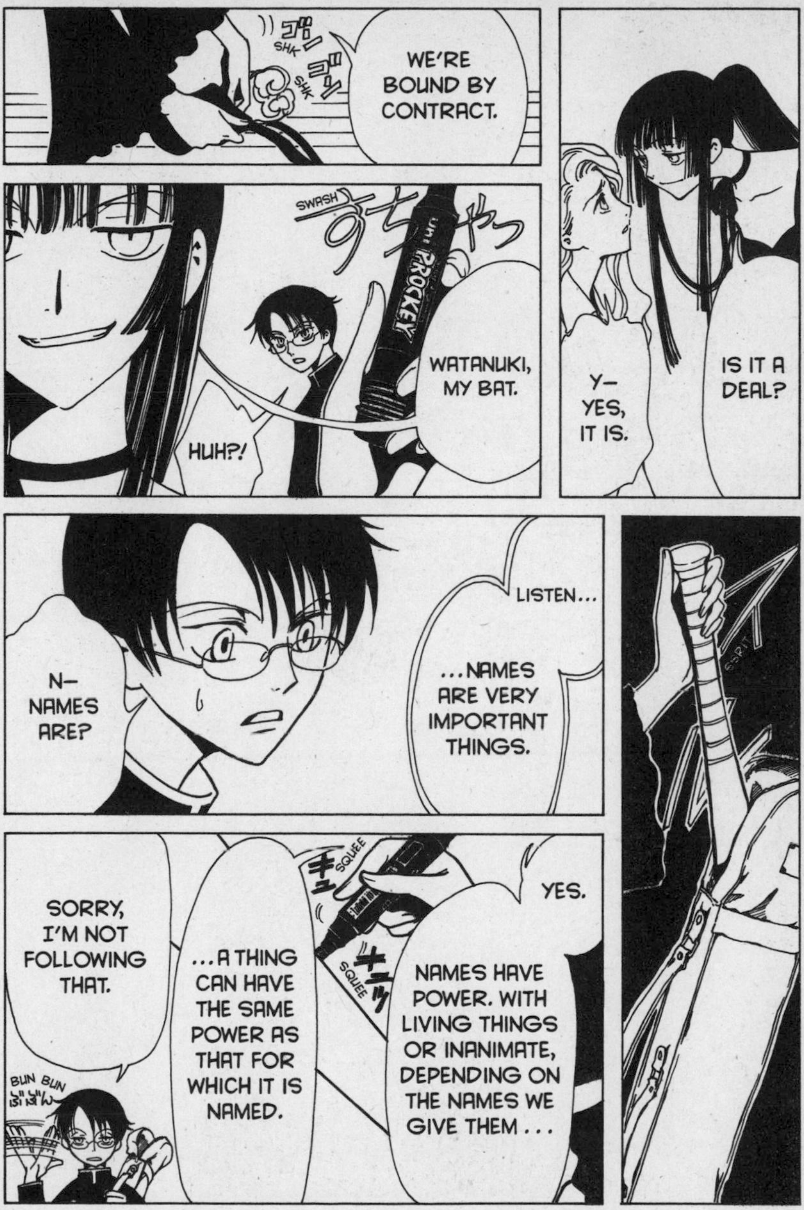
IS IT A DEAL?
Y— YES, IT IS.
SHK SHK
WE'RE BOUND BY CONTRACT.
SWASH
PROCKEY
WATANUKI, MY BAT.
HUH?!
SSPIT
LISTEN...
...NAMES ARE VERY IMPORTANT THINGS.
N— NAMES ARE?
SQUEE SQUEE
YES.
NAMES HAVE POWER. WITH LIVING THINGS OR INANIMATE, DEPENDING ON THE NAMES WE GIVE THEM . . .
...A THING CAN HAVE THE SAME POWER AS THAT FOR WHICH IT IS NAMED.
SORRY, I'M NOT FOLLOWING THAT.
BUN BUN

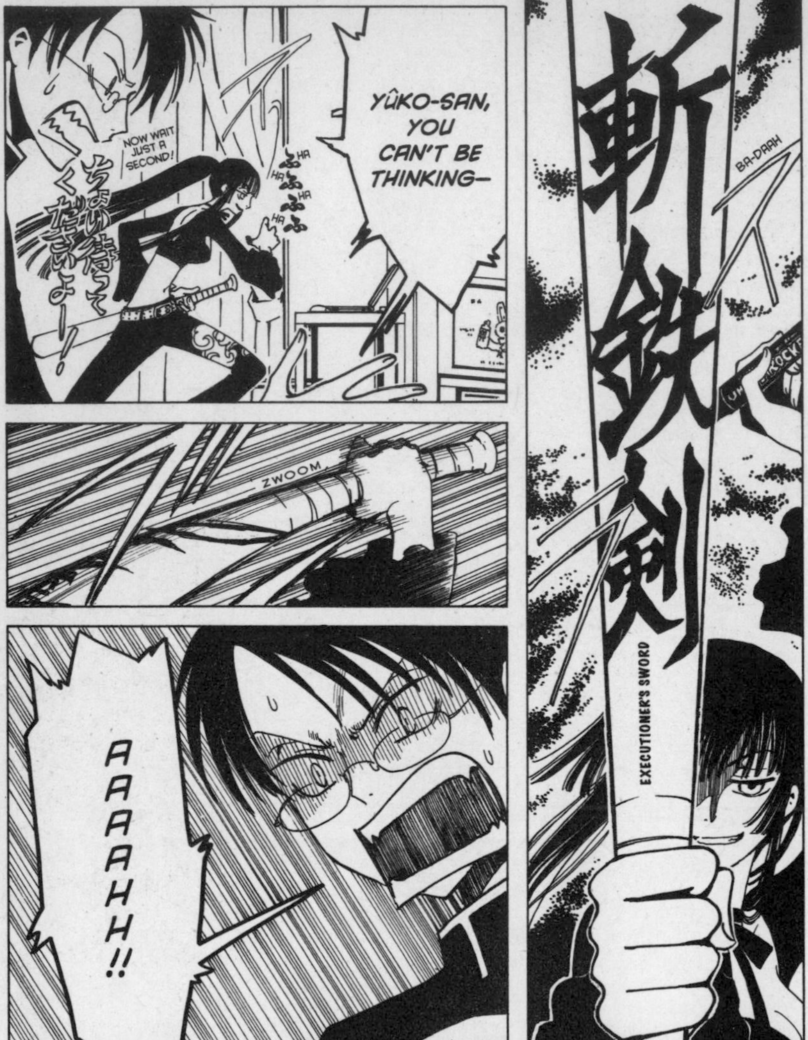
斬鉄剣
EXECUTIONER'S SWORD
BA-DAAH
YÛKO-SAN, YOU CAN'T BE THINKING—
ふふふふ
HA HA HA HA
ちょっと待ってくださいよー!
NOW WAIT JUST A SECOND!
ZWOOM
AAAAAAHH!!

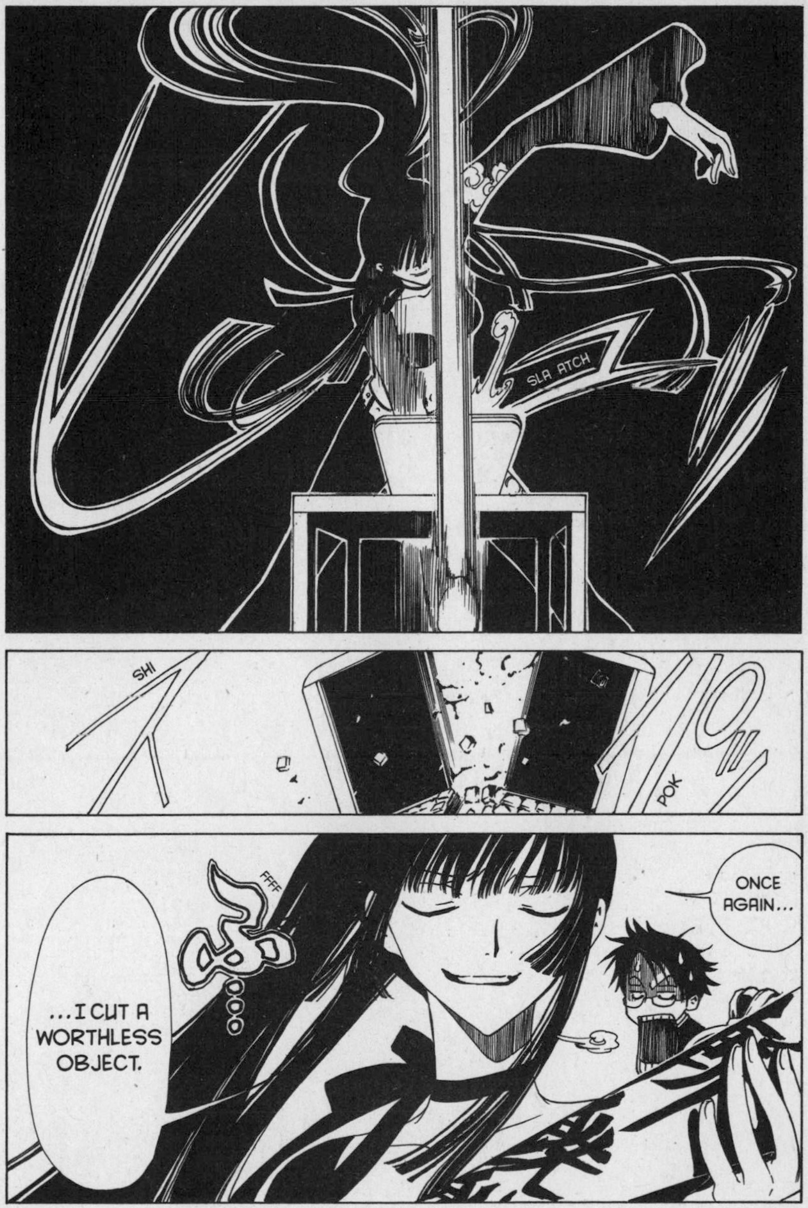
SLA ATCH
POK
SHI
ONCE AGAIN...
FFFF
...I CUT A WORTHLESS OBJECT.

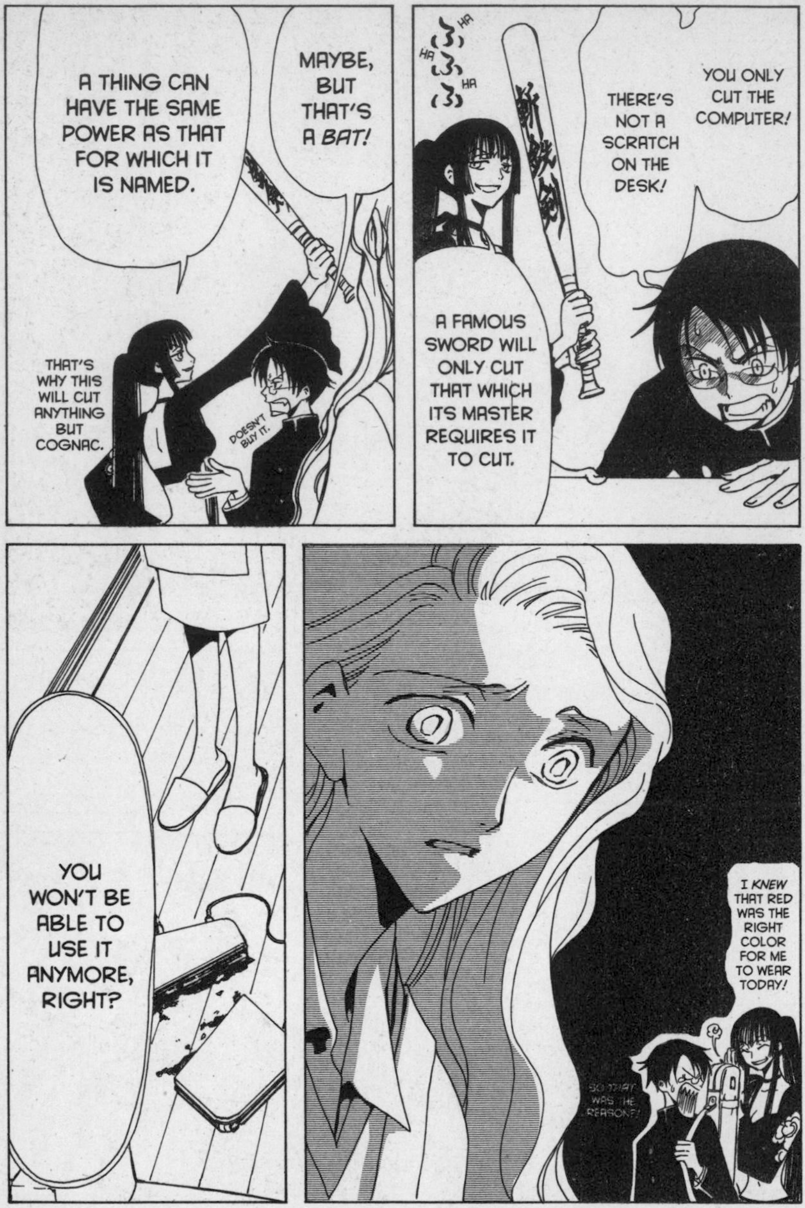
YOU ONLY CUT THE COMPUTER!
THERE'S NOT A SCRATCH ON THE DESK!
ふ HA ふ HA ふ HA
A FAMOUS SWORD WILL ONLY CUT THAT WHICH ITS MASTER REQUIRES IT TO CUT.
MAYBE, BUT THAT'S A *BAT*!
A THING CAN HAVE THE SAME POWER AS THAT FOR WHICH IT IS NAMED.
DOESN'T BUY IT.
THAT'S WHY THIS WILL CUT ANYTHING BUT COGNAC.
I *KNEW* THAT RED WAS THE RIGHT COLOR FOR ME TO WEAR TODAY!
SO THAT WAS THE REASON?!
YOU WON'T BE ABLE TO USE IT ANYMORE, RIGHT?

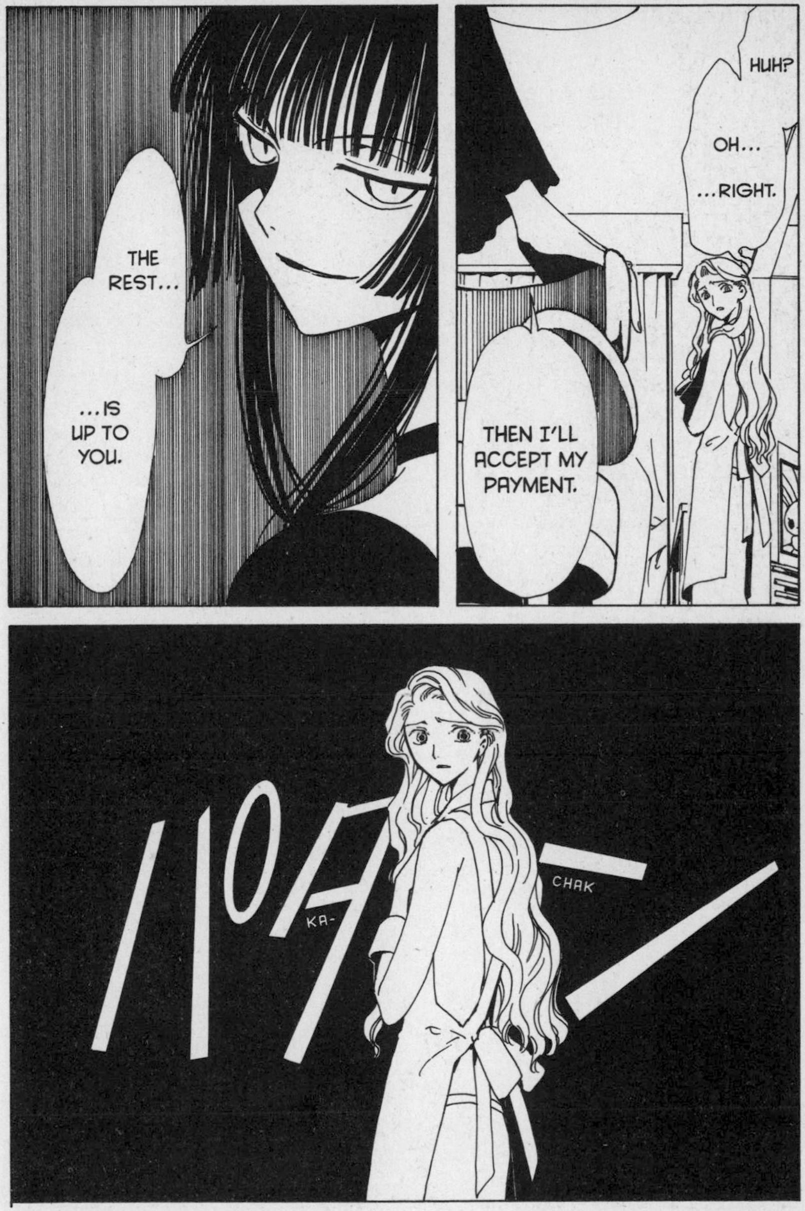
HUH?
OH...
...RIGHT.
THEN I'LL ACCEPT MY PAYMENT.
THE REST...
...IS UP TO YOU.
KA-
CHAK

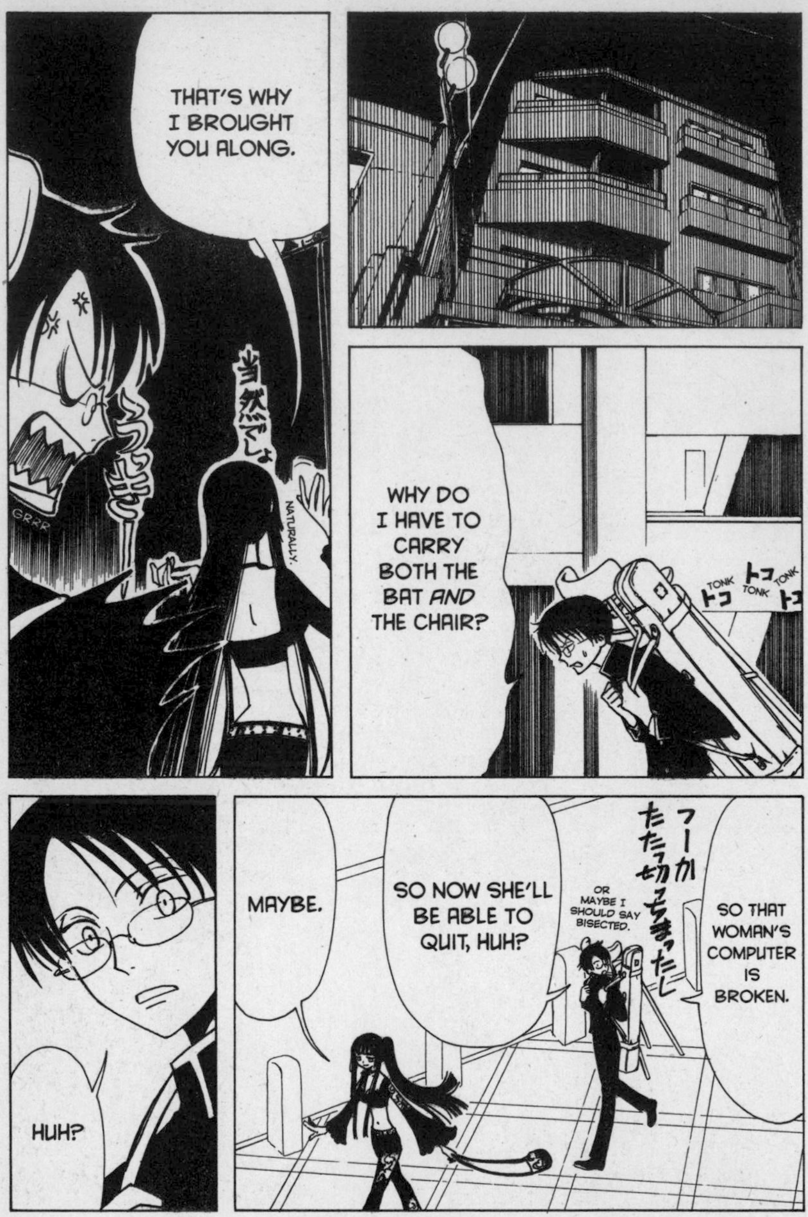
WHY DO I HAVE TO CARRY BOTH THE BAT *AND* THE CHAIR?
TONK TONK TONK
THAT'S WHY I BROUGHT YOU ALONG.
当然でしょ
NATURALLY.
GRRR
SO THAT WOMAN'S COMPUTER IS BROKEN.
OR MAYBE I SHOULD SAY BISECTED.
SO NOW SHE'LL BE ABLE TO QUIT, HUH?
MAYBE.
HUH?

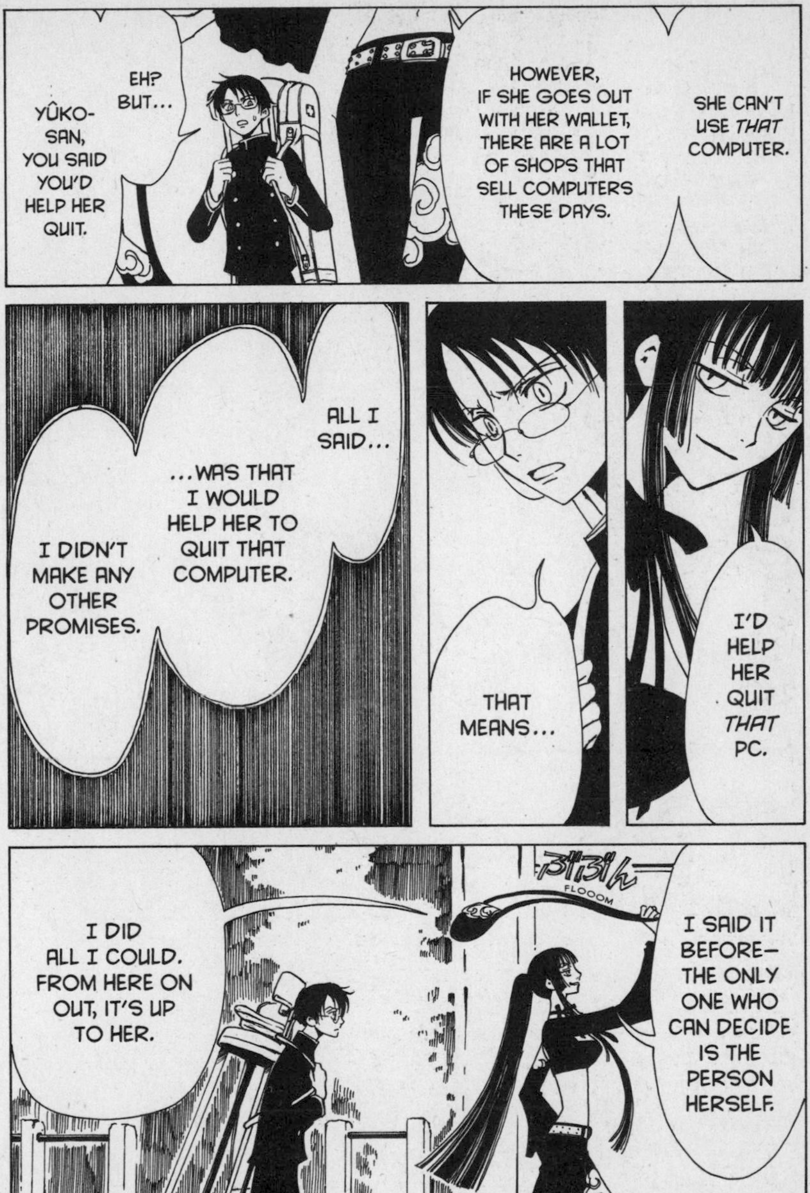
SHE CAN'T USE *THAT* COMPUTER.
HOWEVER, IF SHE GOES OUT WITH HER WALLET, THERE ARE A LOT OF SHOPS THAT SELL COMPUTERS THESE DAYS.
EH? BUT...
YÛKO-SAN, YOU SAID YOU'D HELP HER QUIT.
I'D HELP HER QUIT *THAT* PC.
THAT MEANS...
ALL I SAID...
...WAS THAT I WOULD HELP HER TO QUIT THAT COMPUTER.
I DIDN'T MAKE ANY OTHER PROMISES.
I SAID IT BEFORE— THE ONLY ONE WHO CAN DECIDE IS THE PERSON HERSELF.
ぶぃぶん
FLOOOM
I DID ALL I COULD. FROM HERE ON OUT, IT'S UP TO HER.

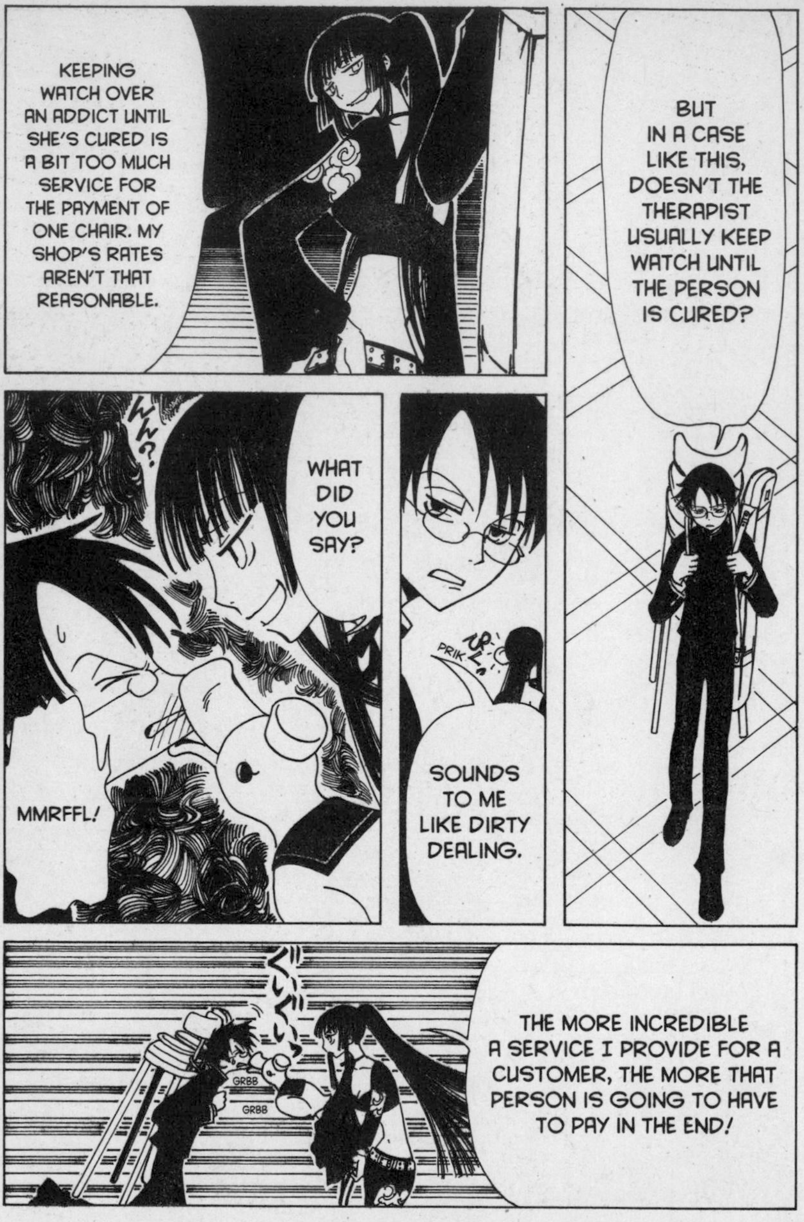
BUT IN A CASE LIKE THIS, DOESN'T THE THERAPIST USUALLY KEEP WATCH UNTIL THE PERSON IS CURED?
KEEPING WATCH OVER AN ADDICT UNTIL SHE'S CURED IS A BIT TOO MUCH SERVICE FOR THE PAYMENT OF ONE CHAIR. MY SHOP'S RATES AREN'T THAT REASONABLE.
PRIK
SOUNDS TO ME LIKE DIRTY DEALING.
WW?
WHAT DID YOU SAY?
MMRFFL!
THE MORE INCREDIBLE A SERVICE I PROVIDE FOR A CUSTOMER, THE MORE THAT PERSON IS GOING TO HAVE TO PAY IN THE END!
GRBB
GRBB

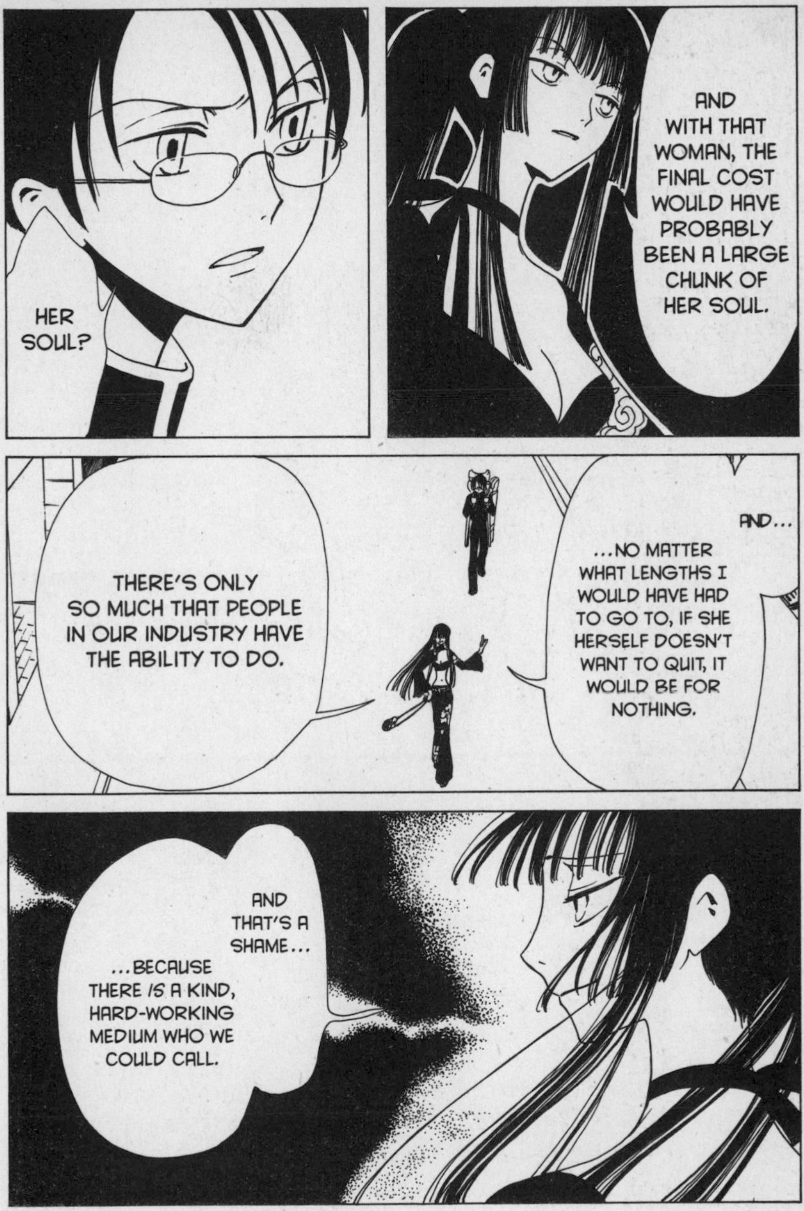
AND WITH THAT WOMAN, THE FINAL COST WOULD HAVE PROBABLY BEEN A LARGE CHUNK OF HER SOUL.
HER SOUL?
AND...
...NO MATTER WHAT LENGTHS I WOULD HAVE HAD TO GO TO, IF SHE HERSELF DOESN'T WANT TO QUIT, IT WOULD BE FOR NOTHING.
THERE'S ONLY SO MUCH THAT PEOPLE IN OUR INDUSTRY HAVE THE ABILITY TO DO.
AND THAT'S A SHAME...
...BECAUSE THERE *IS* A KIND, HARD-WORKING MEDIUM WHO WE COULD CALL.

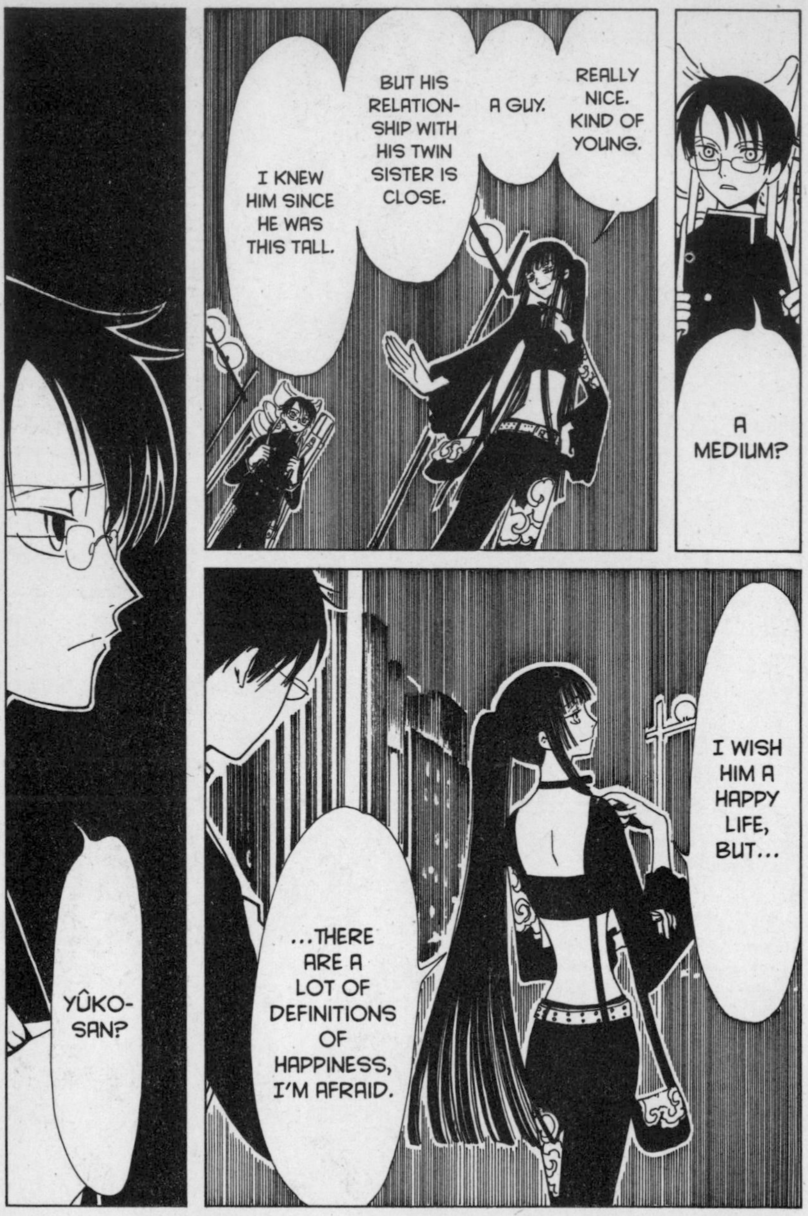
A MEDIUM?
REALLY NICE. KIND OF YOUNG.
A GUY.
BUT HIS RELATION-SHIP WITH HIS TWIN SISTER IS CLOSE.
I KNEW HIM SINCE HE WAS THIS TALL.
I WISH HIM A HAPPY LIFE, BUT...
...THERE ARE A LOT OF DEFINITIONS OF HAPPINESS, I'M AFRAID.
YÛKO-SAN?

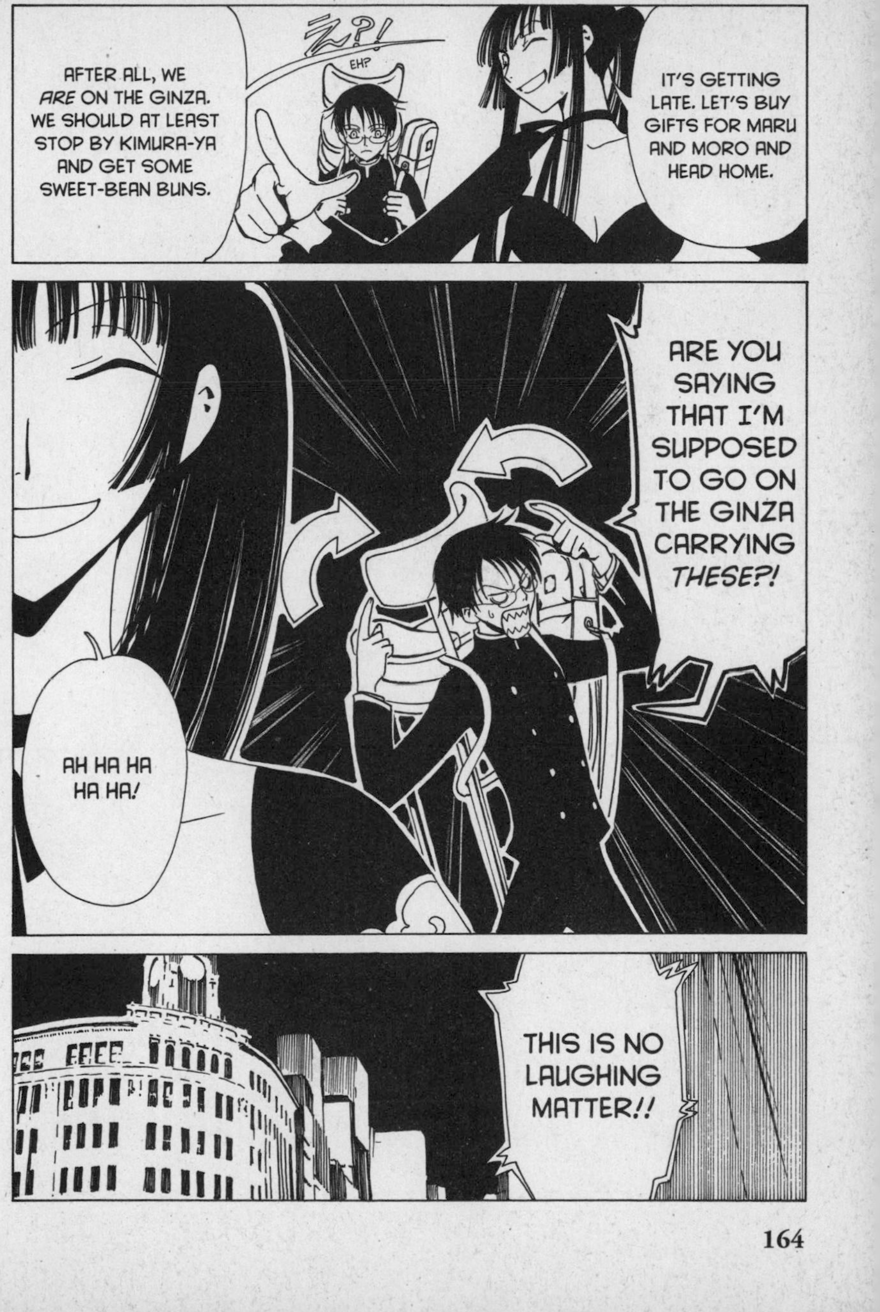

IT'S GETTING LATE. LET'S BUY GIFTS FOR MARU AND MORO AND HEAD HOME.
え?!
EH?
AFTER ALL, WE *ARE* ON THE GINZA. WE SHOULD AT LEAST STOP BY KIMURA-YA AND GET SOME SWEET-BEAN BUNS.
ARE YOU SAYING THAT I'M SUPPOSED TO GO ON THE GINZA CARRYING *THESE?!*
AH HA HA HA HA!
THIS IS NO LAUGHING MATTER!!

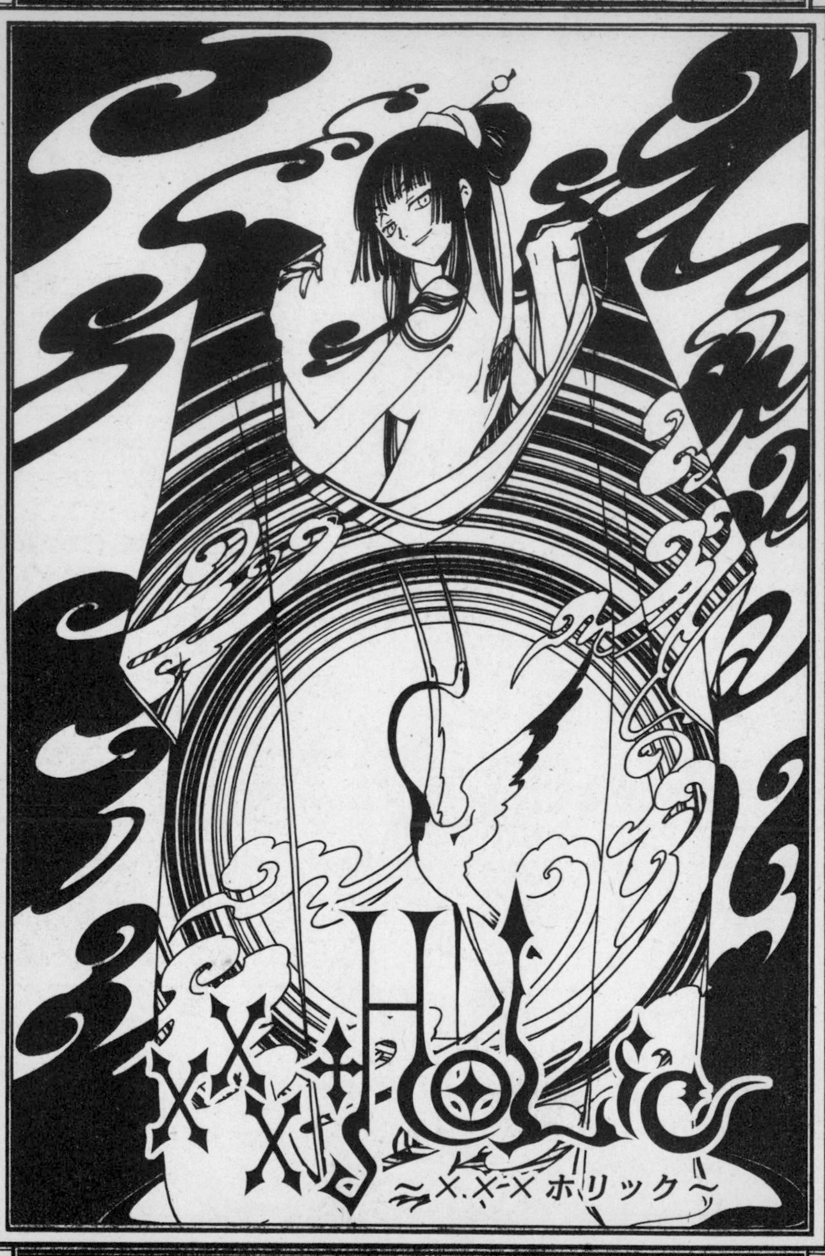
xxxHOLiC
〜×××ホリック〜

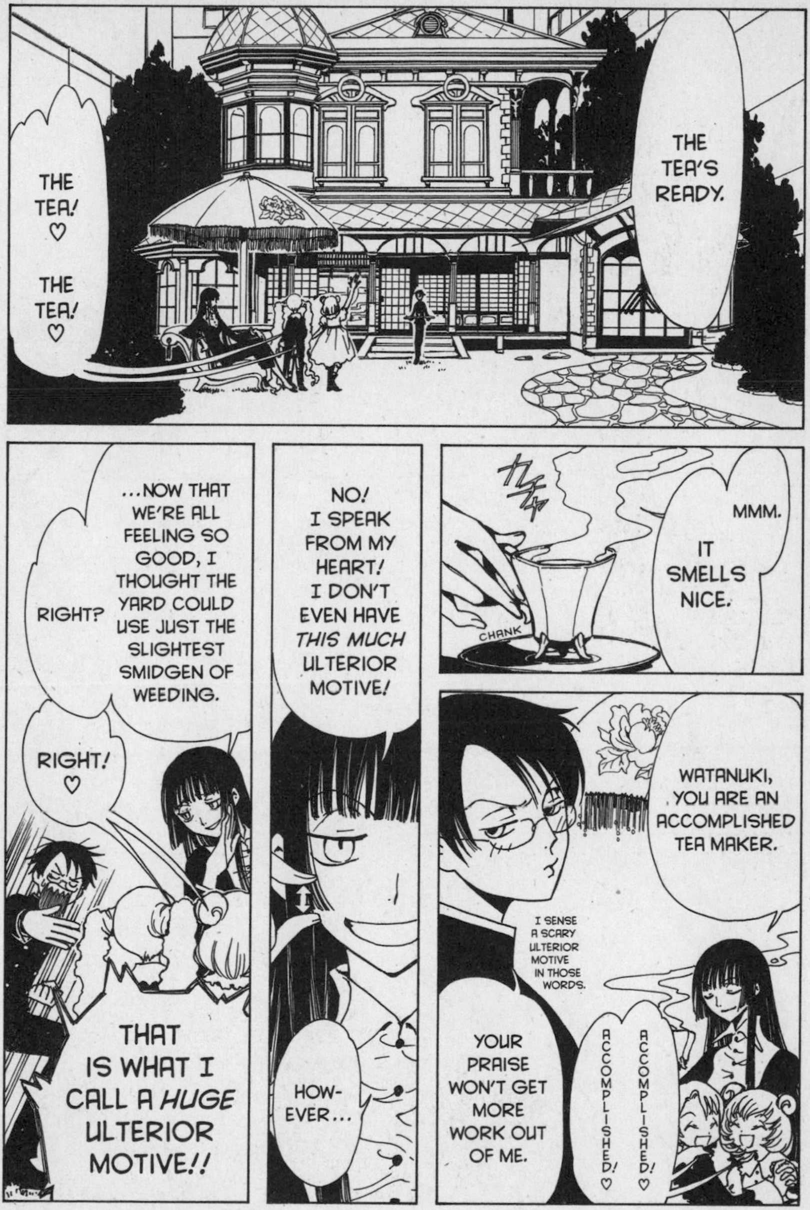
THE TEA'S READY.
THE TEA! ♡
THE TEA! ♡
MMM.
IT SMELLS NICE.
CHANK
WATANUKI, YOU ARE AN ACCOMPLISHED TEA MAKER.
I SENSE A SCARY ULTERIOR MOTIVE IN THOSE WORDS.
ACCOMPLISHED! ♡
ACCOMPLISHED! ♡
YOUR PRAISE WON'T GET MORE WORK OUT OF ME.
NO! I SPEAK FROM MY HEART! I DON'T EVEN HAVE *THIS MUCH* ULTERIOR MOTIVE!
HOW-EVER...
...NOW THAT WE'RE ALL FEELING SO GOOD, I THOUGHT THE YARD COULD USE JUST THE SLIGHTEST SMIDGEN OF WEEDING.
RIGHT?
RIGHT! ♡
THAT IS WHAT I CALL A *HUGE* ULTERIOR MOTIVE!!

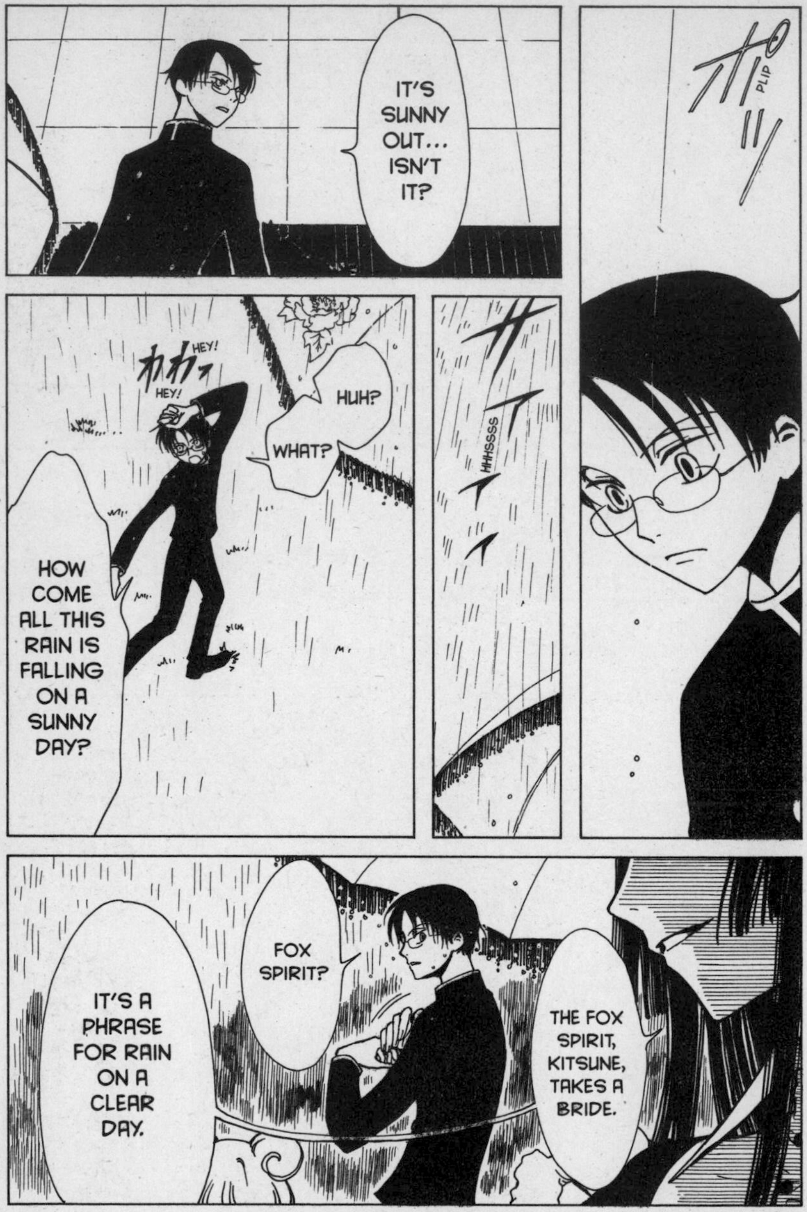
PLIP
IT'S SUNNY OUT... ISN'T IT?
HHHSSSS
HUH?
WHAT?
HEY!
HEY!
HOW COME ALL THIS RAIN IS FALLING ON A SUNNY DAY?
THE FOX SPIRIT, KITSUNE, TAKES A BRIDE.
FOX SPIRIT?
IT'S A PHRASE FOR RAIN ON A CLEAR DAY.

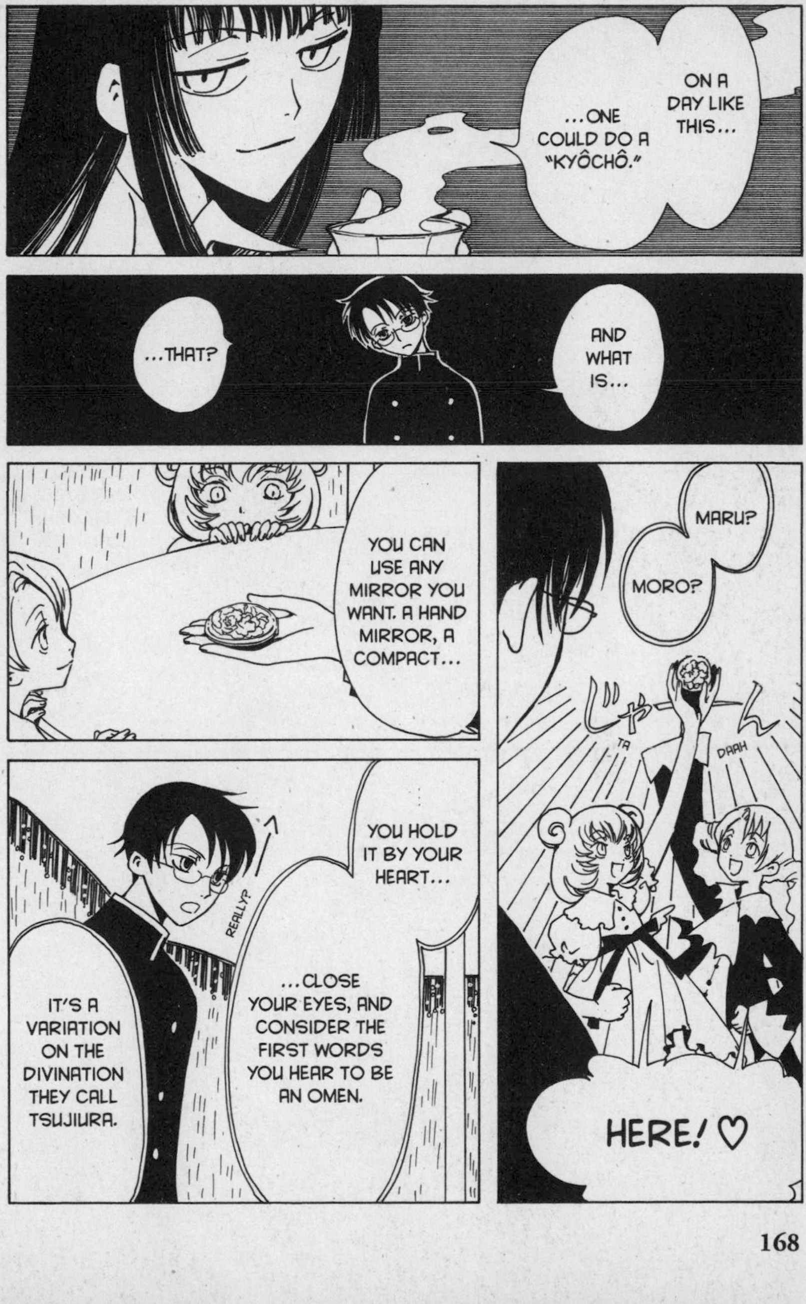
ON A DAY LIKE THIS...
...ONE COULD DO A "KYÔCHÔ."
AND WHAT IS...
...THAT?
MARU?
MORO?
じゃーん
TA DAAH
HERE! ♡
YOU CAN USE ANY MIRROR YOU WANT. A HAND MIRROR, A COMPACT...
YOU HOLD IT BY YOUR HEART...
REALLY?
...CLOSE YOUR EYES, AND CONSIDER THE FIRST WORDS YOU HEAR TO BE AN OMEN.
IT'S A VARIATION ON THE DIVINATION THEY CALL TSUJIURA.

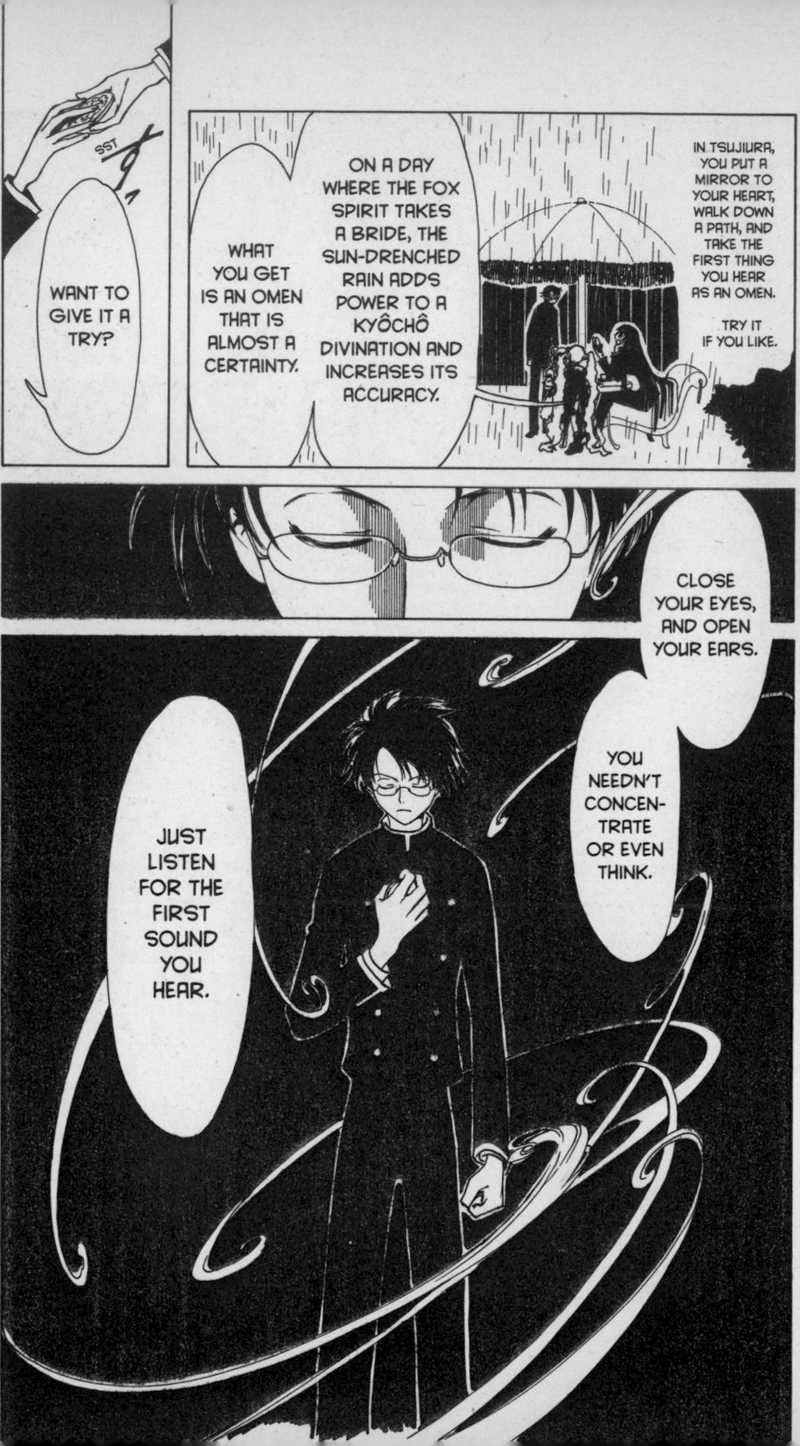
IN TSUJIURA, YOU PUT A MIRROR TO YOUR HEART, WALK DOWN A PATH, AND TAKE THE FIRST THING YOU HEAR AS AN OMEN.
TRY IT IF YOU LIKE.
ON A DAY WHERE THE FOX SPIRIT TAKES A BRIDE, THE SUN-DRENCHED RAIN ADDS POWER TO A KYÔCHÔ DIVINATION AND INCREASES ITS ACCURACY.
WHAT YOU GET IS AN OMEN THAT IS ALMOST A CERTAINTY.
SST
WANT TO GIVE IT A TRY?
CLOSE YOUR EYES, AND OPEN YOUR EARS.
YOU NEEDN'T CONCEN-TRATE OR EVEN THINK.
JUST LISTEN FOR THE FIRST SOUND YOU HEAR.

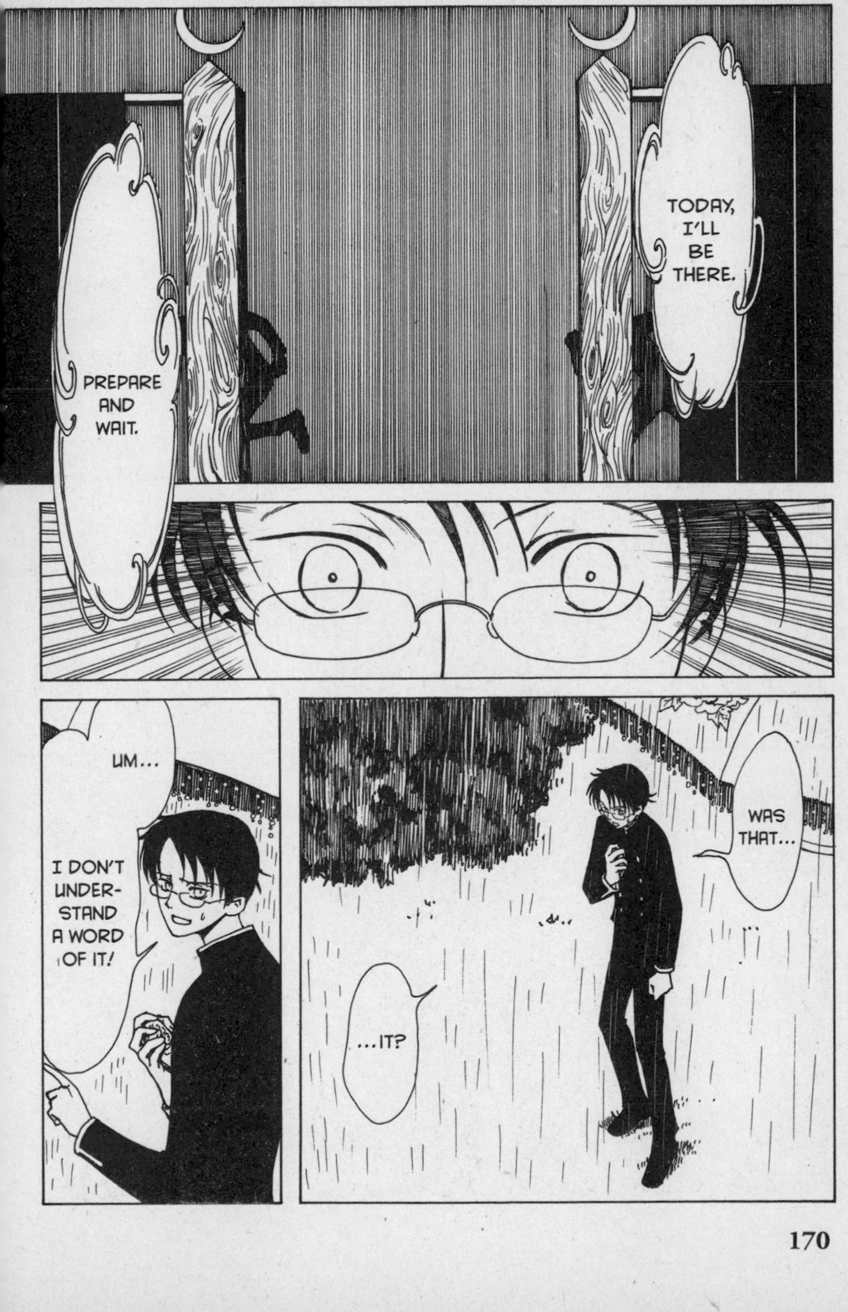
TODAY, I'LL BE THERE.
PREPARE AND WAIT.
WAS THAT...
...IT?
UM...
I DON'T UNDER-STAND A WORD OF IT!

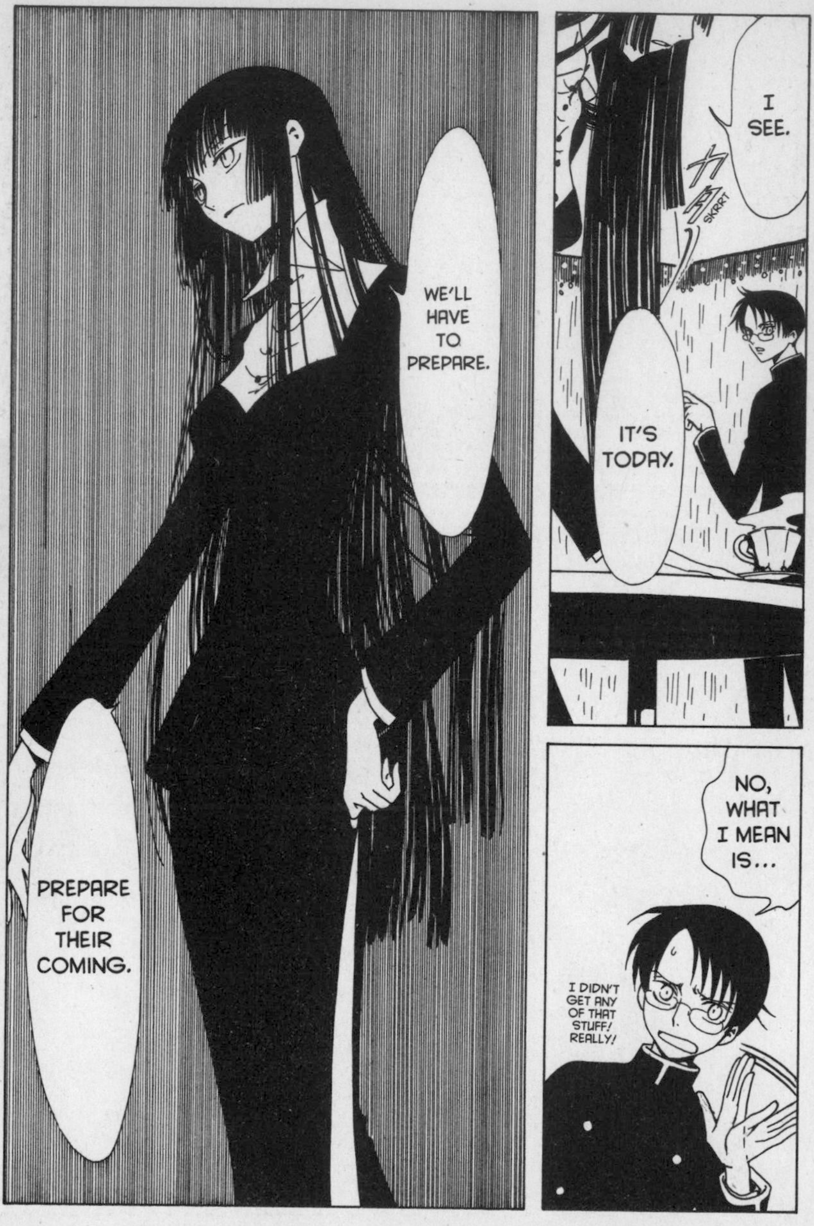
I SEE.
SKRRT
IT'S TODAY.
NO, WHAT I MEAN IS...
I DIDN'T GET ANY OF THAT STUFF! REALLY!
WE'LL HAVE TO PREPARE.
PREPARE FOR THEIR COMING.

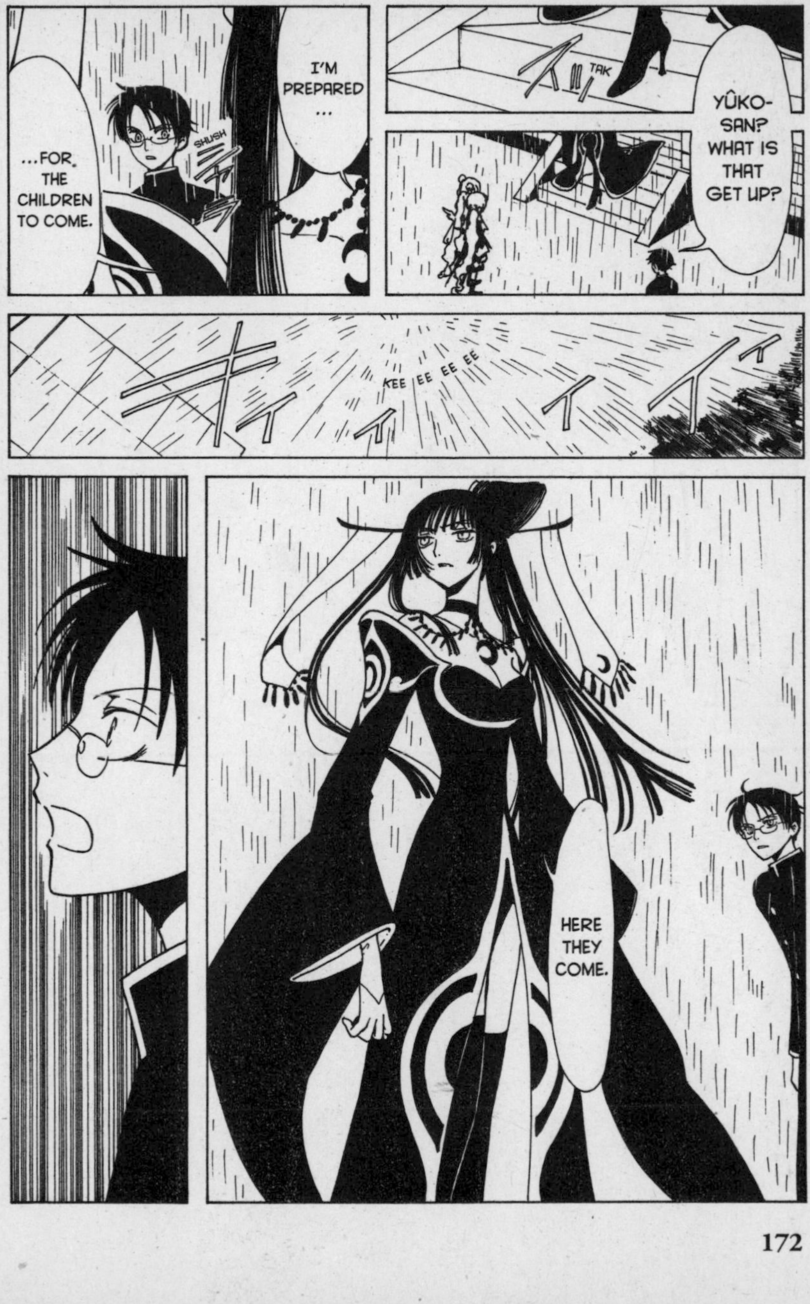
TAK
YÛKO-SAN? WHAT IS THAT GET UP?
I'M PREPARED ...
SHUSH
...FOR THE CHILDREN TO COME.
KEE EE EE EE
HERE THEY COME.

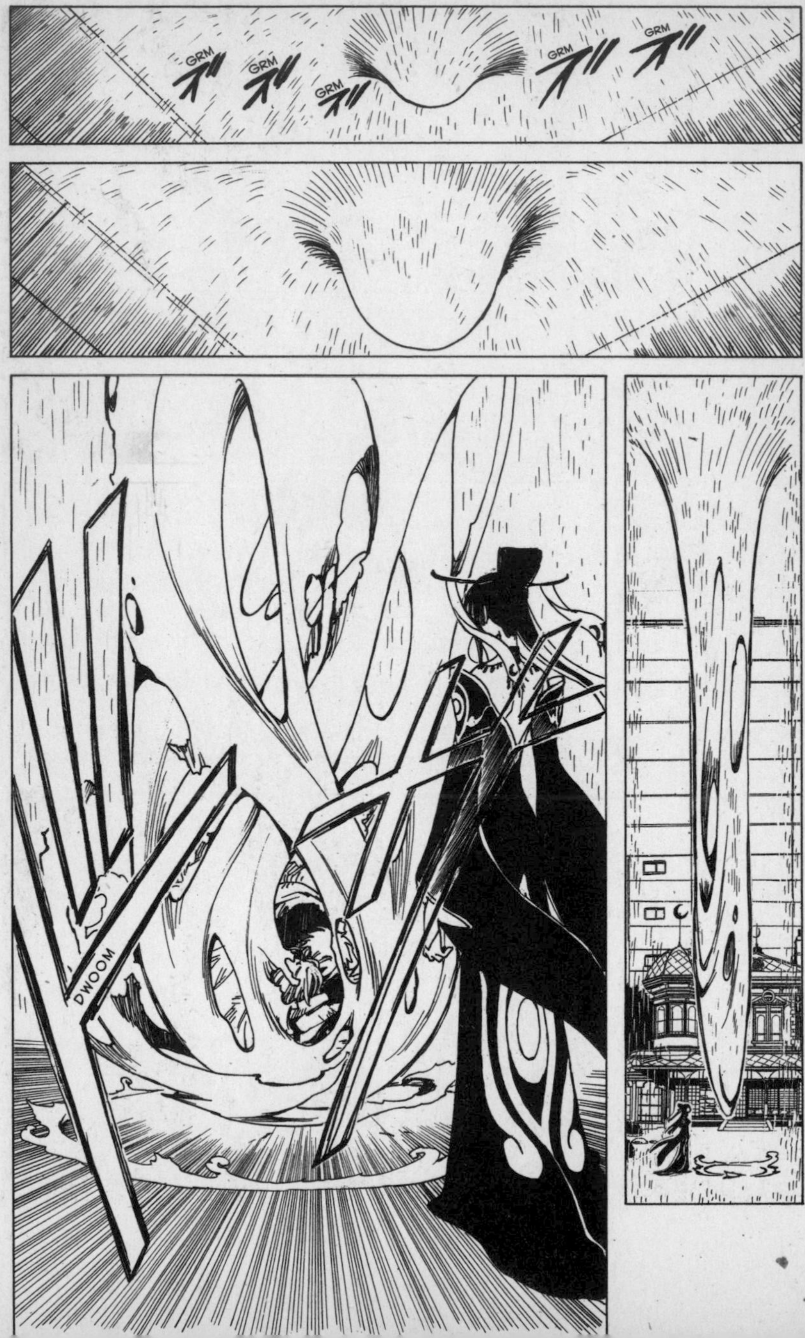
GRM
GRM
GRM
GRM
GRM
DWOOM

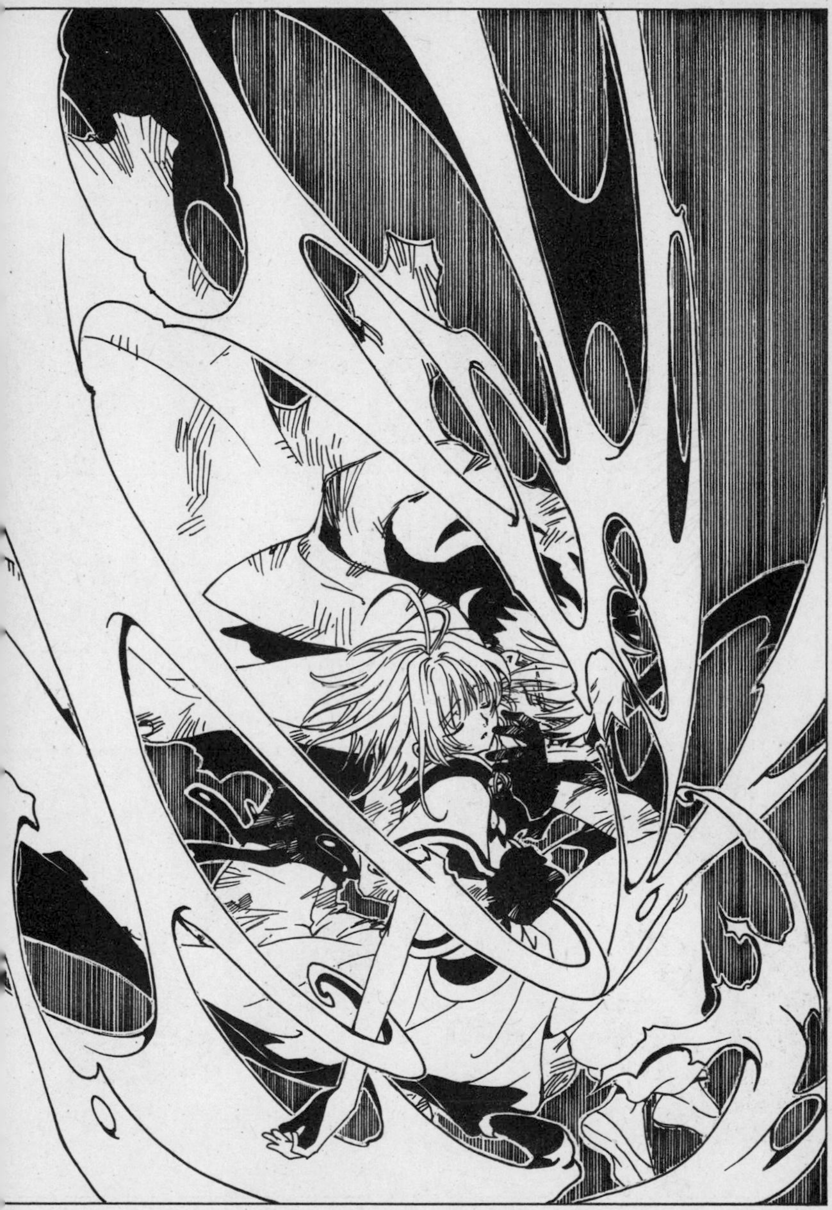

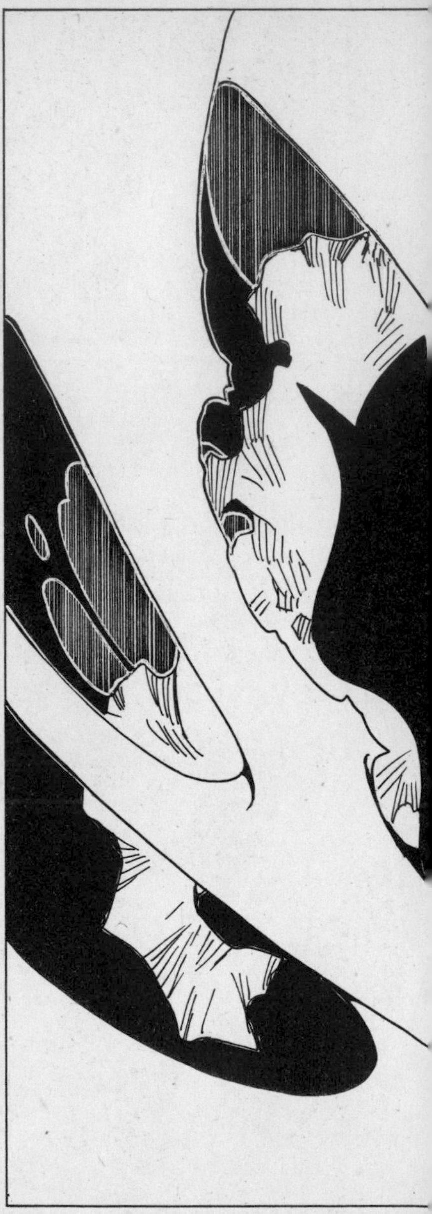

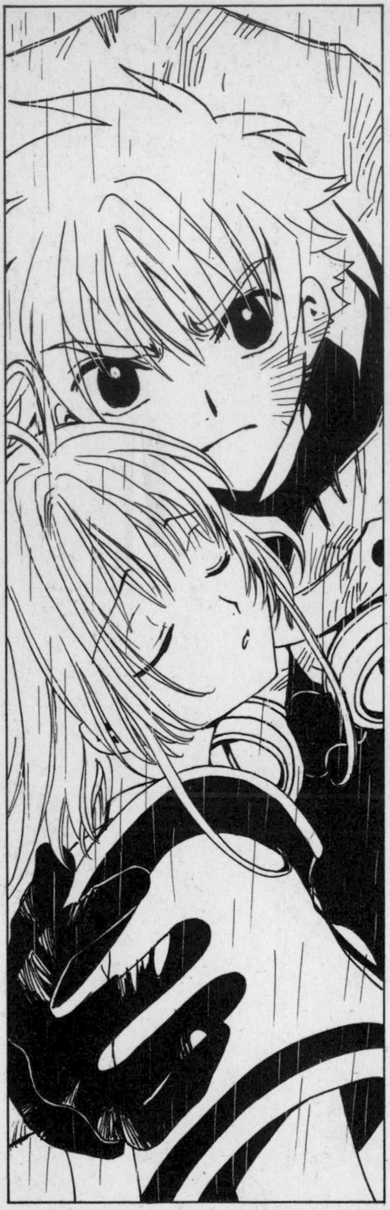

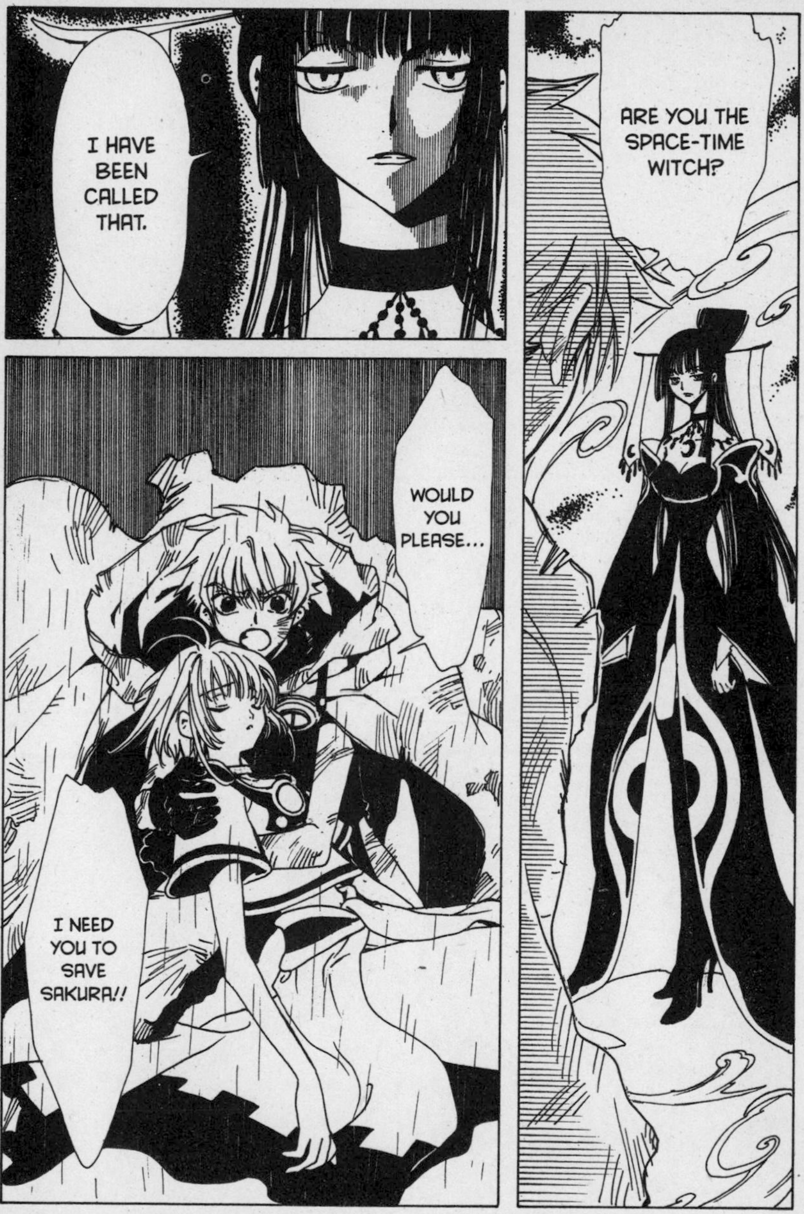
ARE YOU THE SPACE-TIME WITCH?
I HAVE BEEN CALLED THAT.
WOULD YOU PLEASE...
I NEED YOU TO SAVE SAKURA!!

To be continued

Welcome...

...to the launch of the Del Rey Manga line! It all starts here, with four new series from Japan: *Negima!* by Ken Akamatsu! *Gundam SEED* by Masatsuga Iwase! And *Tsubasa: Reservoir Chronicle* and *xxxHOLiC*, both by CLAMP! Together, these four series represent some of the best and most popular manga series published in Japan.

We're dedicated to providing our readers with the most enjoyable, authentic manga experience possible. Our books are printed from right to left, in the Japanese printing format. We strive to keep the translations as true to the original as possible, while giving the English versions the same sense of adventure and fun. We keep Japanese honorifics intact, translate all sound effects, and give you extras at the back of the books to help you understand the context of the stories and keep track of all the characters. It's the next best thing to being able to read Japanese yourself!

For information on upcoming releases, visit www.delreymanga.com, and while you're there be sure to sign up for our newsletter. If you do, you'll be the first to hear all the scoop on Del Rey Manga, and you'll have the opportunity to talk back directly to the editor (that would be me) and say what works for you in our books, and what doesn't. Manga wouldn't be the red-hot phenomenon it is without your support, and we want your feedback.

See you in Volume 2!

Dallas Middaugh

Dallas Middaugh
Director of Manga, Del Rey Books

About the Creators

CLAMP is a group of four women who have become the most popular manga artists in America—Satsuki Igarashi, Mick Nekoi, Mokona Apapa, and Nanase Ohkawa. They started out as doujnishi (fan comics) creators, but their skill and craft brought them to the attention of publishers very quickly. Their first work from a major publisher was *RG Veda*, but their first mass success was with *Magic Knight Rayearth*. From there, they went on to write many series, including *Cardcaptor Sakura* and *Chobits*, two of the most popular manga in the United States. Like many Japanese manga artists, they prefer to avoid the spotlight, and little is known about them personally.

CLAMP is currently publishing three series in Japan: *Tsubasa* and *xxxHOLiC* with Kodansha and *Gohou Drug* with Kadokawa.

Past Works

CLAMP have created many series. Here is a brief overview of one of them.

Cardcaptor Sakura: Master of the Clow

The first volume of *Cardcaptor Sakura* was released in Japan in 1996, and by the time the series was finished it would number twelve volumes in all. The first story arc, wherein Sakura would capture all of the Clow Cards and be named Master of the Clow, encompassed the first six volumes. In the final six volumes, Sakura discovers that there is another type of magic beyond that represented by the Clow Cards, and she must tap an inner power she didn't know she had in order to combat it. In Japan, there were twelve volumes all called *Cardcaptor Sakura*; in America, the second six have been released as *Cardcaptor Sakura: Master of the Clow*.

Romance abounds in this second arc, with Sakura still trying to manage her serious crush on Yukito, and Li Syaoran and new transfer student Eriol Hirragizawa both showing interest in Sakura. When Eriol turns out to be the reincarnation of the wizard Clow Reed, creator of the cards that bear his name, a series of magical tests begin for Sakura, whose purpose becomes apparent only later in the series.

In fact, romance is what it's all about in the closing chapter of the series. Sakura confesses her love for Yukito, only to have Yukito deny her, because he's in love with her older brother Tôya! You'll see the possibility that this love still exists in *Tsubasa*. Eriol finds his true love, Kaho, and Li Syaoran finally finds the courage to tell Sakura how he really feels.

Clearly, CLAMP felt very close to these characters and wanted to go on telling their stories—which they have done in the pages of *Tsubasa*, and, to a lesser extent, in *xxxHOLiC*!

Artifacts and Miscellany

Over in *Tsubasa* you'll find a lot of characters from a variety of CLAMP manga making an appearance. Here in the first volume of *xxxHOLiC*, you'll find a few artifacts and other appearances that might be a bit hard to understand if you haven't read all of CLAMP's work. Don't read these if you haven't read this volume yet—there's a reason we put them at the end of the book!

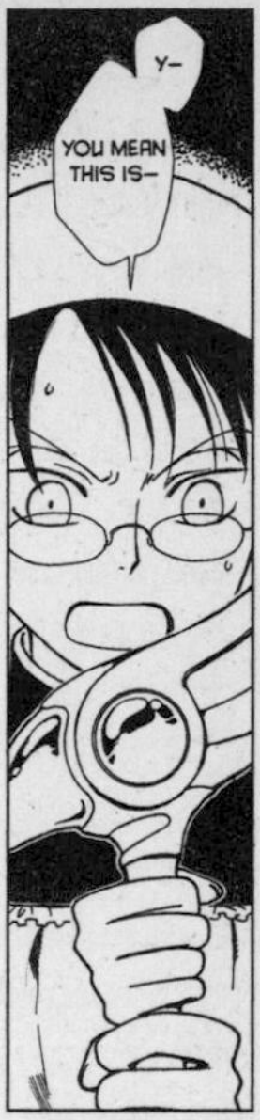
Y-
YOU MEAN THIS IS-

Sakura's Wand

Foreshadowing an event to come in *Tsubasa* Volume 1 and *xxxHOLiC* Volume 2, Watanuki finds an old wand while dusting Yûko's shop. Yûko builds the tension up to the big reveal: It's just a plastic toy wand. But here's the weird thing—Watanuki clearly recognizes it! Is it part of some legend he grew up with? Or does he just watch *Cardcaptor Sakura* on television? It may be revealed in a future volume...or we may never know!

Mokona Modoki

Readers of *Magic Knight Rayearth* will recognize the chubby bunny thing called Mokona. In both the manga and the anime, Mokona exists to guide the Magic Knights through their quests. In the manga, however, his role is a little, shall we say, *expanded*. Mokona is named for Mokona Apapa, a member of CLAMP, and his vocabulary consists entirely of the word "PU!"

As will become clear in *Tsubasa* Volume 1 and future volumes of *xxxHOLiC*, this is definitely not the same Mokona, although there are a lot of similarities.

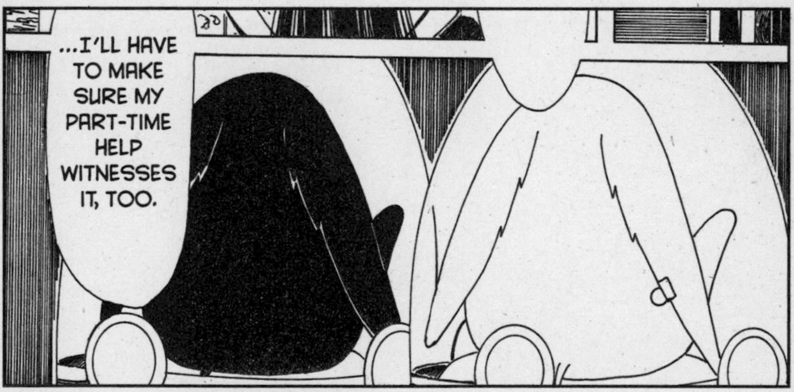
...I'LL HAVE TO MAKE SURE MY PART-TIME HELP WITNESSES IT, TOO.

Maneki Neko

Maneki Neko is not a CLAMP character, but rather a Japanese symbol of good fortune which is very common in that country. When you buy one of these figurines, the arm is usually moving back and forth in a manner that looks to western eyes as though it is waving. In fact, it is actually beckoning in the Japanese manner—by waving its hand with the palm outward. The legend of Maneki Neko is that a man in a thunderstorm took refuge under a tree, only to see a cat beckoning him into a nearby temple. Following the cat, the man turned to watch the tree struck by lightning. Maneki Neko became the symbol of good luck ever after.

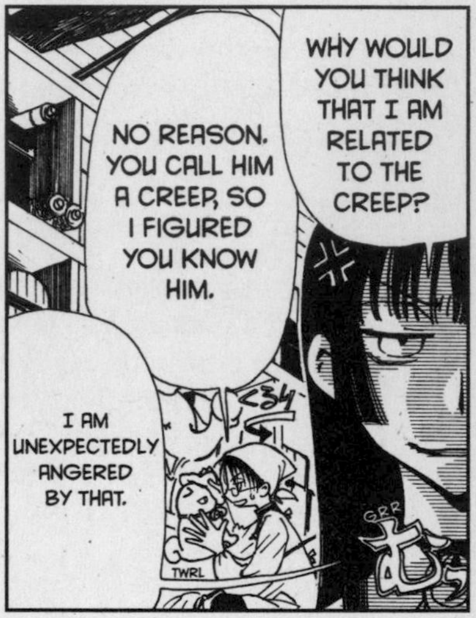
WHY WOULD YOU THINK THAT I AM RELATED TO THE CREEP?
NO REASON. YOU CALL HIM A CREEP, SO I FIGURED YOU KNOW HIM.
GRR
I AM UNEXPECTEDLY ANGERED BY THAT.
TWRL

Translation Notes

For your edification and reading pleasure, here are notes to help understand some of the cultural and story references from our translation of *xxxHOLiC*.

Maru-dashi and Moro-dashi

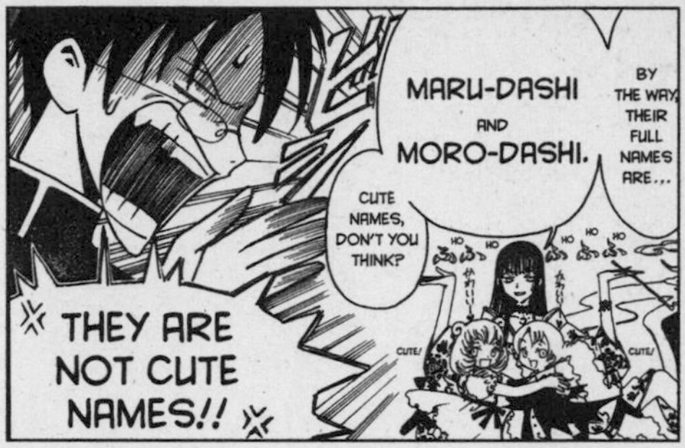
BY THE WAY, THEIR FULL NAMES ARE...
MARU-DASHI AND MORO-DASHI.
CUTE NAMES, DON'T YOU THINK?
THEY ARE NOT CUTE NAMES!!

Maru and Moro are very common syllables found in Japanese names. Watanuki Kimihiro had no reason to assume that their names were the buildup to a joke. But he is absolutely right—they aren't cute names! Both *marudashi* and *morodashi* mean "exposing yourself in public." It's almost as if Yûko has decided to call her two assistants "Streaking" and "Flashing."

Oh, Mirror! Oh, Mirror! Mr. Mirror!

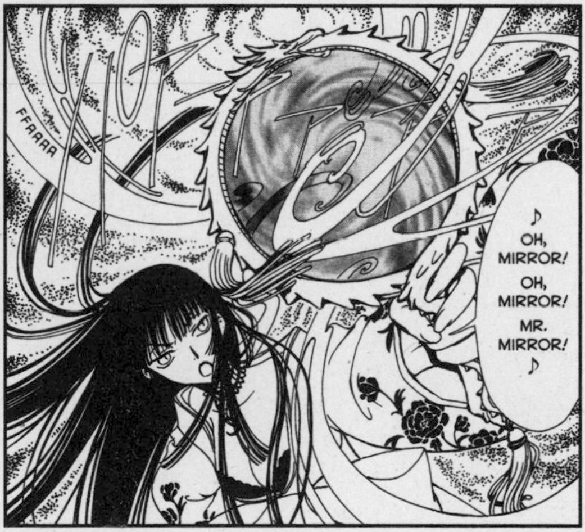
♪ OH, MIRROR! OH, MIRROR! MR. MIRROR! ♪

In the 1970s, there was an American television show for very young children called *Romper Room* in which the host looked at the audience through an empty mirror frame and said, "I see Tommy, and Anne, and Carol, and...etc." Of course, she was listing common names, and those with uncommon names were fated to never be "seen" by the host. Japan's version of *Romper Room* had exactly the same sequence, although the song was a little different (which Maru and Moro sing for us). Do you remember *Romper Room*? No? That's the generation gap for you.

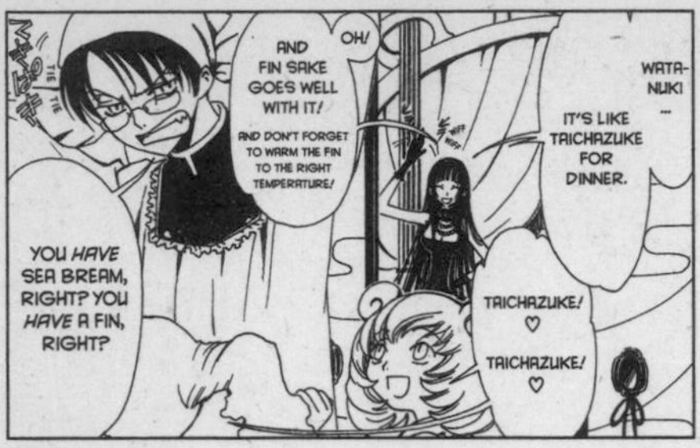
WATA-NUKI ...
IT'S LIKE TAICHAZUKE FOR DINNER.
TAICHAZUKE! ♡
TAICHAZUKE! ♡
OH!
AND FIN SAKE GOES WELL WITH IT!
AND DON'T FORGET TO WARM THE FIN TO THE RIGHT TEMPERATURE!
TIE TIE
YOU HAVE SEA BREAM, RIGHT? YOU HAVE A FIN, RIGHT?

Taichazuke and Hire Sake

Taichazuke is boiled rice poured with tea, and sea bream on top, while hire sake is fin sake.

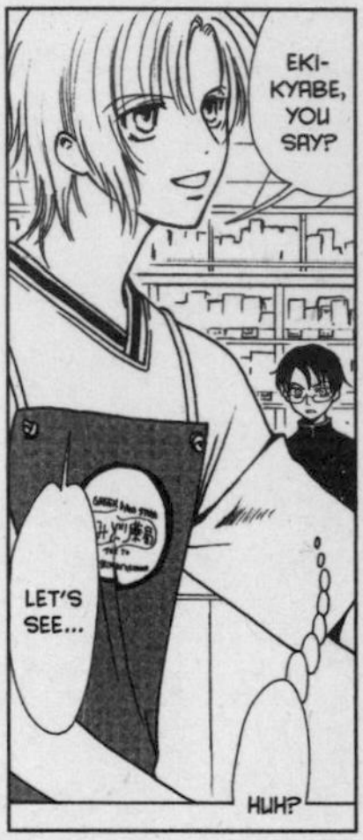
EKI-KYABE, YOU SAY?
LET'S SEE...
HUH?

Eki-Kyabe

A medication for indigestion, commonly used as a cure for hangovers.

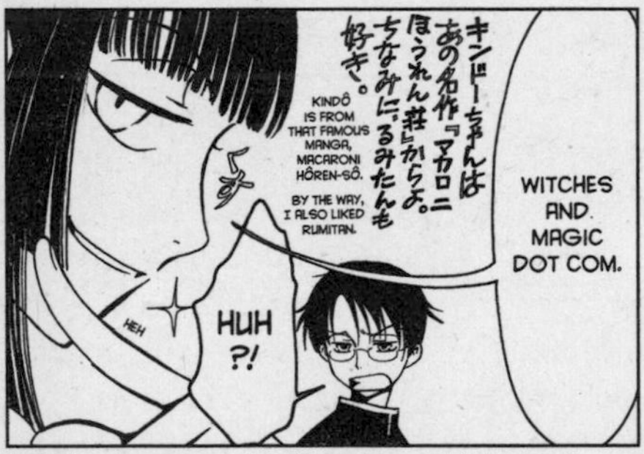
WITCHES AND. MAGIC DOT COM.
キンドーちゃんはあの名作『マカロニほうれん荘』からよ。ちなみに、るみたんも好き。
KINDÔ IS FROM THAT FAMOUS MANGA, MACARONI HÔREN-SÔ.
BY THE WAY, I ALSO LIKED RUMITAN.
HUH ?!
HEH

Macaroni Hôren-so

A comedy manga that started in 1977 and ran for nine volumes in its original release. It is about a young, poor businessman who lives, along with several odd characters, in a *gejuku*, an old-style apartment building, by the name of *Hôren-so*. Although it ran in *Shonen Champion* for only a little over two years, it is one of the seminal comedies of Japanese manga.

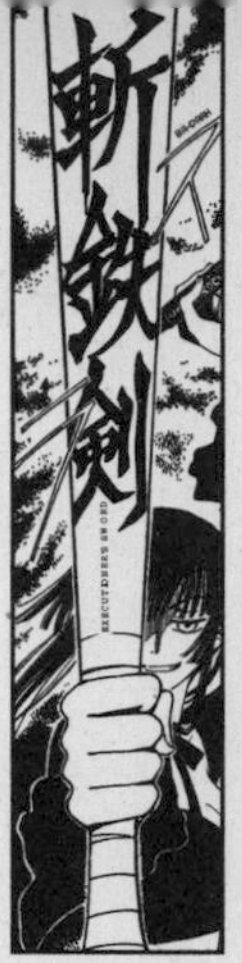
斬鉄剣

Zantetsuken

The Sword That Cuts Iron is the legendary sword of equally legendary thief Goemon Ishikawa. If that name seems familiar, then you have some experience with the comedy/action series *Lupin III* by Monkey Punch. *Lupin*'s Goemon is supposed to be a direct descendant, and his sword also cuts iron—and much, much more. The famous phrase, "Once again, I cut a worthless object" (page 156) is also taken from Goemon's character.

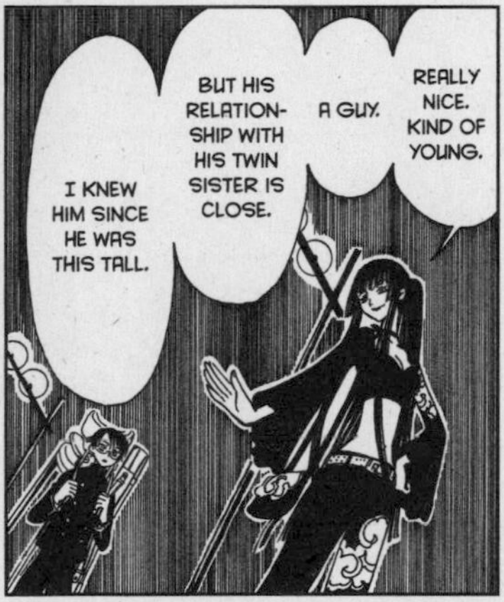
REALLY NICE. KIND OF YOUNG.
A GUY.
BUT HIS RELATION-SHIP WITH HIS TWIN SISTER IS CLOSE.
I KNEW HIM SINCE HE WAS THIS TALL.

The Medium

She's talking about Subaru Sumeragi of X (*X/1999*) and *Tokyo Babylon*. The direct descendant of the nation's highest family of mediums, Subaru was one of a pair of fraternal twins—the other being his irrepressible sister Hokuto.

Kyôchô

The word is made up of the characters for "mirror" and "divination."

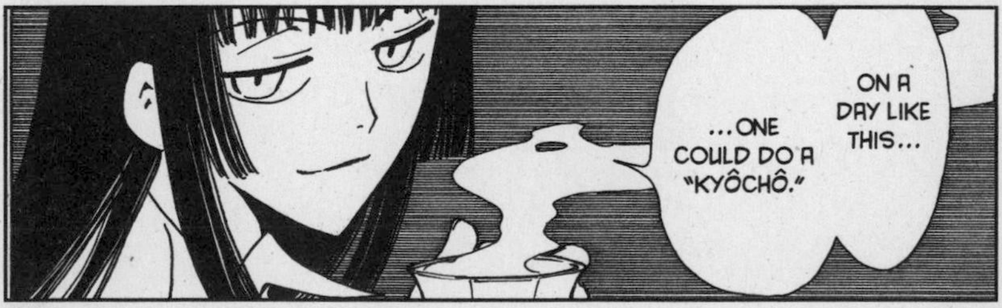
ON A DAY LIKE THIS...
...ONE COULD DO A "KYÔCHÔ."

Preview pages

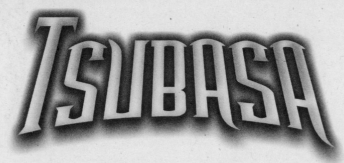

CLAMP

Sakura and Syaoran return—but they're not the people you know! Sakura is the princess of Clow—and possessor of a mysterious power that promises to change the world. Syaoran is her childhood friend and leader of the archaeological dig that took his father's life. They reside in an alternate reality...where whatever you least expect can happen—and *does*. When Sakura ventures to the dig site to declare her love for Syaoran, a puzzling symbol is uncovered which triggers a remarkable quest. Now Syaoran embarks upon a desperate journey through other worlds—all in the name of saving Sakura.

Tsubasa crosses over with *xxxHOLiC*, and here we present a few pages from *Tsubasa* Volume 1, available now!

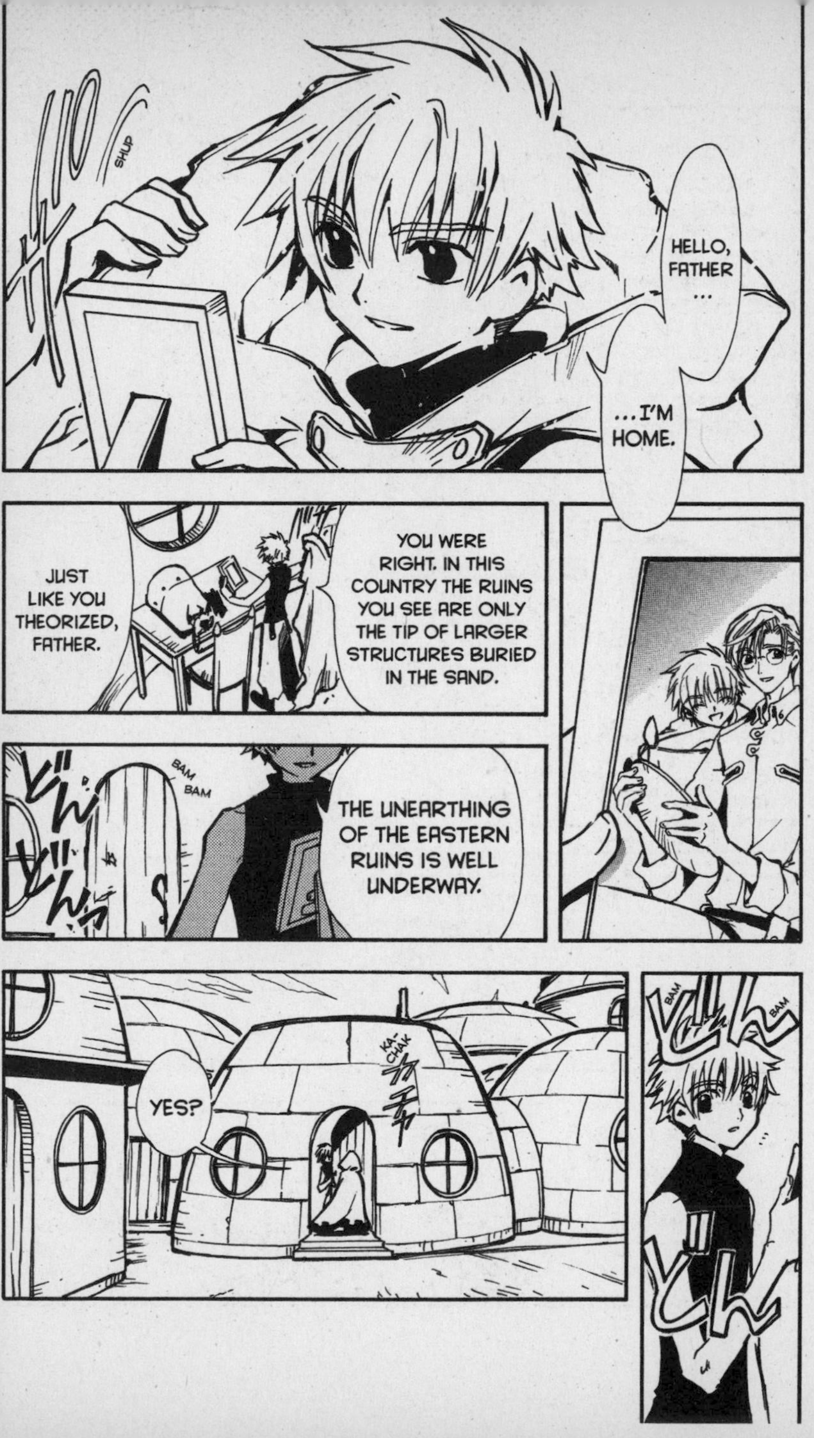
SHUP
HELLO, FATHER ...
...I'M HOME.
YOU WERE RIGHT. IN THIS COUNTRY THE RUINS YOU SEE ARE ONLY THE TIP OF LARGER STRUCTURES BURIED IN THE SAND.
JUST LIKE YOU THEORIZED, FATHER.
THE UNEARTHING OF THE EASTERN RUINS IS WELL UNDERWAY.
BAM BAM
BAM
BAM
KA-CHAK
YES?

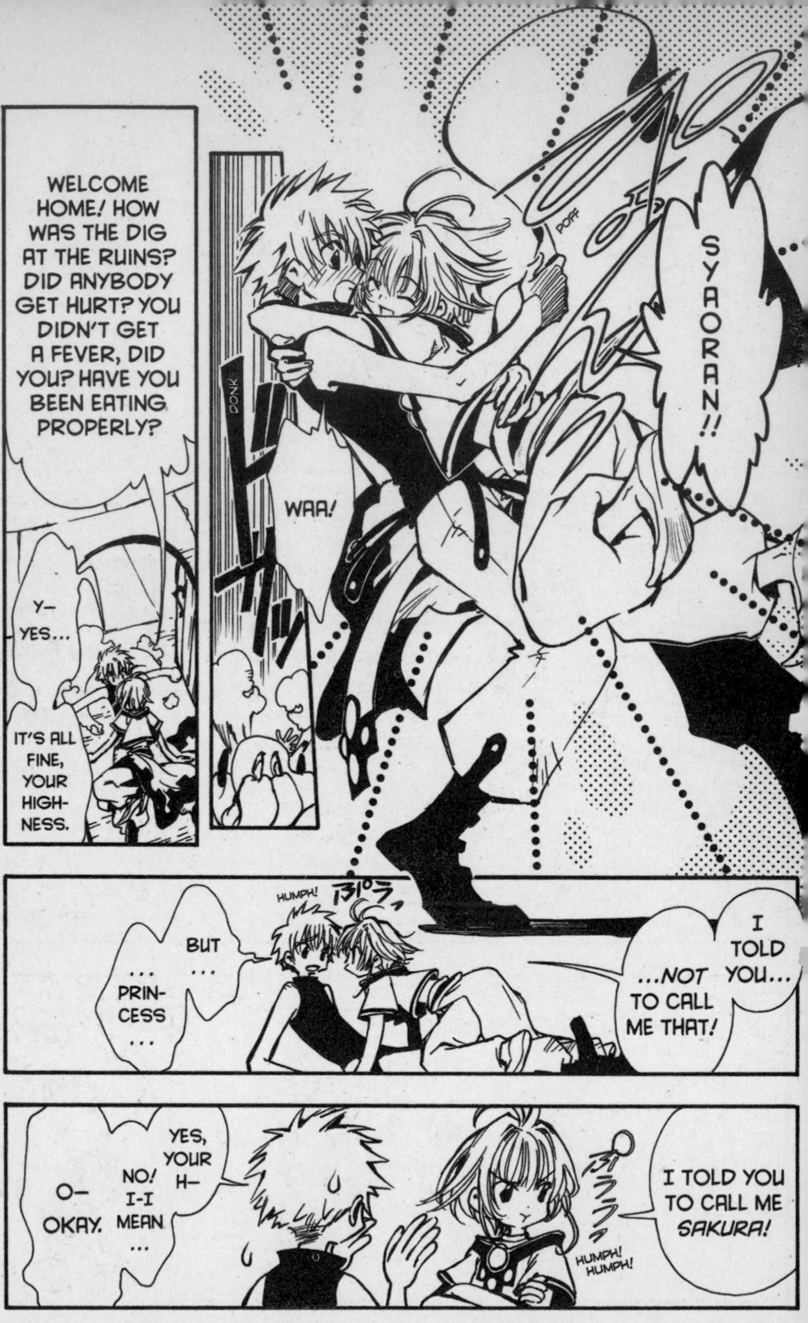
SYAORAN!!
POFF
DONK
WAA!
WELCOME HOME! HOW WAS THE DIG AT THE RUINS? DID ANYBODY GET HURT? YOU DIDN'T GET A FEVER, DID YOU? HAVE YOU BEEN EATING PROPERLY?
Y— YES...
IT'S ALL FINE, YOUR HIGH-NESS.
I TOLD YOU...
...NOT TO CALL ME THAT!
HUMPH!
BUT...
...PRIN-CESS...
I TOLD YOU TO CALL ME SAKURA!
HUMPH! HUMPH!
YES, YOUR H—
NO! I-I MEAN...
O— OKAY.

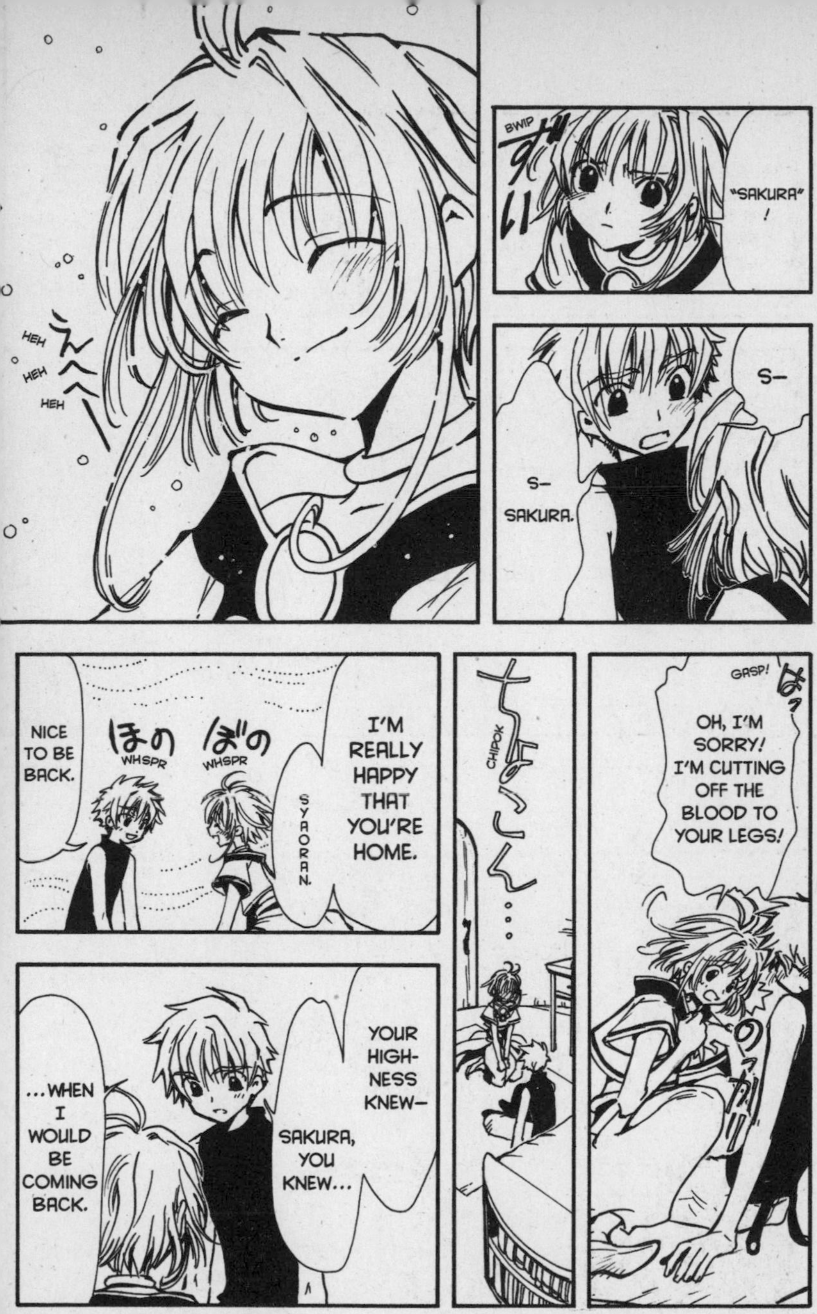
BWIP
"SAKURA"!
S—
S—SAKURA.
HEH
HEH
HEH
GASP!
OH, I'M SORRY! I'M CUTTING OFF THE BLOOD TO YOUR LEGS!
CHIPOK
I'M REALLY HAPPY THAT YOU'RE HOME.
SYAORAN.
WHSPR
WHSPR
NICE TO BE BACK.
YOUR HIGHNESS KNEW—
SAKURA, YOU KNEW...
...WHEN I WOULD BE COMING BACK.

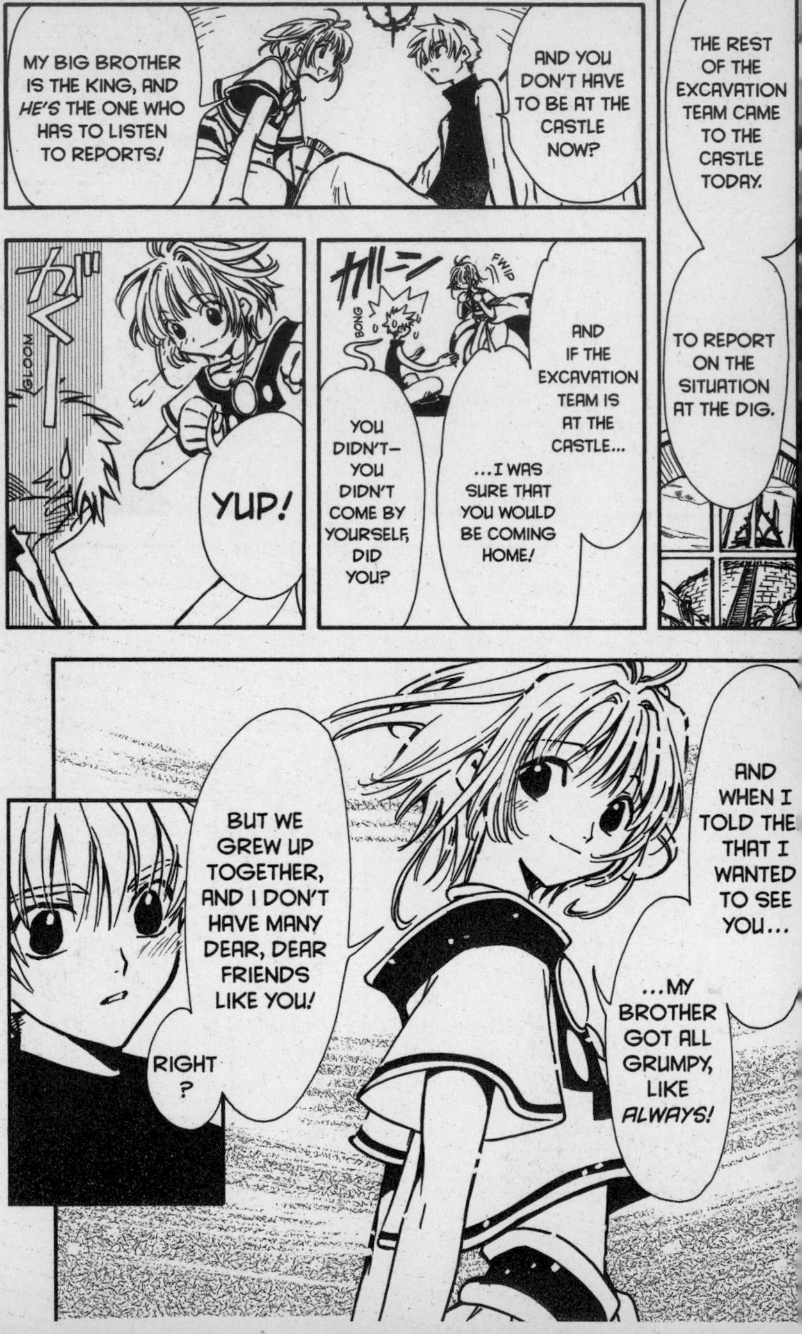
THE REST OF THE EXCAVATION TEAM CAME TO THE CASTLE TODAY.
TO REPORT ON THE SITUATION AT THE DIG.
AND YOU DON'T HAVE TO BE AT THE CASTLE NOW?
MY BIG BROTHER IS THE KING, AND *HE'S* THE ONE WHO HAS TO LISTEN TO REPORTS!
FWIP
AND IF THE EXCAVATION TEAM IS AT THE CASTLE...
...I WAS SURE THAT YOU WOULD BE COMING HOME!
ガーン
BONG
YOU DIDN'T— YOU DIDN'T COME BY YOURSELF, DID YOU?
YUP!
がくー
GLOOM
AND WHEN I TOLD THE THAT I WANTED TO SEE YOU...
...MY BROTHER GOT ALL GRUMPY, LIKE *ALWAYS!*
BUT WE GREW UP TOGETHER, AND I DON'T HAVE MANY DEAR, DEAR FRIENDS LIKE YOU!
RIGHT?

Preview of Volume 2

Because we're running about one year behind the release of the *xxxHOLiC* manga in Japan, we have the opportunity to present to you a preview from Volume 2. This volume will be available in English in July 2004, but for now you'll have to make do with Japanese!

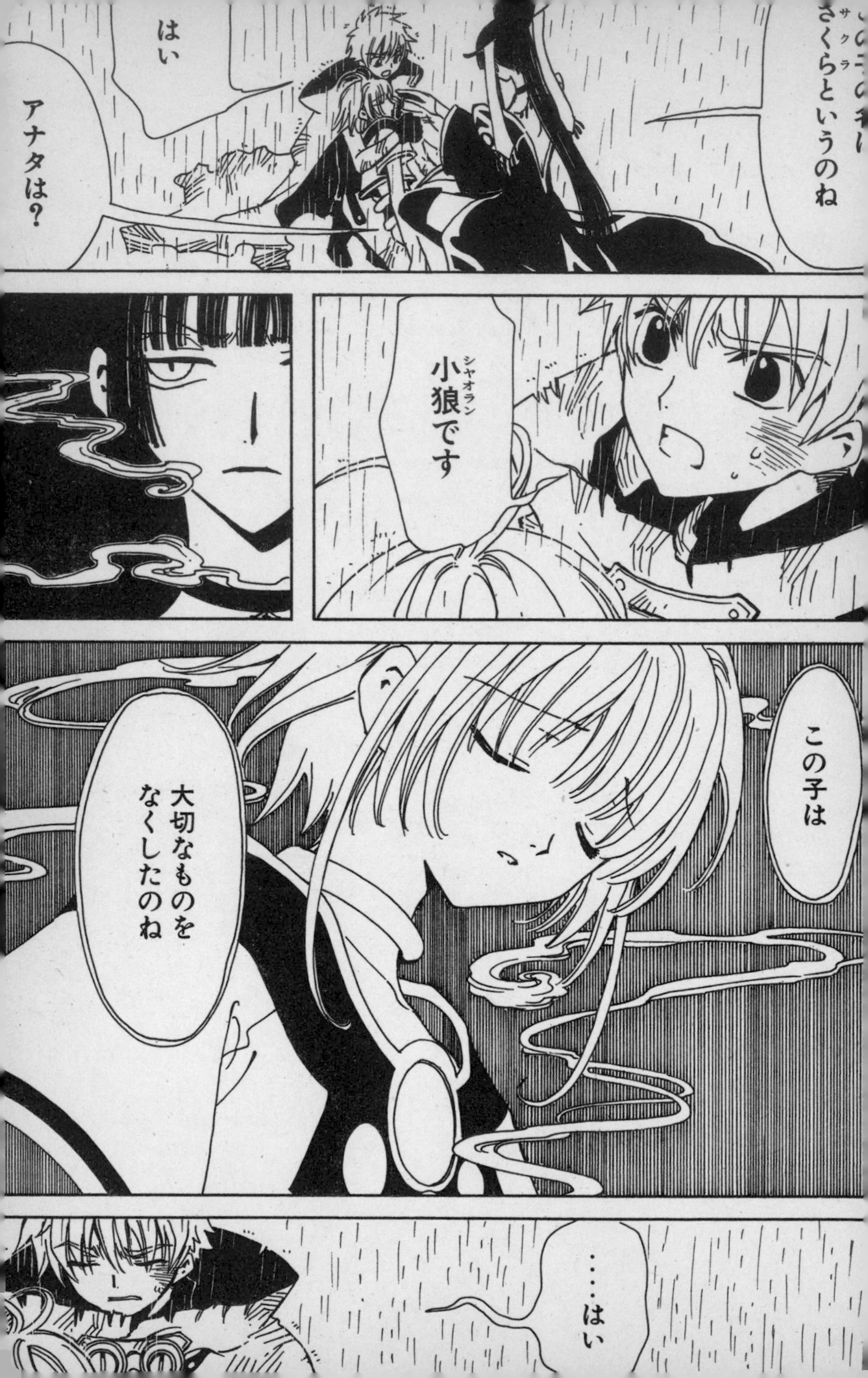
この子は
さくらというのね
はい
アナタは？
小狼です
この子は
大切なものをなくしたのね
……はい

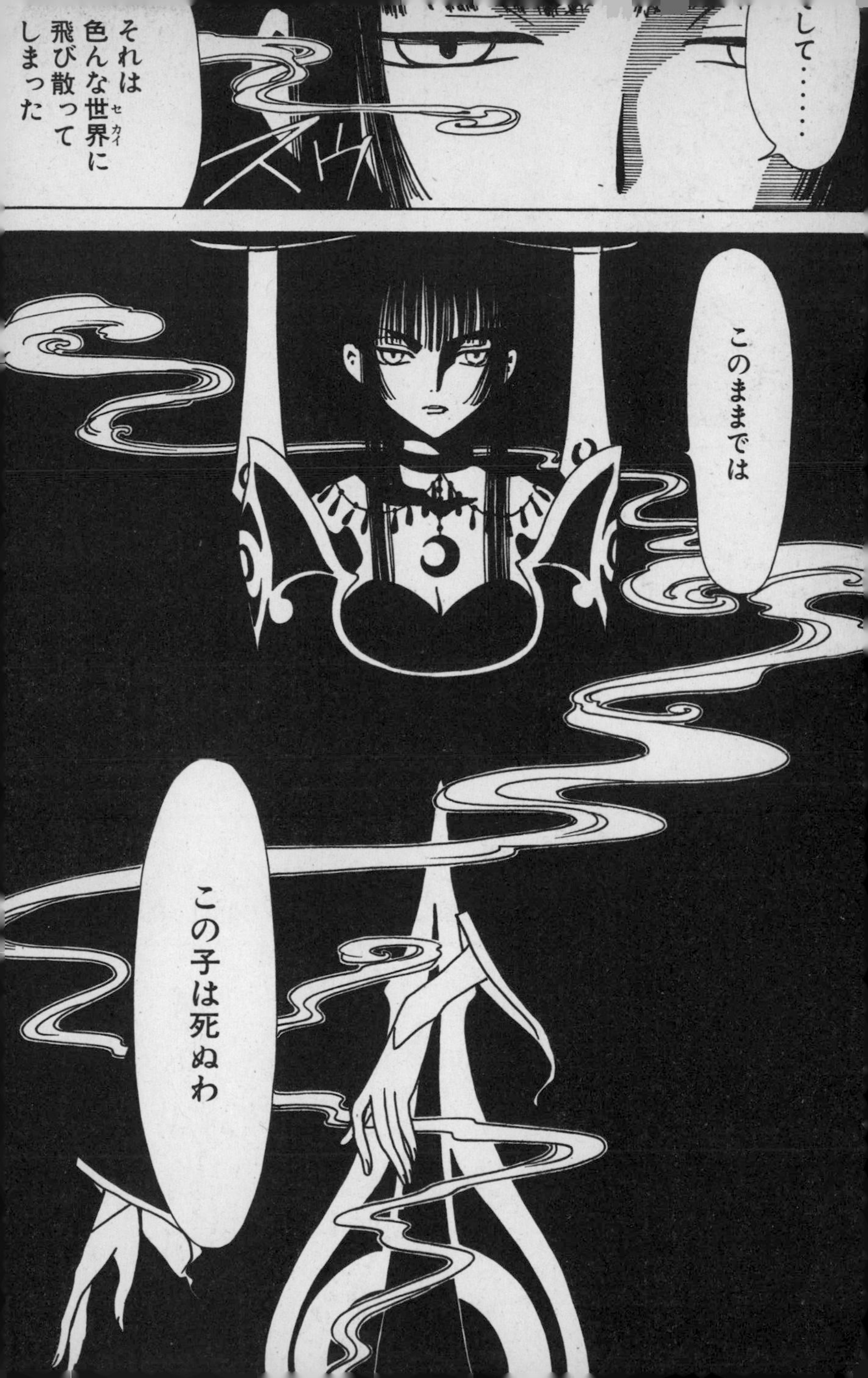
して……
それは色んな世界に飛び散ってしまった
このままでは
この子は死ぬわ

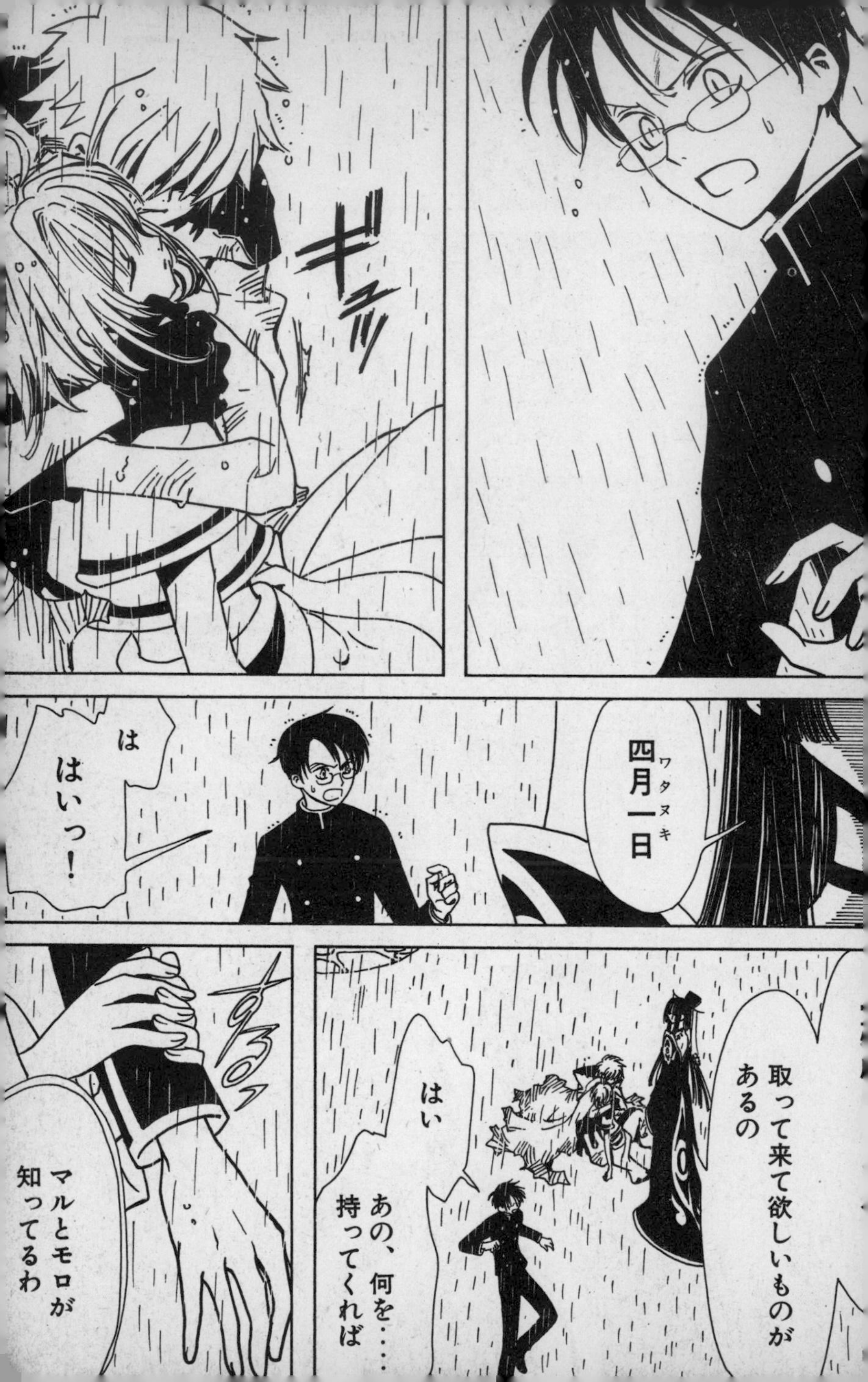
ギュッ
四月一日(ワタヌキ)
は
はいっ!
取って来て欲しいものがあるの
はい
あの、何を…持ってくれば
マルとモロが知ってるわ

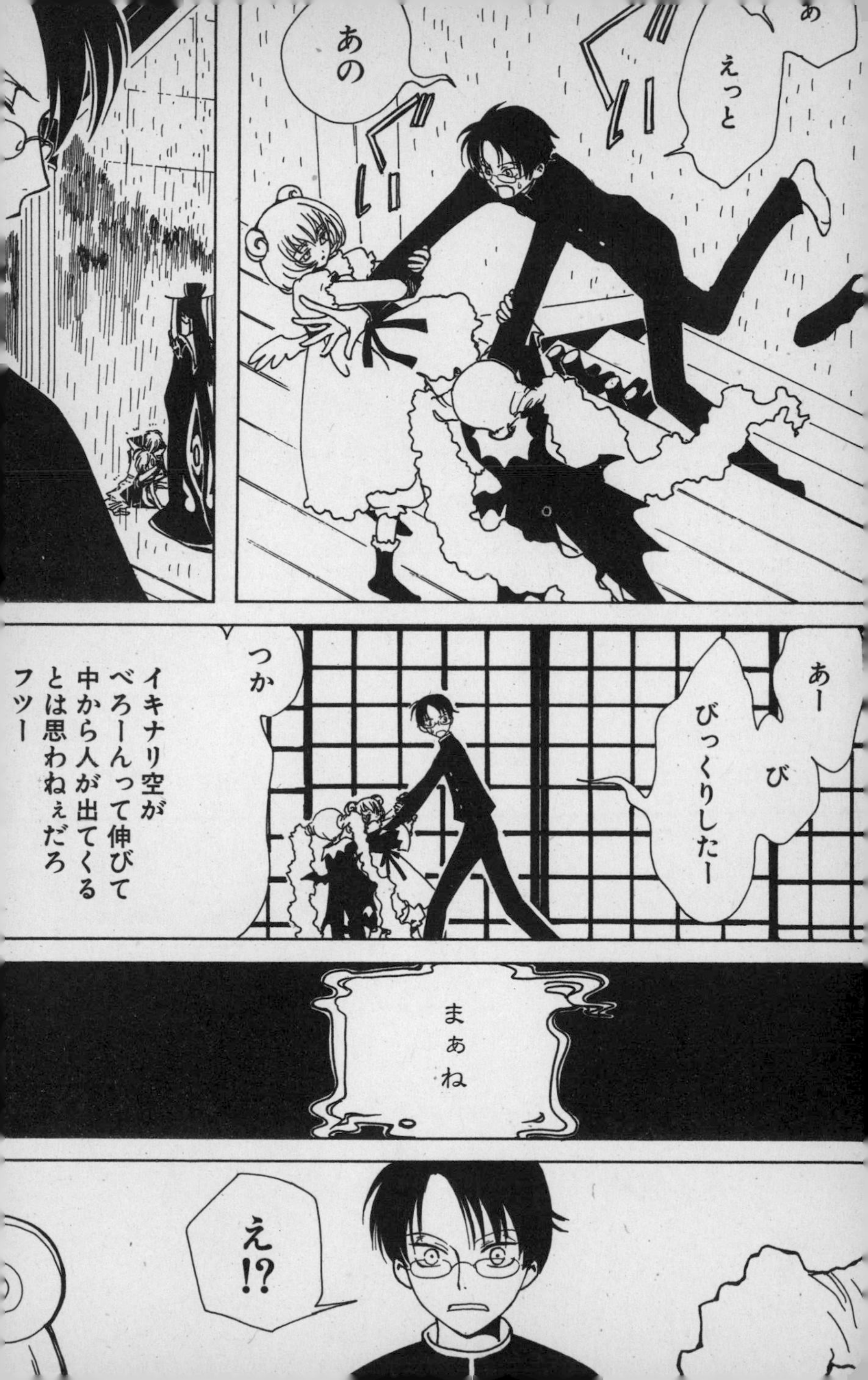
あ
えっと
あの
あー
び
びっくりしたー
つか
イキナリ空がべろーんって伸びて中から人が出てくるとは思わねぇだろフツー
まぁね
え!?

Negima!

by Ken Akamatsu

Creator of *Love Hina!*

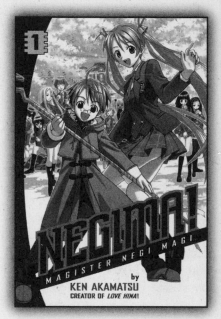

Ten-year-old prodigy Negi Springfield has just graduated from magic academy. He dreams of becoming a master wizard. Instead he's sent to Japan to teach English . . . at an all-girls high school! All the students are delighted with their cute new teacher—except for Asuna, who resents Negi for replacing the teacher she secretly has a crush on. Although he is forbidden to display his magical powers, sometimes Negi can't resist. And when Asuna discovers Negi's secret, she vows to make his life as difficult as possible. But no matter what, it's up to Negi to guide his class through the trials of high school life—and whatever other adventures may come their way.

Volume 1: On sale May 2004 • Volume 2: On sale August 2004
Volume 3: On sale November 2004

 For more information and to sign up for Del Rey's manga e-newsletter, visit www.delreymanga.com

NEGIMA ©2003 Ken Akamatsu. All rights reserved.

Tsubasa: RESERVoir CHRoNiCLE
by CLAMP

Sakura and Syaoran return! But they're not the people you know. Sakura is the princess of Clow—and possessor of a mysterious, misunderstood power that promises to change the world. Syaoran is her childhood friend, and leader of the archaeological dig that took his father's life. They reside in an alternate reality . . . where whatever you least expect can happen—and does. When Sakura ventures to the dig site to declare her love for Syaoran, a puzzling symbol is uncovered—which triggers

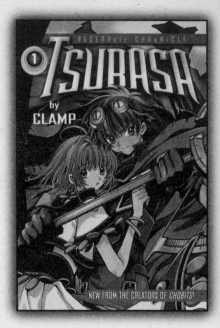

a remarkable quest. Now Syaoran embarks upon a desperate journey through the worlds of *X*, *Chobits*, *Magic Knight Rayearth*, *xxxHOLiC* and many more classic CLAMP series. All in the name of Syaoran's single goal: saving Sakura.

Volume 1: On sale May 2004 • Volume 2: On sale September 2004
Volume 3: On sale December 2004

 For more information and to sign up for Del Rey's manga e-newsletter, visit www.delreymanga.com

TSUBASA © 2003 CLAMP. All rights reserved.

P9-DJA-586

TOMARE!

[STOP!]

You're going the wrong way!

Manga is a completely different type of reading experience.

To start at the *beginning*,
go to the *end*!

That's right! Authentic manga is read the traditional Japanese way—from right to left. Exactly the *opposite* of how American books are read. It's easy to follow: Just go to the other end of the book, and read each page—and each panel—from right side to left side, starting at the top right. Now you're experiencing manga as it was meant to be!